A Heart
So Selfish
Forever Selfish With You
3

JPeach

I

Dedication

To my two amazing kids, DaJah & Da'Vion,
every book I write will forever be dedicated to you.

I love the two of you until death and beyond!

Acknowledgment

To my readers who have stuck with me and given me unlimited support and encouragement, no amount of words could EVER begin to describe how much I love and appreciate every one of you!

Thank you all so much for sticking with me! I genuinely appreciate y'all.

Contact Information

Website: www.authorjpeach.com
Email: j.peach0509@hotmail.com
Instagram: authorjpeach
Facebook: Peach Johnson
Facebook Group: JPeach's Spot
Facebook Author Page: JPeach
Twitter: JPeach1088

Synopsis

Intimacy, adoration, passion, lust, and obsession are everything we give wholly when in love. Yet, don't lose yourself trying to love someone else.

With a clear heart, Kimmy knows who her mind, body, and soul crave for more than anything.

Kim soon realizes that her obsessiveness to keep the man she loves is slowly causing her to lose who she is in the process, which neither she nor her other half likes.

With this realization, Kimmy must get out of her own way to have everything she desires. Yet, with her hormones on high, the task isn't so easily done, causing her to become a threat to the relationship.

Things soon take a turn for the better. Until a blast from the past resurfaces, causing Kimmy to briefly question everything she knew about the man she's spent half of her life with.

Please Read

I want you to all remember this is Kimmy's story. It's not about Bellow and Sabrina's relationship. I added Bellow's POV so you all could get an insight into his mind and feelings, which should give you an understanding of his decisions.

Chapter One

Mike

Battle of The Baby Momma

I didn't have to glance back to know that was Tasha's irritating ass voice. Kimmy blew out a heavy breath while pulling my hand from her panties. "What the fuck are you doing here—matter fact, how the fuck you get in this bitch?"

A sleepy Malik walked into the kitchen, yawning. "I opened the door for her. She called me when she was outside." He came to the island, laying his head down on his arms. A slow smile came to his lips. "So, momma's pregnant? I hope it's a boy." Sighing, he stretched his arms out and yawned again. Standing up, he reached over into a pan.

Kimmy's arm shot out past me, so gotdamn fast, to whack Malik's hands. "Little boy, don't play with me. You know better. Go." She waved at him.

Malik laughed out a groan. "Come on, momma, you could let me slide once. I'm still

1

sleepy." He complained while getting up and going to the sink to wash his hands.

"So, you just gonna sit there and let her hit our fucking son like that?" Tasha snapped, pissed off while she mean mugged the shit out of Kimmy.

A glare formed on Kimmy's face, yet she didn't say anything. Pointing at Tasha, she pushed away from me while taking my plate. "Man, don't come in here starting that bullshit. She ain't hurt his ass, and he knows better to be reaching into shit without washing his gotdamn hands. Fuck all that —what the hell are you doing here this gotdamn early anyway?" It was no later than eight in the morning—on a damn Saturday.

"Had you answered the damn phone, you would've known why. I'm glad I wasn't stuck on the side of the road where anything could've happened to me." She snapped, irritated as she went to my table.

"Don't sit there." Getting up, I snatched her purse off my damn table and put it in a chair at the center island. "Why are you here?"

Sighing, she sat at the counter, looking stressed out. She glanced at Kimmy, then Malik before her gaze settled back on me. "Can we talk in private?"

Going to the sink, I washed my hands. "Tasha, tell me what's up, man." Drying my hands, I sat back down in my spot, and Kimmy sat a plate in front of Malik, then handed me mine. She started to walk off, but I stopped her. "You can eat with me."

Laughing, she smacked my hand off her ass. "Mike, eat." Kissing me, she walked off. "Here." She handed me the syrup.

After covering my bacon with the sweet maple flavor, I handed it to Malik, and he did the same. Kimmy came back with a cup of coffee for me and a hot chocolate for Malik, sitting it in front of us.

"Thanks, momma," Malik said after taking a sip of his hot chocolate.

After eating a piece of bacon, my attention returned to Tasha, who sat mugging Kimmy hard as hell. "What's up, Tasha? Why you here?" I repeated, ignoring her damn attitude.

She rolled her eyes then walked down to me. "I tried to call you before I came over here. My car broke down. I don't know what the hell is wrong with it. I told you that damn car was acting up—"

"Nah, you told me it got fixed a couple of months ago. Where the car at now?" Shorty told me that's where Malik's *'clothes'* money went toward— fixing her gotdamn car. That's how I knew I wasn't fucking tripping.

"I did get it fixed. Now, something else is wrong with it. The damn thing wouldn't start—"

"Is there gas in it?" I asked before eating a fork full of potatoes.

"Don't fucking do that, Mike. I keep gas in my

damn car. If it was the damn gas, do you think I would've caught an Uber over here? I don't know what the hell is wrong with that stupid ass car. Mike, you know I wouldn't have come all the way over here on no bullshit."

"Why didn't you just call roadside assistance to have them tow it to a car shop so they could look at it? That way, you would've known what the issue was?" Kimmy asked, staring at her confused.

That was a good question too. Why come all the way to my crib instead of having the car taken to the shop?

Tasha glared at Kimmy. "Because the last time I did that, Mike snapped on me about not calling him regarding the car's issues. So here I am informing my baby daddy about the issue I'm having with the car I use to get *our son* around. Anything else you wanna know that doesn't have anything to do with you?" She snapped at Kimmy.

She pissed me off talking to Kim like that. Tasha wanted to provoke some shit with Kimmy, and I didn't know why she wanted to fuck with shorty. I was about to stop telling Kimmy to ignore her ignorant ass and let her beat the living fuck out of Tasha. Shorty was lucky Kim was pregnant. Otherwise, I'd let her tag Tasha's tacky ass.

"Why yo' ass so gotdamn hype this fucking morning? Man, you better tone that bullshit down, especially when talking to Kimmy. Whatever the fuck yo' ass coming to me about, trust and believe it involves her mothafuckin' ass too. Because that's the mothafucka I'm going to discuss every fucking thing with. *Our shit*—" I motioned between us, then pointed to Kimmy, "—is her fucking business, period. So, kill that gotdamn attitude before I put yo' ignorant acting ass up out this bitch." I pointed to the chair on the other side of the counter. "Now, sit the fuck down and talk to *us* like you got some gotdamn sense."

LaTasha mugged me hard as hell but walked her ass around to that chair and sat down.

"Malik, go in the dining room and finish eating while we talk," I told him, and he wasted no time getting out of there. Once he was gone, my attention went to Tasha. "The smart thing yo' ass should've done was to call roadside assistance and have them take your car to the shop, so they could tell you what was wrong with it. What was coming over here going to do for your car, Tasha?"

She rolled her damn eyes at me. Baby girl was heated and wasn't hiding that shit well at all. "Like I told her, the last time I took my car to the shop, you got all mad and shit—"

"Stop fucking lying. I was pissed you used Malik's clothes money on your damn car. I said if shit was that bad, you should've called me instead of using his fuckin' money. So, don't twist my gotdamn words around. Regardless of that, I still don't see what's the point of you coming over here for?"

"I have to work at ten, Mike. I needed to make some runs before then. That's when I realized something was wrong with my damn car. I wasn't thinking about calling for assistance, to be honest with you. You were the first person that popped into my head. I tried dialing you before I even came over here. I was just in a rush and wasn't thinking." Tasha sighed while running a hand through her straight hair. "I'm sorry for coming in here bitchy. I'm irritated with that damn car and basically took my frustration out over here."

I noted how she didn't acknowledge Kimmy with her apology.

"Can you at least give me a ride home and to work. I can probably catch a Lyft home from work or have one of my homegirls pick me up..." she trailed off as Malik walked back into the kitchen with his empty plate.

"Breakfast was good, momma. Can I get some more sausage?" He asked, standing by the stove.

"Yeah, baby, go ahead." She told him, and Malik started making himself a whole damn plate.

"Or..." Tasha started with a fake-ass thoughtful look on her face. "Mike, can I use one of your cars until I get mine fixed? That way, I don't have to nag you for rides or keep catching an Uber or Lyft to get around?"

She was out of her gotdamn mind if she thought I would let her drive one of my damn cars —which were all custom done. Hell, I barely let Kim drive my shit.

"You don't need to be taking rides from them.

I keep hearing about folks getting robbed when in an Uber." Malik chimed in, and I glared at his ass. "Maybe she can use the truck? Y'all don't really drive that."

"Malik, go back in the room," Kim told him. Looking at me, Kimmy shook her head. "I need the truck; I have some things that I need to take to the store." Grabbing our plates, Kimmy put them in the sink. "I can't help you with your errands, but I can drop you off at work."

I knew Kimmy was only offering because Malik said something. Once Malik walked by Tasha, she grabbed him, bringing him closer. She kissed his cheek then wrapped her arms around his waist, not letting him leave the room as Kimmy told him to.

Tasha ignored Kimmy. In fact, she didn't even glance at her. Shorty's attention was entirely on me. "I can't use one of your cars, Mike?"

She was out of her damn mind to ask that shit again. "Hell nah! You not about to fuck up my shit."

"You dirty as fuck, Mike. How come whenever I really need you to come through for me, it's always a damn issue—"

"Come through for you? Man, gon' on with that bullshit. You're acting like I'm responsible for yo' ass or some shit. Sweetheart, I'm not obligated to do a gotdamn thing for you—"

"No, you're not, and never once did I say you were. But seeing as I'm the mother of your *only* child, I would think you would want to help me

7

out and make shit less stressful for me as possible. You're dirty as fuck. Now let something be wrong with that bitch's car. You're not gonna have an issue letting that bitch roll in shit." She claimed, jabbing a finger at Kimmy.

"Ma!" Malik yelled, staring at Tasha like she was crazy. "Why you always have to be so mean to her? Dang. You didn't have to get that mad and for no reason. I don't know why you can't ever just talk to my momma without being disrespectful. You talk crazy to them, then expect my daddy to do something nice for you. He doesn't have to. You're not his girlfriend or his child." He fussed, then pushed out of her hold. "I'm about to go play my game." He announced, then stormed out the kitchen.

"And this was why I told him to go into the other damn room. So, he didn't have to see you act a complete fucking fool. Bitch you wanna stand here and act a gotdamn ass in front of him for no damn reason. Disrespect me in my own fucking house, but then expect us to help you the fuck out. You're an ignorant ass hoe." Kimmy raged, pissed off, glaring at Tasha.

"Mike, call this bitch a car ride and get her ass the fuck out of my house. How this bitch gets to and from anywhere ain't your fucking problem. Ignorant ass bitch always wanna pull that—*I'm your baby momma*—bullshit. Hoe, he takes care of his fucking responsibilities when it comes to his gotdamn child like he's supposed to do. Those fucking responsibilities don't include yo' trifling ass. What the hell make you believe they do is beyond fucking me. Ol' ignorant ass bitch!" Kimmy grabbed the frying pan and threw it at Tasha's head without warning.

LaTasha ducked just in time before that damn pan could hit her. Potatoes went flying across the room as the pan hit the wall. "Oh, my God."

"Get the fuck out my house, you stupid ass bitch!" Kimmy yelled, charging for Tasha.

I quickly grabbed Kim before she could snatch Tasha's ass up. "What the fuck is wrong with you?"

Kimmy mugged me while pointing to herself. "Me? What the fuck is wrong with me? What the fuck is wrong with that bitch should be your fucking question. That hoe strolls in this bitch practically demanding shit, calling me all out my fucking name, and still had the fucking audacity to act like you fucking owe her trifling ass some bullshit! I'm sick of her ass. I will fuck that bitch up!" As if realizing she was talking to me with that ending bit, she redirected her glare to Tasha. "I will dog walk yo' ass all through this bitch—" Picking up a glass cup, she threw it at Tasha.

Kimmy was wilding the fuck out. Lifting Kim off her feet, I carried her ass outback. The entire time her ass went clean off on Tasha. Once outside, I closed the back door.

"What the fuck is wrong with you, man?" I repeated. Yeah, Tasha ass talked shit to get under

Kimmy's skin but never had Kim ever let shorty get her that riled the fuck up.

That was the second time Kimmy went off like that and started throwing shit. The first was when she threw that damn pool ball at Tasha's head.

"Mike, let me the fuck go. I don't know why the fuck you're grabbing me when you need to be dragging that fucking bitch out by her gotdamn hair. I'm so sick of that hoe. I'm pissed at yo' ass too for letting that bitch get so gotdamn comfortable with speaking out of her ass to you—and me for that matter." She fought in my grasp, trying to get free. "Mike, let me go before I knock yo' ass out because of that bitch."

"Why the fuck are you letting that bitch get you riled up like this for? You know this is what she wants, and you're giving it to her ass. You're throwing fucking pans and shit, trying to fight that damn girl because she's running her gotdamn mouth. Have you lost your damn mind?"

Kimmy's mouth fell open, and she looked beyond surprised. "You're asking have I lost my mind? How the hell did this even get about me?"

"You're the only mothafucka throwing shit and trying to fight—"

"That bitch stormed in here talking shit, yet somehow I'm the one losing my mind. Are you fucking serious right now, Michael? We're getting disrespected in our shit, but somehow this is on me, though? Like, you're really going to get pissed off at me, like this bullshit is my fucking fault...ooh, I swear—" Kim's lips pursed together as tears ran down her face.

Staring at Kimmy at that moment, I realized her actions had to be a damn hormonal thing. At the realization, I found her to be ironic as hell. My hand rubbed over my mouth so that I wouldn't outright laugh.

Kimmy's tear-stricken face formed into a glare, and she mugged me hard. "The shit ain't funny, Michael. Like, I was really trying to help that hoe out, and she gon' pop slick and call me a bitch. I swear I wanna beat her ass so bad, ooh. Yours too. You gonna snap at me like I did something wrong. Ooh, I wanna fight her ass so bad right now." She damn near growled.

I grabbed her arm, and she jerked it away from me. My brow raised at the action, causing Kim to roll her eyes at the gesture, but she came to me no less. "Yo' ass can't let her get you riled up like this, man. Especially not now with you being pregnant. You can't be stressing the baby out over no bullshit." Pulling her head back, I kissed her. As my lips pressed against hers, I broke out laughing. "Man, yo' ass raged the fuck out. G, you're a fucking violent-pregnant person. You throwing pans of food and glass cups at mothafuckas."

Kimmy hit me in the back and groaned, letting her head fall on my chest. "That's not even funny, Mike. I was so damn mad. It's just her gotdamn audacity. Like you owe her some shit because she had a kid by you. I can't stand when she does that shit. You're not fucking obligated to provide anything for her ass, and she needs to realize that bullshit. But Tasha's behavior ain't entirely her fault either. You got her ass thinking the bullshit she does is cool because you're always bending to do shit she wants—for Malik's sake. That shit shows because of how she came in here."

"I'll handle Tasha's ass; you just control your gotdamn hormones and instincts to throw some shit. Bet?" Kimmy's eyes rolled. Grabbing her chin, I pulled her head back, kissing her while slapping her booty.

Sighing, she wrapped her arms around my neck, getting into the kiss. After pecking my lips twice more, her head moved back. "I'm not making no promises to anything. Now go get that bitch out my shit." With that, she pushed her lips against mine again.

Laughing, I pulled away from her, then led us into the house. Tasha sat at the counter, looking pissed off. My finger raised at her once I saw that damn mouth open. "Don't say shit to her. Yo' ass gon' learn to shut the fuck up, especially when she's not paying yo' ass no mind." I sat in the chair beside her. "Check this, though. I don't owe yo' ass a fucking thing, Tasha. One, you ain't my girl. Two, I ain't fucking you. I help yo' ass out with some shit because you're Malik's momma. You being his mother don't give yo' ass no type of claim to me or shit I have."

Grabbing Kimmy, I pulled her to my side. "When it comes to shorty, yeah, you're right about everything you said. She's entitled to every fucking thing I have. One, that's wifey, period; ain't no question to it. Two, I'm fucking her, so, yeah, she's getting everything she wants out my ass." My finger jabbed at her. "You walking in this bitch like you're running some shit ain't it, sweetheart. Yo' ass better learn to control that attitude you have when it comes to Kimmy.

"Y'all are two different mothafuckas who play two entirely different roles in my gotdamn life," I told them before pointing to Tasha. "It's been twelve fucking years, and if you haven't figured out what your role is, then," I shrugged, I didn't know what the fuck to tell her ass on that front, so I left that shit empty for Tasha to fill in herself. "But this damn entitled demeanor you have when it comes to me, that shit dead."

A heavy breath left Tasha, and her arms crossed over her chest as her foot bounced. LaTasha's entire posture screamed attitude, but I didn't care.

"Can I speak now?" She questioned smartly, making me laugh. I gave a short nod. LaTasha's chest expanded as she released a breath. Kimmy's lips popped at her actions, and I glared at her, making her eyes roll.

"Firstly, I don't think I'm entitled to you or shit you have. Never once have I claimed to be either. Secondly, I feel comfortable coming to you

13

and asking for your help simply because I didn't think it was an issue. From day one, when you learned that I was pregnant, you constantly let me know that no matter our status, you would be here for me, and if I ever needed anything, I didn't have to hesitate to ask you for a gotdamn thing. And for the past twelve years, you've lived up to your word. But never have I ever asked you for more than needed when it came to me personally.

"Mike, you know that shit. Yeah, I came in here out of line, I can admit, and I apologized to you for that. My anger shouldn't have been directed at you. I'm just irritated about my damn car. However!" Her eyes shifted to Kimmy, and a mean ass scowl covered her face. "That doesn't give that— girl a fucking right to act a gotdamn fool and start throwing shit when I was never speaking to her ass to fucking begin with—"

"Bitch—"

"I was fucking talking!" Tasha snapped, pushing up out of her seat like she was ready to do some shit to Kimmy.

Kimmy bucked right back. "Hoe, I will beat yo' ass—"

"Bitch, you can try it—"

"The both of y'all need to shut the fuck up. Man, sit the fuck down." I yelled, pissed off while pushing the pair, making them stumble back. "Y'all mothafuckas acting like fucking kids." I was ready to choke both of their asses. "I said sit the fuck

14

down!"

Tasha snatched her chair, pulled it back to the island, then sat down, pissed off.

"Don't fucking talk to me like—" Kimmy smart mouth ass tried going off.

My hand grabbed the loose ponytail atop her head, and I jerked her ass to me. "Don't make me beat yo' ass right now. You better jump back inside yo' fuckin' body and remember who the fuck you're talking to. Now, sit the fuck down." I pushed her head back to the side, then snatched a chair from the counter for her. Kimmy's face puffed up, and she jerked the chair out my grasp, then sat down, mumbling under her damn breath like a child. I chose to ignore her smart-ass remarks. Knowing her, she was probably calling me all types of stupid-ass bitches.

My finger jabbed at Tasha. "Yo' ass talking like she ain't have a damn reason to go off. Nah, you weren't speaking to her directly, yet that didn't stop yo' childish ass from disrespecting her either—"

"That didn't mean she had to throw a damn —"

"I was fucking talking!" I didn't want to hear her bullshit. Tasha's lips snapped shut before they pursed tightly together. "Just like you feel, she didn't have to throw a damn pan at yo' ass. She feels you shouldn't have disrespected her at all. So, I don't wanna hear that shit, man." I pointed between the pair. "You mothafuckas don't have to like each other. I don't give a fuck for none of that shit. But you're going to be cordial with one another, not for me but for Malik's sake. From this point forth, y'all asses gonna be fucking friendly with each other in front of my gotdamn son. The first time either one of you starts acting stupid in front of him, I'm slapping the fuck out of you. It's simple as that."

Snatching my chair up, I sat down. "Tasha, this petty ass shit that you're feeling toward Kim, let that shit go. Shorty ain't going nowhere. She's a part of Malik's life forever. Accept that shit and move the fuck on. That's the way everything's going to be from this point forth. Am I completely fucking clear?" I asked them.

"It doesn't even be me, though—" Kimmy started saying, but shut up once I mugged her ass.

"A simple fucking *yes* would suffice, Kimmy."

Kim's lips popped, and she exhaled a heavy breath. "Yes, Michael, it's completely clear. Although I'm always cordial with her ass."

Rubbing my bottom lip, I nodded at her. She just had to add her damn two cents. "Tasha."

"If that's what you want, then fine." With arms crossed under her chest, she sat there mad.

"Momma!" Malik yelled from somewhere. I knew from the name and tone that he was calling for Kimmy.

Whenever both women were together, Malik called Kimmy momma and Tasha ma.

"What, Malik!" Kimmy shouted back.

"Come here, please!" He called right back. When he said that, I knew it was something that he wanted her to say yes to because he knew I would tell him no.

"Whatever it is, the answer's no," I told her. With a hand wave, she got up and walked out of the kitchen. Looking at Tasha, I just shook my head at her crazy ass. "When I'm finished cleaning up this mess, I'll drop yo' ass off." Walking across the room, I grabbed the broom and dustpan from the closet then started sweeping up the potatoes. I was going to slap the shit out of Kimmy for wasting those good ass fried potatoes.

"Sooo...she's pregnant now?" She questioned, coming over and taking the broom from me.

"You already know the answer to that question." I let her sweep as I put the pan in the sink.

"Is this why you're saying all this shit because she's pregnant? And what does that mean for Malik?" She hit the dustpan against the trashcan harder than necessary.

Leaning against the counter, I stared at her mad ass for a while. That babe was crazy. "Kimmy being pregnant, don't have shit to do with what I said. Yo' simple-minded ass keep poking at her, and when she snaps, you wanna play innocent. You lucky I grabbed her when I did; otherwise, she would've had you leaking all in this bitch."

"No, the hell she wouldn't have, but you can think whatever you want, Mike." She pushed the broom at me but didn't back away. "You didn't answer my question. What does this mean for Malik?"

"It doesn't mean shit for Malik, aside from he's gonna have a brother or sister soon. Kimmy being pregnant, don't have shit to do with Malik, nor you for that matter."

"It has everything to do with Malik. With you having a new baby, the older kid usually gets overlooked. And my son ain't about to be feeling like he's not important or a priority to his father because he done got another chick pregnant—"

"Man, watch out." I pushed by her, putting the broom and dustpan away. "You sound dumb as fuck. Another chick? You mean my damn girl? Yo' ass was just another chick that got pregnant. Kimmy ain't never been that. I've been with that fucking woman for damn near sixteen years. Yo' ass can't ever call her some other gotdamn chick. As far as Malik goes, he doesn't have to worry about our relationship. My baby—his sister or brother isn't gonna change the bond we have. Man, only yo' stupid ass would say some dumb shit like that. And yo' ass bet not start talking that dumb shit to him either." I couldn't stand her ass. She made shit problematic for no gotdamn reason. "Man, come on." I led her into the living room. "Sit yo' ass in here and don't move."

"You can say what you want, but the moment

you change up on our son—"

"Man, shut the fuck up, damn! Yo, when the fuck are you gonna get a nigga so you can stay the fuck out my damn business?"

Grabbing the pillow off the couch, she threw it at me. "You're a fucking asshole, I swear. And I do have a gotdamn man, so you know." My brows raised questioningly. Hearing that confused me. Taking in my expression, she smiled. "Yes, I have a man that I'm loving on constantly."

Licking my lips, I sat the pillow back on the couch as one thought came to mind. "Then why the fuck are you here? Why you ain't call that nigga or Uber yo' ass to him? Especially if you're fucking him. That should've been the first person you thought of instead of me."

That smile quickly left her mouth, and she rolled her eyes. That damn mug returned to her face. "Because he's not my baby daddy, and seeing as I drive our son around in my car, I came to you."

Laughing, I walked out of the living room, leaving her mad ass there. "Yo' lying ass. Man, stay yo' ass in there and don't go walking around my crib." I told her as I jogged up the stairs. She mumbled something incoherent, which I paid no mind to. While heading to my room, I pulled out my phone and shot King a quick text.

Once I went into the room, Kimmy bypassed me, going into the closet. "Where are you going?" I asked, seeing her hair neatly pulled into a ponytail.

My arm slid around her waist, stopping her before she could step around me again.

"I told you I had to stop by the warehouse and take some things to the store…Mike…" she whined as I pulled her to the bed. "Why you wanna play with me? Stop. I'm still mad at you for yelling at me." She slapped at my roaming hands that moved over her booty. "Is your baby momma still here?"

I glared up at her. "You know she is. I'm about to drop her ass off at home—why the fuck you doing all that for?" I questioned as she smacked her lips and tried jerking out my grasp. I wasn't letting her go, though. Instead, I continued to unfasten her shorts and undo the zipper. I pushed them down, completely ignoring her fussing about Tasha.

"Just like that bitch called a car service to get here, she can dial one up to go home. Mike, stop biting my damn stomach. I'm trying to be pissed off —eep!" She squeaked out as I picked her up.

"I ain't tryna hear that shit, though." Laying her on the bed, I pushed her thighs apart, exposing her pretty ass pussy.

Kimmy laughed as her nails clawed down my bare, tattooed chest. "Don't just stand there admiring her. Give her a kiss."

Laughing, I sucked on my thumb, getting it wet, then brought the digit to her clit. Circling the swelling pearl, I moved down to her opening, playing with her pussy, feeling as she became moist. "I'm about to do more than just kiss her sexy ass.

She about to get some dick too."

"Mmm…" A moan sighed from her mouth as I began tongue kissing her pussy. Kimmy's fingers caressed down my head, then cupped the nape of it. "Ooh, baby, just like that. Suck my pussy, baby. Fuck, Mike!" Kimmy tightened her grip on my head; her nails dug into my skin as her body started to quake. "Ooh, fuck, Mike!"

I sucked up her sweet nectar as she came. My lips kissed from her right thigh to the left, then trailed up her body, pushing her shirt up as I came to her stomach. My teeth grazed over the flesh before I bit either side, then kissed up to her breast. Kimmy quickly pulled her top off.

Kimmy's titties looked good as fuck as they spilled from her bra. Pulling her bra down, my mouth latched onto her nipple as my fingers played with the other one.

Finally leaning over her, my tongue ran over her bottom lip, causing hers to part. I then ran it over her top before sliding it into her mouth.

A half whine and moan left Kimmy's mouth as my dick stroked through her slit. But every time my man pushed at her opening, I moved my hips, not trying to enter her.

Kimmy's hips ground along my shaft and raised every time my dick came to her pussy's entrance, trying to get it inside her. Finally, her hand slid between our bodies, and she grabbed my dick. Stroking it, she brought my thick, lengthy soldier to her pulsing pussy.

Capturing her hands, I penned them above her head at the wrist.

"Mike, you're going to kill me if you don't fuck me." She panted, breathless.

I grabbed my dick with my free hand and slapped that thick mothafucka against her swollen clit.

"Mike..." Kim's thighs widened, and she pushed her hips up. She caught the tip and moaned. Slowly her hips moved on the mushroom head. She kept trying to go deep, but I wasn't letting her.

Releasing my dick, I let her fuck on the tip. I grabbed her throat, squeezing it. The action caused her pussy to pulse more. The shit felt good as hell.

A frustrated whine left her mouth. "Baby, please." She begged, sounding desperate. I pushed inside her fully. "Ooh, Michael."

I stroked her deep as my hand tightened around her throat. I sucked on her lips, letting my tongue stroke inside her mouth how she loved. The heels of Kimmy's feet dug into my lower back when she felt my hips retreating. Pulling back from the kiss, I pecked her lips.

"I love you so much." She moaned. Leaning up, she licked my bottom lip, then the top. Before she could get into it, my hand that held her neck pushed her back on the bed.

"I know you do—"

"No, don't stop." She moaned, locking her damn legs at the ankles.

My hand tightened more on her neck. "Remember when we were in the kitchen?" My words caused her eyes to snap open.

"I'm sorry. I was mad and got in my feelings. I was wrong and shouldn't have gotten smart with you." Leaning up, she kissed me again. "I'm sorry."

I found her instant response to be funny as hell. The irony of her apologizing for that specific thing when a lot went on in the kitchen.

Pulling her legs from my waist, I stood up. "Well, I don't have to say shit else since you already know what's up."

"Mike, I swear yo' ass bet not leave me like this. I swear to God, I'm not even playing with you." She looked down at my hard dick, then stood and grabbed it. "I don't want all this to go to waste." She mumbled, stroking my dick.

"He'll be good. Gon' get ready. I'll drive you." I slapped her bare ass, then pulled away.

A second later, her shorts hit my back. "Michael, are you serious? Why would you even work me up like this, then stop? My damn body is aching and horny, and you're just going to leave me like this? For real, man?"

"Next time, watch your fucking mouth."

"Okay, I said I was fucking sorry. I was pissed off when I did that. You know how my mouth gets when I'm mad."

"That ain't no excuse, sweetheart. Plus, yo' ass only sorry because you want some dick."

"Okay, so what!" She snapped, mad as hell. "So, you're not about to fuck me, Michael?"

My head shook as I walked into the closet. "Nah, I'm about to get dressed so we can go."

"I swear I hate your ignorant ass so much!" She whined before a shoe came flying into the closet. I broke out laughing. "Ain't shit funny, stupid ass."

My brows furrowed at the sudden thickness in her tone. I glanced out at her. Kimmy sat on the edge of the bed, head in her hands as her shoulders trembled. "Is yo' ass crying?"

Kimmy's head popped up, and her tear-streaked face glared at me. "So, fucking what? Ugh! I hate this shit." She roughly wiped her eyes which seemed to cause more tears to fall.

"You dead ass crying real tears?" I was surprised as hell. Seeing Kimmy emotional was going to take some getting used to. Shorty was barely a crier, so seeing her burst into tears over some damn dick fucked me up.

"Just leave me alone." She was actually sniffling like her feelings were hurt. "Nah, don't touch me. Move."

Grabbing her arms, I pushed her down on the bed. "Man, calm yo' silly ass down."

"No, I don't want your damn pity dick just because I'm crying." She claimed but didn't push me away as my man ran through her fold. Instantly she became wet.

"You sure? That pussy got my shit glistening already."

"So..." she bit into her bottom lip to muffle a moan.

Grabbing her throat, I pulled her head back, kissing her. "You don't want my dick, Kimmy?" I mumbled against her lips while stroking her warm cave deeply. My pelvis kissed hers, and my hips rolled into her. "You don't want me to fuck you?" My tongue licked inside her mouth before I kissed her lips.

"Mike..." she moaned as I dug into her, not putting any space between our bodies. "Ooh, I do." A pleasurable whine left her mouth. A second later, her body moved up the bed as she tried scooting back.

"Don't tell me you can't take this dick, now?"

Lust blazed in her eyes as she panted erotically. "Daddy, I can handle everything you're going to give me."

Licking my lips caused my tongue to touch her mouth. Pulling out, I pushed back in, stroking her insides. My arms slid under her thighs, pushing her legs up, pinning them beside her waist. "Fuck!" I grunted, sliding deep inside her pulsing cave. The tightness and moisture of her pussy felt so gotdamn good around my dick. My hips pounded into her soaking cave.

"Oh, my, fuck, baby. Ooh, shit—" Kim bit into my forearm as she screamed. Kimmy's arm cuffed underneath mine, holding my arm to her as the other moved to my lower spine. Kimmy's nails dug into my flesh, clawing the hell out of me as my dick drove her ass crazy. "Ooh, okay, okay!" She cried, her palm hitting my back. "Oh, my, fuck, Michael, okay, okay. Baby, it's too much." She panted.

Letting her legs go, I sat back, hitting her thigh. "I thought you could handle everything I gave you? Yo' ass can't talk that sweet shit to me then tap out."

"Shut up, I can." She giggled before moaning as my fingers started to play in her pussy.

Taking hold of her hair, I pulled her upright, guiding her to my dick. Kimmy didn't hesitate to grab my man and handle that bitch skillfully. She sucked, licked, and slurped on my tip while massaging my sack.

"Fuck!" Her lips widened as she slid that mothafucka down my dick. I watched as my shit disappeared between her pretty ass full lips. My hand whacked hard against her bare ass. "Shit!" The hit caused her to moan around my tip. The vibration of that gotdamn sound shot straight into my damn balls, causing my grip on her hair to tighten. "That mouth sinful as fuck. Gotdamn!" I was seconds away from pushing her off my dick. As if knowing, she pulled back and looked up at me, and that mothafucka had the nerve to smile. "Fuck you."

"Okay then, don't talk shit to me. Lay back." She pushed at my stomach, and I did as she requested. Squatting over me, she tapped my legs, and I bent them at the knees. She took hold of the pair, slid down my shit, then started bouncing on my dick. "Sssh—shit." Switching it up, she began a back and forth motion. Kimmy's eyes closed, and her head went back as she continued to ride me.

Grabbing her breast, I squeezed it. The lustful expression that covered her entire face, as well as the rapid pulsing of her pussy, showed just how much she was enjoying fucking my dick. "You sexy as fuck."

Lazily her eyes opened, and she smiled down at me, picking her pace back up. Grabbing her stomach, I squeezed it as my hips pushed up, meeting her downward movement.

"Ooh..." she pressed her hand against my pelvis, trying to push me down. Taking hold of her ass, I squeezed while thrusting inside her. "Mike, baby, fuck!" Kimmy's love box milked my dick, sucking my shit until I finally let off inside of her throbbing pussy.

"Shit!" I slapped her ass, then shook it. "Fuck, man. This shit ain't gonna work for me, fuck no. Shit." I grunted, making Kimmy laugh as she lay on top of me.

"How us fucking ain't gonna work for you?"

My palm slapped her booty again, harder that time, making her pussy pulse more around my sensitive dick. "That ain't the issue. It's me fucking yo' ass without a condom that's gonna be a gotdamn problem. Shit!"

Kimmy's pussy has always been top tier to me. Hell, her grip alone was fucking mind-blowing, and that was with a gotdamn condom. But now that I didn't need to use one because she was already pregnant. My ass was about to get spoiled as fuck, and that was a problem because after she had that baby, going back to the norm wasn't going to be easy.

Kimmy broke out laughing. "Dude, shut the hell up. You get on my nerves. Well, you better enjoy it now because after I have this baby, I'm getting back on birth control, and you're definitely strapping the fuck up. I'm not getting pregnant no damn more. This emotional rollercoaster I'm on is going to drive me insane. Like, I can't even believe my ass cried like that over some damn dick."

I chuckled at that, making her hit me. "Babe, that's not even funny. Like, my damn feelings were really hurt, Mike. You know that's not even me. Then I got mad because I was crying, and that shit just made me cry more. Stop laughing!" She whined, tucking her face into my neck.

"Yeah, that shit definitely will take some getting used to." Groaning, I went to roll her off of me, but she started to whine.

"No, don't. Let's just lay here."

Laughing, I rubbed her booty. "Nah, I need to smoke, and you have to go get your deliveries and take them to the store." Rolling us over, I pulled out of her, then sat up. After grabbing my case from the nightstand, I pulled out a blunt, blazing it. Inhaling on the blunt twice, I held the smoke in then slowly released it.

Kimmy suddenly jumped up quickly, dashing off the bed and into the bathroom. A second later, I could hear her getting sick. I followed her into the bathroom. Once she was done, I helped her off the floor and to the sink.

At that moment, she seemed so gotdamn fragile. That was a completely new look for her.

Kim being pregnant was definitely going to take some getting used to.

Chapter Two

Mike

Emotional Flip...

"Momma!" Malik called from the other side of the door. "Can I come in?"

She waved me off as I glanced at her. "None of your business." She told me. "Yeah, come in." Malik pushed the door open, going straight to Kimmy and handing her his phone.

"What the hell do you want her to do? And why did you ask her and not me?" Grabbing him around the head, I pulled him over to me. "What you dressed up for?"

"Because I didn't wanna ask you. This was something between us." His finger motioned between him and Kimmy, making her laugh.

"Boy, shut up. You're a damn mess, Malik." She cracked up while focusing on his phone.

I was curious about what they had going on more than anything, only because he made it seem like the shit was top-secret. "What the fuck y'all got going on, Malik, and where are you going?" I motioned over the Jordan outfit he had on.

"I'm going with momma to the store." He shrugged as if that was nothing.

It was at that moment I knew shit wasn't right. Malik hated going to the store with her. I pointed at Kimmy. "I'mma kick yo' ass because I told you to tell him no to whatever he wanted. So, what you tell his ass yes too?"

"And that's why he didn't ask you." She laughed, grabbing her purse. "Let's go, baby..." her words trailed off as she looked around the room. "Where's my phone?" Seeing mine, she picked it up.

"That's mine."

She nodded while unlocking it. "I know. Mine must still be in the kitchen. Let's go." She called once more while putting the phone to her ear. "Hey, Jerron..." She was saying while walking out the room.

My glare fell on Malik. "Ace's badass ain't coming over here."

"I know." He shrugged before grabbing my wallet off the nightstand. "Let me hold something —"

Snatching my wallet from him, I laughed. "Man, get the fuck out my damn room. Talking about let you hold something." Grabbing my gun from inside the nightstand, I clipped the .9mm in its holster on my hip, then grabbed my weed case and keys. Once I had my stuff, I pushed Malik out of my room.

"So, you not gonna let me hold no money? I just need a little something. You know I get bored when I'm at the store." He said as if that would make me give him some damn money. "I can pick me up some stuff from the mall." He kept on saying as we bounced down the stairs. "I'mma pay you back."

That made me stop once we got to the living room. My brow popped up before I chuckled. "Say what? You already owe me for yo' whole damn life, fuck are you talking about?" I muffed his head back before opening my wallet. Grabbing a twenty, I gave it to him.

He looked at the money then back to me. "What do you think I can buy with twenty dollars at the mall? Come on, dad, hook me up—I'm just playing!" He cracked up as I snatched my money back. "You know how we play around. I'll take the twenty." He grinned.

"Alright, let's go." Kimmy walked into the living room. "Here." She handed me my phone back then grabbed her wallet out of her purse. Opening it, she pushed through the bills and took out a fifty. "Here." She gave it to Malik. "Now, let's go. I'm driving." She made a grab for my truck keys.

"No, the fuck you ain't driving." I pushed her hand back. "Why you give him fifty dollars for?"

She rolled her eyes at me. "Because it's my money, and I am driving. It'll be quicker if I take us there. I know all the shortcuts." As she was talking, Malik snatched the keys from my hands and threw them to Kimmy. She quickly grabbed me, laughing before I could get his little ass. "Stop, babe, leave him alone. Just let me drive, please?" She whispered against my lips.

"Don't be driving my damn truck stupid either. Let's go." Malik was the first one out the door. I went to walk off, but Kimmy stopped me.

"Aren't you forgetting something?" She stared at me curiously. After feeling my pockets for my wallet and phone, then my sides for my guns, I shook my head. She rolled her eyes. "Your baby momma."

Immediately my eyes darted into the living room. LaTasha was still sitting where I had left her damn near an hour ago. "Oh, fuck. I done forgot yo' ass was even here."

"Wow, that's beyond fucked up, Mike. I'm glad I called off from work this morning. That's cool, though you can pay me for this day, seeing as I'm missing work because you forgot I was here."

Kimmy patted my chest, shook her head then walked out of the house.

"Man, gon' on with that bullshit. You called off before I even forgot about yo' raggedy ass." I motioned for her to come on. When she got close to me, I stopped her from walking past. "Look, when we get in that truck, I don't want no shit. No smart remarks towards Kim—none of that bullshit you do to piss her off."

She rolled her eyes, popping her damn lips. "Why? Because her ass pregnant? Fuck her—"

Grabbing her throat, I roughly pushed her against the wall. "Nah, fuck you." I spat just as harshly as she had. "Tasha, watch yo' gotdamn mouth and don't fuck with her, this my last time telling yo' ass that. When you get in that truck, act like the grown ass woman you're pretending to be, and not some temperamental, jealous ass baby momma. You hear me?"

Tasha's eyes jumped down to my mouth, and her gaze stayed locked on them for several seconds before looking back up. "Okay, I won't say shit to her." She spoke in a low breathless tone as her eyes returned to my mouth. "Are you going to let me go?"

"You staring pretty gotdamn hard at my mouth, ain't you?" Quickly looking away, she tried to play it cool by rolling her eyes. "If you're not curious about how Kimmy's pussy taste, you shouldn't be thinking about kissing me."

She glared at me that time. "What the fuck ever, Mike. Yo' ass probably don't know how to eat pussy anyway." Smiling, I let her go, then motioned toward the front door. Turning, she stormed out of the house like a mad ass child.

All I could do was laugh as I left the living room. Kimmy stood by the door, shaking her damn head at me. "Yo' ass just ignorant for no reason. Move." She pushed me out the way, laughing as she locked up the house.

∞∞∞

"Kimmy, where the fuck do you have us?" I've been going to her warehouse since that bitch opened and the way she was going damn sure wasn't a shortcut.

"Babe, just ride, damn." She reached for the volume dial to turn up the stereo.

I slapped her hand down. "Man, don't play with me. Where the fuck are we going?" As the question left my mouth, we pulled into a familiar residential neighborhood. I turned in my seat and glared at Malik. "I'mma beat yo' ass."

"Mike, leave him alone. He doesn't wanna be up under us all weekend. He wanna have fun with his friends." Kimmy explained as she pulled into Jerron's driveway. "Come on, Malik, I'll walk you to the door."

"You wasn't gonna ask me if yo' ass could go?" I questioned Malik.

He pointed to Kimmy. "I asked momma, and she said yeah—"

"But she's not your parent. You should've asked your daddy or me if it was alright to come over here." Tasha jumped in with an attitude. "You know better, Malik. If either your *dad or I* don't give you the okay, then you're not to go anywhere."

Malik let out a groan, and the glare that came to his face surprised the fuck out of me. "Ma —" Malik's lips closed tight, and so did his eyes as he exhaled a hard breath. "My momma is equally responsible for me, just like my daddy. She's one of my parents—"

"No, she is not—"

"Ma, why do you always have to start this. Dang. Since I was born, she's been in my life, taking care of me just like you and my daddy." Malik let out an aggravated growl. "Man, this ridiculous. I don't even wanna be in this truck with you anymore. Momma, can we go?" He didn't give Tasha a chance to say anything before hopping out of the truck slamming the door behind him.

I glared at the door, and Kimmy hit me. "Don't say shit to him." She snapped at me, then looked at Tasha. "Bitch, you fucking pathetic. You need to grow the fuck up. Like it or not, that's my mothafuckin' son too. Stupid ass hoe." She pushed her door open, then slammed it shut.

"Dumb ass, bitch—eep!" Tasha yelped out loudly as I reached back and snatched her ass to me.

I slapped her dead in the mouth twice. "What the fuck did I tell yo' ass this morning about talking that dumb shit in front of him? You a stupid acting bitch." I pushed her silly ass back. "Why the fuck would you say that bullshit to him for? Yo' stupid ass was trying to hurt her, but you're hurting him in the process. He loves the fuck out of Kimmy and ain't shit gonna change that."

"I don't give a fuck how much he likes her ass or how long she's been in his life. She ain't his fucking parent, period. I don't care how you feel about me saying that either. She's not a parent and won't be until she has her baby. This some straight bullshit."

I just stared at her ass before I laughed. "You an ignorant ass bitch, man, and that shit got you ugly as fuck."

"Whatever, Mike. I don't know why you even made me ride with y'all. You could've let me use one of your cars or trucks, and I could've been on my way."

"I wish I would let yo' ignorant ass whip any of my damn vehicles. You don't know how to act. But you could always get the fuck out and call you a gotdamn Uber."

"You real fucked up for that shit. Yo' ass treat me like straight shit, then just expect me to act all sweet and shit—"

I turned around in my seat to look at her. "How the fuck I treat yo' ass like shit? Man, get on with that bullshit. I don't ever think about yo' ass for real."

"Exactly, Mike!" She yelled at me. "Why do I have to show my ass to feel like I'm being seen or heard by you. It's like I'm not even a fucking thought to you. Mike, we have a whole ass son together, and you can't even be bothered to have a relationship with me." Tasha snapped, angry. The shit was fucking ironic to see how mad she was behind her words.

"Our relationship is how it is because of how yo' ass act. Even with all the bullshit you done pulled on my ass over the fucking years, I still look out for you and help yo' ass out way more than I need to. But you can't look past the fact I'm with Kimmy to see that you're the fucking problem. Man, yo' ass trying to be in competition with a mothafucka you can't ever compete with.

"Damn, I don't know what part of that you won't comprehend. Tasha, you're my son's mother, and that's all you'll ever be to me. So, kill all this imaginary bullshit you wanna have with me because it's never going to happen, sweetheart. Being Malik's momma is all you need to be, and as long as you're doing that shit right, I don't have a fucking problem looking out for yo' ass. But, if you keep on with this extra shit and disrespecting my girl, helping yo' ass out is over."

I had more than enough to look out for her when need be. But all that petty bullshit she wanted to play at, that shit was about to be dead.

"Okay, Mike. I completely understand." With a nod of her head, she pushed open the door and got out. My hand scrubbed over my head out of irritation. That crazy fucking woman was going to cause my gotdamn death. I had just grabbed a blunt when I realized that Tasha wasn't walking off but was headed to Ron's front door.

"Maaaan." Groaning, I pushed the door open. "I ain't got time for this bullshit." Slamming the door shut, I jogged to the front door.

"Malik!" I could hear Tasha yelling from inside the house.

Snatching the door open, I went inside. Grabbing Tasha, I pulled her back. "What the fuck are you doing, man? You really about to act an ass in here?" It was taking everything in me not to choke her ass to death.

"Let me go!" She snapped in a harsh but hushed tone.

"Ma..." Malik called, walking into the room. Kimmy and Jerron soon followed him, the trio looking confused as hell.

Tasha snatched away from me, then went over to Malik. "Baby, what I said to you in the truck, I was wrong. I didn't mean it—even if I had—I should have never said that to you. You're right, Kimmy has been in your life since you were a baby, and it's understandable why you would view her as one of your parents. Those are your feelings, and you have every right to feel the way you do. I'm so sorry if I made you feel like you shouldn't. Okay?"

Malik's eyes shifted to me. "You made her say this?" He accused, mugging me hard.

My hands raised at his accusation. Hell, I was completely surprised too. "I didn't have shit to do with that, dead ass."

"You really mean that?" He questioned, staring at her suspiciously.

Tasha nodded. "I do, and your daddy didn't make me do anything. He did make me realize how foolish I've been over the years, though. Dragging you in it was wrong on my part. I'm sorry. Forgive me?" She stroked his arms, using a soft tone as if she meant it.

With Tasha's ass, though, I didn't know. Even so, I wasn't going to say anything.

"Yeah, I do," Malik told Tasha while giving her a crooked smile.

"Malik..." Ace ran into the room but quickly came to a halt. He glanced at all of us. "Why all y'all in here?" Although he asked the question, seemingly to everyone, he was looking dead at me, mugging.

"Man, don't make me beat yo' ass." I laughed at him. He did not like me because of his little crush on Kimmy.

"We're about to go play," Malik announced, pushing Ace and laughing. "Dude, she's too old for you. Plus, my dad will shoot yo' young ass over her."

"Age ain't nothing but a number, kid. And she'll be worth every bullet." Ace responded, patting Malik on the shoulder as they disappeared out of the room.

My glare turned on Ron and his hands raised. "Shid, when I got him, he was already like that."

Kimmy broke out laughing, hitting Jerron's arm. "Don't do him like that. Ace's ass is a damn mess. Alright, Ron, we're about to get out of here. If you need anything—which I know you won't—call me."

"A'ight. I'll drop him off tomorrow." Jerron told her as he walked us to the door. Kimmy walked out the door first, then Tasha. Before I could, Ron grabbed my arm. "Yo' ass got to be insane to have those crazy mothafuckas in the car with you."

My head shook as my hand rubbed over my mouth. "Man, you don't know the half of it. I've been dealing with these crazy mothafuckas all gotdamn morning since Tasha popped up at the crib. Kimmy damn near took shorty's head off with a pan. How the fuck do you deal with this bullshit?"

Ron shrugged, then glanced back to ensure the kids weren't around. "Shid, my baby mom's dead, so I don't have to deal with this shit. Aye, that's always a solution."

"HA!" I barked out, laughing wholeheartedly at that. I felt him because I was ready to murder Tasha every time I saw her. "Shid, I may hit yo' ass up to take care of that for me." It was no longer a secret what Jerron did for a living. I would definitely hit him up if I wanted Tasha's ass gone for good.

"You a gotdamn fool. Gone head before those two kill each other, and you won't need me." Shaking up with him, I left out and went to the truck. I hopped into the driver's seat and took off.

I reached over and grabbed Kimmy's bare thigh, squeezing it. "Why you just ain't tell me he wanted to go over Ron's crib. I would've let him go." I asked as my phone went off. Grabbing it, I read the message.

"Because it was our business." Turning in the seat, she leaned over and kissed me. "You gonna help me at the store, or you're just dropping me off?"

"I'll let you know when we get there. I got to meet with King right quick, though."

"Okay, so when exactly are you dropping me off? I'm ready to go the fuck home." Tasha grumbled, irritated.

"After I meet with King," I told her.

Catching my stare in the mirror, she rolled her eyes. "And don't yo' ass ever in your life slap me again like that."

"You slapped her?" Kimmy cut in, sounding surprised.

I shrugged. "She shouldn't have started acting stupid in front of Malik. I told y'all this morning, that dumb shit dead." Turning up the radio, Kevin Gates blasted through the speakers as I finally lit my blunt. That first gotdamn inhale was heaven.

Kimmy turned down the radio, facing me. "Why are we here?" She questioned as we pulled up at the courts.

"To meet King," I told her while parking next to the black Jeep Cherokee. Kimmy's eyes squinted as she stared at the vehicle next to us. Before she could say anything, I hopped out of the truck and went to the Jeep, where King was getting out the driver's side. I shook up with him. "Good looking, dead ass. This shit was unexpected as fuck, but thanks for coming through."

"It ain't shit, I was already on that side of town, so I didn't have to go out the way to get to the garage." He tossed me the key. No matter what, King always comes through whenever I need him, whether big or small. He's been that way since we were in grade school, which was why I fucked with him so tough.

Leaning against the jeep, I laughed at his whipped ass. "Yo' dumb ass stayed at Ebony's crib?"

King's hand rubbed over his mouth as he chuckled. "Yeah, Keema wanted me to stay the night. I couldn't tell my baby girl no. You know how it is when it comes to the shorties."

My head shook at his ignorant ass. "Nigga, at some point, you ain't gonna be able to use Keema to stay a night over there."

"I ain't using her to get to Ebony." He laughed. "Real shit though, Keema ass be using me. One day I'mma tell her spoiled ass no. Dead ass, watch."

My mouth twisted up at his gotdamn lie. "Shid, you don't need to try and convince me of that bullshit you're talking about."

"Man, fuck you. Where the fuck is Tasha's crazy ass at?" He pulled a blunt from behind his ear, lighting it.

I nodded over my shoulder. "In the truck with Kimmy."

King started choking hard on his inhale. His fist hit against the center of his chest a few times as he got himself together. Waving the blunt in front of us, he pointed to my truck. "You left those crazy mothafuckas in there alone?"

"Man, they ain't gon' start no bullshit. If anything, their asses gonna sit in the bitch silent as fuck. If they do anything, I'mma beat the fuck out of both their asses."

King exhaled a cloud of smoke, jabbing the blunt at me. "What the fuck yo' ass got going on? How did you even get them in the same car together?"

"Oh, I didn't tell yo' ass." I ran down the morning's events to him. "All that unnecessary bullshit she's been doing is going to stop. Otherwise, her ass is about to see what a fucking struggle really looks like."

"Shid, you got that babe like that. Once shorty got pregnant yo' ass done practically took care of her. That gotdamn house they're in, you got and furnished that bitch. The car she's driving, you bought. Nigga, that chick in love with yo' ass. She's been waiting on you to leave Kimmy so she can step in."

I didn't see how she was in love with me when we never had a real relationship. We fucked around in high school for a short ass second, which wasn't long enough for her to fall in love. Then when she popped up again a few years later, we fucked one gotdamn time, and that was the end of it.

"That ain't gonna happen, which she already knows. Even if me and Kimmy aren't together, I won't start fucking around with her."

King motioned between us. "Yeah, we know that. She doesn't give a fuck about none of that shit. Now you're about to give her ass this bitch—"

"Michael!" Kimmy yelled, standing on the truck's passenger side with her hands raised. "How long do you expect us to sit in this hot ass truck. It ain't that much conversing in the world. Talking like y'all don't see each other every fucking day." She fussed, irritated.

"Shut the fuck up, yelling. It ain't even hot in that bitch, and if it is, turn on the fucking air." Kimmy's fussing I was going to chop up to her being pregnant. *I'm not ready for that shit.* "Ol' temperamental ass."

"She gon' beat yo' ass." King laughed. "What the fuck is that babe doing?" He questioned, digging into his pocket and retrieving his phone. "I had

Ebony's ass take me to the garage in my truck, and she was supposed to trail me up here. It's taking her ass way too long to get here."

"Shorty went joyriding. That's the last mothafucka you should've let whip yo' shit."

His head shook as he put the phone to his ear. "Nah, because she knew Peach was going to pick her up when she dropped Blaze off."

"That don't mean shit. She 'bout know Peaches will be cool watching y'all ball."

"Where the fuck you at?" He asked into the line. "Out where? Don't fucking play with me, Ebony. If yo' ass ain't pulling up here in the next minute, I'm beating yo' ass. Keep playing with me—hello?" He pulled the phone from his ear, looking at it. "That mothafucka hung up on me."

All I could do was shake my head at them. "Yo, Tasha! Come here." She got out of the truck and came over to us. A second later, I heard the passenger door slamming shut.

"Oh, shit…" King mumbled as Kimmy got out as well.

I tossed Tasha the keys to the Jeep. "You can drive this for the moment. Ain't shit wrong with it, this bitch damn near new—"

"You're giving me a car?" Tasha's damn cheeks were pushed up to her eyes.

"No. This damn jeep ain't yours. It's a fucking loaner, so don't fuck it up. You can push this until you figure out what's wrong with your car and get that fix."

Tasha's lips pursed together. "Whatever you say, Mike. As a matter of fact, you said the same thing about the car I have now. Thank you, Mike..." her words trailed off, and she glanced at Kimmy, who stood beside me, seeming to have an attitude. "Kim, you cool with him giving me this jeep?"

Kimmy's gaze slid to the jeep, then back to Tasha before her irises disappeared into her head. "Girl, I don't care. I don't drive the jeep. It sits in a damn garage."

"What the hell is wrong with you?" I was about to choke that attitude right up out of her ass.

"I'm ready to go. I told you what I had to do today." She snapped. "This is exactly why I should've drove my damn self—keep your damn hands off me." Kimmy slapped my hand as I muffed her head to the side.

"Yo, lose that gotdamn attitude, we ain't even been here for ten minutes and yo' ass bitchin'. You're acting like you got a time frame for the shit you have to do."

"That's not the fucking point—"

"Man, go get yo' ass back in the truck. Ain't nobody trying to hear that bullshit. I said I'mma take yo' stupid acting ass—"

Kimmy punched me hard as hell in my chest. "Who the fuck are you talking to—eep!" A loud squeak left her mouth as my hand grasped her throat tightly, the other taking holds of her wrist as she tried swinging on me. I pushed Kimmy down against the jeep's hood while pinning her wrist to her chest.

"I'm talking to yo' mothafuckin' ass." That babe lost her gotdamn mind. Shorty was acting an ass for no reason. "I don't know what the fuck yo' issue is, but you need to get that bitch together. Kimberly, you better get back inside yo' fuckin' body before I hurt yo' stupid acting ass."

"Mike, let me the fuck go." She yelled, bucking against me and jerking her wrist, trying to get free.

"Calm yo' goofy ass down." I held her wrist tighter while adding more pressure to her throat. Kim's struggling slowed, and as she glared at me, her face puffed up. "What the fuck is your problem?" Her mouth opened, and I choked her ass, making her eyes widen. "If you fuckin' yell, I'm beating yo' ass. You better talk to me like you got some fucking sense. Now, what the fuck is your problem?"

"Nothing is wrong with me." She claimed still mad as hell. "Can you let me go, please?" Once she asked the question, she bit into her bottom lip.

I let her wrist go but kept my grip on her throat. Pulling her to me, I stayed in her face. "What the fuck is wrong with you?"

Kim's irises once again disappeared into her head. She then blew out a breath as her eyes became glossy. "Your ugly ass trying to show out in front of King's dirty ass, and you gonna fucking yell at me."

I felt my mouth moving, yet I couldn't think of shit to say to that. I was stuck as fuck.

Tasha started laughing. Looking at her, she held up a hand as if saying, never mind her. "I'm sorry," she spoke, then cleared her throat. "I'm sorry, it's not funny, but...this sounds hormonal."

"It sounds like you need to shut the fuck up and mind your own gotdamn business, you stupid ass bitch." Kimmy bit out, mugging the hell out of Tasha. "Why the fuck are you still here? You got a fucking car that yo' ass cried about. Now, go, bye!"

"Man, hell nah." Kimmy's demeanor switched so damn fast. She looked like her feelings were hurt one second—I thought she was about to cry. Only to have her flip that emotion and go to being pissed off. Not once did I remember Tasha's feelings changing like that when she was pregnant, and homegirl hated Kimmy throughout her entire pregnancy. Shit, she still didn't like her.

Kimmy was on some straight bipolar shit. I didn't have too much experience with pregnant women, so I didn't know if Kimmy's quick, emotional flip was normal or not. If it was, I didn't want to deal with that shit.

My gaze diverted to the ground as my fingers dug into my forehead. I couldn't even look at her straight as I asked my question. "So, all of this is because you think I hurt yo' feelings—"

Kimmy hit me. "Ain't shit funny, Michael."

I was suddenly hit in the back and shoved forward. "Don't be a fucking asshole, Mike. That shit ain't even cool. I swear niggas can be so gotdamn insensitive at times." Peaches fussed, going to Kimmy. "Babe, are you okay?" Peaches asked, hugging her. "I started to come over here sooner, but Blaze dumb ass stopped me."

"Peaches, make me strangle yo' nappy-headed ass. How the fuck am I insensitive when I didn't do shit?"

"Come on, babe, tell me what happened." Peaches said, ignoring me and pulling Kimmy away from us.

The fucked up thing about it was that Kimmy let Peaches drag her off as if I really did some shit.

"How many months is she?" Tasha asked.

"About four."

She chuckled. "That whole pretending to not be bothered by anything—front she puts on is definitely about to come crumbling down." She claimed, patting my chest. "I hope you're ready to meet the real Kimmy."

"Don't lie and tell him no bullshit like that. You no gotdamn well y'all can't control those hormones. That shit turns y'all bipolar as hell." King snapped at her. "Why the fuck are you still here? Didn't she tell yo' ass to leave with her truck that she gave you? Bitch, get yo' ass from up here before I have my girl beat yo' dumb ass." He pointed straight ahead, causing Tasha to look back.

I did the same, seeing King's truck pulling in. "I'm not listening to shit Tasha's saying, and if she stays here, that's on her," I told them before walking over to where Peaches and Kimmy were.

"Babe...it sounds like you kind of went off on him first." Peaches told her.

Kimmy shrugged. "So, what though, that's not even the point, Peach. He didn't even have to talk to me like that."

Peaches looked up at that moment, locking eyes with me. "I'm so sorry." She mouthed before her attention returned to Kimmy. "Kim..." She broke out laughing before her hand covered her mouth.

Kimmy pushed her. "Bitch, ain't shit funny."

"I'm sorry, I swear. You're right, but Kim, you're acting as if he talks to you any differently in that type of situation."

"Ugh! I know! And knowing that only makes the shit worse because my damn feelings still get all twisted with emotions. Bitch, how the fuck y'all do this shit? I don't want this."

Peaches broke out laughing again. "I'm sorry, but this is hilarious, Kim. Remember when I was pregnant with the twins and overly emotional about Blaze and y'all hoes were laughing at me?" She motioned over Kimmy. "Payback's a bitch,

51

literally."

"Well, y'all might as well make room for her ass because she can't stay with me. Especially not with her emotions flip-flopping like this."

Peaches started laughing, and Kimmy hit her. "Don't laugh at his ignorant ass. Peaches, for your information, that was different." She snapped at her before turning her glare on me. "Mike, I have a whole house that I can go back to."

I nodded in agreeance. "You do, and you can definitely go back to that mothafucka—"

Kimmy started laughing. "I swear you get on my nerves." Coming over to me, she wrapped her arms around my waist. "I'm sorry. I shouldn't have gone off on you like that. Forgive me?"

All I could do was chuckle at her crazy ass. "We're good."

Smiling, she kissed me. Still staring, her hand waved in an expecting manner. My brow cocked questioningly. "You're not going to apologize too?"

Peaches hollered out a laugh. "Bitch, leave that damn man alone. Yo' ass started with him, the fuck! But you want him to apologize for checking you."

Kimmy glared at her. "Girl, stay out of our damn business, irritating ass. Get away from us." She pushed Peaches as a chuckle slipped through her lips. "That shit is kind of right, though. But still, he hurt my wrist." She claimed, holding her wrist up for me to see.

My arm went around her shoulder, pulling her into my side. "Yo' ass better get those hormones under control before they get you hurt."

"Mhm..." She hummed, leaning up kissing me.

"And that's why I told yo' ass to stay out their shit." Blaze said, sitting a cooler down beside Peaches.

Peaches waved him off. "Nah, I thought he was messing with her. I sure was about to jump on you, Mike. Blaze saved you." Peaches' hands clapped together as she cracked up. "Bitch, you should've seen my ass jump out that damn truck. I'm like, *hell no, I know his ass don't have my bitch pinned down on that truck like that.* Kimmy, I should beat your ass because I was sure about to get involved in y'all shit."

"Girl, you're just dramatic, which is why yo' ass reacted like that. Now, of all people, you know me and know I wouldn't have wanted you to get involved anyway. Dramatic ass."

"You ain't lied, she dramatic as fuck." Blaze chimed in, laughing as Peaches hit him.

"Blaze, shut up, you get on my nerves. Don't you have a game to play? Gone." She pushed him away from her.

"You ready to go?" I motioned toward the truck.

"What y'all about to do?" Peaches asked before Kim could respond.

"I have to drop some stuff off at the store, then," she shrugged, pointing to me, "whatever he wants to do."

"If you want, I can take you to the store once their game is over." Peaches offered, but I knew she was silently telling Kimmy to stay. The stare she was giving said it all.

"Nah, I'mma ride with him. We can get up later, though." Kimmy told her.

Peaches' head started bobbing, but she didn't seem happy about Kim not wanting to stay. "Okay, I guess. I mean, we can because momma has the kids, and I'm off, so yeah."

"Damn, look at all that ass!"

Kimmy yelped and jumped, turning around. "Bitch! Missy, I'mma fuck yo' ass up." Kim snapped out a laugh while rubbing her booty. "Heavy-handed ass, hoe got my booty stinging." She said, hitting Missy.

"I'm sorry, baby, I couldn't help myself. It was just sitting there begging me to grab it." She chuckled, hugging Kim. "Hey, Mike." She waved at me. After tossing her two fingers, she looked back to Kimmy. "Why the fuck is Tasha's raggedy ass up here?"

My hand pressed hard into Missy's face, muffing the hell out of her. "Man, don't bring yo' ass over here with that bullshit. She ain't bothering you, so don't worry about her."

Kimmy hit me, laughing. "Why the hell would you muff her like that? You about to get yo' ass beat out here."

"I swear! Mike, you better keep yo' damn hands off me before—"

"Before what? I'll beat all y'all asses." Just to show her I wasn't moved by their warning, I muffed her again.

"I'm about to beat yo' ass." Missy dropped her bag on top of the cooler then came at me. Grabbing the top of her head, I forced her to bend, then pushed her to the ground. "Mike, let me go with yo' stupid ass! I'mma beat yo' ass as soon as I get up, watch."

"And you still gonna talk shit?" I asked as she hit my legs.

"Mike, let her go. Yo' ass so childish." Kimmy laughed, trying to push me away from Missy. "Let her go before I help her beat yo' ass, Michael!" She pushed me again, then grabbed my wrist, trying to get me to let Missy go. "Mike!" She hollered as I snatched her to me.

Quickly letting Missy go, I clipped Kimmy, making her fall beside Missy. Of course, I didn't make her fall hard on the ground. I damn near laid her down. But the moment was so fast, it shocked her. "Oh, my God. Mike!" She yelled, surprised.

"No, the fuck you don't!" King's close voice caused me to look back just in time to see him snatch Ebony up.

"Eep!" She screeched out. "Put me down, King!" She hollered, laughing.

"Watch back." He said, bringing her over. I moved back, and he dropped her on Missy and Kimmy. "She was about to get yo' ass." King laughed as he pushed Missy back down.

"Good looking. I didn't even see her sneaky ass." I shook up with him.

"I swear y'all act like fucking children. Ugly dirty asses!" Ebony snapped, trying to get up.

Kimmy suddenly broke out laughing hard as hell. "I promise they do. Mike, I swear I'm beating your ass. Why would you push us on this dirty ass ground, though?"

"Right, especially when he knew I was just playing with him." Missy chimed in, glaring at me before she started laughing. "Kimmy, shut up, bitch ain't shit funny."

"It's not, for real, though, but he didn't even have to drop me like that. I swear I'mma beat his ass watch. Missy, you gonna learn to shut up. Always starting something."

"Bitch, he muffed me first." Missy defended herself.

"Girl, so. You should've ignored him." Kimmy laughed as her arms came out for me. "Get me off this ground." Grabbing her hands, I pulled her up, then helped Missy to her feet.

"Next time, the both of y'all should shut the fuck up." My palm brushed against Kimmy's ass, wiping the small pebbles from her shorts and thighs.

"Dude, fuck you. You don't run shit but Kimmy's ass." She jumped at me. "He gets on my nerves. I should knock him out. But I'mma let you slide because I don't feel like beating yo' ass." Missy fussed before she ended up laughing. "Anyways. Why the fuck Tasha ass here?"

"Girl, something was wrong with her car, and Mike let her use my jeep." Kim ran down to her.

Ebony's lips suddenly popped. "Girl, if I knew that was why King had me ride with him, I wouldn't have gone."

"But why is she still here?" Missy asked, pointing toward the parking lot.

Kimmy simply shrugged in response. "Hell, if I know."

My head shook at them. They were messy as fuck for no gotdamn reason. "Why do you care, though? Shorty ain't bothering yo' ass, so why you worried about her?"

Missy waved me off but didn't respond to what I said. If Tasha wasn't bothering Kimmy or me, I didn't care about her being there.

"Why are they here?" Ebony suddenly asked

with a hard roll of her eyes. The girls followed her gaze to the three chicks walking through the grass.

King muffed the fuck out of Ebony. "Don't start that bullshit. They can be here just like y'all ass." He told her but was addressing all the girls.

"It's so funny that when we didn't know shit about them, we never saw their asses. Now those bitches just be popping up everywhere." Missy claimed with a hard roll of her eyes.

Kimmy's wrist flicked, brushing off what they were saying. "It doesn't matter. They came to watch their man play basketball, so leave them be."

It took me a second to realize what was up once I saw Bellow. I recognize the girl on his side and the other chick with them. The third babe, I didn't know who she was. The chick next to Bellow's girl was the babe that tried to drop that bombshell on my ass.

"Aye, yo!" I called across the court.

"Why would you yell that loud in my ear for? And who are you calling?" Kimmy asked, rubbing her ear.

"I'll be right back." Letting her go, I took off toward the parking lot.

Chapter Three

Kimmy

Our Closed Chapter

I stared after Mike, watching as he jogged to the parking lot. For a second, I thought he was going to Tasha until I saw Twitch. "I wanna know what they got going on." Although the words were spoken aloud, I wasn't directing them to anyone.

"I don't know, but Twitch knows he's still fine as fuck." Ebony grunted, watching as Twitch and Mike shook up. "I wanna sample the fuck out of him in real life."

Pushing her, I started laughing. "Hoe, you're so damn stupid."

"I'm serious as hell too." She claimed.

"Akil sexy too, no lie." Missy chimed in, nodding toward the dread-headed man standing next to Mike. "Anyway..." Missy stated, facing me. "Leave them be? What's that about?"

Leave it to Missy to bring up my saying that. "It's not about anything. I just don't see a reason to be pissed off at them. I mean," I shrugged, "what would the point be?" Of course, the reason would be over Bellow. Even still, I was over feeling some type of way about his girl and him. My anger should have never been aimed at her to begin with. Hell, I shouldn't have been pissed at all.

"Okay, bitch, what the fuck?" Ebony questioned as Peaches came back over to us.

Ignoring E's question, my attention was on Peaches. "You good, babe?"

Immediately her eyes found Blaze, who was on the other side of the court, talking to Bellow. "Yeah. His ass is getting on my damn nerves, though. Fuck him."

From the attitude rolling off of Peaches, I knew Blaze must have said something regarding her feelings toward Sabrina. Although Peaches hadn't said anything when she saw them, her hard eye roll said a lot.

Once again, I decided not to address that whole thing. I honestly didn't want to feel like I was to blame for their dislike toward that woman.

"What y'all over here talking about?" Peaches put the question out there, glancing at us.

"Kim was just about to tell us why she's saying leave ol' girl and them alone." Ebony informed her, making me glare at her raggedy ass.

"Because we don't have a reason to bother them. That whole shit I started was dumb ass hell and should have never gone down at all. I've learned from my dumb-ass mistake, and I'm moving forward."

"And Bellow?" She tacked on.

Easily my gaze found him. As usual, he looked good in his basketball shorts and beater. "Same." Although a part of me cared for him, I knew that our time had come to an end.

It was ironic how it took us having sex that one day and me walking away to fully accept that. Strangely, I was alright with us being done. The urge to burst into tears was no more, and my heart didn't ache with longing like before either.

Still having love for Bellow was something I could never erase entirely. Neither would I want to. Everything with him was an experience that I would never want to forget. He would have a piece of my heart forever. However, I could breathe easily without him.

Yet, Mike had my heart entirely. Hell, the man had my damn lungs. He was the one I couldn't live or breathe without. That irritating ass man was everything to me.

Without even realizing it, my gaze found Mike. My vision went black as my damn eyes rolled at the excitement that coursed through me.

The feeling that filled me at that moment said

so much. That was why I was at peace closing that chapter with Bellow.

Missy's face suddenly came into mine. Blinking, my head jerked before my palm pressed into her mug, pushing her back. "Girl, get out my damn face."

"Well, hoe don't ignore us. Standing there all awestruck and shit." She chuckled.

I waved her off. "Oh, what you said?"

She rolled her eyes. "We asked what you mean by the same."

I shrugged. "The exact same thing applies to him also. I'm learning from my mistake and behavior and moving forward. So, there doesn't have to be an issue when we're all together. Or when his girl and her friends are around. We can all be cordial." I honestly meant everything I said. In truth, I didn't have an issue with his girl anymore.

Just because Bell and I weren't going to be messing around didn't mean that we couldn't hang with our friends together without there being an issue.

"I was really outside my damn body during that whole situation with them. I feel stupid as hell for it too. But that's part of the learning process, I guess."

"Babe, you really mean that, don't you?" Peaches asked, seeming to already know the answer as her head bobbed.

I nodded. "Yeah, I do."

"Well, I'm glad you've gotten to that space where you can feel like this. Bitch, I'm proud of you." Ebony claimed, smiling. A chuckle left her mouth. "Okay, confession. I'm glad you came to this realization because, for one, I was ready to fight you for being out here looking damn dumb. Two, my nails miss her. She used to hook my shit up, man—"

I broke out laughing, pushing her away from me. "You're so damn ignorant, man. Ugh. Bitch, go get your nails done, then hoe."

She laughed with me. "Oh, after you've said all that, I am. Nah, but seriously, Kimmy, I'm glad you're letting that shit go because how you were acting wasn't the Kim I knew. And I've been knowing you since Elementary. You surprised the hell out of me with acting that way—bitch!" She hit me as she seemed to realize something. "Of —fucking—course!" Ebony's hands shot out as she came to some sort of conclusion.

"Y'all, the bitch was pregnant. That must be why she took everything over the fucking top. Think about it. Before, yeah, she was hurt and irritated, I mean heartbroken. But then the bitch just started bawling about everything about him. Whole-time we're thinking our bitch losing her mind, but she was pregnant." Ebony whispered in an excited hushed tone as if she cracked open a top-secret.

"Bitch, that actually makes a lot of damn

sense. Remember after that slip, homegirl was over it, bitch almost lost her damn life confessing that bullshit to Mike and everything—"

"Ugh hoe, I hate you!" I hollered at Missy's overly detailed two cents. "Like, really? You didn't even have to bring that bullshit up. That shit is traumatic as hell. I thought that damn man was going to kill my ass." My head fell on Ebony's shoulder as I groaned. "But I kind of think so too, though. I was just overly emotional. I'm better with controlling it now—"

"Girl, don't you stand there and lie. Mike had yo' ass hemmed the fuck up because of your damn emotions." Peaches blasted me, laughing.

Once again, I groaned. "So, ugh bitch, shut up. No, but for real, though, my emotions be all over the place. Y'all, I'll go into this gotdamn rage that I can't even control. Bitch, I threw a damn pan full of fried potatoes at Tasha's head this morning, but before that, I threw a pool ball at her dome, trying to bust her head straight open. Now, y'all know I never let that girl get to me. But now, every time she opens her mouth, I'm ready to fight." I ran down to them. "I don't see how y'all survived this bullshit. I'm ready to say fuck it. I can't do this shit." Thinking about earlier events with Tasha, I hollered out laughing.

"Wait, bitches, so I told y'all about what happened with Tasha. My smart-ass mouth had Mike on some get-back shit, right. Y'all, why the fuck did I start crying because his ass wouldn't give me no dick. When I say my damn feelings were hurt, y'all, I mean that shit literally. Like, my damn soul just felt so torn—"

The girls fell out laughing. "Bitch, no the fuck you didn't. What Mike ass say?"

Thinking about it at that moment had me crying laughing. "Mike was like, you dead ass crying real tears. That damn man was so gotdamn confused. His entire face was stuck, y'all. Like he didn't know how to react because I was really crying."

"Well, did he give yo' ass the dick?" Missy cracked up.

"Yeah—fuck y'all. After crying, I didn't even want that shit, though—shut up!" I pushed Peaches as she fell against me, laughing her ass up.

"Lying ass talking about you didn't want it. Knowing damn well you took that shit." Peaches claimed.

"So, what, man. Y'all, don't laugh at me. I promise this shit is going to drive me crazy for real." I was not prepared to be pregnant at all. Yet given I've watched Peach and Ebony go through their pregnancy journeys, one might think I would know what to expect. I didn't. Everything just felt surprising to me.

"Y'all subject change, here comes my boyfriend," Ebony whispered, nodding ahead at Mike, Twitch, and Akil making their way to us.

"Girl, here yo' hot ass go." Peaches shook her head at Ebony.

Once they finally reached us, I hugged Twitch. "Where the hell you've been hiding at?" Mike and Twitch weren't the best of friends, but they were cool enough that they used to occasionally link up, drink and smoke whenever Twitch popped up.

He chuckled at that, returning my hug. "I'm always around. You just too damn busy to see me." Letting me go, he tossed up two fingers at the girls. "Ladies."

"Hey, Akil." I waved at him. He was another dude I've known for years through Mike. However, my girls became familiar with him in the past year or so. After Missy got caught up in the middle of some shit he had going on that nearly killed her.

"What's up, sweetheart." He smiled at me.

Before I could give Akil a hug, Mike grabbed me by the waist, pulling me into his chest. "You don't hug that mothafucka."

Akil's smirk widened as he chuckled. "You met my shorty—"

Mike pointed at him. "And that's why she can't hug yo' ass."

I hit Mike's arm. "Shut up. He ain't thinking about me when he got that thick, voluptuous ass chick at home."

Mike squeezed my thigh as he pushed my

head to the side with his. "You just described yourself. Once he hugs you, he's gonna say some slick shit." He claimed before biting into my neck.

What Mike said caused Akil to laugh, which made me believe he wasn't lying. I just rolled my eyes at them.

"Hell no! Sam, don't be fouling him!" Peaches shouted on the court. "I saw that shit, cheating ass." She looked back at us, pointing to the game. "Y'all saw that? Sam's ass a cheater."

I missed the whole damn play.

"Bitch, take your ass over there with the other yelling girlfriends if you're gonna be screaming like that." Ebony motioned over to where Sabrina and her girls stood, laughing and yelling at the game as Peaches had done.

At that moment, they paused the game, which caused them to come over to where we stood since the drink cooler was next to us.

Nyeisha, Sabrina's sister, jumped on King's back as he made his way over. Once they reached us, she got off his back, glanced at me, and rolled her eyes hard.

I had to laugh at that, yet I wasn't going to say shit to her. I didn't feel like getting out of character for her immature ass.

"Hey, fellas." She spoke, waving. "How come y'all not out there playing?" She questioned, making it known she was talking to the men only.

"Maybe because we didn't come here to play. That's a thought." Twitch put out there with a shrug.

She held up her hands in a surrendering gesture. "Okay, I was just trying to make conversation, is all. Y'all over here just looking bored and shit."

King muffed her head to the side. "Man, take yo' ass back over there." He told her.

"So, what? This group don't like that one?" Akil asked, motioning from us to across the courts.

"No, it's nothing like that—Mike, dude, you hear me talking. Don't bite me again." I elbowed him.

Nyeisha's eyes rolled once again at me before she looked at Mike. "So, you still with her?"

Mike stopped his biting on my neck and stood up straight. "What?" The tone of his voice had me rubbing my forehead. Why she wanted to be petty and stir up some shit by talking to Mike was beyond me. But I wasn't going to say shit.

She shrugged. "I'm just saying, I'm surprised you're still with her. I thought you would've started looking for something better by now." The clear suggestion in her tone had my head shaking.

I glanced at my girls to see their mouths ready to pop off. My eyes squinted slightly at them, telling their asses to shut up. Homegirl wanted to speak to Mike directly, so I would let her.

"Sweetheart, you ain't even my type, dead ass. And you damn sho' ain't shit better than where I'm at, in no fucking way. So, gon' on with that bullshit yo' ass trying to start." He laughed, shaking his head. "You goofy bitches stay minding other mothafuckas business. Bitch, who the fuck I'm with ain't yo' gotdamn concern. If either one of us ain't ever fucked you, what happened ain't got shit to do with yo' ass. As a matter of fact," Mike pointed across the field to Sabrina. "You should be over there with yo' sister, telling her ass that shit, because it doesn't seem like she started looking for shit better. Gon' mind her business and not mine. Gon' on." He shooed her off like she was a pestering gnat.

"Dude, fuck you! I don't know who the fuck you think you're talking to like that—"

"Bitch, I'm talking to yo' ass like that—"

"Nuh-uh, Mike, don't say shit else to her. You answered her question already. But you're not going to argue with this bitch because she's upset about something that don't have shit to do with her. Like, why the fuck are you over here bothering us for? Especially when your sister looks happily in love. Matter of fact—Bellow!" I yelled across the courts to him, getting all of their attention.

"Come get this bitch before I stomp her fucking face into this cement!" I told him before looking back at Nyeisha. "That was your only warning. Now please walk away. Like, don't say anything else to us, or I'mma hit you dead in the mouth."

"Bitch—"

I knocked her dead in the fucking mouth. That was all I had the chance to do as Mike snatched me up quick as hell. The man lifted my ass up and spun us around so damn fast that everything blurred for a second.

"Mike, what are you doing? Let me go!" I shouted. I was beyond pissed that he stopped me. I've been wanting to hit Eisha in the mouth ever since she tried to drop that bombshell on Mike a while back.

"Let me the fuck go! Hoe, you gon' hit me! Let that trifling ass bitch go so I can drag that hoe! Dude, put me down!" Homegirl was going off. "Bitch, I will fuck you up!" Baby girl was screaming, making all types of threats to beat my ass.

I wanted to give her everything she was begging for too. "Hoe, you ain't even about that— Mike, let me go, please!" He was starting to piss me off by holding me.

"You ain't about to fight that bitch because she wanna run her damn mouth." Of course, Mike would say that because he didn't care about her talking.

Usually, I wouldn't either, but she just bothered my soul. I didn't understand why she cared so much about my fucking affair when she wasn't down her sister's gotdamn throat. "Michael, please! I'm just gonna talk to her. Babe, please just let me go." Mike's grip on my arms—pinned to my sides—had me immobile. All I could do was thrust my damn legs. I didn't like the desperate feeling my upper body felt for movement.

"Man, fuck her. Calm yo' goofy-ass down." He snapped at me.

"Michael! Please!" I screamed at him.

"Not until you calm the fuck down. If I have to keep telling you that, I'm going to beat yo' ass." He threatened, and I wanted to hit him, hell or talk shit, but I didn't feel like getting jerked up again in front of everybody.

"Ooh, I swear to God, man." My damn feelings were so hurt, simply because I was angry and couldn't release that shit. "She didn't even have to come over here with that bullshit, though. That dumb ass bitch raging like it was her fucking nigga. When her damn sister ain't even said shit. Like why the fuck is she so gotdamn mad. Stupid ass bitch projecting her anger at the wrong mothafucka. Ooh, man, I swear."

"Man, fuck that bitch. How are you gonna let that bitch make you this angry? If I let yo' ass go, you better control your gotdamn self." He let me down, and I instantly started looking for her ass. Mike grabbed my damn chin in a tight vice grip, bringing my attention to him. "What the fuck did I just tell you? Don't make me fuck you up out here, Kimmy. You ain't about to fight that bitch, or nobody else for that matter, now calm the fuck down."

The fact that my punk ass wanted to cry because I craved to fight her pissed me off far more than need be. "I'm calm." Mike raised a questioning brow. "I promise, I'm calm."

"But why would you even go over there? The bullshit is dead. Why do you keep trying to bring the shit back up, Eisha? Damn, you're acting like the bullshit happened to you. Leave them the fuck alone and let the shit drop." Sabrina was going off on her sister.

That was what I didn't understand. How was Nyeisha popping off behind a man that wasn't even hers?

"That bitch is insane," I spoke aloud, not caring for who heard me. Yet, my words grabbed their attention.

"I'mma show yo' hoe ass just how insane I am too. You trifling ass bitch!" She yelled, totally enraged.

I broke out laughing. "Baby, you mean that shit with all your heart too. Oh, my God." I cracked the fuck up. "Woo, baby, I love the passion you have." My sights fell on Sabrina. "Looks to me like you need to try and figure out why she's so hurt behind some shit your man did—"

"Because I don't like trifling ass hoes like you. And unlike my sister, I'm very fucking problematic —" Baby girl was going off.

"Tell yo' girls bye, 'cause we're out," Mike

instructed, turning us toward the girls. I cut my eyes at him.

"How you just gonna make her tell us bye, though?" Missy laughed, coming closer to us.

"Because her ass don't know how to act. Ol' violent ass knows she shouldn't be fighting. She gon' make me fuck her ass up." He threatened, mugging me. "Gon' tell their asses bye." He commanded with a wave of his hand.

"We'll get together later tonight—" I started saying.

"No, the fuck y'all won't. Until you can control your gotdamn emotions, yo' ass grounded." The fact that he sounded so serious had me laughing. But the raising of his brow had my chuckling slowing. "Oh, I'm serious as fuck."

"Bitch, not he done grounded her ass." The girls fell out laughing, thinking he was playing. Mike was every bit serious.

I wasn't even about to embarrass myself any further in front of them all. Hell, it wasn't only my girls out there. "Alright, I'll call y'all later when I get home," I said, hugging them.

"Ugh, why do you sound so sad?" Leave it to Peaches to ask that shit out loud.

I waved her off. "I don't. But for real, I'll call y'all later."

Once we walked away, Mike pulled me into his side. "Look, you ain't about to be out here fighting bitches because they say some shit to you. Just like you used to ignore that shit, continue to. Sweetheart, it's not just about you anymore. I'm telling you now if anything happens to my shorty while you're carrying him or her, I'm going to fuck you up. So, you better start thinking before you react to dumb shit." Mike yanked open my door, letting me in.

I wasn't even in the truck good enough before he slammed the door in my face. That's when I knew he was really pissed off with me. It was strange how I didn't think about my pregnancy when my body went into a rage. Hell, I was going off instinct only.

Mike was right. I couldn't keep letting stupid shit get to me. Even I knew stress on the body wasn't good for the baby.

"You're right. I wasn't thinking. Hell, don't too much go through my mind when I get to that point of anger which you know. Still, that shouldn't be an excuse. You're right, though it's not just about me anymore. I have a whole other being that I'm carrying." Grabbing his hand, I kissed his knuckles. "I can't promise my anger won't get the best of me at times, but I'm going to try not to fight while I'm pregnant. I promise." I meant every word that left my mouth. It was stupid trying to fight that damn girl. What if we did come to blows, and she hit me in my stomach the wrong way or something, causing me to miscarry?

"Mike, you hear me?" It was a dumb question

to ask. Of course, he heard me talking to him. Hell, the radio was down low, so he had no choice but to listen to me. "So, you're just going to ignore me?" I wanted to push him but thought better of doing that. Yet, knowing Mike, he probably really wanted me to think about my actions.

My gaze was fixed on the side of his head as I waited for him to acknowledge what I said. Hell, even look at me, for that matter. He did neither. Once again, I got that strong urge to punch him hard as hell, and yet again, I ignored the feeling, knowing it was probably best not to provoke him.

Heavily sighing, I slumped back in my seat and let what happened replay in my head.

As I thought about everything, I had to admit that the whole mess with Nyeisha was entirely unnecessary. I had to leave it all in the past and continue to move forward in my life. That was making plans with Mike and for our baby.

Everything else no longer mattered.

The whole Bellow, Sabrina, Kimmy, and Nyeisha situation was a closed chapter in my book.

Chapter Four

Bellow

I Can't Keep Being Selfish with You

Once Kimmy started yelling over at me, I knew some bullshit was about to happen. "What the fuck is wrong with yo' stupid ass sister? Why the fuck is she even over there?" I was pissed that Eisha kept bringing our bullshit up, especially when it didn't have shit to do with her.

"Oh, shit!" Blaze stated as Kim knocked Eisha in the face.

"Fuck!" Sabrina went to take off running, but I grabbed her. "Don't take yo' ass over there and do shit, Brina. Eisha shouldn't have walked her stupid ass over there talking shit."

Sabrina punched the shit out of me in my chest. "You better let me the fuck go." Jerking away from me, she ran over to her sister, who King held.

"Bitch, I will drag yo' stank ass!" Eisha was

shouting as Kim's nigga pulled her off. "Let me the fuck go, King, damn! Like, what the fuck?" She hollered, pissed off.

Sabrina reached her sister and snatched the girl from King. Instantly Eisha tried to run after Kimmy, but Brina stopped her. "Eisha, would you fucking stop! What the fuck is wrong with you—"

"That bitch hit me!" Eisha snapped, jerking away from Sabrina.

"Yeah, after your ass went over there on some dumb shit, Nyeisha! You had no reason to go over there other than to start some mess. Like, the bullshit is fucking dead. Why do you keep on trying to keep the shit alive, Eisha? Damn, you're acting like the shit happened to you. Bitch, it didn't. It's my shit that I've already handled with the only mothafucka out here that wronged me, Eisha, me, not you, not them but me. So, if I'm not over here acting stupid and showing my mothafuckin' ass, neither should anyone else—"

"That's the point, Brina, you're not going to fucking do shit! These mothafuckas sit around talking hella shit, they sit in your fucking face rolling their eyes, giving you attitude, putting the fucking affair in your face like you're the mothafucka that's wrong. Still, you don't say anything, Sabrina." Eisha screamed at her sister.

I knew that was why Nyeisha was going so damn hard behind Sabrina, because of the disrespect Kim's girls were giving off.

Sabrina let out a laugh. "Because I do not fucking care, Eisha, what part of that aren't you understanding. Eye rolls won't hurt my feelings, nor does talking shit cause lashes on my skin. Baby, as long as no one is swinging on me, I don't have an issue with any of them. As I said, the only person I will take issue with is my man. You might not like how I deal with my shit, and you don't have to, baby, but it's my own shit to deal with. So, leave that girl the fuck alone and let the shit drop." Sabrina told Eisha in the finalizing tone that I knew she hated.

"As a matter of fact, if you wanna fight with somebody, fight Bellow's ass. Whenever you're feeling froggy and wanna pounce, talk shit to his ass, swing on that nigga because he's the mothafucka that's wrong." She waved her hand toward me, telling her sister to do something.

Eisha looked at me for a long few seconds before rolling her damn eyes. "Brina, I hear everything you're saying, but I don't like that shit either. I especially don't want any of them to think you're some type of punk ass bitch, because you're not saying anything—"

"Either of them is doing anything, Eisha. Why should I prove I'm not a punk to anyone that I don't have a gotdamn problem with? If any of them have an issue with me, that's something they need to deal with, not me, baby. Now, if you're not going to fight my man, let it go. Are you going to fight him?"

Once again, Eisha stared at me as if

considering it before her eyes rolled again. "Whatever, Sabrina, you're right, this is your shit, and I'm done saying anything." She claimed before her sights set on Peaches and her girls. "But I'm going to beat that bitch ass for hitting me—"

"Nah, you ain't gonna do a mothafuckin' thing; otherwise, I'mma fuck you up. I've already told you to leave that fuckin' babe alone. Shorty popped you in yo' shit because you went fuckin' with her. Had you shut the fuck up and stayed in yo' place, you wouldn't have gotten hit. So, dead that bullshit. If you see that mothafucka go the other way. If I find out you popped stupid on her behind our shit, I'm telling you, Nyeisha, I'm beating the fuck out of you." I warned, and that would be the last warning I gave. I was over her fucking attitude and her going at Kimmy behind our shit. Kimmy should've knocked her shit in.

"Seriously, Bellow? That bitch hit me—"

"Because yo' stupid ass went fucking with her. That babe wasn't thinking about yo' ass until you opened yo' fuckin' mouth. Now leave this bullshit alone." My arm slid around Sabrina's neck, and I pulled her into my chest.

From Eisha's harsh glare, I knew she wasn't happy about me telling her to let the shit go. "Fucking fine. I swear I hate yo' ass sometimes." She pushed away from us and stormed toward the parking lot.

"Alright, cool, great," Sabrina said to Nyeisha's retreating back before her gaze settled on everyone who stared at us. She pulled out of my hold. "Now that the show is over, can we get back to this game? My baby was beating y'all asses—ah!" She squeaked before jumping out the way. "What the fuck, B?" She snapped at Blaze.

"Nigga, did you just throw a fuckin' ball at her?" I glared at his ass.

He nodded while pointing to Sabrina. "She's always talking that bullshit. His ass wasn't winning a mothafuckin' thing. Take yo' baldheaded ass home, Sabrina!" He fussed at her.

Sabrina hollered out a laugh. "Nigga, not yo' ass mad and wanna throw damn balls at women. Don't get pissed because my cheering is boosting my baby skills, and he's whooping y'all sucka asses." She told him while jumping into my arms. "You better beat their asses otherwise, all that dope morning toe-curling top I give you, gonna stop for a good two weeks." She sucked on my bottom lip, then top.

"Hell nah! I knew that mothafucka had been cheating. You can't tell that nigga no bullshit like that. Hell yeah, shorty got to go, now!" King chimed in after overhearing what Sabrina had said.

Sabrina started laughing against my lips. "King, mind your manners and close yo' gotdamn ears. This don't have anything to do with you."

I hiked Sabrina up on me, securing my hands at her ass. Then glared at Blaze. "Nigga, I'mma beat yo' ass. Throw something else at her." I threatened.

Blaze laughed at that while pointing to

Sabrina. "Make her ass go the fuck home. I don't know why you brought her." I glanced over to Peaches, who was staring at us. "Nigga, that's different. Peaches don't get involved in us playing. Sabrina's ass is always talking shit. Man, fuck all that, send her ass home. Bye, Brina, take Eisha and Kass with you—"

"What the fuck I do? I haven't said not one thing." Kass chimed in, pointing to herself. "B, you better leave me alone. I'm not going anywhere unless it's with Sam. And since he's on the winning team, I'm about to start yelling too." She claimed, wrapping her arms around his waist.

"Let's switch shit up then, Sabrina, bring yo' ass on and get in the game. My shorty knows how to hoop too." Blaze suggested.

My head was already shaking. Given how Peaches acted toward Sabrina, I didn't see her playing the game just for fun. "Nah, she ain't balling —"

"I can, though—" She said, wanting to play.

I glared at Sabrina. "But yo' ass not playing. You gonna sit yo' ass down over there and watch us."

Sabrina's face formed into a harsh glare. "Seriously, Bell? We can play." I walked us off, and she let out an irritated groan. "What? Why can't I play?"

I glared down at her. "You know why I don't want yo' ass playing." My eyes drifted down to her stomach. "I don't trust Peaches ass to play straight up without being on no bullshit. I'm not risking you getting hurt, especially not while you're carrying my shorty. Look, after you have my baby, cool, I'll let you hoop with us."

"Baby, I'm only five weeks. Besides, it's basketball. There's minimal contact in this game. Like, come on, babe—"

"No. Five weeks or six months, you're still pregnant with my baby, so you're not balling." Sabrina's mouth opened to say something, but my lips covered hers. Once she moaned into the kiss, I squeezed her ass before slapping it. "Sweetheart, I'm not arguing with you about this shit. You're not hooping. You're gonna stand yo' fine ass on the sidelines and yell for me. A'ight?"

Sabrina's eyes rolled, but she chuckled no less. "What's been up with you lately? You've been far more overbearing behind me a lot, and this was before knowing I was pregnant."

It wouldn't be Sabrina not to notice the small things and call me out on my shit. "I wouldn't say I'm being overbearing, just...shid, I don't know. I guess I'm trying to be better for you." She nodded in response.

"I've noticed that too. Especially after you bought my gifts." She stroked over the pink sapphire gem that sat against her chest, then the matching ring on her finger, finally the bracelet that decorated her wrist. "You've been apologizing a lot, which you should be doing. Still, this is different, though. You're different. Hm..." she suddenly hummed before a light laugh left her mouth. "I don't know how I didn't see it sooner. You're growing up."

I chuckled at those words because I was trying to. I had no choice in the matter. It was either keep doing dumb shit or lose Sabrina entirely. I couldn't do the latter. My ass was too gotdamn selfish to let her go.

"I am. I saw it all in your face that you were tired and was going to take off on my ass." Once Sabrina learned that Kimmy was cool with Blaze's wife, Peaches. I knew then shorty was about to take off. I couldn't have that. Losing Sabrina was never going to be an option for me.

Messing around with Kimmy was never supposed to have gone on for so damn long. I couldn't change those years, regardless of how much I wanted to.

Even though I cared about Kimmy, she wasn't Sabrina. Us fucking at Red Pin was the last time we'd ever fuck again. The only reason it happened was because of our first slip-up. I still felt like shit for handling that babe the way I had. I couldn't let that be our last time.

No, Sabrina didn't know about that, nor did she need to. That was one thing I would never tell her about. Even so, Kimmy and I were officially done.

Sabrina's lips pressed together as she nodded.

When I glared at her, she simply shrugged. "No, seriously, after that whole bullshit at the beach. I started preparing myself to leave, Bellow. Baby, that shit was beyond fucking embarrassing to me. The fact that you would play in my face like that, to begin with, was foul as fuck. A random bitch is one thing, but homegirl wasn't random. She was too close to home. I told you not to let that bullshit reach our home, and it had. So, yeah, leaving was my next step. A few days after the whole beach thing, I started looking for homes—"

"Dead ass?" I knew she was tired, but I didn't think she had taken shit as far as looking at cribs. Sabrina nodded before shrugging at the glare I was giving her. She had every right to feel that way, hell to even take that step. I was foul as fuck, I admit. Yet, that didn't change the peak of anger that formed in me. "You know I wouldn't have let you leave me, though. Sweetheart, it ain't no Bellow without Sabrina—"

"But there's a Sabrina without Bellow. Baby, I love you, but I'm not lost without you. No, I wouldn't want us to end. Still, I'll be fine standing on my own and starting over if needed. I think you might have forgotten that because of the shit I overlooked."

That was what I loved about shorty, she was a realist, so I knew everything she said wasn't a lie. Hell, I saw the shit in her eyes. Sabrina, not being lost without me, was never a thought. I knew if she wanted to end our relationship, she could definitely stand on her own and start over. Although Brina allowed me to do my own shit, shorty was far from weak-minded. So, I knew she could stand on her own without me.

Throughout our entire relationship, Sabrina never became dependent. All she ever wanted was love and protection, which I constantly gave her.

Regardless of the bullshit between Kimmy and me, Sabrina never came second to that babe. Shit, most of the time Kimmy and I were together, Sabrina was either out with her girls, building up her shop, or in the City—where Eisha lived at the time.

"Sweetheart, I've never forgotten that. I know who the fuck I'm with. You bouncing off, I know you wouldn't hesitate to do. I won't be able to let that shit happen, though. There's no me without you, sweetheart. You've had me since high school. So yo' ass know that. I fucked up bad this time, I know that. I'm done with all that shit, though. It took me a minute to realize how selfish my dumb ass has been with you through the years. I'm about to make up for all that bullshit. We're starting over." I glanced down at her stomach. "You, me and our shorty, this is our new beginning. I'mma be a better me for—"

"Yourself first, then us. It won't be genuine if you're doing it just to keep me, Bellow." Sabrina pulled my head back and stared into my eyes. The stare told me how serious she was. "Which won't keep me if I'm ready to go."

I chuckled at that. Of course, Brina would say

that and mean it. What she said was true, though. If I wasn't going to do it for myself, I would undoubtedly revert back to doing the same bullshit. So, I agreed with her, although she was why I had to get myself together.

As I stated, there was no Bellow without Sabrina. She was it for me, my forever, and I wasn't willing to lose her behind Kimmy and my bullshit. "Sweetheart, I love you."

Sabrina's head lowered, and she kissed me. "I know you do." She whispered as her lips came back on mine.

"Are we balling, or you mothafuckas gonna cake all gotdamn game? Ol pussy whipped ass nigga." King called over to us.

Sabrina broke out laughing against my lips. "I can't stand your damn friends, I swear." Pressing her lips against mine once more, she pulled back. "Do they know I'm pregnant?"

My head shook. It had only been two weeks since I've found out. "Nah, but I'mma let them know."

"Man, bring y'all ass on!" Blaze yelled.

Laughing, Sabrina stuck up her middle finger at him. "Impatient damn fools." Rolling her eyes, she looked back at me. "I wanna play—"

Turning around, I headed toward the courts while shaking my head. "No, you're not playing. Don't ask me no more—"

"Dude, I never asked you whether I could play or not." She laughed. "I can play if I wanna, though." My brows raised at that statement. Again, her eyes rolled as she chuckled. "Whatever, man. I just don't feel like arguing with you."

"That's what I thought." My hand slapped against her booty as I took us back to the group.

"So, what we're doing? Shorty balling, or she's gonna bitch out?" Blaze asked as I placed Brina back on her feet.

Sabrina's mouth opened, and my hand covered it. "Nah, she's going to sit this one out. Be glad that she's not, and I'm really saving you mothafuckas. You niggas chest tight now, if baby ball with us, you bitches will be in tears." I kissed the side of her head as she rolled her neck.

"He's definitely saving y'all. I'm going to stand over there on my sideline where I'll be boosting my baby from. Come on, y'all." Sabrina turned and walked off with Eisha and Kass following her.

"Give me that damn ball. I'll knock her ass out." Blaze claimed, grabbing the basketball.

"Nigga, I'll fuck you up if yo' ass throw that bitch at her." I snatched the ball from him then tossed it to Sam.

"Why the fuck you ain't letting her play? I'll foul the fuck out of her nappy-headed ass." Blaze spoke loud enough for Sabrina to hear. She stuck up her middle finger while laughing.

His question, however, had my gaze shifting on their girls. I motioned to the side while walking away from them. I wasn't saying shit in front of those girls. I wasn't trying to give them shit to talk about. Once we were in the center of the court, I nodded to Sabrina. "Shorty pregnant—"

"Damn, that babe let you trap her ass." Blaze was an ignorant ass dude.

I laughed no less. "Nigga, yo' ass stupid. Nah, but shorty been wanting a baby for damn near ten years, and she kept putting it off because of me. It's about time we filled the crib up with a few of my shorties."

"Nigga, welcome to the damn daddy club," Blaze said, making us laugh.

I pushed his ass away from me. "Yo' ass ignorant. Man, let's ball."

"Bell, you remember what I said. Two weeks —"

King grabbed the ball from me and tossed it across the field. "Shut the fuck up! With yo' cheating ass!" He snapped, causing Sabrina and her girls to break out laughing.

I punched the nigga. Even so, I laughed too. "You sound mad as fuck. Don't pout, ball up, baby." I caught the ball Sabrina threw back and gave it to Sam.

As he took the ball out, my gaze shifted to a

laughing Sabrina. Baby was beautiful as hell. Shorty deserved so much better than my ass. Even with knowing that, I was too selfish to not have her.

My head soon started nodding as I agreed with myself. I had to get my shit together and do right by her. She deserved that and some.

I loved shorty to gotdamn much to lose her. I won't lose her. I couldn't keep being selfish with her.

Chapter Five

Kimmy

I-Spy... A Dead Man

Two Months Later

"I wanna be your main thing. Boy, you know you drive me crazy. Boy, you know you're my baby." I sang Ann Marie's song Main Thing to Mike as I grind and wind my hips on his hardening soldier.

"Keep playing here, Kimmy I'mma have you on your neck." He warned, and I licked his bottom lip.

"Now, don't tease me because we can go." After sucking on his bottom lip, I gave him a peck. "So, what you trying to do?" Mike tapped my leg, and I started laughing. "I'm playing, babe. Stop." He was ready to go.

Once those words left my mouth, those beautiful bright blue eyes formed into slits on his sexy chocolate face. "A'ight, bet. I see how you wanna play. Now, you remember this moment here." He nodded, making me laugh.

"I'm just playing, I promise." Leaning into him, I pecked his lips before getting off his lap, deciding to leave him alone. I had already played around with him enough, and I didn't want him to fuck me up when we got home.

Mike and I sat in a private section at the Lion's Den, enjoying the night with Akil and his girl Nya. The club was in full swing, which wasn't surprising. Akil's spot has been jumping since he opened it a little over a year ago. I loved the club, to be honest. There was barely any bullshit that popped off there, which was a huge plus for me. I didn't want to be dancing one second, then dodging bullets the next.

Standing and fixing my dress, I grabbed Mike's hand. "Let's go dance. I didn't come out to just sit and look good."

"You've been dancing since we got here." Mike's hand rubbed over his face as he chuckled. He was high and didn't want to do shit.

Although true, I shrugged at what he said. I didn't care. All I wanted to do was dance. "Babe, I can't drink, you won't let me smoke, all I can do is dance. So, come on." My hand thrust out for his once more. Shaking his head, he grabbed it, then jerked me down onto his lap. "Why would you do that!" I hit him in the chest. "Dude, I could've broken my damn ankle or something, stupid high ass."

Mike's hand slapped against my ass hard. "Man—" he broke out laughing. He was high as hell. "Yo' eyes got big as fuck, yo, damn. You were scared?" He chuckled in my face, and I hit him once again. "Damn, baby, my bad. I didn't think you would come down like that for real. I'm sorry, dead ass." Fixing the back of my dress, he closed my legs then sat me sideways on his lap. Once I was settled to his comfortability, he rubbed and squeezed my ass.

He had me laid on him as if we were at home. "You don't need to smoke shit else tonight. Because..." my head shook at him before a slight giggle left my mouth. "I promise you're irritating. Give me a kiss." My arm snaked around his neck as his head came down. Mike's tongue came out, and instantly I sucked it into my mouth, moaning as it twisted with mine.

Abruptly Mike pulled back from the kiss, looking to the side of him. A groan left my mouth from the interruption.

Mike tapped my thigh, making me whine out loud because I knew we weren't about to finish that damn kiss. Glancing down at me, he chuckled. "Let me handle this right quick, then we can go dance. Bet?"

Leaning up, I pecked his lips. "I want more than just a dance."

He chuckled while helping me off his lap, making sure my ass didn't flash anyone. "You definitely gonna get more than just a dance." Kissing me, he squeezed my booty. "Don't take yo' ass nowhere. Stay right there until I get back." He motioned for me to sit back on the couch.

"Dude, don't start, gon' somewhere." When he glared at me, I rolled my eyes but laughed no less. "I'mma be good, promise, now go." I shooed him off. After that whole thing with Nyeisha's crazy tail, Mike didn't seem to want me out of his sight, thinking I would try to fight.

A few weeks had gone by since then, and he was the only person I was ready to fight. I swear he was on my ass like a damn parole officer.

"Nya..." Mike called to Akil's girl, then pointed to me.

I pushed him. "Man, gone somewhere. She doesn't need to watch me. I'll be right here when you get back, though." Kissing him once more, he walked off, going into the private room in our section. Turning to Nya, I grabbed her arm, giving it a slight tug. "Come on, we're not about to sit here looking sexy as fuck for no reason. We're going to dance." Mike was out of his gotdamn mind if he thought I was about to sit there bored and wait on him.

Nya looked confused, then glanced into the room where the men had gone. "But you just told him you weren't going anywhere."

"I lied. Now come on."

She started laughing. "Girl, yo' ass is hell. Let's go." She finished off her drink then let me pull her to the dance floor.

∞∞∞

I didn't know how long we stayed on the dance floor while grinding against each other, but we were having a damn ball. I was surprised at how much I was actually enjoying myself, seeing as I was completely sober.

Nya, on the other hand, was utterly wasted. Even so, she was aware of everything going on. "We're going to the bathroom." She yelled loudly into my ear. "We're going!" She repeated and started dragging me off the floor. Drunk and all, homegirl was strong. I didn't even have time to respond to her before she began pulling me.

However, I didn't complain. I let her drag me along. Once we got into the bathroom, she let me go. "You're going to be okay right here?"

Glancing around the empty rest area, I nodded with a laugh. "I think I'm safe. Girl, go pee."

She quickly ran into the bathroom, slamming the door. "Baby, I had to piss!" She hollered, laughing out of relief. "How far along are you?"

"What?" I questioned, staring into the mirror at my furrowed expression.

"You're pregnant, right? That's why you're not drinking and why he doesn't want you off on your own."

"Oh, I'm approaching five months. And yes,

to the drinking, but that's not why Mike's being like that—well, I guess it is kind of. But, since I've been pregnant, I will rage the hell out at any little thing. I'm getting better, though. It's been a few weeks since I've tried to fight anyone, including him." I confessed with a groan.

Nya laughed as she washed her hands. "Those damn hormones ain't no hoe."

"Girl! Tell me about it. I be ready to fight my damn self because of them. These damn hormones and the morning sickness I can do without." Although I was complaining, I wasn't miserable like I expected to be. Especially giving everything I had to worry about with the baby and who it belonged to. That was one thing that wasn't constantly on my mind oddly.

"Do y'all know what you're having?" She questioned.

My brows furrowed because not once have I thought about the baby's gender. "No, we don't. Oddly we haven't even talked about what it could be or what either of us is hoping it to be. This whole damn pregnancy was one big ass surprise, honestly."

"Well, it's still early. Y'all have more than enough time to talk about it." Tossing the towel paper in the trash, she fixed her dress. "Let's go to the bar. I need another drink."

After leaving the restroom, we made a beeline to the bar. Nya ordered herself another margarita.

"You buying me a drink too?"

Smiling at the irritating voice in my ear, I laughed. Turning, I pushed King away from me. "Man, move. You should be buying my damn drink."

"What's up, sweetheart." He leaned over and gave Nya a hug, which she gladly returned. "So, you're drinking?" He questioned curiously.

My eyes rolled at him as I got his meaning. King was all for me getting that abortion, especially given I told him the baby couldn't have been Mike's. We hadn't talked about it since that day.

Grabbing his arm, I pulled him away from Nya so that I wasn't overheard. "He knows everything. Hell, he knew I was pregnant before I even had a clue." King stared at me questioningly. "After the fight and he came back to the house. Well, he knew. The nigga even brought me a test." I ran the short version down to him. "But he knows of the possibilities—just know that he knows every single thing. So, you don't have to feel like you're keeping some big ass secret from him."

King just stared at me. "Shorty, yo' ass is insane. At some point, you're going to have to realize the truth ain't always best. I dead believe you told him everything too."

My eyes slanted as I nodded. "Because I did. But it was after he brought me the damn test."

"You be careful with the shit you're doing. That mothafucka is crazy behind yo' ass, Kimmy.

If you gonna be with that nigga. Leave that other bullshit alone—"

I knew instantly he was talking about Bellow. "I am, King, I promise. I'm done with all that. Believe me, I know how bad I fucked up, and I'm doing everything to make shit right. So, letting that whole situation go, I've done it, I swear." He needed to know that. I was done looking stupid and fucking up.

Nodding, he pulled me to him, kissing my forehead. "Good, because I didn't want to have to kill my nigga for murdering yo' ass."

Pushing him away from me, I rolled my eyes at his ass. "Bye, King. Who the hell you up here with?"

"My damn self. Where yo' nigga at, though?"

I pointed to our section. "He's back there doing something with Akil and them. Hey, do you know what he got going on with Parker?"

King muffed my head back. "Yo' nosey ass. I don't know shit. Ask him if you wanna know. Wait. What? He told you to mind yo' damn business?" He laughed, making me glare at his childish ass.

"So, what? Still, though, I don't want him doing shit with them. Those mothafuckas be having niggas shooting at them. Niggas don't be shooting at Mike—"

"That you know about." King saying that shut my ass up quick. Staring over my expression, King started laughing. I hit him.

"Yo' ass childish as hell. That's exactly why I don't like you now. Bye, man. I don't know why you'll even play with me like that."

King started backing away from me. "Who said I was playing, though?" He shrugged before turning around and walking away.

"I can't stand his ass." I was definitely going to ask Mike about that. He didn't play in the streets to have folks wanting to shoot at him. Either way, I was going to find out. "My bad, King's ass irritating," I told Nya, who still waited for me. "Hey!" I waved the barman over. "Let me get—"

"Something with tequila in it?"

King's dirty, lying ass. I should've known he wasn't there by himself. My gaze fell on Bellow. The man was just a walking gotdamn sin. "Actually, no," my focus went to the barman, and I pointed to the drink on the menu. "Watermelon Margarita. A virgin."

"A virgin? You ain't drinking?" He questioned, looking me over.

I shrugged, trying to play it cool. "No, I'm not." Looking away from him, I mentally groaned. It was so odd how I suddenly felt stuck. I didn't know how I was supposed to act.

"How you been?" He asked as the man sat a drink in front of him.

"I've been good, actually." The smile that

graced my lips was genuine. It felt great saying and meaning those words.

"You look it." My eyes rolled at the compliment. Even so, my damn face heated up. "Don't do all that. I mean it, you look good, though, and I'm not just talking about appearance." Grabbing his drink, he motioned his head to the side for me to follow him.

Every nerve in my body screamed that going with him wasn't a good idea. Yet, the small piece of my heart he held wanted to go with him. "I'll be right back," I told Nya.

"Just stay visible." She responded, watching me curiously. After shaking my head at her, I followed Bellow to a sitting area right across from the bar.

"Look, that whole thing with Nyeisha—"

I waved off the apology he was about to give. "It's forgotten. Don't worry about that. But maybe your girl needs to talk to her because shorty seems to hurt."

Bellow pulled out a blunt and lit it. "Yeah, her crazy ass was out of line for that bullshit. Sabrina told her to let the shit go. If you see Eisha, ignore her, but if she pops stupid, call me, and I'll handle it."

"I'm not worried about her doing shit to be real with you—"

"Regardless of that, call me because I told her

to leave yo' ass alone." He explained, staring at me.

Rolling my eyes, I looked away from him. "Alright," I stated simply, although I wouldn't call him behind Eisha. Bellow held out the blunt for me. "No, I'm good."

His brows furrowed at that. "You're not drinking or smoking, dead ass?"

Of course, I wasn't going to tell him I was pregnant. Did he have a right to know? Absolutely. Yet, that didn't change my thoughts. The truth was, I already knew where his mind would've gone instantly. Abortion. Which I was all up for until I learned that my baby could've been Mike's.

"Yeah, not tonight." *What the hell are you doing, Kimmy?* Sitting there with him, I suddenly felt so damn stupid. Mike was there, right at the other end of the club. "I should probably go. Mike's here, and I would hate for him to see me sitting with you." Hell, I needed to let Mike know he could trust me completely, and sitting with Bellow wasn't the best start.

Bellow nodded, not seeming bothered by what I said or anything. "You can take off. I saw you and just wanted to see how you were." His head bobbed as he stared at his blunt. His gaze then came to me, a curious look taking over his handsome features.

He was genuinely concerned about my mental state, I realized. Of course, he would be especially given how my emotions took such a drastic turn on him. A light chuckle left my mouth as I smiled at Bellow. Standing, I fixed my dress.

"You don't have to worry about me, Bell. I'm good, really, I am. It's not an act, seriously."

Brushing himself off, he nodded once more, then stood. "I think I believe you." He chuckled, licking his lips. He let his eyes roam over me once more. "Let me ask you this." Bellow's eyes squinted as he rubbed his bottom lip. "You still got me blocked?"

That time a laugh burst from my mouth. "Of course, I do." Smiling at him, I grabbed his hand, giving it a reassuring squeeze. "I have to go."

Licking his lips, he nodded. "You're getting good with that."

My brow raised questioningly at his comment. "With what?"

"Walking away." He claimed.

Smiling, I nodded in agreeance. "Of course, I am. Walking away from this is better than losing my everything. You know what that's like."

"You know I do." Giving my hand a tug, Bellow pulled me into a hug. "This the Kimmy I know. That other mothafucka was insane. Don't let that mothafucka come back."

Laughing, I hit him in the back. He was right. I had really lost my damn mind for a while, which I'm blaming entirely on being pregnant. That was the only explanation for my drastic behavior.

"Oh, you don't have to worry about that," I assured him. Kissing my forehead, he let me go. "Bye, Bell." Pulling away, I turned and started walking away.

"Aye," he called, causing me to glance back at him. "There's something different with you. I don't know what it is, but it's looking good as fuck on you."

Waving, I made my way back to the bar. I didn't feel the need to address what he said. I took it as the compliment that it was and kept going.

I was so gotdamn proud of myself. Every single encounter we've had after our breakup, I've made a damn fool out of myself by crying, hell begging him to give us—our damn affair another chance. Acting utterly desperate for a man that had already let go.

It felt so good to look at him and not want to burst out bawling. It felt simply amazing to not feel so gotdamn heartbroken or hurt and made to look like a damn fool. Thinking about my past actions—which seemed like yesterday—made me feel embarrassed.

Grabbing my drink, I smiled at Nya. "Thanks for waiting—"

She waved me off. "If we left that section together, we gonna stick together and return just the same." I agreed with that. It was the same with my girls and me.

Going back to the dance floor, we began dancing with one another. I was enjoying myself dancing all over that damn floor while keeping a hold on my drink. Nya wasn't losing a step either, as she twirled her hips like a damn professional dancer.

After a while, the floor started to get too gotdamn crowded, which didn't bother me. What did, however, was the persistent sonofabitch that wouldn't get off my ass.

"Dude, back the fuck up, damn!" I finally snapped because obviously my damn moving away or elbowing homeboy wasn't telling him shit.

The dude's hands raised as he grinned at me. "My bad, sweetheart, no disrespect intended. I just like the way your body moves and wanted to dance." His hands held out for me to take. "Dance with me."

My lips pursed together, and my eyes rolled as my head shook. "No, thanks. My man would disapprove."

"One dance, I'm sure he won't mind." He insisted.

"I'm sure he would. It's a bunch of sexy ass women in here moving just as good. Go find one." Turning away from him, I looked at Nya, and my eyes went up as if asking *what the fuck.*

She rolled hers in understanding. "The niggas in here be thirsty as fuck. They don't care if you have a man or not."

"Ah!" I screeched as my drink spilled down the front of my dress from somebody bumping into me. "You stupid bitch!" I hollered, ready to go clean the fuck off, thinking it was the guy I brushed off.

"Damn, shorty, my bad, I didn't mean to do that. That bitch bumped me." The dude claimed, motioning behind him. "I'll buy you another drink —"

"No, it's cool." That was all I said before grabbing Nya's arm and dragging her off.

"Please slow down, babe. You're moving way too fast." She claimed, but I ignored her as I made it back to our private section. Once we made it to the couch, I let Nya's arm go and grabbed my phone. Immediately, I pulled up the girl's group chat.

Me: Why the fuck did Martell just bump into me.

Literally, a second later, my phone instantly started pinging. I wasn't expecting such a rapid response. Still, I ignored them as I snatched up a handful of paper towels and tried drying myself off.

The front of my dress was soaked. I was irritated and ready to go. Growling, I tossed the towel paper on the table and grabbed my phone.

Ang: *What? Where? Tf? I didn't even know he was back in the state.*

Miss: *Bitch, where are you?*

E: *Right, where tf you at?*

Peaches: *Do we need to come get you?*

Me: *Ang, I didn't know that either. I thought that nigga was out of state hiding. But nope, here his ass is out in the fucking open at the Lion's Den. I don't know if he realized who I was or not, but as soon as I noticed him, I took the fuck off. Hell, I don't know if he remembers that me and Missy was shooting at him and Mook's ass that one time. But I wasn't about to stick around for him to realize the shit either.*

Ang: *Are you sure it was even him though? I mean...how good can you see in a dimly lit club?*

After I hit send, I saw Martell again. He was leaning against the balcony rails, looking at the partygoers below.

Me: *I'm 1000 percent sure. I'm dead looking at the man right now. Bitch, hold on...*

Once the message was sent, I quickly pulled up my camera. "Shit..." I mumbled, realizing how obvious it would be if I just started taking pictures of the man. I glanced at Nya, who was still sipping while dancing in her seat.

I tapped her thigh. "Let me take a picture of you real quick." I urged, rushing her to get up. She stared at me curiously, then shrugged. She got up, and I positioned her so that I could snap the picture of Martell. When taking the photo, he looked right in my damn direction.

"Turn to the side so I can get all that!" I yelled at Nya, motioning to her ass, trying to play it off.

And the bitch was a damn trooper because baby girl was posing her drunk ass off.

"Let me see." She came to me, looking over the images. "Send these to me."

Taking my phone, I sat down then pulled up the images. I sent the ones I took of only Martell in the group chat.

Me: Is this not him or am I seeing shit?

After several long seconds, I got a collective of Bitch!

Ang: Bitch, I feel like I wanna show this shit to Parker, but then I don't wanna. Y'all, the last time he went after Martell's crazy ass, the shit wasn't pretty. Parker became so obsessive trying to find him. Like, I don't want this bullshit to start back up.

I didn't respond right away because I understood where she was coming from. When no messages came through, I knew the other girls felt the same way and wanted to let Angel come to her own decision on what to do.

Ang: Ugh! I wish that man would drop fucking dead already. Like why is he even back though? Not fucking knowing is bothering me. Ugh!

Ang: And his ass just out at the damn club. Y'all know that nigga hate my fucking baby. I'mma have to tell Parker just in case Martell tries some shit. I fucking hate this.

Me: Do what you feel you need to. Like, his ass isn't hiding anymore it seems.

E: What you gonna do, Ang?

Ang: *I'mma text y'all later.*

I knew the thought of Parker being on Martell's trail again stressed Angel out. Yet, without a doubt, I knew she would tell Parker about Martell being back so he could watch himself.

A heavy sigh left my mouth as I began feeling bad for her. I hated the bullshit that my girl was put into, and I couldn't even blame Parker for the shit. It was a collective of shit between the couple that had Martell wanting them dead.

Seeing all the bullshit that my girl had gone through just to finally get a happily ever after. Made me glad for the way Mike was. He didn't deal with many people, nor did he have enemies. Mike had his super small circle and left it at that. He never let folks get too close to him, which I loved.

I was happy that I didn't have to experience half the shit they've gone through. I'll take dealing with a crazy ass baby momma over dodging damn bullets or mothafuckas trying to blow my ass up any day.

Looking into the private room that Mike was in with Akil and his people, still. A heavy sigh left my mouth because I was ready to go. My dress was wet and sticking to me, making my body feel so damn yucky.

Me: *How much longer are you going to be?*

I shot Mike a text hoping they were almost

done. I watched as he looked at his phone, then went back to his conversation.

Me: *This dude made me spill my drink all over my damn dress.*

Mike read the text, then glanced around the front of the room before his eyes jumped to the other end, settling on me. He said something to the guys then walked out of the room.

"How did somebody waste some shit on you?" He pulled me up, looking at my dress.

"We were dancing—"

"Yo' ass wasn't supposed to go nowhere, though."

My lips popped, and my head cocked to the side, asking if he was serious. The glare on his face told me he was. "That's not the point. I'm wet and ready to go."

"You hardheaded as hell." Shaking his head, he pulled me into him, then walked over to Akil and his boy, who sat on the couch. "We're about to take off. I'll get up with you later in the week. Bet?"

"A'ight. I'll let you know when everything is set up." Akil told him.

That had me curious. I wanted to know what type of business the pair had going on.

"We gon' head out this way to avoid that damn crowd." He told Akil, pointing to a door.

Akil walked over with us, pushing the door

open. "Gon' head get out of here. We'll get up later." After the pair shook up, Mike led us down a flight of stairs to a door that opened on the side of the building.

Once inside the truck, I raised my dress. "Give me your shirt," I told Mike, pulling the wet dress off. I reached into the back seat, grabbed some wipes, and cleaned my chest off. "Stop." I slapped Mike's hand as he grabbed my breast.

"How you gonna have that shit all in my face then tell me to stop?"

Laughing, I popped his hand again. "If you look straight ahead, my titties won't be in your face." After cleaning up as best I could, I pulled on his shirt. "Oh, I saw King at the bar. Did he come down and talk to you?"

"Nah, he didn't." Mike grabbed my dress, then tossed it in the back. "My bad, for inside, shit ran longer than I thought. You know I planned on dancing with you."

I knew he did. Hell, the man had danced with me majority of the time we'd been at the club. "I know. That's why I'm not down your throat. We danced damn near the whole night together." Leaning over to him, I kissed his jaw, then sat back down. "What business you and Akil got going on?"

"My damn business, that's what." He chuckled, shaking his head at me. "G, you nosey as fuck. What made you ask that?"

"Because I wanna know. Plus, I know you. If it

was nothing, we all would've still been hanging out, enjoying the night together. But y'all had to go into the private room. You, Michael, only do that when it involves business." I broke down to him.

Since Mike and I have been together, he's never done business in front of me. He might tell me about a custom gun he's done or doing, aside from that, when it comes to the actual business. I didn't know anything.

"So, what y'all got going on?" However, I really wanted to know what was up for some reason.

"It ain't shit you have to worry about." My lips popped as my vision went black from the hard roll of my eyes. Mike's hand pressed against my face, and he muffed my head back. "Why the fuck you doing all that for?"

"Because you can never give me a straight answer."

He shrugged at that. "Shid, that was a straight answer and the only one you'll get."

"So, it's business? He wants some guns or something?" That was Mike's business and the only one I wanted him to keep. Looking away from me, he turned up the radio ending the conversation. "You're so damn rude, I swear." I hit the off button for the radio. "Do you be having dudes shooting at you?" Mike's eyes were focused straight away, yet I watched as his brows creased together. "Mike?"

"What the fuck are you talking about? What

niggas be shooting at me?" He sounded serious as hell, and his face showed his confusion.

"I don't know, that's why I'm asking. Do niggas be shooting at you?"

Mike shrugged. "Not that I know of." His uncaring tone irritated the hell out of me.

After seeing Martell at the club and knowing Mike was conversing with Twitch, who's related to them, I didn't like it. Nor did I want him to have anything to do with Parker and his people.

I didn't want Martell's crazy ass to think Mike had shit to do with them and start coming after him.

"So, you know the situation Parker and his people have with Martell—"

"Kimmy, that's not our business. Whatever they have going on is their shit." He seemed so unbothered.

Sighing, I turned, looking at him. "I know that. I also know you've been talking to Twitch too. And now with Martell being out here—"

Stopping at a red light, Mike looked at me. "What makes you think he's out here?"

I pointed behind us, in the club's direction. "I just saw him."

"You saw Martell?"

Slowly my head bobbed as I motioned toward my dress. "He's the one who bumped into me."

Mike's fingers scrubbed over his head. "Kimmy, stay out of their shit. I'm not gonna ask because I already know yo' ass texted Angel already. Why the fuck are you worrying that gotdamn girl about that nigga for? Man, you need to start thinking before reacting to shit. Now, you're about to stress that mothafucka out for no gotdamn reason—"

"For no reason? Are you serious? The last time Martell came around, he damn near got her killed before he went after Parker. Who's to say he's not back for the same gotdamn reason, Mike? If this was your friend, you would've done the same gotdamn thing."

The harsh glare that covered Mike's face said so much and had me feeling like I'd done something wrong. Which shouldn't have because I knew I hadn't.

"I don't give a fuck for none of that shit you're saying. That's their shit. It don't have a gotdamn thing to do with Kimmy. I'mma tell yo' ass this, though. If something happens to yo' dumb ass or my mothafuckin' baby from you trying to be in their bullshit, I'm going to kill yo' ass."

"Now you're just being dramatic. Talking about you're going to kill me. What the hell could happen from me simply telling Angel I saw Martell and taking a couple of pictures of him? It's not like he's going to know."

"The problem with you mothafuckas is that

y'all don't ever do simple shit like just sending a fucking picture. Y'all asses got to get involved in niggas shit. Just like you and Missy's ass shooting at those mothafuckas—"

"That was different. They were shooting at—"

"Kimmy, shut the fuck up, those niggas weren't shooting at y'all mothafuckas." Mike snapped, pissed off. He was furious. "But that ain't stop yo' simple ass from going out there, though. That bullshit damn near got Missy's ass killed—if yo' ass tell me that shit was different, I'm slapping the fuck out of you. My point is, let those niggas handle that shit. You sent off some pictures, cool, leave the shit at that.

"You gotdamn females need to sit the fuck down somewhere. That's why you mothafuckas always end up getting hurt." With a shake of his head, Mike let out a low chuckle. "The fact that y'all think you're slick is the funny part. Half the time you're playing the role, a mothafucka setup for you to play without even knowing it." Pulling into the driveway, Mike parked in the garage.

"So, you think Martell planned to run into me?" Mike shrugged as he shut off the truck. My mind replayed the short encounter, and I couldn't see how he could have, especially not within that time frame. "Everything happened so fast, though I don't think he had time to even recognize me?"

"Not fast enough because you recognized him. My point is, stay out this shit with Martell and Parker. Put that shit far out yo' mind." His hand came to my stomach, rubbing it. "When you go back to the doctor?"

My eyes rolled at him for trying to change the subject. I didn't like how he talked about me staying out of shit when it came to my best friends. Especially when I knew for a fact had it been King, Leon, or Jerron, Mike would be all in their shit, ready to ride for them with no questions asked.

"Don't say shit else about it, Kimmy." Getting out of the truck, he came around to my side, opening the door for me. My hand slapped into his, harder than needed, as I hopped out. The action caused Mike to chuckle and pull me into him. "I don't give a fuck about you being pissed. Sweetheart, you trying to be there for yo' homegirls, I get that shit. I love how protective and loyal you are to them. That's yo' family, so I get it, Kimmy.

"Still, you getting involved in niggas shit, I don't like it. I mean, the mothafuckas they're going at don't give a fuck for you. Sweetheart, yo' damn life doesn't mean shit to none of those mothafuckas. To me, though, your life means everything, and if it's lost behind something, that has nothing to do with you. How the fuck do you think my mental is going to let me mourn, Kimmy?"

When he broke it down like that, I understood where he was coming from. My thing wasn't to get in the middle of Parker's beef because I knew how they got down. Not only that, I saw how Martell liked to play in the background.

"I won't get involved, I promise. That was

never my plan. I just—I don't know—I guess when I saw Martell, I was surprised. After all that shit happened, that man vanished and hasn't been seen for years. Then to suddenly have him in my face. I felt Angel needed to know. That's all I was doing. Trust me, I know just how ruthless they can get. I would never put myself in their mess because of that. Especially not now." Mike's hand pressed against my stomach, and I nodded, letting him know the baby was the reason.

Grabbing my throat, he pulled me to him, pressing his lips to mine. All too soon, Mike broke the kiss. He pushed the door open, then motioned inside the house. "Gon' inside and shower. I'm right behind you."

At times, I really hated how dismissive he was with shit. "Don't be too long." Nodding, he motioned to the opened door once more. Sighing, I walked into the house. Once I did, Mike closed the door, staying inside the garage. My eyes rolled at the closed door before going upstairs.

Once in our room, I went into the bathroom, deciding to run me a bath. I had just finished pulling off my heels when my phone went off. Grabbing it, I answered the FaceTime from Angel.

"What's up, babe?" I answered, sitting the phone on the counter, then continued undressing.

"Y'all at home already?" She questioned.

Picking up the phone, I rolled my eyes into the device so she could see me. "Of course. Martell made me spill my drink all down my dress." Setting my phone on its stand, I sat it on the floor.

Shutting off the water, I sunk into the hot bubbled bath. Sighing, I sank further into the deep tub.

"Ugh, what you got going on over there?" Ang grunted, making me laugh.

"Girl, shit, just got in the tub. The water feels so damn good too." I boosted.

"Let me see."

I broke out laughing. "Yo' nasty ass. Bitch, what the fuck do you want? Did you talk to Parker?" I grabbed my phone just in time to see her eyes rolling long and hard. "What happened?"

"He gets on my gotdamn nerves. So, I told him about Martell being back, bitch showed the man the pictures and everything. But he already knew. You think Mike told him?"

My eyes slanted in thought. I didn't see how Mike could've when I didn't tell him about me running into Martell until after the fact. "To be honest, Ang, I doubt it for real. I told you damn near a half-hour before telling Mike about it. I mean, we were on the way home when I said something. So, I don't know, maybe King—I don't know, maybe he saw him and thought to tell Parker."

Angel's head shook into the screen as she stared thoughtfully at me. "King and Parker don't really talk like that. Parker and Blaze mostly converse. So, King was at the club with y'all when you saw him?"

"No, I ran into him while I was there. And that was before I even saw Martell. To be honest, I don't know if King saw him. I'm just guessing because I know Mike couldn't have told Parker anything." I didn't know who told Parker, but I knew it couldn't have been Mike. "What did Parker say when you told him?"

Angel glared into the phone. "After telling me he already knew, he went off on my ass. Told me not to worry about Martell. Talking about some, *you and those bitches always got y'all fucking nose in shit that don't have a gotdamn thing to do with y'all. That's why you stupid mothafuckas always end up getting fucked up—*"

"Bitch! Not Mike's ass went off and said damn near that exact same thing to me. It's like, I'm not even trying to get involved. I just wanted to let my best friend know that the nigga who tried to kill them was fucking back. Ang, I promise that's all I was doing—letting you know so yo' ass can tell Parker."

"I know, Kimmy. Which I did, next time though, I ain't gonna tell him shit—bitch don't make that face." She broke out laughing because we both knew she was lying. "Girl, he gets on my damn nerves. I hate when he goes off on my ass. Parker has this way of fussing that makes me feel so damn little. Like, I'm a gotdamn child. I hate that shit. They're acting like we're about to be out hunting for this man or some shit."

It was my turn to laugh. "Ang, it's not like he's far off, though either. Bitch, remember when all this shit first started. The plan you had, then Missy's ass took over and damn near got herself killed. Then with us shooting at Martell and Mook."

"That was different though—hoe don't laugh, I'm so serious. Fuck you, Kim. But so, what though, fuck them. We can do what we wanna." After she said that, she glanced behind her. "Peewee, I'mma whoop you. I thought you were your daddy. Why are you creeping around the house for?"

I broke out laughing. "Not yo' ass got scared."

"Girl, fuck you. I sure thought that was Parker bursting into the room." She laughed as Peewee climbed into her lap.

"Hey, auntie Kimmy." He waved, grinning.

Smiling, I waved my bubbled covered hand at him. "Hey, baby. Why are you up this late?" Angel knew she birthed some beautiful babies. Peewee was the spitting image of Parker.

Peewee's brows knitted together before his face pressed into the phone. "You in the tub?"

"Boy, move. Get over there." Angel pushed Peewee off of her, which made him laugh. "I'm about to whoop his ass." She threatened, glaring at him. All the while, Peewee was cracking up. Rolling her eyes, she looked at me. "You should've seen how his ass grabbed my damn phone. Girl, he was looking down like his ass was about to see something."

I pointed to her. "That's all your fault. That's what you be saying, then be like, let me see." She couldn't help but laugh, knowing it was true. "With his handsome little self. Baby, you and Parker gonna have trouble with those babies when they get older." I told her while washing myself up.

She rolled her eyes. "How about now? Peewee and Ant are already talking about they have girlfriends. Like, y'all are in kindergarten and first grade. What do you know about a girlfriend? These kids too much—Peewee, get out your daddy stuff. He's gonna get you."

"Why the hell is he even up? It's like...one in the morning."

Peewee's face popped back into the phone. "My daddy said I can be up to watch my momma."

"Boy, move." Angel pushed him out the way, laughing. "He's irritating."

Peewee grabbed Angel's face and kissed her on the lips. "I love you."

"Awe." I cooed. That was just so damn cute.

"I love you too, baby." She kissed him back. "Where are you going?" His muffled response, I couldn't hear. "Girl, this damn boy just be all over the place. Peewee, where your daddy at?" Looking at me, she rolled her eyes. "Out of all the kids, he's the only one that stays up, walking around this big ass house alone. Girl, I'm surprised he don't be scared."

"Ang, go put your son to bed, and we'll talk later."

"Alright, babe, love you."

"Love you too, babe. Bye—"

"Wait." She called before I hung up. "Show me something real quick. Remind me of what I'm missing."

I broke out laughing. "Bitch! And that's why your gotdamn son a mess now. Bye, hoe." I ended the FaceTime and finished with my bath.

Chapter Six

Kimmy

Threat

One Month Later

The slow, caressing stroke along my bare stomach, up to my breast, caused a relaxing sigh to leave my mouth. I moved closer to Mike, taking in his comfortable warmth. Again, I exhaled that content breath loving the feel of his warm fingers caressing my skin.

Although his fingers rubbed over my breast, the manner wasn't sexual. It was soothing. "Good morning." I sighed. Mike kissed my shoulder but didn't say anything. "What are you thinking about?"

"You being pregnant." His hand continued to stroke my stomach as he placed kisses along my shoulder.

"Are they good thoughts?"

Mike chuckled, biting my shoulder. "Shid, I don't even know—oof." He grunted as I elbowed him in the stomach. "I'm bullshitting with you, sweetheart. Of course, they're good thoughts. Why wouldn't they be?"

I shrugged, not knowing how to respond right away. "How come you haven't brought up me moving in again?" I thought to question instead, deciding to keep my real worries to myself for the moment.

"Because the shit will be pointless." My lips popped, and I rolled over to glare at him. "I don't know why you're staring at me like that. Kimmy, I'm not gonna beg you to live with me. You have your reasons for not wanting to move in. Apparently, when you're ready, you'll ask me if you can come home—"

"I have to ask you to come home? I can't just move in when I wanna?" I picked, finding it funny how he worded that. He knew, just like I did, those words would never leave my mouth. Hell, we were already living together in a sense.

To be honest, the only reason I hadn't moved back in with him entirely was because of the pregnancy.

Mike's head shook in response. "Nah, you have to ask me to come back." Pushing my chin up, he kissed me. "Matter fact, I think yo' ass might just have to beg to come back." Grabbing my thigh, he brought it up to his waist. "What do you think?"

Smiling, I pecked his lips. "I'll definitely beg if I have to."

Laughing, Mike slapped my bare ass. "I'll let you know when it's time for that."

I popped his arm. "You're irritating. Don't play with me like that." My head rolled on the pillow as I stared at the ceiling, sighing.

Mike let out a grunt then released his hold on me. I didn't have to look at him to see his irritation. I had to admit that I loved how Mike was paying more attention to me. Although great, it made keeping shit from him harder. Especially when it came to my thoughts. When he wanted to, he could read the hell out of me.

"When you go back to the doctor?" He combed a hand down his face before sitting upright.

"In a couple of weeks. Why?"

His shoulders rolled as he sat on the edge of the bed. "You need to call and see how soon we can get this DNA test done."

I sat up as well. "Where did that even come from?"

"Don't play stupid with me, Kimmy. You know where it's coming from. Look, the sooner we find out, the easier it'll be for us to move forward. Whether that's together or apart—"

I pushed him hard in the back. He just had to take shit too damn far at times. "Like, why would you even say all that extra shit, though? That bullshit wasn't even called for."

"Neither is the fact you're constantly

thinking that fucking baby is ol' boys. So, to ease the both of our minds, schedule to have the fucking test done." Mike got off the bed, in all his naked glory, pissed.

"Hey," I grabbed his arm before he could walk off. "Wait. Don't just walk off. Talk to me..." my words ran off from the harsh look he gave me. Swallowing my nerves, I gave his arm a tug. Of course, I knew why he was mad. Even so, I was about to play dumb for a moment. "You just snapped for no reason, Mike. I haven't even said shit to make you go off and say all that."

He pulled his arm from my grasp. "I ain't about to play this dumb act with you, Kimmy. We both know what the fuck you're thinking whenever the baby is mentioned."

My hands went up, feign confused. "My mind didn't even have time to go anywhere before you went off, though, Mike."

He stared at me for the longest time, not saying anything. Yet, his facial expression said it all. "Dead ass, Kimmy?" That—are you really about to play me for a dummy—expression didn't leave his handsome face. Rubbing his bottom lip, he laughed. "A'ight. It's too gotdamn early for this bullshit you tryna play at. As a matter of fact, I'm not about to do this bullshit with you at all." With that, he walked off.

"What is that supposed to mean?" The bathroom door closed as I finished asking the question. Groaning, I got off the bed and went to the door, pushing it harder than necessary. The resistance I got back wasn't expected at all. I tried the door again. Sure enough, it didn't open. "Mike, you really locked the damn door?" I twisted the knob as if that would magically unlock the door. "You really locked the fucking door, though!" My insides peaked with irritation as I heard the shower come on. I couldn't believe he wanted to behave like that.

His reaction was why I redirected our conversation from the baby to me moving back in. I loved Mike and knew he would do right by the baby and me if the outcome wasn't what either of us wanted. That was why I began feeling distant when talking about the baby lately. Which I knew Mike felt.

I just didn't want Mike to get attached to the baby if he didn't plan on staying with me—us if the child wasn't his. Mike has stated multiple times that we wouldn't be together if the baby wasn't his. So, I wanted to protect myself and my baby from further hurt. Hell, I was already going to be crushed if it turned out not to be his baby. So, I was really trying to prepare myself.

My palm slapped against the wood hard. "Mike, open the door! I have to pee. Damn!" He didn't say anything, which I wasn't surprised by. My forehead fell against the door as I groaned. I was beyond irritated with him and myself. For the life of me, I wish that I wasn't in this damn situation to begin with.

I understand Mike's frustrations, yet I couldn't just forget about the possibilities of my baby being Bellow's, like he may have wanted.

I hated the situation so much that I honestly wasn't excited about the pregnancy like I should've been. Although kids weren't on my mind, I still wanted to feel excited about being pregnant since it was my first time.

In truth, I didn't want a damn DNA test from fear of what it might say. I wish like hell I could start these past few months over. I would have stopped myself from having sex with Bellow—hell, I would've let him go altogether and focused on fixing my relationship with Mike.

Deciding to let Mike have his space, I grabbed some clothes and went into the guest room to shower.

"Lizzie, don't get me wrong, I can understand his frustrations with everything. I mean, when I found out he had gotten Tasha pregnant, it wasn't the easiest time for us. So, I understand why he got so pissed with me. But, I also want him to at least try to see my standpoint as well. Yes, I hate this situation, and I don't like that there's a possibility of my baby being Bellow's, yet, I can't change that. Not only that, Mike has made it clear that if the baby turns out not to be his, he's not going to stay with me.

"So, I also have to think about that every time this baby is mentioned." My fingers raked through my hair as I tried to keep my stress levels at bay. That wasn't the hard part, however. The terrible part was I didn't want to be pregnant anymore because of the situation I put myself in. The shit was to gotdamn stressful, and I hated it. I didn't want to bring my baby into it.

Elizabeth's fingers tapped on the sofa's arm as she stared at the table in thought. "Given the years I've known you and how much we've talked about Mike a lot. I think I can assume that I know him quite a bit. Would you agree?" My head was nodding before she could even finish her sentence.

Since the beginning of our sessions, Mike has always been a topic of discussion. Not only that, she knew the mental state I had been in when I learned about Tasha being pregnant.

"I'm going to speak freely with you—"

"You always do, Lizzie." That was another reason we got along so well. Elizabeth didn't hold back with me. She always spoke her honest thoughts, and I loved that she did.

"Mike knows the possibilities. And although he feels like the baby is his, he also knows the chance that it's not. Maybe..." she fell silent for a while as she stared at me. Sighing, she moved to the edge of her seat. "Have you thought that maybe, he doesn't want to know the outcome? That it's a possibility, he's already accepted the child as his, yet your constant thoughts of Bellow being the father is what's making him mad. I mean, Kimmy, Mike has pretty much told you that in more ways than one. You know what? Let me ask you this. Are you okay with Bellow not knowing that he could be your baby's father?"

My mouth opened to respond, yet I had no response. Was I alright with Bellow not knowing if the baby was his?

"Would you be alright with Mike raising Bellow's child as his own; without him ever knowing?"

I didn't know. Even though I didn't want to tell Bellow that I was pregnant. If the baby turned out to be Bellow's, then, yeah, he had the right to know. But at what cost? Losing Mike? Or even making his relationship with Sabrina more complicated? I didn't want either of those to happen. While I felt in my heart if Bellow knew the baby was his, he would have likely told me to get an abortion to save his relationship. Yet, I knew he would do the right thing by taking care of the baby.

Groaning, my hands gripped my head. I was going to drive myself gotdamn crazy with the way my mind formed different scenarios, questions, and thoughts. I didn't like it.

Would I be alright with him not knowing if the baby was his?

Sighing, I sat up, licking my lips. "No, but I would if that's what Mike wanted."

A hum left Elizabeth's mouth. "I've realized that much of what you've said starts with Mike. Everything revolves around what Mike might think. What about Kimberly? What is it that Kimmy wants?"

Ironically, I didn't know exactly.

"You keep making assumptions on how you think Mike feels or what he may want."

My eyes rolled automatically at that. "Those aren't assumptions. Mike made it completely clear that he was done with me if the baby wasn't his. That's another reason I barely want to talk about the baby with him."

"Okay, Mike says if the child isn't his, the relationship is over. Why is that exactly? Is it because he doesn't want to raise a baby that isn't his?"

My brows furrowed, all the while my head shook. "No, that's not it at all. Mike being here for the baby isn't even a question, honestly." He made it perfectly clear that the baby would be taken care of. Even if he hadn't, I know without a doubt Mike would always be there for the baby.

"The baby isn't the issue. It's me. He'll end it because of my and Bellow's relationship. He knew how I cared about Bell. For that, he wouldn't trust us to leave it at just co-parenting. So, he feels that ending our relationship is what's best for him."

Lizzie's lips pursed, and her head slightly tilted as if understanding. I didn't like that action. I felt like she was in agreeance with him.

"No, don't think that. I wouldn't cheat on Mike again." The parting of Elizabeth's lips caused my explanation to stop, knowing she wanted to say something. "What?" She shook her head. "No, say it."

A visible sigh left her mouth. "But you have, Kim. After you sat here and explained to me just how much you loved Mike. Not long after, you did cheat and on your date at that. From me knowing that and how unexpected it happened, you can't blame me for thinking Mike has a point."

Hearing her say that made me feel like shit. I knew what I did was wrong. Yet, I needed that. Yes, that was a selfish way of thinking, but I needed that from Bellow. It was my closure, in a sense. Of course, Mike wouldn't understand that and would see it for what the action truly was. Cheating.

My actions were definitely selfish. Then again, so was my whole outlook on what I've done.

"Lizzie, I know how bad I messed up and hurt him. I know I've been completely selfish this entire time. I know this and see it, and I hate myself for how selfish I've become. For that, I wouldn't do it again. I know what's important to me and where my heart, body, and soul belong when it comes to those men. It took me a while to realize it, which is crazy." I admitted shamefully. "Although he has a piece of me, I can live without Bellow." My head shook as I felt myself becoming emotional. "I cannot see my life without Mike, though. He is my everything—"

"Yet, you're trying to exclude Mike from something that means a lot to him. Well, the both of you, all because of a possibility—which he doesn't seem to care about. Kimmy, you're undermining something that doesn't need to be sabotaged. What I mean by that is Mike wants to experience this pregnancy with you, yet every time he tries forming that bond, you're blocking him, and the bad thing about that is; you don't realize it. That's the reason you can't see why he's frustrated.

"It has nothing to do with Bellow or the possibility of the baby being his, but you, shutting him out. This will be his first real pregnancy experience. Mike didn't have that with Tasha. He couldn't because he was with you, and Tasha wouldn't allow him to." Lizzie's legs crossed over her knee, and she locked her fingers together. "I usually let you gather your thoughts and go the route it sends you on. But, as a friend, Kimberly, I want you to take my advice without questions and go that path. Alright?"

Without conscious thought, my head was moving up and down. Given how well Lizzie knew me, I believed whatever advice she'd give wouldn't lead me wrong.

"When y'all are together, and the baby comes up, I want you to get out of your head and take Bellow out of your mind and stay in that moment with Mike. That's the first thing. The second is to stop making decisions based on what you think Mike may want. Kim, you are a smart and very educated woman, but when it comes to Mike— at times, you seem to forget that. I want you to start using that big, beautiful mind of yours. Your thoughts don't have to match Mike's." Grabbing my hand, she gentle squeeze it as a small smile graced her lips.

"Sweetheart, that's not going to make him stay with you." She exclaimed sadly. "I know that's not what you want to hear, but trust me when I say, doing so won't change how he feels about you. However, what may do that is you not being Kimmy, the woman he fell in love with. Instead of being that person, you have become a desperate shell of her. I know you want to prove that he can trust you again. Kimmy, that's great. Do it, but don't become someone else by trying to appease him. As I said, that's not going to make him stay.

"Be your authentic and loving self. That's all you have to do. And even if that doesn't work, life won't stop because y'all aren't together. Yes, you'll be heartbroken for a moment, yet you'll move on in time." She claimed sincerely before a small laugh left her mouth. "But in truth, given how much that man loves you, Kim. I doubt he'll leave you alone. Y'all will work this out as long as you take my advice. Alright?"

Letting go of Elizabeth's hand, I leaned back on the couch, allowing her words to replay in my mind. I didn't want to believe that I was becoming some yes person with Mike, let alone desperate. Yet, while listening to Elizabeth speak, I hated to admit that she was right. My whole demeanor had changed because I wanted Mike to see how serious I was about being with just him. Hell, I was desperate for him to see it. So, no, I hadn't been myself entirely, because I couldn't lose Mike...

A laugh left my mouth as realization finally

hit me. I was desperate as hell. That last thought about Mike proved that. I was definitely becoming someone else, hell, somebody I was barely recognizing. No doubt someone Mike probably didn't like, which frustrated him most. I was trying to appease him, and that's something he wouldn't like.

Elizabeth was right. I had to be myself. I needed to stop thinking about not being with Mike. That's what made me so damn desperate, which wasn't me.

I had to be Kimberly. That strong-minded—don't need a man for shit—person again. Not this desperate shell of a fucking person who was losing her gotdamn mind over a man.

Although I didn't want to picture life without Mike, and my feelings for him would never change, that didn't mean I had to lose myself to keep him either.

Again, I laughed because a part of me knew that my emotional changes were because of my damn pregnancy. Even so, I knew I had to let my guilt of hurting Mike go and really move forward. That was the only way we would get through everything.

Ironically, Lizzie made me realize that *I* was a *threat* to my relationship without even knowing it.

"Miss, let me ask you this and be completely honest with me." Flipping through the racks of clothes, I stopped at a pair of black jeans and glanced at Missy, who was already staring at me. "Do you think I've become desperate for Mike? Like to satisfy him?"

"Umm..." Missy's mouth closed, and she moved down the clothes rack. "I mean..." my brow raised at her hesitation, and she groaned. "I wanna say yes, but I don't want to; given your situation—"

"Missy, seriously? Don't think about me being pregnant. Go off my actions. Do you feel that I've been acting desperate to please Mike?" I didn't want her to beat around the bush with me. I wanted her honesty only. Which I knew she didn't mind giving. Hell, her hesitation pretty much answered the question already.

"Yeah, kind of. I feel like you're trying so hard to show him that you're serious about being faithful and wanting to build his trust back that it's coming off as desperation. We all know that you love and want to be with his crazy ass. But I don't think you need to change who you are to do that. Besides, I think if a chance comes for you to cheat with Bellow again, I don't think you'll take it." She expressed, staring at me with a curious look. "It's like you've come to some resolve about him, I don't know exactly, but you're not the same when Bell's brought up. That's why I don't see you risking your relationship with Mike for Bellow again. Especially now that you know, he'll leave your ass."

She was right. If the opportunity did arise, I wouldn't take it.

"I'm going to assume that you already realized this. So, what? You wanted me to clarify your own thoughts?"

I nodded. "Sort of. I wasn't overbearing with it, though, right?" I didn't believe that I was. Either way, I wanted to be sure.

Missy hummed thoughtfully. "Not really. Well, not to me anyway. Hell, most of your clinginess I chopped up to you being pregnant. As for how Mike feels. You'll have to ask him." A sigh left my mouth as I thought about asking Mike. "What's that about?" Missy questioned, catching the action.

My shoulders moved up, then down before I chuckled. "Honestly, I don't want to know how he feels. Mike's ass is too gotdamn truthful, and with the way my emotions are set up, I don't feel like fighting him for hurting my feelings—" Missy broke out laughing, making me glare at her, "—that shit not funny, man. Seriously though, what really brought all this up was because we kind of got into it this morning. I didn't realize it before, but I've been sort of shutting him out when it comes to the baby. Like, although he knows everything and pretty much accepted it all. Yet, I try to divert the topic whenever the baby is brought up."

"That's understandable. I mean, with the possibility of the baby being Bell's, y'all don't wanna...I don't know." She stopped looking through clothes and glanced at me. "Yeah, I don't understand that. What you mean y'all don't talk about the baby?"

Humming, I nodded. "Exactly what I said. We don't discuss the baby at all. That's mainly because of me, which I now know is because of my damn guilt. I wonder if Mike ass felt this much shame when he got that hoe pregnant because this shit is horrible."

Missy laughed. "Bitch, I would think so. The shit isn't supposed to feel good, Kim. But you're right. You need to let that shit go. And if you are shutting Mike out, you need to stop before you end up pushing him away completely. Which we all know you don't want."

That was what I didn't want to do. "I know, and I'm changing that starting today. Plus, I think Mike's getting tired of my ass." I confessed, knowing that was true.

"Girl, just give that man some bomb ass—I'm sorry—head, and he'll be happy, trust me." Missy grinned, making me laugh.

"Yo' ass irritating in real life. Plus, I've been giving him some stupid dome, and I still think he's tired of me. Hell, the head, sex, and baby are probably the only reason he's still dealing with my ass." Missy hummed as if she agreed with that last bit. "Anyway, enough about my complicated relationship. Hoe, when are we going to get a damn wedding date? Bitch, we're pushing at what? Shit,

I've lost count."

Missy groaned. "We're not even about to get into that shit. Don't get me wrong, I'm so ready to start planning my over-the-top wedding, but after that shit happened with Eric, my heart isn't into planning. Like, I'm already lying to him, but to marry him knowing what I do. I can't, Kimmy. It's so fucked up because I love the hell out of that man and wanna become Mrs. Roman Darrell Price. But I know once he finds out, it's going to be over with us, and I'm not ready to lose him."

My lips formed into a pout as I came up behind Missy, enclosing my arms around her waist and laying my head on her shoulder. I knew how crazy in love my girl was with her man. I actually felt bad for her because I knew the secret she kept was tearing her up inside. In truth, had the roles been reversed, I probably would've told him what happened right off the bat. Just to get the shit over with. Yet, I understood Missy's fear of not wanting to lose Roman.

"I'm sorry, babe. I know how hard this situation is for you, but you'll figure it out. And if Roman doesn't understand your reasons for not telling him right after, he just doesn't deserve you. Hell, he knew his damn cousin wasn't wrapped tight—"

"Nuh-uh, hoe don't do that. Eric had serious issues, and Roman wanted to help him. Hell, that was his favorite cousin. So, regardless of his mental stability, Roman still felt he could've done something somehow. Like, he won't see the wrong in what Eric did entirely. But that's not here nor there, meaning I don't wanna talk about it. The shit is only going to stress me out." Her head fell back, landing against mine. "So, how's my niece or nephew doing? Bitch, when do we find out what you're having? I'm ready to shop for my baby." She groaned out a laugh.

Letting her go, I pushed away from her, chuckling myself. "Mike asked me that same damn question this morning. I go back to the doctor in a couple of weeks. But even still, I don't think I wanna know. I kind of want to be surprised, honestly."

Missy's hand came to my stomach as her eyes rolled hard. "Well, bitch, I don't. I wanna know now. I'm ready to spoil my baby." She whined, leaning down to my stomach. "What are you Tinka stinka shit?"

"Ha!" I broke out laughing. "Hoe, get away from me. Ugh! Move!" Pushing her back, I walked around her, putting the clothing items I picked up back on the rack. "Are we finished in here? I'm not getting none of this. I wanted them at first, now I don't." I was so picky when it came to clothes. I could walk through a store and pick up a bunch of shit, but half the time, I'll end up putting everything back—which was ironic because I loved clothes.

Missy looked at the stuff I put back and shook her head. "Girl, get those damn jeans, they're cute, and I got a pair like it. I'll get them for you." She grabbed the black destruct jeans and the top I had. Hell, I wasn't going to tell her ass not to get them. "You're coming to dinner with us tomorrow night, right?"

My head shook, and she glared at me. "Girl, I don't want Mike around Roman—"

"Bitch, why not? Hoe, it ain't like Mike ass don't know every fucking thing, nor is Roman the type to bring up your affair in front of Mike either."

I waved her off. "I know that. It's just I don't want to keep putting it in Mike's face, either. With this dinner, it will be all of the girls and their men, none of who Mike messes with. I could see if King would be there, but he's not going. Mike won't have anybody to converse with. So, it'll be awkward as hell." I explained as we made it to the counter.

Missy shrugged. "Kim, seriously? You're acting like any of them have an issue with Mike. Hell, to be honest, all of them are antisocial as fuck. Blaze and Roman may converse, but those mothafuckas ain't buddy-buddy in real life. Hell, they're mutual because of Bellow. Just like Blaze and Mike, they're cordial because of King. So, excuse me if I'm missing your point. Plus, we're not asking none of them to become best damn friends—"

"Okay, fine, damn. Just shut the hell up." I knew if I disagreed, she would keep on talking about it. "But, I'm not promising Mike is gonna come. He loves y'all, but he doesn't like being around y'all for real." Although true, I found it funny because Mike has known them for years, so one would think he was used to them. However true that might've been, Mike still didn't like being around them.

"Don't nobody care. His ugly ass ain't fun to be around either, though. Mike's ass is irritating. Just tell him we're going to a club. I bet he'll come then."

"Leave my baby alone. He's not that bad, though. Hell, his ass better than damn Blaze."

Missy's lips pursed together, and she nodded. "Yeah, he is, and Mike doesn't talk that much shit to us unless we start with him." She pointed out.

My brow raised at that. "Hoe, you start half the shit with all those niggas, though."

"Okay, and? It's fun sometimes. Oh, and one day next week, I plan to go down to see Ang and my babies. I told Peach and E this morning. Y'all can come with me if you wanna. But I'm out of here next week." She laughed, making my eyes roll.

That didn't come as a surprise to me at all. Missy ass practically lived out there with Angel. The pair was truly inseparable. I was really surprised that Missy hadn't moved out there yet.

"I'll come with. I wanna see my sweet niece and her badass brothers."

Missy hit me. "Don't do my boys like that. They're so sweet." She cooed.

Linking arms with her, we walked out of the store. "Yeah, when they wanna be. Girl, I talked to Ang the other day, late as hell. Peewee's ass up, just all over the damn place—Ooh, excuse me." I apologized as I bumped into someone. Yet, I didn't bother stopping to see if whoever heard me as I continued walking. That was until my wrist was grabbed, halting me.

"It's cool, sweetheart, no harm done." The handsome brown-skinned man smiled a sexy dimpled grin at me while rubbing my arm in a caressing manner. Although what would've flattered any woman, it instantly irritated me.

I jerked my arm from his grasp as a glare covered my face. "I remember you. Mr. I can't take a hint."

His hand went to his chest, and he rubbed over his heart as that grin seemed to widen. "Ooh, you made my heart jump. I didn't think you would remember me, straight up. Real shit, I didn't think it was you at first." He claimed, licking his lips while his eyes scanned over my figure. Biting into his bottom lip, he smiled, then rubbed his wet mouth. "Damn, dim light didn't do you justice. You're sexy as hell—" He began to compliment me while taking hold of my hand again.

"And I'm happily taken, which I told you that night at the club." Out of all the people to run into on a random ass day. It would be the creep from the club. With a roll of my eyes, I removed my hand from his. "We have to go. Again, my bad for bumping into you." I said dismissively, ready to get the hell away from him.

"Don." Missy suddenly said as if coming to

some conclusion. "I knew that damn face, but for the life of me, I couldn't figure out who the hell you were." She claimed, staring at him before her eyes settled on me. From the motion of her eyes, I knew it was time to go.

I glanced at Don to see a mug on his face as he took Missy in. *Okay...who the fuck is Don?* I couldn't help but wonder, but not enough to ask her questions in front of him.

"Don! Nigga, where the fuck you take off too." Martell was saying until his eyes landed on me, then Missy. The murderous expression that covered his mug was pure hatred.

We definitely needed to get the fuck gone.

"I told you, I needed to holla at somebody." He motioned to me.

My mouth formed into an O as it clicked. "So, me bumping into you wasn't a mistake. You ran into me intentionally."

That dimpled grin was back on display. "Of course. You're beautiful as hell. I had to come and talk to you again." My eyes rolled at that, making him laugh. "I heard you, you're taken, but that doesn't matter to me, I promise."

"Kimmy, let's go." Missy urged, and I was there with her.

Martell moved in Missy's path, however. "So, we not speaking?" The venom in his voice was very well noted.

Missy shrugged, not seeming bothered by him, yet, I knew the truth, however. "No." She shook her head. "There's no reason for us too. You know that and why." She pointed out facts. After that shit he pulled, he knew damn well there wasn't shit to be said between none of us.

Martell laughed, nodding his agreement. "You're right. I owe yo' ass too. You already know that shit, though. I mean, you did play a role in my cousin's death. I don't know how—then again, the how don't matter, but I know yo' ass set him up. You should've stayed in a little girl's place and not tried to play a man's game. So, know your day is coming."

That was a clear-ass threat, yet I needed to be sure. "Did you just threaten her?"

Martell chuckled as he rubbed his wet bottom lip. "Of course, I did. Mook was my favorite cousin. It's only right I do the bitch that got him killed."

Don suddenly let out a growl. "My favorite brother too. So, you know yo' ass good as dead. We ain't gonna do shit to you now, though. I want you terrified as shit, dead ass." He laughed before his sights came to me. His fingers rubbed my chin in a caressing manner. "She ain't have shit to do with it though, right, Tell? I really don't wanna hurt her. She's beautiful as fuck—"

Martell grabbed Don's wrist, pushing his hand away from me. "She doesn't have shit to do with none of this. Plus, shorty's off-limits. That's Mike's ol' lady, so leave her the fuck alone." The glare he gave his cousin was a clear warning that he seemed to want Don to take seriously. "Let's go." He told him before his gaze fell on Missy again. "I'll be seeing you, sweetheart." A wide and genuine smile graced his face as he spoke to her. "Oh, tell my little chocolate baby, I said hey, and I miss her." The fact he looked to really mean that didn't sit right with me.

"And Parker? What do you want me to tell him?" Missy asked, her mug mean as hell.

That vicious glare returned to Martell's face. "Bitch, there that mouth of yours go." Laughing, he started walking away. "Don, come on." He growled.

It was then I realized Don still stood there staring at me. "You be good out here, beautiful. Hopefully, the next time we see each other, your situation may be different. It's cool to leave that nigga if you wanna."

"Ha!" I barked out a laugh without intending to. My hand covered my mouth to muffle my laughter. The fact that he seemed so damn serious was what did it for me. His entire expression was so serious. Not only that, the way he spoke wasn't in a threatening manner either. Not toward Mike or me.

"Damn, even yo' laugh sexy—"

"Don!" Martell yelled, sounding pissed off.

However, Don didn't seem bothered or in a rush to go. "I ain't gonna hold you." Grabbing my hand, he kissed it. "Gone head, and enjoy the rest of your day." Giving it a gentle squeeze, he smiled and started backing away. "Oh, tell yo' nigga I said what's up." With a wink, he turned and walked off toward Martell.

"Bitch, we need to leave," I told her.

Missy's head was shaking as she pulled out her phone. "We're not leaving this damn mall by ourselves. Well, I'm not. Obviously, they ain't gonna do shit to you. That mothafucka threatened my ass." She fussed, freaked out. "Fuck!" She groaned, tapping her phone screen rapidly. "Roman's at work, so he's not gonna answer."

"Hey, babe, it's okay. Calm down. I won't let shit happen to you—"

"Bitch, you won't be able to stop him if he tries to kill me. Hell, Don ass will probably just— shit, I don't know, but he likes your ass apparently. That mothafucka outright threatened me, though." She went off, pacing.

Seeing how scared she was, I grabbed my phone and called Mike.

"Yeah?" He answered after the second ring. From the tone of his voice, I knew he was still irritated with me, yet I was glad he answered.

"Babe, I'm at the mall with Missy, and we just ran into Martell and Don—"

"I'm on my way up there."

"Okay—"

"Stay on the damn phone." He snapped as if he thought I was about to hang up. "Those mothafuckas didn't do shit to you?" He damn near growled.

Instantly my head shook. "No, they didn't. Martell said I was your girl and was cool and not to be messed with. But he threatened Missy."

"Fuck. He ain't do shit to her?"

"No. He threatened her that's it." I sighed, rubbing my forehead.

"A'ight. Y'all go to the food court and stay there. I should be there in about fifteen minutes. I'mma stay on the phone, though." He insisted.

After telling Missy what Mike said, we made our way to the food court. "You texted, Angel?"

"I'm calling her now. I can't believe that nigga. This bitch ain't answering..." she trailed off, looking at her phone before her fingers began moving across the screen hastily. That let me know she was texting. "She's at the doctor with the kids. I'mma text Chris."

"Bitch, no the fuck you don't. If you call his ass, he'll be down here and acting a fool, looking for those niggas. We don't need his ass here yet. Especially when we don't even know where they're at." I liked Chris. Homeboy was cool as hell. Still, he was a gotdamn psycho when it came to Martell. Not only that, the man was crazy about Missy. So knowing Martell threatened her, there was no doubt in my mind that he wouldn't be here acting the hell up.

Missy's hands went up frustratingly. "No, duh, Kimmy. But how do you think his ass will react if somebody else tells him? He's gonna go clean the fuck off on my ass. I don't have time for that bullshit." She snapped at me before her attention went to her phone, and those damn fingers started moving once again.

"Do shorty not realize that man ain't her nigga?" Mike's voice came through my AirPod. He had been so damn quiet, I forgot he was even on the line.

"Mike, shut up, please. What I don't understand is why Martell just overlooked me?" That's what confused me. I was sure he knew just how tight the girls and I were, so what would make him consider me not to be a threat?

Mike's sudden chuckle baffled me because it wasn't funny. It actually pissed me off. "I'm glad you find some humor in this bullshit."

"Man, calm yo' ass down. I ain't laughing at the situation but your question. Martell might be crazy, but that mothafucka ain't stupid. He knows who to fuck with and who not to. And I'm on that not too list." He chuckled, which caused my lips to pop. "Sweetheart, I have no mothafuckin' limits when it comes to you or my son's safety. Everybody knows that to be a fact." The calmness he spoke held so much surety and promise that it caused a chill to run through me.

I never doubted that Mike would pop the fuck

off behind Malik or me. Yet, had I not seen how Martell warned Don, I wouldn't have taken Mike's words as serious. Still, it baffled me that anyone would take Mike in that manner, mainly because he wasn't one to mix with drama. He wasn't a hood nigga, nor did he play in the streets. Well, not that I knew of. Yeah, he conversed with dealers because half of them were his clientele.

My damn head began to spin as I tried to understand Martell's reaction. One thing that was cause for relief was that he hadn't known I shot at him and Mook a few years back.

"Chris, don't fuckin' yell at me. How would I know the mothafucka would be at the mall? I wasn't by my damn self, I'm with Kimmy—boy—nigga it just fuckin' happened—I'm not leaving—Mike's coming to get us—he on his fuckin' way now." Missy growled out of frustration.

"Shorty dead arguing with that dude like he's her nigga for real." Mike chuckled, and I had to agree with him.

Missy's damn face had turned red, and I knew she was pissed off. Chris and Missy's relationship would be strange to anyone looking from the outside. Not to us, though. The pair had such undeniable chemistry, their bond was strong, and it was because Chris let Missy see his vulnerable side, which he had closed off for years.

That was what made their relationship so unique. I actually believed Missy was the only female Chris could really be himself with. I also felt that scared him the most. I didn't know the reason behind his fear, but I knew that played a huge part in him letting Missy go.

"Babe, how close are you?"

"I just got off the escalator. I'll be there in a minute."

I breathed out a sigh of relief. "Mike's here—"

"Aye, why the fuck is Chris calling me?" Mike's amused voice came through the line.

I rubbed my forehead, feeling a damn headache coming. "Missy, why is Chris calling Mike?"

She rolled her eyes in irritation. "Girl, I don't fucking know. I hung up on his ignorant ass. Mothafucka gonna go off on me like I was supposed to know Martell would be at the damn mall. I thought the nigga was still hiding for real."

"Well, hit his ass back and tell him not to fuckin' call me. It ain't shit I can tell his ass." Mike told her as he reached us. "You straight?" He questioned while his eyes examined me.

"Yeah, I'm alright. I told you they didn't pay me no mind. They just had words for Missy, then left." I clarified.

Mike nodded at the explanation as his arm went around my shoulder, pulling me into his side. "What yo' smart mouth ass say to him?" He questioned Missy while grabbing our bags.

"Shit, I don't even remember what I said to

be real with you. I know that crazy mothafucka threatened me. He thinks I had something to do with Mook getting killed."

Mike's laughter had me hitting him in the stomach. "How are you finding this shit funny? That man popped up—"

"That nigga ain't pop up on y'all asses. You mothafuckas just ran into each other. That nigga crazy, but his ass ain't stupid. If he's gonna do some shit, it's not going to be in a mall full of witnesses." Staring at Missy, Mike's head shook. "But, riding around by yourself, you shouldn't do. Not with that nigga out here. He'll definitely snatch yo' ass up. So, don't be out here by yo' damn self and watch your surroundings to make sure ain't nobody following you."

Missy looked so damn stressed as her head bobbed from what Mike said. "I know. I won't put shit past his psycho ass."

Mike's hand pushed my chin up so that I was staring at him. "And you sho' he ain't say shit to you?"

My head shook, yet before I could respond, Missy snorted loudly. "Hell no, he didn't say anything to her. Shit, Don ass was just trying to holler at her. But Martell told him who she was and said Kim didn't have shit to do with it."

"Don tried talking to you?" His brow raised questioningly at that.

My eyes just rolled as I shrugged. "He tried,

but I told him that I already have a man. He was the dude all over me at the club. That's how I ended up running into Martell and spilling my drink. I didn't know they were together or who he was; otherwise, I would've said something. Oh, he said, what's up, too."

Mike's hum and nod had me staring at him more closely. I knew something was up, I just didn't know what, and I wanted to know.

"That's it?" He asked, and I nodded. "Alright." He guided us out of the mall to his truck. The passenger door opened once we got there, and Leon hopped out of the front seat. "Missy, give Leon yo' keys and show him where you parked. He'll drive your car back to my crib."

Missy didn't argue or hesitate to give Leon her keys. Hell, she didn't even warn him not to mess her car up like normal. She simply passed him the sets then got in the backseat. "Mike, I parked in the front." She told him.

Mike motioned for Leon to get in and drove us to Missy's car.

Chapter Seven

Kimmy

The Friend of my Enemy is my...Man

"Missy, you can hang here until yo' dude gets off." Mike offered, like that wasn't already the plan. Missy glanced at me, and I waved my hand, telling her to ignore him. "Why the hell is Chris calling me?" Mike questioned.

Missy let out a heavy groan. "Ignore him." She told him, sounding irritated as hell. Once Mike's phone stopped ringing a second later, Missy's started. Laughing out a groan, she answered. "Dude, what?"

Mike let out a chuckle, and I hit him. "Shut up."

"What? I'm not about to come out there, Christian. No, I'm not asking Mike to bring me either. Dude, get off my phone—look, I'm not about to argue with you, and I'm not coming out there either."

Tapping Mike's arm, I motioned for him to follow me out. "Let her argue with him." I led him into Malik's game room and closed the door. "I wanna talk to you about earlier—"

Mike's head shook, and he walked around me. "Ain't shit to talk about. I'm going to guess and say that you talked to somebody earlier, and they made you realize something, which got you feeling bad. I don't wanna hear that shit. Apparently, it's some shit you need to deal with on your own, not with me. So there's nothing we need to discuss." He shrugged, then walked around me to leave the room.

"Mike, seriously?"

"Kimmy, I don't know what makes yo' ass think I wanna keep going on about the same damn thing with you. Just because you've had some type of realization don't change shit for me. I'm done going in this circle with you about this damn baby and the possibility with dude ass. I knew what the fuck everything was when you told me, and I stated where shit stood. Yet, yo' ass can't seem to grasp what the fuck I'm saying because you're so stuck in yo' own gotdamn head. So, work that shit out on yo' own. Sweetheart, those yo' issues, not mine. Leave me the fuck alone with this shit." He pulled away from me and opened the door.

"Mike, would you just stop and talk to me—"

"That's the point, Kimmy. I don't wanna

fucking talk to you about this shit anymore." Mike laughed, shaking his head. "Of course, yo' ass don't hear that though because you've come to some type of resolve. So now you have to discuss that shit with me, and that's what I don't want because I don't give a fuck."

It took everything in me not to punch his stupid ass in the damn face. He didn't have the decency to even pretend to hear me out. That shit pissed me off to the max when he got like that. His actions shouldn't have surprised me because he's been that way for years.

Closing my eyes, I inhaled a deep breath then exhaled it slowly. When I finally opened my eyes again, I saw Mike's retreating back. That mothafucka just walked away. Pissed, I glanced around the hallway, looking for something, anything. Taking my shoe off, I threw it hard, hitting him in the back.

Mike stopped, looked down at the shoe for a second, then kept going into the living room. "Leon, let's go."

I know he is not about to leave...

Quickly, I made my way to the living room to see him grab his phone and keys off the table. "Where are you about to go?"

"Away from yo' dumb ass." He stated flatly, and I knew he meant that shit. Mike could be mean as hell when he wanted to be. The nigga could've at least lied to me.

All I wanted to do was apologize to his ass about how I've been acting. That was all.

"Seriously? Your really going to act like this? All because I wanted to apologize for earlier?" He didn't say anything. Hell, he didn't even look at me. He motioned for Leon to follow him out. "Mike..." he brushed by me, still not saying anything. "Michael!" I believed he was trying to piss me off. I made a grab for his keys, but he pushed me off of him and went to the front door. Before realizing it, I had taken off my other shoe and threw it at his ass, that time hitting him in the back of his head.

"Kimmy!" Missy yelled at me, surprised.

"Shorty, what the fuck is wrong with you?" Leon asked, staring at me like I was crazy.

I ignored the pair as my gaze was fixed on Mike. He stared at me, rubbing the back of his head. Laughing, he snatched open the door and walked out. My ass was right behind him too.

"Kimmy, just let him go," Missy said, grabbing my wrist trying to stop me.

I jerked away from her and followed behind Mike to his truck. I reached him just as he opened the driver's door. Pushing it closed, I got in front of the door.

Mike stared down at me for a while with a blank expression that I couldn't read. A laugh suddenly left his damn mouth, and I pushed him.

"Ain't shit funny—"

Mike muffed the hell out of me, then grabbed my wrist before I could hit him. "Yeah, it is because you don't even want shit. You just put on a whole gotdamn show for no reason."

"How the hell can you say what I want or not when you didn't want to listen to me—"

"Sweetheart, because I already know. Look, I'm not about to argue with yo' ass. And I'm definitely not about to hear you express some pointless ass shit to me just so you can feel better about yourself. Shorty, I don't wanna hear yo' ass apologize for shit. I already told you that. I've moved past that bullshit. Now, can you move so I can go?"

A heavy sigh left my mouth because he was right. I felt like shit for how I was being when it came to the baby. And I wanted to apologize to him for that, but I also wanted him to say all was forgiven so that I felt better about it.

"I'm sorry I threw my shoes at you." My arms went around his waist as my hands slid under his shirt. Standing on my tiptoes, I kissed his chin. "You don't have to leave." Mike didn't say anything, just stared down at me. Yep, he was definitely over my damn antics. "Babe, I'm serious, I'm sorry. I promise I'mma get better with everything, I swear." My teeth grabbed my bottom lip as I stared up at him through my lashes. All the while, my nails continued to caress up and down his spine.

Mike rubbed his head, licking his lips. "A'ight,

Kimmy."

My lips popped at the dryness of his tone. "Don't say it like that. Say you believe me, Mike."

"Man, what I just tell you? I ain't tryna make yo' ass feel better—" My lips pressed into his to stop him from talking. Pulling back, he rubbed his mouth. "A'ight, Kimmy, I believe you. Can you move now?"

Once again, my lips popped from his sarcasm. Although he probably wasn't trying to be sarcastic, I still felt like he wanted to irritate me. "Where are you in such a big rush to get too—"

"None of your damn business. Kim, now get yo' ass out of the way before I move you." He threatened, and I could see the annoyance on his face.

I wasn't trying to irritate him, but I didn't want him to leave either, especially if he was pissed at me. "You can go as long as you're not leaving because of me." Standing on my tiptoes, I kissed his chin as my nails lightly dug into his lower back.

"Shorty, it doesn't have shit to do with you anymore. Now move." He motioned for me to get out the way.

"Fine. Gimme a kiss, then you can go." My lips puckered, and I stood on my tiptoes

Laughing, Mike's hand went around my neck, and he jerked me to him. "Yo' ass irritating as fuck. You're lucky yo' ass pregnant; otherwise, I'd choke the fuck out of you right now." Lowering his head, he pecked my lips, then pulled back. "Now, go in the house." My lips popped, and he kissed me again. "I'm not about to fuck you, Kimmy. So it's no point in kissing yo' ass how you want me to."

I broke out laughing while letting my head fall against his chest. "Don't do that. My mind wasn't even going there for real. I really just want a kiss, I promise."

"You promise?" He stated as if he knew I was lying. Which I didn't think I was, so I nodded. "Is that why yo' ass been standing here scratching my damn back this whole time?"

My nails stopped moving, and my fingers locked together around his frame. "I didn't even realize I was doing that. Alright, go, and we'll talk when you get back. I still want a real kiss before you leave." I was beginning to see what Missy and Elizabeth were talking about. I was starting to irritate my own damn self with how I was acting.

Tilting my head back, his grip on my throat tightened as he kissed me. Immediately my agitation left, and my gotdamn body melted as he sucked and kissed on my lips before his tongue slid into my mouth, tangling with my own, intimately.

Like a match falling on gasoline, my body ignited with flames, and that heat went straight to my core. Moaning into his mouth, my hands ran up his bare skin to his shoulders. My arms soon snaked around his neck.

I was about to jump my big ass into Mike's arms and hoped like hell he caught me. That was my plan until Mike's big lips left mine too soon. A desperate moan escaped my mouth as I tried to pull his lips back on mine.

Laughing, he moved my arms from his neck, pulled me from his truck, then turned us around. "That's yo' kiss, now get yo' nasty ass in the house. I'll be back later."

I already didn't want him to leave to begin with. That feeling only grew more with my added horniness. "Fine, go. But don't be gone long. With everything that happened—"

"Dead ass, Kim? You gonna use that?" Mike thought the shit was funny, but I was serious about him not being gone long. Of course, it had nothing to do with what happened earlier.

"So what. Just don't be too long." Leaning up, I pecked Mike's lips, but his phone started ringing before I could try to take things further.

Mike kissed my forehead as he grabbed his phone. "I'll be back in a couple of hours, and you can have this mothafucka." He put my hand on his hard dick.

I couldn't help but rub his thick soldier. Even so, the name on his phone screen confused me. *Don.* Why the fuck was he calling Mike for?

"He has your number? Why? Wait, you have his number saved. Why?" I couldn't help but ask.

Why would Don be calling Mike after our run-in? Better yet, why the hell did Mike have his fucking number stored in his phone. "Mike—"

"It doesn't have shit to do with you, so don't worry about it."

How could he fix his mouth to say that shit to me? Martell just threatened to kill my best friend less than two hours ago. Not only that, his ass almost killed my other best friend and her fucking husband. Now he was calling Mike. How was that something I didn't need to worry about? If he knew where the fuck they were, we should've been telling Parker so they could kill that mothafucka.

"Mike, why do you have Don's number? Why is he calling you—"

"Sweetheart, it ain't none of your business why. Gone in the house. I'll be back." Opening the driver's door, he hopped in and blew the horn.

Things with him weren't making sense. First, Mike reached out to Parker and Chris, now this shit with Don and Martell. Mike knew the pair hated each other. Not only that, he knew all the shit Angel went through because of Martell. So for him to be in contact with Don just wasn't right.

Pulling open the door, I leaned against it. "What's going on? Babe, you can talk to me, you know that. Why are you talking to Don?"

Pushing my head back, he kissed me. "I know, and if I had something to talk to you about, I would. Now get in the house and don't be stressed about shit. That ain't good for the baby." Kissing me once more, he nodded toward the house just as Leon got in the front seat. "Go."

I didn't want to let that shit go. I needed to know what the hell was going on. I knew Mike, though, and he wasn't going to tell me anything.

I was going to have to find out for myself. "Okay. Call when you're on your way back. I love you."

Mike's eye squinted as he nodded slowly. "A'ight. I love you, too."

Closing the door, I tried to slow my pace as I quickly went into the house. I stood at the front door for a long second. My mind was trying to think of different logical reasons Mike would talk to Don.

The first thing I thought about was business. Mike was selling him guns. But why would Mike do that when he knew about their beef with Parker. If he sold them guns, there was no doubt that they would use them against Parker.

Still, Mike knew Angel would be dragged into that shit. So why deal with them, to begin with?

The second thing, maybe he was trying to help Parker, even though he didn't care for them. He knew I loved Angel, so perhaps he would try to protect her by setting Don up...

However, that thought was quickly erased because Mike wasn't the type to get in the middle of folk's shit. For as long as I've known him, I've never seen him get involved with bullshit. Especially when it came to mothafuckas shooting. Although, Mike wasn't scary or a pushover in the least bit. He just didn't gravitate to drama. He seemed to always stay clear of it all.

"Kimmy, what's wrong?"

My mouth opened but closed because I didn't want to tell her something when I didn't know what was what. "I don't know. Are you cool to be here by yourself for a minute? I promise I'll be right back." Missy looked confused as she stared me over. "Call Ebony and Peaches to come over. I'll go pick us up something to eat while I'm out." Grabbing a set of keys and my purse, I quickly left the house, not giving her a chance to ask me anything else.

Jumping in Mike's all-black car, I quickly pulled out the driveway. I knew driving mine would be too damn noticeable.

Pulling up the find my phone app, I quickly tracked Mike's device. "Damn..." I mumbled, seeing how far he had gotten. The nigga was flying because I wasn't in the house for no more than a minute. Groaning, I hit the gas, setting out to follow him.

∞∞∞

It took me a minute before I got caught up with Mike. When I finally found him, he was at the Lion's Den, Akil's club. It was the middle of the day, so I knew the club wasn't open yet. Then again, I guess that didn't matter when you're friendly with the owner.

I was so tempted to go inside the club, but I wasn't that damn stupid. I knew there was a ninety percent chance that I'd get caught, and I couldn't have that. I needed to know what the hell Mike ass was up to. I just prayed like hell he wasn't involved with Don and Martell, but something else altogether.

I didn't know what I would do if it wasn't the latter. Mike wasn't a snake, though. So I knew I could get that thought out of my head.

"Oh, my God!" I was about to drive my damn self crazy. "Like, dude, what the fuck are you doing?" I was beyond frustrated.

After an hour of sitting outside the club and not seeing anyone go inside, I figured he wasn't meeting with anyone, and he just needed some space away from me. Even if that was the case, he could've told me that instead of letting me think the worse thing imaginable. He knew what I would've been thinking once I saw Don's name pop up.

Sighing, I made myself comfortable as possible as I continued to watch the club and Mike's truck.

Another hour and a half passed when the club's doors finally opened. My damn heart dropped to the pit of my stomach when Don walked out, then Mike.

"What the fuck, Mike?" I whispered lowly. My

head quickly ducked down once the pair scanned over in my direction. After a second, I felt dumb because the windows were tinted dark, that no one could see inside the car.

Don's hand came out for Mike to take. He looked at the outstretched palm then bumped past him. I let my window down a bit to hear what Don was saying.

"I didn't know that babe was yo' shorty. When I found out, I stepped the fuck off. Nigga, you've already busted my fuckin' lip, and I let you have that. So, let all be forgiven, Mike." Don was saying, all the while chuckling.

Mike walked to his truck and put the large gun case in the back of his vehicle. "Once you get back, hit me up, and I'll let you know when you can come to the range and test everything out." He told him while closing the truck's back.

So he was selling him damn guns. Why would he do that shit? There was no doubt that those guns would be used to start a damn war with Parker and his boys.

What the fuck was Mike thinking?

Mike wouldn't do that, though at least I didn't think he would. "What the fuck are you doing, Michael?" I mumbled to myself as I watched Don move closer to him continuing to converse. However, the pair were close that I couldn't understand what they began saying. Mike and Don talked for several seconds longer before they parted ways, getting in their vehicles.

Yet neither pulled away. My phone rang with Mike's name on the screen a few seconds later. After the third ring, I answered.

"Hey, babe, what's up?" I tried to sound collected, although I was anything but that.

"I'm on my way back to the crib. You want something while I'm out?" He questioned.

"Um...no, no, you don't have to get anything. I was actually on my way out to pick up the pizza I ordered for the girls—"

"I'll get it since I'm already out. Where did you get it from?"

I put the phone on speaker and quickly pulled up the girl's group chat.

My Bitches: *One of y'all call and order two pizzas from Godfather's right now and put it in my name. Hurry up! Peach and E, if you bitches ain't at Mike's house, get there, please! Bring the kids if you have to. I don't care. Just get there.*

I was not about to get caught up in a damn lie.

"No, I got it. I'm in the car now about to leave —"

"Don't yo' ass leave that fucking house by yourself. And don't take those fucking girls with you. Stay yo' ass there. I'll pick y'all shit up."

My hands squeezed air to stop myself from groaning in frustration.

"Mike, no, for real. I'll get it. While out, I was going to stop at the L and get them something to drink. I want to try and ease Missy's mind. She's not taking this threat from Martell lightly. Babe, she's really freaking out, so we're trying to get her drunk." I quickly thought to say. "Babe, come home. I got this."

Mike finally pulled out of the parking lot, with Don following behind him. I waited for a few seconds, then followed the direction they drove off in. Don was on Mike's ass, following him.

Why was he following him? Did Mike know he was being followed?

"Kimmy, you hear me?" Mike snapped into the line, grabbing my attention.

Clearing my head, I focused on the call. "Sorry, what you say?"

"I said you bet not leave those fucking girls in my crib by themselves. Especially not Missy's black ass. All my gotdamn weed better be where I left it. I'll stop by the L and get them something to drink and pick up the pizza. You probably got that shit from Godfather's or Luigi's anyway. I'll be there in a minute." He ended the call with that.

"Oh, my God!" I groaned, frustrated as hell that he hung up and just didn't listen to me. Don suddenly switched lanes, merging onto the highway to Chicago. "Fuck me!" I didn't know whether I should follow Don or not. At least if I did, I would know where the fuck they were, and I could tell Parker. I hit my blinker and switched lanes. My phone rang immediately after, Mike's name flashing on the radio. "Yeah?" I answered.

"I'm about to swing by the crib and pick you up—"

"What? No!" I practically yelled. *Fuck! He was fucking everything up.* Quickly, I jumped back in my lane, getting over just in time. "I mean, no, just go get the stuff. We're starving. That's why I was going to pick it up. So, go get the pizza, drinks, and hurry up." I ended the call before he could say anything else. I then called Missy.

"Bitch, where the fuck you at? Yo' ass said you'll be gone for a little while. Hoe, you've been gone for fucking hours. I'm glad that nigga didn't come here and kill me." She snapped into the line, causing the girls to laugh.

"Hoe, Martell don't even know where Mike stays. Okay, y'all listen, I'm on my way back right now. Look, Mike gonna pick up some food and drinks for us. But I need y'all to smoke some of his weed. He got a case—"

"Bitch, Missy found that shit a long time ago. This hoe on her third blunt now."

My eyes rolled, but I chuckled no less. Missy stayed taking weed from our men. That was why Mike didn't want her alone at the house.

"Okay, cool, but don't smoke anymore, Miss. Y'all, It's a bottle of Henny in the kitchen opened, start drinking that shit—"

"Missy already did. Kim, what the fuck do you have going on, and where are you at? Bitch, you know Mike will flip the fuck out if he knew you left us here by ourselves. Are you with Bellow?" Peaches questioned, making my eyes roll hard.

"Bitch, no, I'm not with him. Bell and I are done and over with. I had something else to do. But I'll be there in about ten minutes. Missy, don't smoke no more damn weed. I don't feel like hearing that niggas mouth about you smoking his shit up."

"Girl, I'm stressed. I need this shit more than him at this point." She claimed, making me laugh.

"Wait!" E yelled before I could hang up. "What you had to do that took up nearly three hours of your time?"

"Bye, y'all!" I ended the call. I wasn't about to tell them anything, especially when I didn't know the whole story behind Mike's actions.

I literally floored it all the way back home. I wasn't about to take any chances on Mike beating me to the house. After backing the car into its spot, I rushed into the house. Only to see the girls peaking into the hallway.

"Bitch, I thought yo' ass was Mike. Where the hell have you been?" Missy asked, coming fully into the hall.

"I told you I had something to do." Kicking off my shoes, I pulled off my shirt as I walked into the laundry room. Finding one of my lounge around the house t-shirt dresses, I pulled it on then took off my pants.

Taking my hair out of its neat ponytail, I ran my fingers through it several times then pulled it into a messy bun atop my head.

"Okay, what the fuck, Kimmy?" They questioned as I finished fixing myself up.

"Nothing, I just need it to seem like I've been here with y'all, comfortable," I explained, putting my clothes in the dirty hamper. I turned toward them to see the trio looking me over. Laughing, I brushed by them. "Y'all, it's nothing for real. I just don't want Mike to know I wasn't here with y'all. Let's get back in the living room."

"So, you're not going to tell us where you've been?" Peaches questioned.

Shaking my head, I went into the living area and plopped down on the couch. "Nope." The girls shared glances before their gaze fell on me. I simply shrugged because I wouldn't tell them shit until I knew more. It would be dumb to start speaking on assumptions when I could be wrong.

A part of me knew I was wrong and merely just overreacting. Hell, I knew Mike. There was definitely a good reason for whatever he was doing. He knew how much I loved Angel and Missy, so he wouldn't be conversing with a nigga that wanted to harm them.

Mentally I groaned. My fucking mind was on overdrive, and I hated it. Only because I knew there was no way of knowing until it was too gotdamn late.

From the glares on the girl's faces, I could tell they felt some type of way about me not spilling my gotdamn guts to them. I didn't care, and they shouldn't be mad. They knew me, so they should've known I wasn't going to say shit until I was ready... then again, that was probably the reason for their mugging. They knew I wasn't saying shit.

I started laughing at their glares.

"Bitch, fuck you. Hoe, we tell yo' ass everything—" The girls started saying.

That only made me chuckle more. "Okay, hoe. I tell y'all asses shit too. Not everything that goes on in my life is on a need-to-know basis."

"Well bitch, I can go the fuck home because I'm not covering for your ass if I don't know what's going on." Peaches claimed.

Once again, I shrugged. "If you wanna go, you can. Either way, if I don't wanna tell yo' ass shit, I'm not going to." I told her while making myself comfortable on the couch and pushing the whole bullshit with Mike to the back of my mind. "Anyways, Miss, what the fuck you been in here doing?" I motioned to the Coke-A-Cola that sat right next to a bottle of beer and the Henny.

"That's all he had in there—oh and some gotdamn whiskey. Don't nobody even drink Jack Daniels. But I needed a drink, so," She motioned to everything on the table. Grabbing the bottled water from the table, she took a long drink. "Mike got the kitchen and pantry stocked like he don't ever have company over here."

I couldn't help but laugh at that. "Hoe, he doesn't. Aside from King, Leon, and Jerron, all of whom drink that shit."

"Bitch, you live here too, and I don't see no damn tequila, Vodka, or shit." She snapped, sounding so serious.

I broke out laughing. "I barely drink when I'm here. Plus, y'all hardly ever come here. We're always at my house for real. I'mma stock up here, though, for when y'all do come. *And* I'll have him get you your own personal weed stash, so you're not in his shit." I told her before kicking Peaches' moody ass in the thigh. "Peach, can you give me my phone?" I pointed to my device on the table.

"Nope. Get it yourself. I don't wanna be all in your business." Peaches ass was so gotdamn dramatic it didn't make any sense.

I wasn't even pissed at her behavior simply because she's always been like that. Peaches ass was so gotdamn entitled the shit wasn't even funny. Homegirl thought she was permitted to have all your info and business just because she was okay laying her shit out. It wasn't her fault entirely, but King's.

The jingling of keys had me forgetting about Peaches and looking to the entrance where Mike was coming through the door. For a second, my mind went blank because I didn't know what I would say to him. Especially given what I'd seen. How the hell was I supposed to act? I had no clue at all.

Mike walked into the living room and sat the pizza on the table without saying anything. Yet, the man was pissed off. The hard mug on his face showed that much. He dropped the bag of liquor on the sofa.

"Hey, Mike." Peaches spoke.

He didn't bother acknowledging her either. Oh, yeah, he was pissed. "Kimmy, come here." He turned and began walking out of the living room.

I wasn't about to go nowhere with him when he was like that. "Why? What's wrong with you?"

"If yo' ass ain't behind me when I walk in that room, I'm fucking you up. Shorty, don't play with me." With that, he walked out of the living room.

I could feel the girls burning a hole into me with questions. "Mike..." he was already jogging up the stairs. I knew he couldn't be pissed at me. Hell, I hadn't even done shit.

"Kimmy, what the fuck did you do?" The girls questioned, sounding concerned.

All I could do was shrug. For the life of me, I didn't know why he was pissed. "I didn't do shit."

"Bitch, where did you go when you left here?" Peaches wanted to know.

"Peach, shut up. Kim, get yo' ass the fuck

upstairs before he brings his ass back down here and drags you up there." Missy urged, giving me a push.

Her advice, I took. I knew Mike ass didn't have a problem dragging my black ass up those stairs. I wasn't trying to get embarrassed. Getting up, I quickly made my way up the stairs.

"Kimmy!" Mike hollered. I had just made it to the top of the stairs when he walked out of the room. "Get yo' ass in here."

"First off, you don't have to keep fucking talking to me like I'm your gotdamn child—" I was going off as I walked into the room.

The room door slammed, and Mike had me hemmed up against it as soon as it shut. His hand gripped my throat tight.

"You following me now?" I felt my eyes widen, and he nodded, noticing as well. My mouth opened, then closed, at a loss for words. "What? You didn't think I wouldn't notice my own fucking car, Kimmy? But not only that, yo' stupid ass was about to follow that mothafucka until I called yo' ass back. Are you fucking stupid, Kim?"

Oh, he was pissed off. And my stupid ass couldn't even lie my way out of this bullshit. What the fuck was I thinking? Of course, he would notice his own damn car.

"You know those mothafuckas will kill yo' ass without blinking, right? Man!" Mike punched the door beside my head, making me jump. Biting his lip, he choked the fuck out of me before moving back quickly. He was pissed off. "I wanna beat the fuck out of yo' ass right now."

I was definitely about to deflect and turn things around on him like a mothafucka. "Why were you even meeting with him, Mike? Especially knowing who he's with? You know what they tried to do to Ang and Missy—" Mike turned on me so fast, I quickly moved out of his arm's reach because he looked like he was ready to smack fire from my ass. "I wouldn't have followed you if I knew what was going on. But you won't tell me—"

"Because it ain't yo' fuckin' business, Kimberly. What part of that aren't you fucking understanding?" He snapped, and I moved to the other side of the room, away from him. Mike laughed as his hands roughly scrubbed over his head. "You doing dumb ass shit like following that mothafucka is why I don't tell yo' stupid ass shit—"

"You can really stop calling me stupid. Because I'm not fucking dumb. Okay, maybe trying to follow him wasn't the best idea. But the nigga just threatened my best fucking friend."

"And that's reason enough to stay the fuck away from them. Not follow the mothafucka, Kimmy. Man, I wanna knock the fuck out of yo' ass. What the fuck did you tell them?" He pointed to the door.

"Nothing." He mugged me hard as hell. "I swear, I didn't tell them anything because I don't know shit, Mike."

He stared at me for a long time before nodding as if believing me. "You mothafuckas can't help but put yourselves in the middle of bullshit. I ain't tell yo' ass about the shit because I knew you would do some bullshit like this. You can never just leave shit alone."

"Mike, you're still not telling me anything, though. I just need to know why you were meeting with him..." taking in his anger, I wanted to slap myself. "Of course..." my words trailed off as what was going on clicked. "You're going to try to set them up? Why?" If Martell found that out, I knew he would no doubt try to kill Mike.

Mike glared hard at me. "Why the fuck do you think, Kimmy?" I simply shrugged. I was tired of guessing. My damn head was starting to hurt from all the thinking I had been doing.

"You don't even know Parker and them like that—"

"I don't give a fuck about Parker or none of his fuckin' boys. I'm tryna help yo' fuckin' girl out because I know how twisted Martell's ass is. It doesn't have shit to do with them niggas. It's Angel I'm trying to look out for. Now Missy's big mouth ass. Sweetheart, that's all you need to know. And don't go running yo' fuckin' mouth to those gotdamn girls either. You mothafuckas will fuck everything up. Like with yo' stupid ass about to follow him."

I definitely felt stupid for following Mike and

then thinking about trailing Don's ass. Sighing, I flopped down on the bed. "Why couldn't you just tell me what was going on?" I didn't understand why he would keep that a secret from me, of all people.

"Because it doesn't have shit to do with you, Kimmy. Those may be yo' fuckin' homegirls, but this ain't your business. It ain't even mine, but I don't wanna see Angel get fucked up behind some shit her nigga in."

I wanted to slap him, so gotdamn bad. How could he think I had nothing to do with it? If it involved my bitches, and there was a way to help them out, I was all in. My mouth opened to snap at him, but I stopped myself as Mike responded back to my angry thoughts.

"I didn't tell yo' ass because I knew you would tell them. And you mothafuckas always coming up with something that put y'all right in the middle of niggas shit. Like the shit with Missy pulled with Mook and yo' dumb ass about to follow Don. I saw yo' ass hit that blinker without a second thought. You were probably thinking, you could follow him, find out where they were posted, then tell Angel's dumb ass."

"No!" I practically yelled defensively. That was precisely what I planned on doing. "No," I repeated, causing his glare to deepen. My eyes rolled at him. I didn't like how he knew what I thought of doing. "Point is if you're doing something like this. I should know what's going on; otherwise, stuff like this happens. Had you not seen me, I could've still fucked shit up, Mike, damn." Did I have a right to be mad at him? Yeah. I could have really ruined his plan had I followed Don and told Angel what I knew.

Mike looked at me like I was stupid. His mouth opened, then closed, and he took a deep breath as he walked to the other side of the room, away from me. "Kimberly, I'mma tell you this one more time, and it's the fucking last. Stay the fuck out of this shit. If you keep on and you're the cause of something happening to yourself or my fucking baby. Kimmy, G, I put this on my son's life. I'm going to fucking kill you. And I mean that shit whole-fucking-heartedly. Baby, this isn't a playful ass threat. Listen to me clearly. I put this on Malik's fucking life. If you're the cause of something happening to you or my kid, I'm going to kill you. So, sit yo' ass down some fucking where."

Had he not swore on Malik's life twice, I wouldn't have taken his threat seriously at all. There was no reason or point in me telling him what he should or shouldn't say, nor questioning if he meant it. He was serious as hell.

"Nothing is going to happen to either of us." My hand went to my stomach, assuring him that we would be alright.

"Then stop doing dumb shit. I had every mind of beating yo' ass when I got here. My baby is the only thing that saved you. But know, I'll take the both of you out this mothafucka before I let another nigga do it, Kimmy." The way he was stressing that fact left no room for doubt. I knew Mike, and although that would be the hardest thing he would have to do in life, he'd still do it.

"I'm going to stay out of it now that I know what's really going on. Babe, I hear you. I don't even think Martell would suspect me, though. He pretty much made it clear I wasn't a threat."

A light disbelieving chuckle left his mouth, and his head shook. "Sweetheart, Martell knows you're close with Angel. The nigga ain't stupid. Of course, you're a fucking threat to him, Kim. You thinking otherwise shows how fucking naïve you're being. Even though you're a threat to him, he's not gonna fuck with you because of me. Still, that doesn't mean if he feels you're trying to do some dumb shit like catching him up, the nigga won't hesitate to retaliate. Martell knows if he does something to you, he's going to have to come for me because I'm going to be at his fuckin' head."

The shit was stressing me out. How could Martell know I was a threat but not see Mike as one? "Babe, you're a threat to him too, though."

His brows raised at that before his head shook. "I'm not. I don't get involved in niggas bullshit. Because I don't give a fuck about none of them. Martell, Don, Parker, Chris, their bullshit is theirs alone. I don't give a fuck if any of those niggas die. Angel, on the other hand, I like. Plus, I know how fucking gruesome Martell will be with her. That nigga and his family are fuckin' lunatics. Those mothafuckas beef and kill each other like the shit is normal. I know this because of our past. That you don't need to know about. So, that's why I'm not a threat to them."

My heart did a damn somersault as I listened to him talk. Knowing Mike was risking himself for my best friend's safety said so much about him and his character. That just made me love him more. I mean, who would go through the trouble of setting up some gotdamn psychos? A fucking lunatic, that's who.

"You be careful dealing with all of them too. That includes Parker and his people. I don't need you getting hurt behind this. Don't get me wrong, I love that you're putting yourself out there for Ang. Baby, that means everything to me. But we—Malik, me or our baby—can't lose you either." I brought his hand to my stomach as I kissed him.

"And y'all won't if you sit the fuck down."

I kissed him again. "I will, promise. Now that I know everything, I won't put you at risk."

Mike kissed me once more, then stood up. "A'ight, now gone get down there with those girls. And take my fucking weed from Missy's ass. That mothafucka just lit up. I can smell that shit all the way up here." Pulling off his shirt, he headed to the bathroom and turned on the shower. "Oh, tell Peaches I said what's up."

I leaned over the bed and stared at his tattooed back through the opened bathroom door as he undid his jeans. "You want me to get in with you?" Hell, forget my girls I was about to get fucked.

Mike pulled his pants and boxer briefs off, getting completely naked, then turned and faced me. "Nah, yo' ass on punishment. You've been showing yo' ass a lot lately. Until you get yourself together, you don't get shit from me. I mean that."

"Man—" Mike slammed the bathroom door shut as soon as those words left my mouth. My eyes rolled as I laughed. Pulling off my dress, I went to the bathroom door. I jiggled the handle hard several times before it dawned on me. His ass locked the damn door. "Mike, really? Dude, you're childish as hell. Open the door."

"Get yo' ass downstairs with them fuckin' girls."

My palm smacked against the door hard, not believing him. I was irritated as hell. "Stupid ass fucka!" I mumbled that last bit to myself as I hit the door again. Snatching my dress back on, I slapped the bedroom door as I walked out.

The only reason I didn't put up a bigger fight was because of the dumb shit I had done. So, I was going to give Mike that for the day.

I still couldn't believe that he kept his whole plan from me. It was crazy to think of Mike in the middle of some beef that had nothing to do with him.

"Everything's cool?" The girls asked once I made it downstairs.

I nodded while sitting on the couch. "Yeah, we're straight." The trio glanced at each other then began examining me. "We're good, y'all. Stop looking at me like that."

"We're just making sure y'all wasn't up there fighting or shit like that. We know yo' ass won't tell us shit if y'all were. So we have to make sure for ourselves." Ebony claimed.

Missy's lips popped loud, and I glanced at her just as her eyes disappeared into her head. "Bitch, if they were fighting, you would hear that shit. Because this bitch gonna be throwing shit. And she doesn't tell y'all ass shit because you two bitches always judging."

I laughed at Missy's low hooded eyes. Baby girl was drunk and high as hell. "We didn't fight. Mike ain't gonna touch me while I'm pregnant. Besides, we barely come to blows. Mike will yoke my ass up and shake the hell out of me. Aside from that, he's not going to do shit." Mike will definitely choke my ass up. Aside from that, things rarely got physical. Unless I'm the aggressor. I'll definitely swing on Mike or throw some shit at him when I'm pissed.

"So, how come he came in here all mad?" Peaches questioned.

"Because he was pissed at me," I told her flatly. Of course, I wouldn't tell them what Mike and I talked about. Not until the shit was done and over with. "Missy, Mike said don't smoke no more of his fucking weed." She stuck up her middle finger then puffed on the blunt she held. I just smiled at her, all the while my mind went back to Mike.

I was beginning to see that there was a part of Mike I didn't know at all. I didn't like that one bit either. I really believed it took a damn lunatic to go after Martell or try to set him up, knowing how crazy and calculated that man was.

Mike was just the fucking lunatic to do that shit. Seeing how devious he was being, Mike could definitely pull it off.

Mike was right. He didn't have any emotional ties toward those men, so their lives meant nothing to him. For that, his plan was actually perfect.

The friend of my enemy is my man.

Chapter Eight

Kimmy

Love On My ~~Body~~ Baby

I lay on the medical bed, twisting my thumbs together nervously, waiting for the doctor to come in. Since I've decided to keep my baby, I was excited about my appointment. One because I wanted to know how my baby was doing. I could admit I had neglected to go to a few doctor appointments because of the whole DNA thing —which was no longer the topic of discussion. Two, Mike was there with me.

Yet, I was nervous and couldn't explain why. Then again, maybe it was because Mike was there, and it'll be his first time seeing the baby on a monitor. Hell, I didn't know.

My gaze shifted to Mike, who had been silent majority of the time there. Aside from asking the doctor about doing an ultrasound to determine the baby's gender. He sat in a chair at the bed's foot, absent-mindedly rubbing my legs, while strolling through his phone.

In truth, I didn't want to know what we were having. I wanted it to be a surprise. Not Mike's impatient ass, though. He just needed to know.

"Man, if you roll yo' damn eyes at me one more time, I'mma pop them out." His sudden threat caused a burst of laughter to leave my mouth. Especially since he hadn't taken one glance at me. "And stop fuckin' mugging my ass like you wanna do some shit. Your damn glare got the side of my face hot." He glanced at me then. "I don't have to stare at you to feel that shit. What's wrong with you?"

"There's nothing wrong with me. I'm just ready to go home." Yeah, I felt anxious; I was also tired too. My body wasn't up to doing anything. I lacked energy in the worse way, and I wasn't used to that. I also didn't like the fragileness I'd been feeling as of late.

In truth, I was gotdamn miserable as hell. I knew everything was symptoms due to my pregnancy. Still, I couldn't stand them. I hated the flip of emotions, nausea, frailness.

Mike's hand slid under my shirt, and he began rubbing my stomach. My gaze focused on him, but his eyes were trained on his phone.

"What's on your phone?" I finally asked as his hand continued to caress my belly.

He didn't say anything at first as his brows bunched together. "Numbers, apps—"

"You're irritating. You could've just said none of my business. Move." I pushed his arm, still chuckling. "Man, this doctor needs to hurry up. I'm ready to go home." I complained, groaning.

"She'll be in, so calm down."

I let out a heavy breath. "Mike..." Glancing at me, he started laughing as his head shook. "Why the hell you do that for?" Sitting up, he leaned over my body, kissing me. My head jerked back, and I tried my hardest to glare at him but ended up laughing. "I did not ask you to kiss me—"

"It's what you wanted, though. Whenever you call my name like that, you either wanna fuck or a damn kiss. And seeing where we're at, on top of your irritating mood, yo' ass wanted a kiss." He broke down like he actually knew what he was talking about. "Now, am I wrong?" He so cockily asked with a knowing smirk.

I whined out a laugh. "So, what. You didn't have to say it. And I'm not irritated..." his brow rose questioningly once more. There wasn't a point in lying to him, especially when he knew me. "Babe, I am. I don't like it either. Nor do I like laying on this damn bed. Man, I'm ready to go home and get out these clothes." I was saying as his phone vibrated. My lips popped, and I rolled my eyes at him.

Mike muffed my head to the side. "What I tell you about rolling yo' damn eyes at me? Sweetheart, it ain't shit I can do about yo' damn irritation—"

"You can start by staying off your damn

phone while we're at the doctor." I fussed.

Mike chuckled as he quickly texted on his phone. "As soon as you ain't pregnant no more, I'm fucking yo' moody ass up. Me being on this phone isn't your issue, so stop trying to make it out to be. But, for argument's sake, I'm texting Malik. He wanted to know if everything was good with the baby and yo' ass. On top of some other stuff." Mike turned his phone toward me, and sure enough, Malik's chat box was on the screen.

A groan left my mouth, and I was about to apologize as another message came through. Immediately I glared at the device. "I can't stand that little boy. Give me that." I went to snatch the phone to reply to his damn message.

Mike pulled back and read Malik's message aloud. "She hasn't been crying today, has she? She's been crying a lot lately. Dad, it's terrible." he laughed. "Baby, he doesn't know any better for real." He claimed, defending him.

"Yes, the hell he does. I'm going to whoop him, watch. When is his big-headed ass coming back over?" Mike started laughing just as the room door came open. I pushed Mike while rolling my eyes. Even so, I couldn't help but chuckle as well. Malik got on my damn nerves. He was most definitely his father's son. Once I saw the ultrasound machine, I groaned. "Mike, you're really going to find out now?" I just didn't want to know what I was having.

He nodded. "Look, I wanna know what I'm

having. I'm not going to tell you what it is." He claimed with a shrug.

"You're so damn impatient—don't look at me like that." I broke out laughing at the—*no, the fuck you didn't just say that*—stare. "I can be impatient. I'm pregnant."

That made him and the doctor laugh. "Kim, I promise not to reveal anything to you. Once I know, I'll snap the shots and tell daddy only." She insisted. "Ready?"

Sighing, I nodded. I was ready to get it over with. After applying the gel to my stomach, Doc grabbed the transducer and moved it around my stomach.

"Okay, here goes, baby…" she began saying before her words faded.

The sudden silence immediately worried me. Subconsciously, I grabbed Mike's hand to calm myself down.

"Is the baby alright?" Mike questioned, taking the words out of my mouth.

"Babies—"

"What?" I had to have heard her wrong. "Baby?" I rephrased for her.

She let out a chuckle at my correction. "No, babies, as in two, plural. Here's baby A…" she pointed to the screen before clicking on the keyboard. "And there's baby B—"

I was so damn confused. "How? During the

first ultrasound, there wasn't a second baby. We didn't see another baby." There couldn't be another baby in my stomach.

"At times, we don't see the second baby until eighteen to twenty weeks. And then there are times when we don't see the second child at all. It's not uncommon. They sometimes hide behind each other." She explained. "Do you need a moment to process it all?"

My lips were moving, yet no words left my mouth. So, I settled on shaking my head in response to her question. I was about to have two damn babies. Exhaling, I got myself together. "I'm fine, surprised as hell, but I'm okay." Clearing my throat, I looked back at the monitor.

"Are the babies alright, though?" Mike and I looked at each other, then laughed as we asked the same question at once.

"Yes, babies look to be developing very well in size and length...baby A is a bit bigger than baby B—that's normal." She explained, still moving the transducer around. "Does twins run in the family?" She questioned, glancing between us.

Without thinking, I pointed to Mike. "His side. His mother is a twin, and he was a twin." My mouth snapped shut after that came out. Looking at Mike, I felt terrible for oversharing his business. "I'm sorry." However, he didn't look mad. Instead, he stared at me, amused.

"Don't be, sweetheart. You're good." Leaning

down, he kissed me.

"Daddy, I know what you're having—"

"What?" I asked, looking at the screen. Since she pointed out we were having twins, I could see both babies clearly. The sight was honestly amazing to see them both there.

"Don't worry about it. You'll know once you have them." He kissed my forehead, then turned his attention to the doctor. "Show me what they are." Mike tried to move over to her, but I quickly grabbed his arm.

"Michael, don't play. If you're finding out, so am I. If I can't know, neither should you. I don't care what I said earlier. That was before I knew they were twins. Just like they changed, I changed my mind. Doc, tell me what I'm having."

She chuckled at us, yet she focused on me. "Kim, are you positive you want to know? Don't wait until I get ready to say it and yell, don't tell you. So, I need to know you're one hundred percent sure. Are you?"

I nodded. "I want to know seriously. If I'm having twins, I need to prepare myself for if I'm going to get two of me, two of him or a combination —" The doctor and Mike broke out laughing. Where they laughed, I didn't, hell I couldn't. I was beyond serious.

"Congrats, mom and dad, you're having twin boys."

Mike's loud and visible exhale surprised the hell out of me. He seemed so relieved with the reveal. "Thank God." He breathed before chuckling more to himself.

"Well, I take it that you wanted a boy to begin with." I was surprised by how he acted.

He nodded. "Yeah, I did. Man, I couldn't have a damn girl. Every time I thought about it, all I kept seeing was Keema's ass. That shit scared me."

"Oh, my God!" My hand covered my mouth as I broke out laughing. "I can't believe you." The fact that he was so honest and relieved did it for me. All I could do was laugh.

"I'll go print these out while you clean yourself up. I want to see you again when you're twenty-eight weeks. You can make your appointment upfront." She explained while tallying off several other health-related things before leaving.

Once she did, I hit Mike. "What is wrong with you? Don't do my Keema like that. She's not that bad." I told him while cleaning the gel off my stomach.

"Nah, she's not bad. Keema's spoiled as fuck, and she makes saying no hard. I don't like that shit. Now, boys, I can handle." He nodded as if agreeing with himself.

I just stared at him in disbelief. "Michael, have you not met Malik. Homeboy ain't no diva, like Keema, but baby Malik barely get told no, and he's spoiled as hell." Staring at him, I just broke out laughing again. "I could believe you've let out that damn breath, though, Mike."

"Shid, I didn't realize I wasn't breathing until she said, boys. Kimmy, I don't care. I'm not trying to have no damn girls. Do you know how insane I would be if I had a gotdamn girl? Yo' spoiled ass is more than enough for me." After pulling my pants over my belly, then fixing my shirt, Mike helped me sit upright. "You remembered me telling you that I was a twin?"

"Of course, I do. That was one of the first things you told me when we started hanging out." Once I was off the bed, my arms went around his waist, and I kissed his chin. "I'm sorry for just putting it out like that. Honestly, I wasn't thinking when I responded. She asked, and it was an automatic reply." I felt embarrassed as hell for saying that without thinking.

Milly, Mike's mother, was pregnant with twins before she miscarried during her first trimester, resulting in her losing one baby.

"It's cool. Stop apologizing. You're acting like you did or said something wrong. You didn't, Kimmy. Shid, if anything, I was surprised you remembered that shit." Mike's hand went to my stomach, and a big wide grin came to his face. "You about to give me two damn babies. Yo' ass definitely about to get spoiled. What do you want?"

I broke out laughing. "You're so irritating, I

swear." Standing on my tiptoes, I kissed his lips.

After kissing me, he pulled back. "I'm dead ass. What you want?"

My brows raised, not expecting him to be serious. "Anything? Seriously?" He nodded. "I want a newer Benz like the one Angel got, but red—"

"You're out yo' gotdamn mind. I'm not buying you a damn Benz. I meant anything except for a damn car." Mike explained while pulling away from me.

Ever since Parker let Angel push his car damn near five years ago, I wasn't letting up on getting one. Mike wasn't caving, and I was too damn cheap to buy it for myself. I wanted him to purchase it for me.

"Don't say shit. I'm not about to argue with you in this damn office." Mike quickly tacked on as he took in my glare. At that moment, the doctor walked in, and I laughed. She didn't even know that she had saved Mike's ass. I sure was about to snap on him.

After the doctor gave us the sonogram and I scheduled the follow-up appointment, we left the office. Once we were in the truck, Mike glanced at me, grinning hard as hell.

I couldn't help but laugh at his expression. That man hadn't stopped smiling since the doctor informed us of the twins and them being boys.

Mike's hand reached over, and he began

rubbing my swollen belly. "Twin boys. Damn. I'm not even gonna front. I'm happy as fuck."

I burst out laughing at his wide-ass grin. He was genuinely happy about the fact I was pregnant with twin boys. His excitement couldn't be faked. His reaction caused my body to become jittery as I continued to laugh.

Leaning over to Mike, I kissed him, then leaned back into my seat. "I feel your excitement, and that got me feeling giddy too. I know once the excitement dies down, I'm going to freak out. Like, I'm about to have two damn babies." I knew myself, and given how my damn hormones were set up, I already knew the freak out would come.

"Twin boys?" Mike's momma, Milly exclaimed happily as she looked over the sonogram. "Big Mike, you see, they're giving us twins?" The glint in her eyes had me laughing at her excitement.

Poppa grabbed the ultrasound and looked at it. "It's about damn time. It was getting too damn quiet around here." He sounded just as excited as his wife. They were already happy learning that I was pregnant but finding out we're having twins added to that.

"We have to think of names," Milly claimed, looking at Mike Sr. and ignoring us completely.

My eyes slid to Mike's only to meet his raised brows. "Who babies are these?" He questioned, and I laughed before pointing to his mom and dad.

It was apparent that our babies were no longer ours.

Chapter Nine

Kimmy

Date Night

"I'm still pissed at you for not coming out with us the other week." Missy glared at me hard before turning her mug on Mike. "I know it was because of you. What? You didn't want to hang with us?" She asked me.

Mike gave her a confused look before looking at me. "What the fuck is she talking about?"

I shot Missy a mean glare for bringing that up. I never told Mike about the dinner she wanted to have. The truth was, I didn't want to go. I just wasn't feeling up to it.

"It wasn't him. I wasn't up to it for real. Plus, we needed time to figure out our shit." There was so much constantly on my mind those last few weeks. Having a couples dinner wasn't one of them. One thing was what I learned about Martell. The second was saving our relationship. After realizing I was the threat to it, I needed to fix that before we went on a couple's date with my girls. Now that Mike and I were on the same page, we as a couple was a lot better, which was why I felt good about going on a dinner date with my girls.

"Oh, my bad, Mike. I know how funny acting you be sometimes, so I thought you didn't want to be around us." She told him seriously.

I broke out laughing at her ignorant ass. Missy couldn't help herself, she just loved fucking with our men. "Girl, leave him along before he slaps your ass," I warned.

Mike's arm went around my shoulder, and he pulled me into his side. "Shhh, don't tell her that. I've been wanting to knock her in those big ass lips." Smiling at her, he winked. "Baby, keep talking yo' shit."

My head started shaking at Missy, warning her to shut up. "Where's Roman at?" I asked as we walked down to lane two.

Since I missed the couples dinner night. Missy wanted to plan another date night for us, and I suggested Red Pin, Sam's new spot. I liked the place, especially given the different activities they had for us to do. I loved that we all didn't have to be packed in one space.

"He is—" Missy stretched out while glancing around before finally pointing ahead, "—right there talking to Sam."

Missy's ass was determined to get all of our men together and have them on friendly terms.

Yet, she failed to realize that none of them had a problem with each other. They just didn't hang in the same circle. Still, she wanted them all to be friendly and hang out for some odd reason. Hell, I didn't care. I liked all their men, and they were fun to be around.

"Hey, hoes!" Ebony yelled, waving, causing us to laugh. "Hey, Mikey!" She excitedly spoke, hugging Mike, then me. "Hey, niece or nephew." She whispered to my stomach.

Mike's eyes met with mine before we looked at her. "Okay bitch, why yo' ass so gotdamn happy?"

"She just got some dick," Mike claimed, looking her over.

Ebony glared at him. "Dude, shut the fuck up. Didn't nobody ask you shit." She snapped, making him laugh.

She definitely had that bomb ass dick glow. I turned to Mike. "How the hell you know?"

"That mothafucka to gotdamn happy. She got that same gotdamn cheeky smile you get after being fucked good. Plus, her ass just hugged me. Ebony, don't ever hug me. So, her ass got to still be dick high. Kim, her ass just hugged me." He pointed that last bit out as if it was important.

I glanced at Missy, and we seemed to realize the same damn thing at once. "Bitch, when are we gonna meet this nigga? If he got yo' ass glowing like this and hugging on Mike's mean ass. Then bitch, it's time to bring his ass into the fold." I was beyond excited for her. I knew she was seeing somebody, yet I didn't think it was serious, because she never introduced us to him.

"Y'all, I do really like him. But I'm not ready to show him off just yet. Not until King's possessiveness tone down hella notches. Like, I don't feel like fighting with that nigga about this or run my baby off. I'm going to have to ease this on him first, then once the drama settles down from his damn blowout—which we all know is going to happen, then I'll bring my man around." She explained.

I understood that wholeheartedly. King was a damn fool in general and was an even bigger one when it came to Ebony. Now that she also has a baby with him, I knew his craziness went up to a million.

Ebony's gaze soon went to Mike, and I immediately waved her worry off. "He isn't going to say anything because it doesn't have shit to do with him." Mike wasn't one to run his mouth. He didn't care for the simple fact he knew King wasn't faithful.

"Bitches!" Angel's loud screaming voice had my ass hollering.

Pushing away from Mike and Ebony, I met her halfway, my arms enclosing around her waist. "Bitch, why you didn't tell me you were coming down?" I fussed, not believing she was there. I was honestly surprised that Parker let her come back to Indiana, especially because Martell was back in Gary.

Ang laughed into my ear before we pulled apart. "Hoe, surprise much. I had to do a lot of sucking, fucking, and crying before Parker agreed to bring me down. So, you owe me. Yo' ass and Missy." She claimed, pointing to Missy. "Hey, Mike." She hugged him, and he returned her embrace.

"What's up." He kissed her cheek, then let her go. "I'm about to get something to drink. You want me to bring you something back?" He questioned, motioning to the food lounge.

Humming, I looked around to see what folks were walking around with. "Um...just get me water for right now. I'll have to look over the menu to see what I really want."

Mike kissed me, then stepped back. "I'll be right back." With that, he walked off.

Looking at Ang, I pulled her back to me. "Bitch, I'mma need you to move back here. I've been missing the fuck out of you for real." I groaned, hugging her.

She laughed, hugging me back. "Girl, yo' ass always free to come down and visit me too. You and Mike. Hell, Parker's ass won't care—"

"I won't care about what?" Parker asked, walking through us.

Angel pointed to me. "You won't care if Kim and Mike come down and stay at the house for a few days." She repeated to him.

Parker waved me off. "She already knows

that shit. Shid, Missy's the one that's about to be limited."

"Ooh! Parker, she comes down there too much?" I questioned, laughing.

"Hell yeah, every other week she's there, and her ass don't ever ask to come. She just pops the fuck up." He stated.

We broke out laughing as Missy hit him. "Fuck you, Parker. You know y'all love when I come down. Otherwise, y'all ass would be bored out your damn minds." She claimed, making him laugh.

"Believe that if you wanna." He said, pushing past her, going to the couches, and sitting down. "Syn." He called Angel, beckoning her to him.

She waved him off before her attention went to Missy. "You know Parker's ass just talking shit. He loves your ass like a damn sister now." She laughed before taking in the area. "This is a nice little spot. Where did you find this place?"

"This is Sam's spot. I brought Mike here a while ago. I thought this would be a fun little place for us to come and enjoy ourselves. It's better than a damn restaurant for dinner." I told her while looking at Missy.

She mugged me before sticking up her middle finger. "Fuck you, hoe. The dinner was nice, though. Wasn't it y'all?" She asked the girls, and they all agreed with her.

"Next time, we'll come for real," I told her as

we finally went to the couch and sat beside Parker. "I'm ready to get this damn bowling game going for real." I was ready for the damn fun to begin.

"Peaches just got here. Once she comes in, we can start." Missy said, looking away from her phone screen. "So, how's my niece or nephew doing?" She questioned, reaching over and rubbing my stomach.

My head shook as I started laughing. I hadn't told them I was having twins yet. I still needed to get used to thoughts of having two babies instead of one.

I planned on showing them the sonogram later during the night. Yet, I didn't expect Missy to ask about the baby so damn early.

Mike pushed Missy's hand off of my stomach. "Stop touching shit." He told her before handing me my water.

Laughing, I hit him. "Don't be doing her like that. She can rub all on me if she wanna." I told him.

"Bitch, you better tell his big-headed ass." She pushed him, laughing.

Grabbing my arms, Mike pulled me up, then sat down. He tapped the side of my booty, then tugged at my jeans. Laughing, I sat on his lap as he wanted.

"Peach!" Ebony yelled, waving her over.

"Hey, bitches!" Peaches yelled, quickly coming over to us. Missy and Ebony stood up to hug her, but she moved around them. "Ang!" She practically threw herself on the damn girl. "Why y'all ain't tell me she was coming?"

"I'm really starting to feel some type of way. Like, bitch, I don't ever get this type of reaction from none of you hoes." Ebony claimed, mugging us.

"Bitch, move away, and you will." Peach told her before releasing Angel. "Kimmy, yo' ass lucky you came out because if you hadn't, I was coming right on over there to whoop yo' ass." She threatened before hugging me. "Hey, Tinka baby." She spoke to my stomach.

Laughing, I pushed her away from me. "Girl, you're so irritating. Move."

She popped my hand. "Stop, hoe. How's my baby doing?"

Grabbing my purse, I took out the sonogram and held it out. The girls eagerly grabbed for it at the same time. Laughing, I quickly snatched it back. "If you hoes tear my picture, I'm going to be pissed the fuck off. So, calm down." Parker suddenly grabbed the ultrasound out of my hand. I glared at him, ready to pop slick. "Dude—"

Parker held up his finger as he turned his phone's flashlight on. His brows knitted together before he looked at me. "Damn, no shit?"

"What?" The girls asked at once. They got up to move toward him, but he stood up.

"Man, move the fuck back." He held it

up childishly. "You mothafuckas acting like some gotdamn fiends."

I broke out laughing. "Parker, stop being childish. Give it to them."

"Dude, stop fucking playing. I wanna know what we're having, shit." Angel fussed before going up to Parker and snatching the photo from him. The girls quickly gathered around her.

"Bitch!" They called in unisons. Ebony turned on her flashlight. "Nuh-uh…" they said, surprised before looking at me.

All I could do was nod. "Y'all seeing it right."

"Eep!" They squeaked out excitedly.

"Oh, my God. Twin boys, Kimmy?" Angel questioned excitedly, and I nodded. "Damn, y'all went from having one kid to now three. Mike, you excited—"

I broke out laughing at her question. "Wait, y'all." I cut in before he could answer her. "Bitch, why when we found out they were boys, Mike let out this loud ass sigh. Like, you could see his breath of relief. Y'all this man don't want no damn girls." I told them, cracking up thinking about Mike's relieved exhale.

"Why not?" Ang, Peach, and E questioned, seeing as they all have girls.

Mike and I pointed to Ebony. She returned the gesture, pointing to herself. "Hell yeah, you," Mike told her. "When I thought we could be having a girl, all I saw was Keema's bad spoiled ass—"

The girls broke out laughing. "Dude!" They hollered, cracking the hell up.

"No, y'all, he's so damn serious right now. Like y'all didn't see his damn relieved expression when the doctor said the babies were boys. I believe he doesn't want a girl for real. He claims he'll be too damn weak behind her." I told them with a roll of my eyes.

"Shid, his ass ain't fucking lying. Pixie is spoiled as fuck, and it's hard telling her ass no. Hell, boys are easier to deal with. But Pix on top of Syn's ass." Parker's head shook. "Man, that shit will fuck with yo' gotdamn sanity." Parker further explained.

"Ex-fucking-actly!" Mike blurted out. "That's the same gotdamn thing I told Kimmy. Shid, I'm already insane behind her ass. Man, adding another fucking girl to the mix will make my ass straight psychotic. Man, hell nah."

Once again, the girls broke out laughing at how stressed he sounded.

"But what does my child have to do with it, though?" Ebony asked, still laughing.

Mike's head just shook. "Shid, it's your damn daughter that made me realize that shit. Keema's ass got a nigga wrapped around her damn finger. Ebony, yo' fucking daughter got a whole ass bedroom at my crib on top of hella clothes and toys. If I'm like that with a shorty that's not even mine, I can only imagine how I'd be with my own girl. Hell nah." He stressed.

"Mike ain't wrong, though." Peaches chimed in. "Keema got Blaze mean ass the same damn way. And Brianna already has him wrapped around her damn hand." She told us which we already knew.

"So, y'all see my damn point. Kimmy's bad enough. I can't deal with two of her." Mike stressed that fact, making them crack up again.

I turned on him so fast. "Nigga, don't you even do that bullshit. So, it's cool with me dealing with three versions of you, though?"

Looking me dead in the eyes, he had the audacity to nod. "Shid, I'm not that bad. I'm just protective as fuck. Yo' ass spoiled—"

"I wish you would stop saying that because I'm really not spoiled for real." My eyes rolled at him, and I looked back to my girls. "He's so damn irritating. This nigga claims I'm so spoiled but check this. We found out we're having twins, homeboy excited as fuck and told me—you can have whatever you want—" Mike broke out laughing, causing me to glare at him. "—so, I tell him I want a newer Benz, like Ang's but I want it red. Y'all know that's my color. This mothafucka gonna say—"

Parker started cracking the fuck up, cutting me off. "Yo' ass should've talked to Mane then. He would've had you pushing that bitch in no time." Angel whacked the shit out of Parker, making him laugh more.

"And that mothafucka would've been leaking

in no time," Mike told him.

"Mike, he's just playing for real," Angel said, rolling her eyes at Parker. "I don't know why y'all still hung up on that damn car. That shit was years ago." Angel laughed. "But not you're still trying to get that man to buy yo' ass a Benz."

"Yeah, the fuck she is," Mike told her.

I glared at him. "His ugly ass won't get me one. But he wanna holler how spoiled I am. If I was that damn spoiled, why I don't have my dream car?" I pointed out.

"Shorty has a point, though. Why won't you get it for her? I got a nigga that'll hook yo' ass up." Parker offered.

Mike waved him off. "I ain't thinking about Kimmy's black ass getting no new fucking car. Kim always wants some shit she sees, but the mothafucka will never drive it. You mothafuckas don't know how many cars and trucks Kim's ass actually have and don't drive any of them. The only whip she pushes is that gotdamn black Audi." He broke down to them.

"I ain't thinking about her ass and no gotdamn cars. That's just like my truck. She saw it and wanted one. I got it for her. Where that bitch at now, though? In my damn garage. She'll drive my fucking truck before she drives that one. Claiming mine bigger, but it's the same exact truck."

The girls broke out laughing. "Kimmy, he does have a point, though." They claimed at once.

My eyes rolled at them. "Man, so, that's not even the point—fuck y'all." They weren't wrong. I liked what I did. Even though I didn't drive the cars or trucks, he got me frequently, I still loved my vehicles.

"Man, let's get this damn game going so I can kick y'all asses. Y'all lame ass men against us." I told them before turning to Mike. Grabbing the nape of his neck, I leaned into him. "You didn't even have to put my business out like that."

Mike laughed as he squeezed my thighs. "Man, gone. You did that shit." Taking hold of my ponytail, he pulled my head back then kissed me. "You ain't gonna start crying when we win, are you?"

Laughing, I hit him. "Nope—ooh." I sat upright and faced the girls. "Give me my sonogram before I forget."

"Girl, you could've let me keep this," Angel said, reaching into her purse.

"On what yo' ass was about to steal it, though?" Mike asked, laughing.

Angel held the image out toward us. "So, she should've brought copies."

Reaching around me, Mike snatched the photo from her. "Let's get this damn game going. I didn't come here to just sit around looking at y'all asses." He told them before getting up and going over to Missy. "Put my name at the top." He pointed to the bowling screen.

Looking at the girls, I just shook my head, telling them to ignore him. Going up behind Mike, my arms went around his waist, causing him to glance down at me. Standing on my tiptoes, my lips puckered for him. Laughing, Mike kissed me.

"You gonna help me win?" I questioned while licking his bottom lip.

∞∞∞

"Y'all niggas sucking tonight. First, we whooped y'all asses in bowling, now pool. Come on now, y'all starting to really look bad." I picked, laughing, as I shot another ball in.

Mike muffed my head to the side. "You talking real big shit ain't you? If I was you, I would shut the fuck up before I start taking this game seriously." He warned, making me laugh.

"Kimmy's been talking big shit all night like we didn't hear her asking Mike for help." Peaches clowned, causing the girls to laugh.

"Right. The only reason her ass winning is because she's giving him twin boys." Angel chimed in.

"G, I swear, that's the only reason," Mike agreed.

Turning on him, I glared. "I'm about to beat yo' ass. Don't try to play me like that. When you know I be winning in real life, sometimes."

"Wait, hold the fuck up. Who's having twins?" King questioned. I raised my finger then motioned between Mike and me. "Stop fucking lying."

Mike ass was quick to pull out that damn sonogram and show him. "Why do we have to lie? Look at that shit, twins and both boys, nigga." We broke out laughing at Mike's excited voice.

King took the image and started looking it over. "Damn, no shit?"

"Mike's ass too damn happy about his boys." Angel laughed, laying her head on my shoulder while wrapping her arms around my waist as her hands lay on my stomach. "I'm really happy for y'all, babe. That excitement—" she discreetly pointed to Mike smiling, "—can't be faked. That man is happy as hell." We chuckled, watching Mike grin along with King as they talked while looking at the sonogram.

"Ang, he really is for real. I think that's why I'm so gotdamn relaxed about it because of his excitement. I swear I've been waiting on a damn freak out to happen. Hell, I even warned him it was going to come. It hasn't happened yet, and it's been damn near a week since we've found out about the twins." I told her.

She chuckled at that. "I don't know, Kim. I can't see you freaking out about having twins. I can only picture you freaking out when you first learned about the pregnancy. For one, you were complicated, and two, you weren't ready to have no kids. Malik was the only exception." She chuckled. "But, after that, I can see you being cool about everything. I mean, you already know what type of parents you and Mike will be. Shid, you've watched him raise Malik, and you see how tight their bond is. Then look at how you are with Malik. Girl, twins gonna be a damn piece of cake for y'all."

Smiling, my head lay against hers, agreeing with everything she had to say. "His ass still gets on my damn nerves."

Angel broke out laughing. "Even still, you love that man's dirty ass draws."

My eyes rolled at that. Still, I laughed no less. "So." My laughter slowly faded as I watched Mike. He was really excited, and I felt terrible that not even a month ago, I was trying to take all that excitement from him without realizing it.

"I do, though, Angel. He's really been amazing for real. Even with knowing everything, that man hasn't treated me differently from before, especially when I kept constantly putting the possibility and affair in his face and mind. He hasn't changed. If anything, he's been loving on me harder. Bitch, I can't stand his ass, but my whole damn soul loves him—"

"Um, no shit, Kimmy. If I thought you didn't love him, I know you would've been gone. Regardless of how crazy Mike is behind you, that wouldn't have made you stay with him if you didn't want to. Bitch, you're gotdamn fearless. So even with the affair and all of that shit, I knew you weren't going anywhere. Just like when you started talking all that bullshit saying some—*I don't think I'm in love with him anymore, I think it's just familiarity.*"

A loud snort left her mouth, and she laughed as I lightly elbowed her. "I knew that was bullshit because one, you're not going to stay nowhere you don't want to be. Now, think, aside from us, Mike knows you better than we do. So, if I knew this, don't you think Mike figured that bullshit out too? Especially when you went and started confessing shit." Again, we laughed. "He knows that you would've been gone if you wanted to leave. Maybe... that's why he hasn't changed toward you."

Angel has always been intuitive and spoke her thoughts without remorse. Yet, once she got with Parker, her insightfulness seemed to have amplified by a thousand. Whenever she speaks, I always adsorb her words up.

Yet again, I had to admit she was right. "How come it takes someone else to tell me what they feel I'd do before I realize y'all are right? It's like I know this shit, but it never comes to me until someone else says it." That was the same thing with Lizzie.

"Sometimes it takes someone else to say what we already know before we can see or realize it." She pointed out.

That's what it was too.

"What you hoes over here whispering

about?" Missy questioned, reaching us.

I nodded to Mike, who was still talking to King. "Michael's overly excited ass." I couldn't help but laugh at how true that was. The man hasn't stopped smiling since he found out I was giving him two damn babies. "Mike!" Getting his attention, I waved him over to me. "Come on, so we can finish this game. I'm trying to win something."

Missy and Angel started laughing at that. "Something like what, hoe?"

"Y'all so damn nosey. Move." My palm pressed into Angel's face, and I pushed her off my shoulder.

"Nah, we gonna start over. With all that shit yo' ass was talking, you don't need help winning." King claimed, making everybody laugh.

"Dude, don't be acting like I can't play pool. As much time we spend in Blaze's raggedy ass pool hall —"

"Hold the fuck up, hoe. Don't bring my baby's shit into what y'all got going on. His club ain't raggedy." Peaches jumped in, glaring at me playfully.

"You better tell her baldheaded ass before I snatch those red ass tracks out her fucking head." Blaze snapped, mugging me.

I broke out laughing because Blaze has never really snapped on me before. "B, that's about the nicest you've ever gone off on somebody."

Peaches laughed. "Babe, that is, though."

"Fuck her baldheaded ass." That was all he said, making us laugh.

Mike came behind me, and he fisted my hair. "Nah, nigga ain't shit about this fake. This all her except for the color." Mike pulled my head back, and his lips came down on mine. I was seconds away from snapping at him until his mouth covered mine. My angry words were immediately swallowed as I got into the kiss. All too soon, he pulled back. "You know I'mma help you win." He whispered against my lips.

Once again, I began laughing. I was not expecting him to say that at all. "You better." He pecked my lips again, then pulled back. "Mike, seriously?" I knew damn well he wasn't about to halfway kiss my ass. Especially not after his damn tongue had already got my body excited.

"What?" Glancing down at me, he started laughing. "Man, get yo' ass on." He pulled away from me and went to the pool table, racking the balls. "Come on, we gonna let y'all go first." He motioned between him and King. My lips smacked, and I rolled my eyes at him.

"What the fuck wrong with yo' moody ass now?" King questioned while holding out a pool stick for me. My eyes rolled, and I snatched the stick from him. "What the hell wrong with you?" He repeated.

Mike started laughing. "She's mad because I ain't kiss her nasty ass how she wanted."

King stared at me before he started laughing. "That's why yo' ass pregnant now. Fucking nasty ass." He clowned.

"Who pregnant?" Sam asked, walking into our group. Immediately his eyes landed on Peaches, then Blaze.

"Nuh-uh, don't be looking at us. Nigga, I just had two damn babies. Ain't no more coming out of me no time soon. That's all, Kimmy. Hell, it's her turn to give us babies." Peaches said, pointing to me.

"Then, Missy. Like y'all some damn latecomers. We were supposed to have damn babies at the same time. Our kids were supposed to grow up together." Ebony said, glaring from me to Missy.

"Bitch, yo' ass due for another baby. It's time you play catch up too. Me and Peach have three. Kim's about to have two, and yo' ass still on your one. So, you really don't have no room to talk." Angel told her, making us laugh.

King's arm went around Ebony's shoulder, and he pulled her into his side. "I keep telling her we need to give Keema a sibling. Plus, I want my boy, dead ass."

"Ha'Keem, get away from me for real. I'm not having any more kids—especially not with you. Nigga, you've already given me Princess Chucky."

Turning into Mike, I muffled my laughter into his chest. I was glad Ebony could see her damn child for what she was. My arms went around Mike's waist, and I pushed up on my tiptoes, kissing his chin. Once those beautiful blue orbs fell on me, my lips puckered, making him laugh.

"Yo' ass, man. If you get that mothafucka going, we're leaving. I'm telling you that now." He warned while slapping my ass. Gripping my booty, he shook my cheek. "So, what you trying to do?"

"Go—"

"Get yo' nasty ass away from him." Ebony broke out laughing, pulling me out of Mike's grasp. "Not, your ass trying to leave us to go get some dick. Y'all live together; you can get it later. Bitch, those hormones ain't no punk, are they?"

"They're not. I swear my ass be horny all the time." I groaned. The sound slowly faded as my eyes landed on Bellow. He looked from me to my protruding stomach. Ignoring his gaze, I grabbed my pool stick. "Mike, you gonna help me shoot?" Once he came behind me, I leaned forward.

"Man, y'all mothafuckas dead cheating," Parker said, grabbing our attention.

The girls and I looked around before we broke out laughing once our eyes landed on Ang. Angel was bent over, with her ass all on Parker like I was on Mike.

Looking away from them, I shot the ball, breaking.

"Sam, I don't know if I told you, but this is a nice spot you have," I told him before eating a french-fry.

"Thanks. It's a cool little date spot." He claimed, downplaying the place. Hell, it was nice and big with some of everything inside it.

Once Sam and Bellow showed up at the pool area where we were, so did their girlfriends. Apparently, we weren't the only ones thinking about having a date night. I wasn't bothered by them being there in the least bit.

"How far along are you?" Kassandra, Sam's girlfriend, asked, gesturing to my stomach that Mike was constantly rubbing.

"Seven months and ready to drop this damn load." I grabbed my drink, but it was picked up before I could get it. My gaze went to Mike.

His brow raised at my action. "Man, turn around, this mine. You better crunch on that damn ice."

My eyes rolled at him. "So. We're sharing. I already told you that." Taking the drink from him, I drank some, then put it in front of me and out of his reach.

"Bitch, you are stupid. Give that man his damn drink." Missy took the cup and placed it in front of Mike. He quickly snatched it up and started back drinking. Laughing, I glanced at him, about to tell him not to act like that. But my words were cut short.

"Do you know what you're having?" Kassandra continued to question.

"Boys," Mike answered for me.

The girls started laughing at that. "Mike couldn't have said that any prouder. That man is happy he's having twin boys. I'm starting to get offended as hell. Like, don't try to play my daughter, Michael. She ain't that bad."

Instinctively Mike snorted. "She ain't even bad for real, she just spoiled as fuck—"

"Whose fault is that, though? King's, yours, and Blaze. Y'all have that girl, so gotdamn spoiled it doesn't make any sense. Y'all the damn problem, not her." Ebony glared at the trio.

"What am I missing?" Blaze and King questioned, confused.

"Mike's ass claims he doesn't want a girl because of Keema." She glared at him before laughing. "Irritating ass claiming a girl would make him psychotic."

"Shid, I agree with him. Hell, I know I'm going to war behind Brianna. I mean all, age kids gonna get knocked the fuck out behind her." Blaze stated factually, making us crack up.

Mike pointed to Blaze. "Exactly. I already know how I am behind Keema's ass, and she isn't even mine. Shorty got her own bedroom at my crib, clothes, toys—I mean hella shit—"

"Hold the fuck up. She got a room at your crib?" Blaze asked Mike, looking at him like he was crazy. Mike nodded. "Oh, yeah, you a fool. Shid, shorty ain't got a bedroom at the house. Then again, she can't even spend the night at my house anymore."

The men laughed at that, whereas we rolled our eyes. "What the fuck she do?" Parker questioned, chuckling.

"A while ago, her little badass took a damn crayon and was drawing on the walls. Then blamed the shit on the twins—"

"I told yo' black ass Keema did that bullshit. And you wanted to argue with me." Mike pushed me in my back. "Like the damn pencil jumped up and started writing on the walls by itself."

I was in the middle of biting my fries when he pushed me. "Michael, I'm about to beat yo' ass." I smacked his thigh hard. I knew Keema did that shit, but I didn't want her to get in trouble. "Keep your hands off me. I don't even know what you're talking about. Ugly stupid ass gonna push me like that."

Parker broke out laughing while pointing to me. "Shorty was fucking those damn fries up. Her mothafuckin' eyes got wide as fuck. She didn't know what the fuck was going on. Syn..." He fell back, cracking the hell up.

"Parker!" Angel hit his leg before looking at me. Shaking her head, she started laughing too. "I'm sorry, Kimmy, I swear I wasn't going to laugh with him. But yo' ass was fucking those damn fries up, baby." She claimed, laughing along with Parker's irritating ass.

Mike's arms went back around my waist, and he pressed his face into my back. I felt him shaking, knowing he was laughing. "Y'all asses irritating. First off, fuck you dumb fuckas, I'm pregnant, so I can eat however I want." I snapped at them, causing the group to break out laughing. I could help but join in. "Fuck y'all. These fries are good."

"Back to Keema's ass." Blaze jumped back into the topic at hand. "So, shorty fucked up your walls, and she still got a room at your crib?" He asked with all seriousness.

"Hell yeah." King chimed in. "As a matter of fact, the next day, he took her ass to Walmart and bought her one of those damn four-wheelers."

"Oh, hell nah. I love shorty, but I ain't doing all that shit. Yeah, you a straight bitch." Blaze told him, laughing.

"Nigga, fuck you. Yo' ass about to be a straight bitch behind yo' shorty too." Mike told him.

"Of course, that's my damn kid—"

"Nigga, fuck you. Keema is the damn daughter I don't have." I started choking on my food at Mike's response. His damn tone was so serious. He meant that wholeheartedly. But what had me choking was the hint of anger that slipped in.

"Baby, did you just get mad?" I asked, and that

made him chuckle.

"Hell yeah. With her badass."

"If you ain't got kids her age. What she be doing at your crib?" Sam asked him.

King started laughing. "Whatever the fuck she wants. That's why she loves going over there. And he be having her on his damn four-wheeler. She loves that damn thing."

Peaches suddenly hit Blaze's leg. "Ooh, she sure does. Babe, we went to a park with them so the boys could ride the ATVs. Malik brought one for Blake to ride on. Keema's ass like, I'm riding with Malik. Babe, she gets on his damn bike in front of him. So, he ties her to his body with some type of strap thingy. He takes off and pops a damn wheelie with her on it. Y'all, I damn near had a fucking heart attack. Not Sha'Keema, though; she wasn't scared at all. Baby girl was cracking the hell up. I was the only one scared shitless. Y'all ass to gotdamn dangerous for me." Peaches overly dramatic ass explained, causing my eyes to roll and a light chuckle to leave my mouth.

"You ride bikes?" Blaze questioned, looking from me to Mike, seeming genuinely curious. "Blake ass ain't told me shit about him going riding with y'all."

I pointed to Mike. "He loves four-wheelers. And I don't know why Blake or Peaches didn't tell you about it. When she brings him with her, that's what the boys do. Malik, Ace, and Blake. The trio is either at the dirt trail or in the back of Mike's house in the dirt field riding around." Glancing at Peaches, my brow raised, silently asking her why she didn't tell him. She simply shrugged.

"Let me see your bike," Blaze told Mike, making us laugh.

"Don't get this nigga started. Aside from guns, this mothafucka love motorcycles." King told Blaze.

After wiping my hands on a napkin, I stood up. "I'll be back. I have to go to the bathroom." I told Mike. After kissing him, I went to turn around when he stood. Laughing, I pushed him back down on the couch. "Baby, that was not code for sex. I really have to pee. Sit and show Blaze your bikes." Pushing away from him, I chuckled while waving my girls on. "Y'all, come on."

After using the restroom and washing my hands, the girls and I stood in the front area talking. We wanted to give the guys their space to talk about whatever they wanted. Or, as Missy called it, letting them bond more.

"You and Mike seemed to be... I don't know what to call it." Peach said.

Sitting on the bench, I rubbed my stomach. "Great?" I questioned. "We're a lot better now that I've gotten outside myself. I was making us worse without even realizing it. I was so scared of losing him and thinking the worse when it came to our babies that I wasn't letting him in—which wasn't my intention. So, after I got out of my own damn way and let Mike in, it was like two magnets connecting. We were already in love and weren't going anywhere. Then when we began experiencing the growth of our babies together, we just got on this damn magical ass wave. I've been high ever since." I told her, truthfully.

Elizabeth didn't know it, but she saved our relationship. Had she not broken down everything to me as she did, I would have never understood what Mike was feeling.

"Well, you definitely look happier, and Mike's crazy ass been grinning all gotdamn night. I can't remember the last time he was all smiles when we've been together." Missy pointed out, laughing. "Well, I'm happy the two of you finally got y'all shit together." Sitting beside me, she began rubbing my stomach. "I can't wait to see them. I bet they're going to be so damn handsome. I mean, Mike is kind of sexy with his dark-skinned self and those beautiful ass blue eyes of his."

My head fell back, and I groaned out loudly. "Y'all, I hope my babies have his damn eyes." The babies began moving, making me laugh. Grabbing Missy's hand, I placed it on my stomach. "I think they asses be in there fighting, for real. They move constantly, I swear. That's why Mike is always rubbing on my stomach. It's so cute when we're at home, and they're moving. Mike will raise my shirt, and whenever they kick, he'll push that spot, and they'll kick again."

"How have his crazy baby momma been acting since finding out?" Ebony asked.

I simply shrugged. "I don't know what the man said to that woman, but she's been really cordial. Like, homegirl doesn't talk shit anymore or make any side remarks implying they've been messing around nothing. She'll drop Malik off with a hey and how you're doing. It's the same when I pick him up. I'm not complaining because y'all, I was going to end up killing that gotdamn girl for real. She used to cause so much rage to come out of me that I would just click the hell out—"

"Right, throwing pool balls and hot pots at bitches." Angel said, cracking up.

"Y'all don't laugh at me. I was going through some stuff, and Tasha kept bothering me." I groaned, remembering how I would rage out on Tasha. "Y'all, I'm done after this. I can't do all these damn emotions. I have never been so emotional in my entire life. Like, I'm tired of myself." I chuckled while rubbing my stomach as one of the babies moved up.

"Okay, so I don't wanna be a downer, but," Ebony looked around us before moving in closer. "Did Bellow not know you were pregnant?" She whispered.

I didn't know why, but I expected one of them to ask me that question. "No, he didn't know. To be honest, my pregnancy—my babies aren't his concern. It's mine and Mike's." That was true. After my last session with Elizabeth, I decided to let go of the possibility. There wasn't any. My babies were Mike's, be it biological or not, that didn't matter. He is their father, and they will be raised as Mike's. "Y'all, when I say I closed that chapter with him, I mean that."

"Bitch, we can tell. I haven't seen you glance at that man all damn night. Or roll your eyes when they came over to us. See, this the Kimmy I fucking know." Angel boosted excitedly, making me laugh.

"Y'all, he told me that too when I saw him at the club—"

"Wait, what? When?" They asked at once, making me roll my eyes.

"The night I saw Martell at the club. I ran into him, and we talked. It was cool. He knows where I'm at with everything, mentally. He also knows I can't lose my everything either. Y'all, the crazy thing I realized is that I barely know shit about that man. And in truth, he doesn't know me—Kimberly, he's familiar with Kimmy. He doesn't know who I am, not how Mike does.

"Don't get me wrong, that doesn't knock the fact we did bond and have a relationship. Still, our bond was never on the same level as the one we shared with our significant others. I'm just embarrassed that I couldn't see this a lot sooner before I made a fool out of myself."

"Yeah, because bitch I was ready to fight your ass. I'm not even gonna lie to you." Angel told me, laughing.

"Hey, ladies," Sabrina spoke, waving as she reached us.

They all looked at me as if asking for some type of permission. I swear they didn't listen at times. I ignored them and spoke. "Hey," I gave her a slight wave. I didn't have an issue with the woman. The truth, she was right. She had more reason to be pissed than me. Bell was her gotdamn man, to begin with.

As Sabrina came closer to me, I noticed her belly for the first time during the night. She was pregnant too.

"Can I talk to you for a second?" She questioned while gesturing between the two of us.

"Yeah." I glanced at my girls, nodding at them. "Y'all give us a minute." Once they left, Sabrina sat down beside me.

"I wasn't eavesdropping or anything, but I did catch the ending of what you said. Let me just say I never blamed you for the affair. To be real, you don't own me shit. Bellow does, which was why I never came at you on no, rah-rah bullshit and why I ignored you." She explained before her hand waved. "Okay, I'm not going to drag this out and make small talk, so I'm just going to ask. The babies you're carrying, is there a possibility that they're Bellow's?" She questioned. "And, no, he didn't send me to ask you this. He doesn't even know I'm talking to you right now. But I can tell it's worrying him, me too, though. Although you haven't been paying him any attention, his eyes keep wandering to your stomach. The time frame fits as well. Is there a possibility?"

Looking at my stomach, I slowly caressed over my belly. My gaze fell back on Sabrina, giving her a genuine smile. "No. they're not his." My babies were Mike's.

Besides, I wasn't about to burn that man's house down, especially not when I knew how he felt about her. Bellow loved the fuck out of Sabrina. He made that perfectly clear when he stopped messing around with me. Like me, he didn't want to lose his home because of a mistake.

"My boys are my man's. You nor Bellow have to worry about that. Believe me, if they weren't, Mike's, I wouldn't be having them. Trust and believe that fact."

After that last bit left my mouth, a relieved exhale escaped her. A laughful huff flowed through her lips. "Okay. I believe you. Alright." She repeated, standing up. Sabrina's started walking off but stopped. "Congrats on the babies."

"Thanks. Same to you." With that, she turned and walked off.

Immediately the girls came back over to me. "What was that about? She wasn't trying to be on no bullshit?" Missy questioned.

Getting up, I started walking past them. "No, Melissa, she just wanted to talk. That's it." I told them, not bothering to tell them what she wanted.

"Yeah, I don't think she's the type to start bullshit. Especially not with Kimmy, behind Bellow. If anything, I believe she'll take that shit straight to his ass for real." Peaches told them, and I nodded in agreement. Hell, that's what I'd do if a chick came to me about Mike.

"Okay, so what did she want?" Ebony asked.

My eyes rolled at her as I kept walking. "E, she just wanted to talk. There was no bullshit behind it. Let it drop. Thank you." I blew her a kiss before we made it to the men. We got there right as Sabrina sat on Bellow's lap.

I went to the couch opposite them, sitting beside Mike. Laying into his side, I grabbed his hand, placing it under my left boob. "Move him," I whined. I didn't know why, but one of those damn boys loved moving right underneath my tittie and the shit hurt.

Mike grabbed the hem of my shirt, raising it. "Mike." I glared at him, but I didn't dare get up because he was the only one who could make the baby move once he started massaging that area.

"Here." Angel chuckled and laid Parker's jacket over me.

"Thank you. He plays too much." My eyes rolled as I chuckled. My gaze shifted and met with Bellow's as Sabrina sat whispering to him. A smile came to my lips, and I chuckled lightly at the visible relief that washed over his face. It was apparent she told him that the babies weren't his.

"The baby under your tittie?" Angel asked.

"Girl, one of them, with his irritating ass. Like that shit be hurting. I'll rub the spot trying to get him to move, but nope, his ass will kick or something. A bitch be damn near in tears. Then here comes Mike's ass, rubbing all over my stomach, and both babies gradually moves."

Both Angel and Peaches pointed to their men. "Same shit."

"How the fuck are you gonna call my damn son irritating, though? It's two of them in there. They need more damn room." He claimed, making me groan out a laugh.

I had to admit, I missed being with Mike how we were. It had been years since we've been so carefree around each other. I missed that so damn much.

It was crazy how I didn't even want any parts of couples night, yet I wasn't regretting coming because I was actually enjoying myself with my baby and my homegirls. Date night was definitely worth coming out for.

Chapter Ten

Kimmy

Realizing He's Serious

"Y'all momma getting on y'all damn nerves, huh?" Mike cooed before pressing his ear to my stomach. "Yeah, I know, she's out here getting on mine too, shit. At least y'all can tag-team her ass on the inside and don't have to hear about it out here." He told the babies as they began moving. "That's what's up. Give daddy another five." Mike hit my stomach as the babies seemed to kick at once. Grabbing my stomach, he shook it and kissed the two lumps pressing up.

The whole time I just glared at him. "You're laughing, but I swear it feels like I'm getting jumped. Like they're so active, I promise I wish you could feel this shit. Seeing it is one thing to actually feel them inside moving around is completely different." I was so ready to get those babies out of me. They literally moved nonstop. It was worse at night when I was trying to sleep. They were simply kicking my ass. Although I constantly complained and threatened to spank them daily, I enjoyed the experience.

"Dad! Can Ace come over?" Malik yelled from somewhere in the house.

Mike glared at the game room door as if expecting Malik to bust into the room. Mike and I lay in the game room on the couch watching tv on the huge flat screen.

"How come he don't ever ask me to go over to Ron's crib?" He asked me. Laughing, I rubbed over his head as he kissed my stomach. "Y'all brother gonna make me kick his ass watch." He told the babies.

"You better stop all that cussing. They can hear you, Michael. Their first words are going to be *kick-ass*. Because you're always using them."

Mike glared at me then brought his mouth back to my stomach. "Y'all momma about to get her black ass kicked too."

Once again, I started laughing. "You're so irritating. I promise you are." My fingers continued to stroke over his deep waves as I stared into those ice-blue eyes. "Gimme kiss." My lips puckered for him to kiss me.

"I can give you more than just a kiss." Leaning into me, his lips pressed into mine.

"Dad! Can he? I need to know now." Malik said before he busted into the room.

Mike let out a growl, and I hit him. "Yeah, he can come over. Do we need to pick him up, or is Jerron dropping him off?" I asked him.

"Ron's about to drop him off. What are the babies doing? Still beating you up?" Malik questioned with a grin.

"Yup, I'm spanking both of them as soon as they get here because this is ridiculous." I chuckled as they continued moving.

"What are we naming them? I hope not, Michael." Malik broke out laughing as Mike's head shot up.

"What the fuck is wrong with Michael?" He asked before looking at me.

My head shook, and I pointed to Malik. "Ask him. I love Michael."

Malik let out a loud snort. "Yeah, the man, not the name." My hands covered my face as I tried to hide my laughter, but the fact that I was shaking gave me away. "Be real, momma. They need something new and dope, like my name."

Grabbing Mike's glaring face, I shook my head at him. "Ignore him, baby. I love your name. Even so, he has a point. We do need to figure out names. We have less than two months before I'm due, and we don't have any picked out. If you want a junior, we can name one baby that, but we still have to figure out another name."

Mike grunted as he sat up. "Nah, I don't want no junior otherwise, Malik's ass would've been named Michael." He glared at him before chuckling. "We gonna figure something out, though. As long as their names start with an M, I'm cool."

Smacking my lips, I hit him. "Boy, get yo' ass off me. Their names don't have to start with a damn M. What about a K?"

"Y'all, they're twins. One can start with each letter." Malik laughed as he stood up. "I'mma leave y'all to it. Ace upstairs in my room waiting for me." He told us while walking to the door.

Mike and I glanced at each other. "When the hell did Ace get here?" We asked at once.

Malik stopped at the door, then slowly turned around. "Um...maybe ten minutes ago, maybe..." he gave us a sheepish look seeming embarrassed.

"Bye, Malik." Laughing, I waved him off, and he quickly left the room. "I'm about to have to deal with two more of that. Lord help me." I prayed, looking up at the ceiling.

"That shit ain't even funny. How is he gonna ask if Ace can come over and dude already here?" Getting up, he went and locked the room door.

"Michael, we're not about to get nasty in here. Especially when the boys will be knocking on the door to play the game on this tv." He already knew that, so I wasn't about to get shit started—especially knowing what was going to happen. My arms raised for him to help me up. "Come on, we can go get in the jacuzzi. The warm water and jets really relax my body."

After helping me to my feet, Mike just looked at my stomach. "Sweetheart, yo' damn stomach big as fuck. Baby, that mothafucka huge as hell."

Glaring at him, I hit his chest. "Get the fuck away from me. Nigga, I'm carrying two damn babies. How do you expect my stomach to look, Michael? Yo' ass so damn irritating. Like, why would you even say that to me? I'm already feeling damn huge as a house. You are so damn insensitive. Nah, Mike, move. Don't touch me." That damn man didn't have any type of filter. Like who says that to someone?

Mike's arms enclosed around me. "Baby, I'm not saying it in a bad way. Like you dead sexy as fuck right now. Ten times sexier than before, but that doesn't change the fact your stomach huge as fuck—"

I pushed him down on the couch. "You're an asshole. I swear." Pissed, I stormed to the door, leaving the room. As I bypassed a mirror in the hallway, I broke out laughing. "Oh, my God." I looked huge and pissed, waddling like a damn penguin. "Mike!" His arms came around my waist, yet I felt his body shaking. That let me know he was laughing at how I looked when I stormed off. "I promise, I'm not getting pregnant again. If I do, I'm leaving yo' ass, I promise."

"Then you can be with me. I'll love to be their stepdaddy." Ace said, grinning as he came down the stairs with Malik behind him. Once the pair finally reached the hallway, his palm slapped against Malik's shoulder. "I mean, given how I stay schooling Malik's ass, I'm already playing stepdaddy."

I fell the hell out laughing.

"Ah!" Ace hollered and took off, running back up the stairs as Mike chased him. "I'm just saying, Mike! I'll make her happy." He yelled, cracking the hell up.

Malik chuckled as he came over to me. "That boy crazy. Momma, he's really in love with you." He claimed, making me roll my eyes although I chuckled.

"I'mma get my belt and whoop his little ass." Ace was the sweetest and the funniest teen ever. I loved that flirty little boy. Hell, Ace has been like that since I met him when he was five or six. It was crazy how he didn't change with me, although he's gotten older.

"Mike, I was just bullshitting, for real, dude!" Ace yelled, thrusting around as Mike carried him down the stairs. "Malik, help me, dude!"

"Malik, go open the back door. I'm about to drown this little mothafucka. I keep telling yo' ass to leave my damn girl alone. Now you wanna play stepdaddy? Dead ass?" Mike fussed while dragging him down the hallway.

Ace looked at me and winked. "A'ight, dude, I didn't mean it. I mean, she's fine—I'm playing, Mike!" He laughed out. "Come on, bro, you know how we play around."

I couldn't do shit but laugh as Ace hollered all the way down the hallway. "Mike, you bet not throw him in that damn pool, especially not with his clothes on. I don't need him tracking water through this house after I done swept and mopped these floors."

"Yo' ass lucky I don't feel like hearing her mouth. Otherwise, I'd drown yo' little ass." Mike threatened while letting him go.

Laughing, I shook my head at that fool. I didn't know why he wanted to mess with Ace. "Come on, babe."

"Here I come—I'm playing!" Ace yelled, running into the game room and slamming the door shut in Mike's face.

"I swear that damn boy crazy as hell. Malik, go play. When y'all get hungry, tell me. I'll cook something up for y'all or order in. Just let me know." After kissing the side of his head, I gave him a slight push then headed upstairs.

Once in the room, I went and started filling up the jacuzzi. Going back into the bedroom, I kicked off my slides, then took off my sweats and panties, just as Mike walked into the room.

Mike ass knew he was sexy for no damn reason. "Oh shit, I know that look."

My eyes rolled at him as I laughed. "You don't know nothing. Come give me a kiss, though. You haven't given me one all day." Of course, we both knew that was a damn lie. My arms went out for him to come to me. He stood leaned against the door, just staring at me. My eyes rolled into my head, already knowing what he wanted. "Baby, you know I want it. Come fuck me, Michael." Pulling my shirt off, I moved to the middle of the bed. "Oh, wait, babe, go turn off the water." I quickly remembered.

When Mike returned, he was naked and stroking his hard man. Mike knew he was sexy as sin. I lay on my side with my left leg raised, giving him a clear view of my pulsing pussy. I was so damn horny. "How you want me, big daddy? On the side or all fours?" Sex was beyond amazing with Mike. However, with my big belly, my positions were limited.

"Just like that." Coming to the bed, he grabbed my thigh, pushing it up before bringing his mouth to my throbbing pussy.

"Mmm." My forehead fell against my arm as his tongue played with my clit. Pulling the swollen pearl into his mouth, he started sucking. "Ooh, shit, baby, yes, suck my pussy." My nails dug into his head as I fucked his mouth. The shit was feeling so good. "Ooh, baby." My leg quickly closed around his head as my body shook as I came. "Ooh, shit, baby."

Mike chuckled as he pushed my thigh up. Biting the skin, he kissed it, then ran his tongue from my clit to my pulsating core. Sitting upright, he slapped my ass, then leaned over and kissed my booty before hitting it again, causing a moan to slip through my lips. Leaning over my body, his hand wrapped around my throat as his mouth came to mine.

Mike bit then sucked at my top lip before sucking on the bottom. His tongue ran over my bottom lip, causing the sets to part for him. Once his tongue thrust into my mouth, my love box immediately became wetter.

"Oh, my God." My lips pulled from his, and my hand slid between us, pushing at Mike's pelvis as he filled me.

"Fuck, Kimmy." He grunted as his hips rotated into my pulsating sex. "Your pussy sucking the shit out my dick."

My pussy was definitely contracting without me

having to work my muscles on him. Even so, he was to gotdamn deep. His hips slowly retracted before he thrust back into my pussy at the same pace.

"Michael, baby, fuck," my legs pushed forward, trying to put some space between us. Mike suddenly pulled out of me and got off the bed. I quickly made a grab for him. "Baby, what are you doing?" I watched him go to the headboard and groaned.

"Turn around." His fingers moved in a circle.

Once again, I groaned as I watched him grab the two leather straps from behind the headboard. Even so, I turned around, placing my arms over my head. He did quick work with belting the leather cuffs around my wrist. Once they were secured, he got back on the bed. With me still on my side, he raised my left leg. A second later, I felt the cuff at my ankle.

"Hell nah! Mike, don't play with me. Hell fucking no! Let me go. I don't even wanna have sex with you anymore." I whined. I should've known what was about to happen when he grabbed two straps instead of just one. Mike simply laughed as he successfully cuffed my ankle. "Baby, you really gonna do me like this?" He was about to fuck my shit up, and I was just going to have to take it.

Leaning over me, he grabbed my titties, sucking on the right then left nipple. His hand then moved down my stomach. Looking at me, he licked his lips. "You're sexy as fuck, pregnant, dead ass, Kimmy." As he spoke, his dick played with my clit. Still, his eyes were locked with mine. My lips parted as he pushed deep into my love box. "Fuck." He grunted, rolling his hips into mine before stroking slow and deep into my soaking cave.

"Mike..." the feel of his slow grind was driving me crazy. It felt good, but my damn sex needed more. "Oh, my fuck!" My head dropped on the bed, and my hands gripped the leather straps tightly as his pace sped up. Mike's dick was like a gotdamn match as he struck my sweet spot. Yet, with that damn pleasurable sensation was the underlining pinch of pain as he went deep. Even so, the pleasure outweighed everything else.

My leg jerked, trying to get free, but it went nowhere as that leather strap kept it in place. The pleasure was literally driving me crazy. And the fact I couldn't push him back, scratch, pull—hell bite his ass made me feel so damn frustrated. All I could do was moan loudly while jerking on my confinements.

"Oh, my God, baby!" His fingers came to my clitoris, adding to the amazing sensation. "Michael, please—ooh, fuck!" A loud moan left my mouth, and my hips pushed up as I came. Panting, my head raised, trying to look down at his moving body. But I couldn't see a thing over my swollen belly.

"Ah, fuck!" Mike grunted, pulling out, then thrusting back into my wet, contracting sex. "Yo' damn grip, Kim, fuck." He bit into my calf before his pounding became relentless. With my clit between his fingers, he jerked it, playing with the swollen pearl.

"Wait, wait, baby—ooh!" My head turned, and I bit into my arm. The pleasure was simply too much as he brought me to another mindboggling orgasm.

"Shit!" Mike's hips pushed more into mine as his body twitched, and he released his nut into me.

"Ow..." I whined as my body started rocking.

"Did I hurt you?" Mike's body went completely still as he looked at me, concerned.

My head shook at his question. "No, the babies are under my damn chest, and it hurt." I moaned as my hand tugged on the straps. For some odd reason, a laugh burst from my mouth. Mike sounded concerned about possibly hurting me, yet the man didn't free my arms and leg. Nor did he pull out of me. "Michael, untie me, please." I groaned out a laugh as the babies kicked.

"Oh, shit." He leaned forward.

"Mike!" Grunting, I glared at him. "Pull out, please. And don't lean over me." Mike chuckled at that and pulled out. He then quickly freed me from my bonds. I grunted as my leg came down. "Babe, you can't be tying my damn legs up and fucking me like that. Your ass is going to mess around and send me into premature damn labor." Groaning, I started rubbing my stomach while Mike chuckled. "That's not even funny. You know exactly what you be doing for real. This is the last time you're tying my legs up. Then you be going deep and shit—stop!" I kicked him as he popped my butt.

"If you can't take this dick, that's all you have to say." He bit into my side then kissed the skin. His lips trailed over to my stomach, then up to my breast. "You're sure you don't wanna get tied up no more."

My head shook as I laughed. "Michael, stop..." my

words trailed off as his mouth finally reached mine. After sucking on my lips, his tongue pushed into my mouth, making me moan.

Mike broke the kiss and laughed when I reached for him. "You're positive you don't wanna be tied up?"

Once again, I laughed. "You can tie me up as long as I'm not seven months pregnant with twins. Now kiss me." I grabbed for him, but he pulled out my grasp and got off the bed. "Mike, you're not going to kiss me?"

"Nah!" He called while walking into the bathroom. A second later, I heard the water running.

"Michael, for real?" I glared at the open bathroom door before rolling my eyes. I then grabbed my body pillow, tucking it between my thighs and making myself comfortable.

"I thought yo' ass wanted to get in the jacuzzi?" Mike said, coming back to the bed.

That was my plan, but having been fucked good, I didn't want to do shit but lay there. "You shouldn't have sexed me like that. I don't feel like getting up and doing anything."

Chuckling, Mike moved my leg from the pillow. "Man, get yo' lazy ass up." Taking hold of my arms, he pulled me upright, causing a groan to leave my mouth.

Even so, I got up and let him drag me into the bathroom. Once I stepped into the heated jacuzzi and sat down, a moan slipped through my lips. Mike got in behind me and placed his hand on my stomach.

We sat there in silence for a long time, enjoying

each other's company. Until a thought came to me. "Babe, can I ask you a question? I know you told me it wasn't my business, but I need to know something."

"No." He stated flatly. "It's not your business."

Leaning to the side, I glanced up at him. "How you just gonna say no, though? Like, you don't even know what I was going to ask, for real."

He shrugged. "Is it about Martell?" My lips popped instantly, and that made him chuckle. "That's what I thought." He claimed, kissing the side of my head. His arm covered my breast as his palm continued to caress over my belly.

I hope he didn't think that was going to shut me up. If he did, then he was sadly mistaken. "I just wanna know what's going on. It's been weeks since you've last talked to Don—"

"How the fuck you even know that?" Although he asked the question, it wasn't in a harsh manner. "You went through my phone?" Once again, the tone wasn't sharp, nor was it surprising.

"You already know I did. That's why you asked, and you're not pissed about it. You knew I was going to go through your phone." I stated as a matter of fact.

A hum left his mouth, and he nodded. "And that's why I got another phone. Sweetheart, it's not your fucking business. So, you don't need to know what's going on."

I didn't see how he could even say that. He knew how crazy and slick Martell was. So, how could he not think I wouldn't want to know what was going on? Not only was I worried about my best friend's safety, but for his also. I knew he wanted to help them out, and I loved him so much for that, but I didn't want to lose my baby in the process of their shit either.

"But I do need to know, though, Mike. Telling me stuff isn't going to be putting me in the middle of it. In truth, I don't want you mixed up in any of this shit. Baby, I understand your reason for doing this, and I love you so much for putting yourself out there for my girls. But, shit, babe, I don't want you getting hurt in the process. I heard what you said about them not expecting you to do shit, but we don't know that—"

"Kimmy, I know that. Look, I know how twisted that nigga and his family are. Like I told you before, I have a past with them. They know me getting in the middle of some bullshit that doesn't involve you or me is unlikely. Plus, what would make them think I wanna set them up, Kimmy? Those niggas have been buying guns from me and pops for years. Why would anything be different now?"

"I don't know, but we can't just assume it's not. We need to at least consider that Don and Martell may be thinking it's a setup, especially after that shit with Missy." I stressed to him. I couldn't understand how he wasn't worried about them.

"First off, ain't no fucking we. So, stop saying that shit. Second, Kimmy, did either of them fuck with you?" He questioned me, and my head shook. "Okay then, to their knowledge, I don't give a fuck about Missy's ass. Shorty doesn't matter to me. Shid, when I saw Don's ass later that night, I stole on that nigga a couple of times because he was trying to holla at you. I ain't say shit about Missy. Look, all you have to do is trust me. As long as you don't do shit stupid and stay out of it, everything will go accordingly. So, stop worrying and stressing my damn babies out."

"Why can't you just tell me the plan—"

"Kimmy, shut the fuck up. Gotdamn, man." He finally snapped at me. "What part of this don't have shit to do with yo' ass, aren't you understanding? Stop fucking asking me. Be glad you know the little you do." Mike's grip on my chest tightened as I went to turn around on him because he had lost his damn mind yelling at me like he was crazy. "I know you're worried, but you don't have to be. Martell nor Don would think I'm on no bullshit, Kimmy. Baby, I'mma need you to relax for real, damn.

"Look, I'mma say this, and it's gonna be vague as fuck, so don't ask me to make shit clearer because I'm not gonna do it." He groaned out, and I knew his head fell back on the side of the jacuzzi. "When you told me what happened with you all those years ago. Martell has a twisted ass brother. He did me a solid with doing some violating shit I wanted done to dude. Ever since then, we've been…I won't say friendly because that isn't what we were. But say we have an understanding; I won't get in the middle of their shit, and they'll stay out of mine. It's that simple. And had I not known how much Martell liked Angel, I wouldn't be getting involved, Kimmy. If I thought the nigga would just kill her ass and leave it at that, then shid—" feeling him shrug, had my damn breathing stopping, "—it is what it is. But I know that twisted mothafucka wouldn't make shit that simple for her."

I sat there still for a long time, letting what he said replay in my head. I knew damn well I had to have heard him wrong. Then again, thinking about the first time Mike said he was doing it hit me. His reason was because of how he felt Martell would do Angel. Not because he didn't want her ass to die, but because of how Martell would kill her.

"Baby, if Martell would give her a quick death, will you still try to help them?"

Once again, I felt him shrug. "No. I mean, I wouldn't be happy about the shit. But it's part of the game they play and live by. Families aren't exempt when you live by this shit. I respect the rules of the game, dead ass, and that's why I don't get in the middle of niggas shit when they live by the streets." Again, he shrugged, and I knew he wholeheartedly meant everything he said. "Although there are no rules as to how you get at a mothafucka. What I see Martell doing to Angel won't be cool. I know how those niggas take pleasure in breaking a mothafucka. She doesn't deserve that shit." His tone faded off as his grip on me loosened.

Turning around to face him, Mike had a far off look in his eyes. I was about to ask him how he knew that but stopped realizing he had already told me.

"Your past with them and the favor his brother did for you is how you know?" I knew Mike had Johnathan, my mom's then boyfriend, killed, but I never wanted to know how it was done. Mike wasn't volunteering information either. I just wanted him to suffer, which I knew Mike made him do. As the word *violating* played in my mind, instantly, an image of Johnathan being raped repeatedly flashed in my head.

So Mike had Martell's brother rape Johnathan. Was I surprised by learning that? Of course. Yet, I didn't feel bad, and I hope the shit was violent as hell too.

Realizing Mike had that done for me caused my damn heart to squeeze tight, and I fell more in love with him. I never knew he would go to the extreme of having that done.

Mike's eyes focused back on me. A slight smile came to his lips, and he nodded. "Yeah, that's how I know those mothafuckas twisted as hell and why I keep telling you not to worry. You're homegirls gonna be straight, I promise." The sincerity in his eyes was so sure that it left no room for doubt in those beautiful blues I loved.

"Are you?"

Mike laughed at that as he pulled me back into his chest. "Of course, I am. If I thought otherwise, you'd know more, and I wouldn't be near you either. I wouldn't risk your life like that. Trust me." His head lowered, and his lips pressed against mine. Again, that look was back in his eyes.

"I do. I'mma stop asking questions. But Mike, if something happens to you, I'mma lose my gotdamn mind and go on a killing spree—"

"Ha!" He barked out a loud bellyful laugh. "Damn, you gonna go killing niggas in my honor, huh?" He chuckled.

Glaring at him, I hit his arm. "I'm being serious, babe. I'm killing niggas behind you."

Taking hold of my hair, he pulled my head back, and I licked over his lips. "Yo' ass better, and my damn twins better be out there with knives, stabbing niggas up like Chucky's ass."

I broke out laughing. "Mike, get out! Like Chucky, though, babe? You're so irritating."

"G, I'm dead ass serious." He chuckled, kissing the side of my head.

A sigh left my mouth as I thought about his logic regarding the streets. "Babe, your outlook on shit when it comes to my girls and niggas killing them isn't cool. I would think you would want to help them because you like my girls."

Mike started laughing at that. "Sweetheart, your girls are cool. But once they insert themselves in the middle of nigga's shit, then aye, those mothafuckas are fair game. Now, if they get dragged into the bullshit by default, that's different. Why do you think I went off on you when I found out yo' ass was shooting at those niggas? I damn near beat yo' dumb ass."

My lips popped, and my eyes rolled hard at him as I thought about Missy and me shooting at Mook and Martell at Angel's party all those years ago. Mike and I damn near came to blows when he found out I was shooting instead of staying out the way.

I was happy as hell they didn't see my ass that night, though.

"You don't go putting yourself in the middle of some bullshit, then when a mothafucka retaliate y'all hurt. Fuck out of here." Mike continued, making me roll my eyes. "Like Missy, that shit she did with Mook was dumb as fuck. Shorty made herself a fucking target. She should've left that shit to those nigga's to deal with, especially after he damn near killed her ass the first time." His head shook at that. "Shid, I'm surprised Martell ain't tried to kill her ass sooner for real. Because that nigga and Mook ass was thick as thieves. I'm telling you if it wasn't for the fact, it's Martell's damn family. I'd leave the shit alone. As I said, that's part of the game."

I couldn't even say shit about that because he made some valid points, especially when it came to my girls. They were some fucking riders and couldn't help but try to help their men out as best they could.

Mike ass, on the other hand, wasn't letting me nowhere near his shit. My only involvement in his business was to see some custom jobs he'd done. Aside from that, he left me out of it. I knew it was because they sometimes dealt with some shady people. Even so, that didn't explain why he didn't talk to me privately about shit.

Mike knew the definition of separating work from home.

"I'm telling them too; I hope you know."

"Sweetheart, I don't give a fuck if you do. I'll tell those mothafuckas that shit. Hell, I told Parker's ass that shit. The only reason I was helping was because of Angel."

A groan left my mouth, and I laughed, already knowing he told Parker that for real. "You work my damn nerves, man. I swear. Ugh, move." Pushing away from him, I turned off the jets, then started cleaning myself up as Mike did the same.

∞∞∞

"Malik, I'mma kick yo' ass. Keep playing with me." Grabbing the pillow from beside me, I threw it at him. "Now give it here!"

Malik stood with the big bucket of popcorn, holding it up. "Get up and get it."

My eyes formed into slits as I glared hard at him; I couldn't stand his black ass. He was definitely his father's damn son. I was in the game room minding my own business, watching tv, until I realized I had forgotten my popcorn. Since Mike wasn't in the room with me, I had to get off of the floor and get it myself. Malik walked in as I was rolling over to my damn knees. The once simple act of pushing myself up and getting to my damn knees was difficult. A bitch was tired and out of breath. Yet, the whole damn time, Malik's ass saw me struggling and just watched. It wasn't until I sat on the couch to take a breath that his childish ass laughed.

He was a little asshole, like his damn daddy. "Alright now, you remember this shit. Because you're going to come to me for something. Especially when your daddy tells you no. So, gone head and keep laughing at me."

Malik quickly slid beside me. "You know I was just playing with you. It was funny seeing you rolling over, though. I've never seen anything like that before." He laughed, pulling out his phone.

"Malik, if you recorded me, I'm kicking your ass. I'm not playing. Let me see." I snatched his phone from him, and sure enough, his ass recorded me. I hit him. "Why would you do that? Oh, my God!" I broke out laughing as I watched myself take a damn break once I got on my knees. "Wait, I said, *shit, I'm tired.* I don't even remember saying that. Oh, my God. Why would you record me?" I instantly sent the video to myself and then tried to delete it, but Malik snatched the phone from me.

"Nah, don't delete it. I need to keep it for memory's sake. When the twins get older, they're gonna want to see how you were pregnant." He claimed, cracking up.

Laughing, I rolled my eyes at him before pushing him away from me. "Move and give me my damn popcorn."

Malik chuckled as he made himself comfortable beside me. Glaring down at him, I rolled my eyes but didn't say anything. Laughing, I laid my head on top of his. Mike came into the room with pizza, fried chicken, and fried rice. Of course, I had to be the oddball and want chicken and rice.

"You might as well get yo' ass up," Mike stated, his fingers waving for me to move up so that he could get behind me.

I felt Malik move and glanced at him only to see that he moved all the way over, watching me.

Once again, I broke out laughing, knowing he just wanted to see me get up. "You're an asshole, Malik."

Chapter Eleven

Kimmy

Girl Talk

One Month Later

"Y'all, something is seriously wrong with that man. I'm telling y'all, my babies, first words will be, kick ass for real." I told them while looking through the store's clothing inventory.

"Kimmy! Didn't I tell you to sit down somewhere? I told you we got this." My sister Mya fussed as she took the book from me. "I know your damn feet hurt. You've been waddling your ass around since you got here." She clowned, making the girls laugh.

"That shit ain't even funny. Mya, fuck you. And I told you I'm okay. It's not like I'm picking up heavy stuff." I snatched the book back from her. She was so dramatic. She acted like I was supposed to lounge around with my feet up all day. "And y'all dumb asses gonna laugh with her." I fussed at my girls.

"I didn't. I was over here saying *that hoe better leave you the hell alone.*" Missy defended herself with a straight lie, making me laugh.

Mya chuckled as well. "If you wanted me to say something to you, Missy, just say that."

"Girl, the fuck bye. Something is wrong with your damn sister. But, seriously, Kimmy, shouldn't you be on bed rest or something. You do look like you're ready to pop." Missy let out a light laugh.

"That's the point I'm trying to make. She needs to be at home with her feet up. One of y'all come and get this damn girl out my store." Mya told them before glaring at me. "Go home. I can handle this, Kimberly Jamisha Jones."

"Damn, you must be getting on her nerves, Kimmy. Homegirl said your full government name." Missy chuckled. "Girl, go home, damn. You got a free day to do nothing. You better take that shit."

My eyes rolled at their joking. "No, I'm not leaving. I'm about to hang up on all you hoes and fire Ka'Mya Latavia Jones' raggedy-ass. I don't care if she owns this store with me. Her ass is about to go." Hearing my sister laugh, I glared at her. "Anyways, Angel, when are you coming back down here? I miss you, and I don't like dealing with these other bitches."

"Wait, what did I do?" Peaches chimed in laughing.

"Nothing yet, but it's still early. I'm just

including you because I know yo' ass gonna get on my nerves by the end of the day."

"Who you on the phone with?" Came a little voice entering the chat.

"Boy, if you don't get yo' nosey butt out my face—" Angel started saying until he cut her off.

"Who is this?" Peewee questioned, screening the call.

We all broke out laughing.

"Peewee, give me my damn phone!" Angel yelled before we started hearing shuffling.

"Y'all, I think he took her phone," Ebony said, cracking up.

"On what though he's screening her damn calls. If that ain't Parker's damn son." Missy claimed, cracking up.

"Daddy! Momma on the phone with my aunties talking shit again." Peewee yelled.

"Oh, my God!" My hand went to my stomach as I leaned against the wall laughing my ass off. "I'mma whoop his ass."

"Who ass you gonna whoop?" Peewee asked.

"Yours!" The girls and I yelled in unison.

"Yeah, a'ight." That was Peewee's uncaring reply.

Missy hollered. "Bitches! Y'all why he just gave us the Parker's, *yeah whatever,* response. I can't wait until I get out there this weekend. I'm tearing his ass up."

"Oh, shit!" Peewee yelled as there was a loud thump. "Uncle Chris! Unc!" He hollered.

Seconds later, heavy breathing came through the line. "Y'all, I'mma fuck Peewee's ass up." Angel panted. "His ass snatched my phone off the bed so fast and took off running. Bitches, I'm gotdamn tired. As soon as I catch my breath, I'm whooping his ass, y'all." She breathed out.

Once again, we broke out laughing. "That damn Peewee was something else, with his grown ass."

"I swear he is. Then he'll run to Chris' dirty ass to protect him, and I'mma have to beat both of their asses. E, Peach, y'all want your nephew for a couple of days. He can keep Blake, Keema, hell even the twin's company." Angel asked, groaning.

Ebony and Peaches laughed. "I don't care. You can bring them down." Peaches told her.

"Say less." She laughed. "Ooh, okay, subject change. Miss, you haven't seen Don or Martell again, have you?" Angel questioned her.

"No, I haven't, and I'm not trying to either, with his crazy ass." Missy breathed out, sounding stressed. "What Parker and them saying about him? Do they know where they're at?"

"Y'all, that's the crazy thing. Parker and his boys have been quiet about the shit for real. Y'all know after that nigga tried to kill Parker, my baby went on a rampage trying to find him. Like, it had gotten so bad, I was about to leave his ass, pregnant and all. He's nothing like that now. He's different. It's like he doesn't even care that Martell resurfaced.

"I'm just like this nigga walking around and threatening my damn best friend and y'all sitting around like shit good. He just like, when Martell's ready to make his presence known, he will, and then they'll go from there until then, he's not about to be chasing a damn ghost. Y'all, he pissed me off. I'm like that mothafucka threatened my best friend. Parker likes Missy, but apparently, he's not going to go on a manhunt for her ass—"

"Bitch, just tell me how unimportant I am to him." Missy snapped before she groaned. "Hell, I know that, though."

"I was about to say, Miss, don't act like I'm lying. Anyways, so I went to Chris because that nigga will go to war behind Missy's ass." Missy suddenly let out a groan at that statement. "Yeah, bitch." Angel responded to the sound, confusing me.

"What's that about?" I asked.

Missy made the sound again. "After we ran into Martell at the mall. Chris wanted me to come down there and stay until Martell's taken care of. But I wasn't about to pack up my life and go there for no telling how long. Plus, I couldn't leave Roman. So, Chris got all pissed at me for that. I believe if he didn't have Christiana living with him, his ass would've come here. Y'all that man called Mike trying to get him to bring me down there—"

"That's why he kept blowing up Mike's phone? Mike's like, why the fuck is this nigga calling me. I didn't know he actually talked to him, though. Hell, I don't know why Chris would ask him."

"He was pissed off that Mike wouldn't do it either, especially knowing the situation. Baby, he was ready to fight Mike's ass. I guess Mike told him he wasn't getting involved because my ass shouldn't have gotten in the middle of that bullshit with Mook. Girl, told that man I was fair game." Missy relayed to us.

My damn mouth dropped because I knew she wasn't lying. Yet, I didn't think he would actually tell somebody else that shit.

"But Parker damn near said the same bullshit, though, for real. Don't get me wrong, he appreciated what you did, but he was pissed off too. Like, you made yourself fair game by getting involved in their bullshit. Saying you should've let them deal with it. Girl, that man told me had I done it, he would've killed me, pregnant and all. But would never let another nigga take me from him." Angel ran down to us.

Missy groaned once more into the line. "Chris told me if I got myself killed, it would be my own damn fault. So, I better sit down somewhere and shut the hell up. Y'all, my ass don't go nowhere anymore. Bitches, I go to work and come back home. Unless I'm with one of y'all. That's what my damn life consists of now."

"Wait..." E chimed in. "Is anyone else wondering why Chris called Mike of all people? Like, I didn't know they were cool."

"They're not." Missy, Angel, and I spoke at once before chuckling.

"Y'all asses irritating." We once again chimed in at once.

"Anyways," I stated, chuckling. "They're not cool, but they got in touch a couple of months back. But I'm going to assume Chris asked Mike because Missy was with me when all that happened and then came home with us." I informed them.

"Oh yeah! Kim, did you ever figure out what the hell Mike wanted with Parker?" Angel questioned.

Mentally I sighed because I wanted to tell them so bad what I knew. Still, I wasn't going to because I didn't want them running their mouths to their men—which I knew Angel would do.

"Nope, he would not tell me shit. Y'all, he pissed me off. I hate when he says, *it doesn't have shit to do with you*." I mimicked Mike's voice, making them laugh. "Y'all, that shit ain't funny. He gets on my nerves for real."

"It must be about some damn guns or something like that." Angel assumed. "But y'all, I'm ready to do some shit behind this Martell situation. Like, I'm just not okay with that man walking around—especially not after that nigga almost killed my damn husband. I'm ready for this nigga to be dead already. Y'all know I'm down for a setup—"

"And bitch, Parker is going to kill your ass and ours. Ain't nobody about to play with yo' ass, Ang." Peaches told her, and I could hear the seriousness in her tone.

"I'm with Peach on this one. Plus, I don't feel like fighting my ignorant ass baby's father behind your recklessness. Now, if the nigga pops up while we're out, my gun on go. Going out trying to find that nigga, though, no ma'am." Ebony agreed with Peaches.

"Well, I'm down shit. That crazy ass nigga threatened me in my damn face. His ass has to go asap, for real." Missy added in.

I couldn't help but laugh as I saw what Mike meant. At first, I didn't see it, but he was right. My girls were quick to jump in the middle of their men's shit to help out. Which wasn't surprising at all. Hell, if I knew some dudes were out to kill Mike, I would, without a doubt, be down to ride for him. My beautiful chrome desert eagle, Lucy, would be ready to rip on sight.

"If you two bitches don't sit the fuck down somewhere and leave that bullshit alone. Y'all don't need to put yourself in the middle of this shit. Nine times out of ten, you two bitches will make everything worse, especially if one of you gets hurt. Besides, Ang, yo' ass won't get away with it because Parker's—aware ass—notices everything about you, so if you start acting different, he's gonna know something's up. Remember the last time you tried this shit, and he caught you with Ron? And Missy, I'mma just call and tell Chris on your ass, watch, I promise I'm going to tell. You bitches will not stress me the fuck out."

Peaches and Ebony broke out laughing. "I guess y'all heard that. And Ang, know she can't get shit past Parker. But, Kimmy, not you being a tattletale, though." Peaches cracked up.

"Bitch, I'm snitching, I swear. I don't care." Sitting in front of my computer, I started putting in restock orders for clothing, lingerie, shoes, jewelry, purses, perfume, and other accessories for the store.

"Kimmy." The girls called.

"Hm?" I questioned as I paused placing the orders. "My bad. Y'all know I'm working. What you say?"

"Me and Ang said we're jumping your telling ass after you have our nephews," Missy warned, making me laugh.

"I don't care, man. Y'all hoes reckless. Then y'all don't be telling nobody shit until you're damn near killed, Melissa." I snapped at her as I thought about the shit she pulled with Mook.

She smacked her lips into the line. "Bitch, I lived and learned from that shit. This different because we're telling y'all what we're thinking—"

"Bitch, telling us ain't shit. It's the real

fucking shooters y'all need to be fucking telling, the fuck! Parker, Chris, Mane, and Jason's asses are the ones that need to be on board. Bitch, our dumb asses gonna fuck around and get killed with y'all hoes." I snapped before moaning as the babies started moving.

The girl's loud laughter broke through the line. "Not you trying to go off on our asses, though. Bitch did we piss you off?" Angel questioned.

"Yeah," I said before laughing. "Like, let us handle these nigga's bitches, sisters, aunties, mommas, grannies, or some shit."

"Not the grannies, though, bitch." They cracked up at me.

Rolling my eyes, I couldn't help but laugh. "Fuck y'all, man."

"You're really trying to get us killed. Dudes do not be playing about their grannies." Ebony chuckled.

Rubbing my stomach, I glared at the time to see that it was almost ten. "Hey, y'all, I have to go. It's almost time for the store to open. I have a few more things to do before I get out of here, and talking to you bitches is slowing me down."

"Nah, it's that heavy ass load you're carrying around that's slowing you down." Peaches pointed out, making the girls laugh. "But go ahead. I'll probably stop by there once I drop the kids off at Momma's house."

"Yeah, come get me," Missy told her.

"Alright, I'll be there no later than twelve. Kimmy, we can go get something to eat too."

That sounded like a plan to me. "Cool, we can do that. Alright, y'all. Love you, bitches."

"Love you, too, babe." With that, we ended the call.

∞ ∞ ∞

I finished the work I needed to do, which took me another hour. My ass was tired and ready to go home.

"How are my nephews doing?" Mya walked into my office, coming over and rubbing my stomach.

I couldn't explain why, but folks rubbing on my belly was beginning to irritate me. Even my girls doing it was becoming frustrating. Nobody ever asked; they just started stroking me.

"They're getting big," I told her. Although the babies moved, they weren't as active as a few weeks ago. However, I saw their body parts lump up in my stomach as they moved. "They've been kind of still today, which I'm thankful for."

"My babies don't have any room to move around no more. At this point, they're stretched to capacity." Mya clowned, making me laugh.

"You're so stupid. Move fool." I pushed her hand off my stomach. She was so damn goofy.

"I'm on babysitting duties as soon as they get here. I can't wait until you have my babies." She cooed, making me laugh. I knew without a doubt that Mya would treat my babies like they were hers. She was definitely going to have them spoiled as hell. The girl had a nursery for the boys and tons of gotdamn clothes and toys at her house.

"Oh, you're definitely will be. I told you to move in with us for a few weeks." Although I had experience from when Malik was a baby. The situation was different because I would have two babies instead of one, and I would have the twins daily instead of a couple of days out of the week.

So, I wanted my sister to stay with us because, for one, I knew I was going to be exhausted handling two babies. Two, I knew I wouldn't be alright letting my babies go anywhere without me. They definitely weren't going to be sleeping at anybody's house.

"Mike said it was cool." I lied. I didn't tell Mike shit. He was going to have a damn fit once she popped up at the house with her bags. Which was the plan.

"Kim, I've been knowing that man just as long as you. Mike doesn't like nobody at his home. Now, if it was his party house out in Gary, then yeah, he wouldn't care." She shook her head while standing up. "You're not about to set me up like that. I would have to fight Mike's rude ass. I can hear him yelling now. No, thank you." She chuckled, making me laugh as well because homeboy was going to go clean off on my ass. "Come on, I'm hungry, and I know you haven't eaten anything since you've been here."

I looked at the time to see that it was nearly twelve-thirty. "Peaches and Missy was supposed to be coming up, so we can get something to eat." I wasn't about to wait on their asses, and I was hungry. "Come on, they've probably at Bianca's house." I knew once the girls got with Blaze's mother, Momma B—Bianca—they could talk nonstop.

"What do you have a taste for?" She questioned as we left the store.

I pointed down the hall to the seafood restaurant. "We can go there. I want some crab legs and shrimp. Girl, we're about to fuck this shit up." My hand went to my stomach, rubbing my babies. They were a part of the *we* I was referring to.

Mya caught on and chuckled as we went into the bathroom and washed our hands. We then went and sat down at a table. After looking over my menu for a second, I knew what I was getting and called the waiter over.

I ordered my seafood boil, and my sister got what she was getting. Shortly after the waiter brought us our drinks, Mya started messing around on her phone, yet I could tell she wasn't doing anything on it. Fidgeting was something Mya didn't often do. So when she couldn't be still, I knew she was contemplating telling me something that I wasn't going to like.

"Mya, you might as well say what's on your mind and get it over with. Like, you're stressing me out, and I don't even know what it is."

Glancing at me for a long second, she looked away, tapping on the table. I should've known it was something because she agreed to come to a seafood restaurant, which she hated.

"Have y'all come up with some names yet?" She asked instead, making me glare at her. "Have y'all?"

My eyes rolled as I sucked my teeth. "No, not yet. My mind is completely blank when it comes to naming them. Like, I can't think of a single damn name. Mike's talking about he doesn't care as long as their names start with M. I don't care what they start with as long as they're cute." Once again, she started up that damn tapping. Covering her hand with mine, I stopped her moving fingers. "Mya, either tell me what's bothering you or let it go."

After letting out an exhale, a pissed-off look covered her face. "Cassie's been popping up at the store." She informed me, and the anger she was trying to hide was on full display.

My brows furrowed in confusion as to why she was telling me that. Let alone why she was pissed off. As those thoughts came to me, something else popped into my mind. "Is that why you've been trying to keep me out of the store?" For damn near three weeks, my sister has been trying to keep me home, saying I didn't need to come in. Hell, I thought it was because she didn't want me to work. Not because of Cassie's ass.

"Kind of. I didn't want you to stress if you saw her or shit like that. Your due date is around the corner, and we don't need you stressing. Her pop-ups have been random, and I didn't want you at the store if she decided to come up there. That's why I've been here so much." She explained further, looking both angry and stressed.

Taking a sip of my drink, I just stared at my sister. I didn't know how she thought I would react, let alone how she wanted me to act by the news of our mom showing up.

After what happened with Cassie's then boyfriend, I've probably seen her a handful of times once I moved in with Mya. Truth, I held no ill feelings toward my mother for what happened. Still, I didn't deal with her and never wanted to see the woman again. The bitch was twisted and had shit she needed to deal with on a mental level.

I could think that way and feel as such because of Elizabeth. Therapy played a massive part in my healing when it came to Cassie.

"Mya, I don't understand. I mean...I don't know." I chuckled, confused. "Why would I be stressed about seeing her. I'm not a kid anymore, so she can't scare or intimidate me. Why she's popping up at the shop is beyond me—"

"She wants to get back into our lives."

Immediately I started choking on my tea, knowing that I had to have heard her wrong. But the serious look on her face told me I hadn't. A laugh left my mouth once I got myself together. "Oh, my God. Why?"

"She just said she wanted to make things right with us, you especially. Says she's changed and even dating a preacher." She continued to relay.

Nodding, I shrugged. "That's good for her. I wish her nothing but the best. She has nothing to make right with me. I've done my healing without her and made everything within myself right. So, I don't need to hear her words or apology if she plans on giving one." I didn't need either. Although I've done my healing, I didn't want her in my life at all.

Seeing the waiter, I instantly got excited. "Foods coming." My lips popped as I became happy for my food.

"Kareem just came home too." She rushed out.

Now that was surprising to hear. Hell, I haven't spoken to our dad since I was eight. That was when he and Cassie split up. Although Cassie kept us away from him, I felt that he didn't put forth much effort to try and see us either. Cassie told our father to stay away, and homeboy did just that.

I've always felt like when she told Kareem that, it relieved him. Like he'd gotten his freedom back to where he didn't have to worry about anyone but himself. So, he did what was easy for him and took off, not thinking about us or the crazy bitch he was leaving us with.

When I finally turned fifteen and made the decision to find him. He was sent to prison for arson. Kareem's crazy tail tried to burn the house down that he shared with his girlfriend at the time. He was sentenced to twenty years for that bullshit. So how he was getting out five years early puzzled me.

Learning that he tried to kill his girlfriend for having a man in their house let me know he was a gotdamn psycho as well. I knew then I didn't want anything to do with him. I already had too much bullshit in my life at that time.

Not only that, but learning that he lived in the same damn city and state as us. Yet, he didn't bother to come to check on us at all. Made the decision a lot easier for me.

"Okay. Good for him." I told her as I sanitized my hands. I grabbed the plastic bib, tied it around my neck, then stared at the oversized gloves and tossed them to the side. "So, what? He wanna see us too now?"

I didn't have to look at her to know the answer. That was the only reason why she brought him up. Aside from not being around, I really didn't hold any ill feelings toward our father either. Hell, he abandoned me when I was younger, and I did the same when he got locked up.

Of course, I could've visited him throughout the years, but I didn't. I didn't care too. Even so, I didn't hate the man.

"Yeah, he do. He's been home for about two months. He found me on Facebook, ironically. He's supposedly staying with a sister he has out here."

Cracking a crab leg, I hummed. That was news to me. Hell, I didn't know our father had a sister that lived in Indiana.

"I was going to have dinner with him Friday." She told me, and I nodded as I sucked the juice out of the leg. Grabbing a shrimp, I peeled it, then ate it. "Kimmy." The way she called my name was in the manner of saying, *bitch*.

I stopped mid-bite of another shrimp and looked at her. "What? I said okay."

That made Mya laugh. "Hoe, you didn't say not one damn word aside from sucking on that damn shrimp. But I'm looking for you to say more than just okay, Kimmy."

Humming, I broke off another crab leg then sucked the juice and meat off the top before glancing at my sister with a bored expression. "I'm not coming. Now, his ass will stress me out. I don't wanna go into premature labor—"

Mya started laughing. "Kim, dead ass? You can come with me at least. I told him I'd bring you."

My eyes rolled at her as I continued eating my food. I wasn't about to talk to her anymore. I just wanted to eat, that was all.

∞ ∞ ∞

"Now that you're done eating, can we talk about Kareem?" She asked as we walked back down to our store.

"There's nothing to talk about, Mya. If you wanna go to dinner with him, baby, that's your right. You don't need me to come with you." I told her while walking into the store.

Mya quickly stepped in front of me before I could head toward the back. "Why don't you want to go?"

I shrugged. "No real reason, really. My body is tired right now, and I know by the time Friday night comes, I'mma be exhausted and only going to want to layup with Mike—" my words trailed off as a thought came to me.

Mya's eyes started rolling hard as hell. "What do you want, Kimmy. I swear your ass is irritating."

Linking my arms with hers, I lay my head on her shoulder. "I'll go to dinner if you come and stay with us for a few weeks once I have the babies. And no, we're not telling Mike until you show up. That's the only way I'll go to dinner with you. So, yeah or nah?"

"Fine—"

"Great. Let me know the time and place—as a

matter of fact, you can pick me up because I'm not driving no-damn-where." Walking away from her, I went into my office and locked my purse into the drawer.

"Why the fuck are you here?" Mya sudden loud and angry tone had me groaning.

I prayed like hell she wasn't about to get into a fight with one of her damn girlfriends. Letting out a heavy breath, I made my way back to the front. "Mya, why are you shouting?" My words trailed off as I finally made it to the front of the store.

"Kimberly..."

Chapter Twelve

Kimmy

An Unexpected Family Reunion

"Cassie, what are you doing here?" Mya spoke her ass up. Not once have that woman showed up to the store since I've been working. Yet as soon as Mya speaks her name, she pops up. "You know what? Don't answer that. Mya already told me what was up with you. Cassie, I'm happy you've found yourself, God, and your pastor. But I don't want to have anything to do with you. I'm giving you my forgiveness, so go be happy with yourself."

It was funny how I wholeheartedly meant that.

"You're pregnant. Mya didn't tell me you were." She claimed, seeming surprised.

"Why would she tell you anything that's going on with me?" Turning away from her, I went to the front counter. "Ronny, Hannah hasn't come in yet?" From the roll of her eyes, I knew the girl hadn't shown up. When I didn't see Hannah, I was hoping she was in the back, and I missed her. "Go, take your break. I'll work the front until you come back."

"Are you sure, Kim? I don't mind staying a bit longer." Ronny was such a sweet girl. She worked at the store part-time while going to college. Taking in my, *get the hell out of here,* expression, her hands raised as she smiled. "I'm going, I'm going." Chuckling, she walked off.

When she was off to the back, I glared at Mya. "Hannah didn't show up, Mya, and this is the second time this week. Not only that, she didn't call off. Homegirl's done. Either you tell her, or I will." I couldn't stand that gotdamn girl, but because she was Mya's little friend, she stayed well past her gotdamn welcome. I've been waiting to fire that little hoe for months.

"Right now isn't the time to be talking about that, Kimmy." She pointed out before looking back to Cassie, who stood in the middle of the store, seeming to be waiting on some form of acknowledgment.

"If you're not buying anything, then you can leave. Unless Mya wants to talk to you. Then, hey, be my guest stay with her. But there's nothing for the three of us to talk about." I told her while glaring at Mya. "Call Hannah."

Cassie moved closer to me as I sat on the stool behind the counter. "Kim, please don't be like that. I just want the three of us to be a family. I know I have a lot to make up for. Please, let me do that, Ka'Mya and Kimberly." I could hear the pleading in her tone. She seemed to really mean what she said.

"Absolutely not, Cassie. Look, you don't have shit to make up for. When I was growing up, you were a fucked up human being. I've forgiven you for being the messed up mother you were. That's all I'm offering because it's all I want to give you. I don't want you in my life, my babies' lives, nothing. Now, if Mya wants that, fine. She's a grown ass woman who can decide for herself. Baby, go be happy, hell build you a new family. Do whatever you want without me." I told her as a customer came to the counter.

"Mya, take Cassie somewhere that's not here. We do have a business to run. I don't want our family drama displayed in front of our customers." I waved the pair off before I started ringing the woman up. "Did you find everything okay?" Giving me a friendly smile, she said she had.

"When did she become so...mean and nonchalant?" I heard Cassie asking over the customer's response as I handed the receipt to her.

"Cassie?"

"Daddy." The excitement in Mya's voice surprised me. "What are you doing here?" She asked him, forgetting all about Cassie as she walked away. Quickly she went over and hugged our dad.

"When you told me you worked here, I figured I could surprise you, and maybe we could grab something quick to eat and talk." He told her.

Funny how I thought all that shit about my daddy. Yet, seeing him for the first time in nearly twenty-two years. I didn't feel like that grown, confident ass woman that just basically said fuck him. Instead, I instantly felt like a little girl.

Ironically, he still looked the same. The years —hell prison seemed to have done him good because he aged well.

His dark brown skin was smooth, even with the new scar on his cheek. His face was fuller than I remembered, and a thick salt and pepper color beard now surrounded his mouth. Long salt and pepper neatly braided dreads covered his head. His stocky build fitted his 6'3 frame nicely.

"It's not a problem that I came up here, is it?" He questioned, not seeming sure. His eyes glanced over to me before they went back on Mya.

"No, of course not." Mya quickly eased his worry.

However, I didn't think he heard her as his gaze fell back on me. "Kimmy..." he looked down at Mya as if asking was it me, all the while making his way over. Once his eyes settled back on me, my head nodded, answering his question. "Damn, baby girl. You done grew up."

I damn near fell off the stool as it tilted forward while I was getting down. I caught my balance just as my dad reached me. "Hey, daddy." Once those words left my mouth, I damn near fell into his arms as they went out for me.

"Let me look at you." He stated before holding me at arm's length. His brows knitted together, and he glanced at Mya before his sights fell on me again. "You're pregnant." He said, then looked back to Mya. "She's pregnant. You didn't tell me she was pregnant. She's pregnant as hell too." I couldn't help but laugh at that. He sounded so surprised. "Damn, baby girl." He said, pulling me into another hug. That one was tighter than the one before.

"Ka'Mya, get over here. Damn, it's been too gotdamn long." He kissed the top of my forehead just as I felt Mya beside me. Our dad's arms loosened for a second before he was squeezing the fuck out of us. Although the embrace was lovely, it became smothering. I was pressed so tightly into his chest; I began inhaling his shirt into my nostrils.

"Daddy, I can't breathe." I exhaled out as I tried putting some space between my face and his chest. His lips pressed into my forehead once more before letting us out of that death grip.

Taking a step back, he wiped his cheeks as his red eyes stared between us. "Y'all have really grown into some beautiful women. And Kimmy, you're pregnant." I knew his mind was blown from seeing us from how fast he spoke. "Mya, you don't have any kids you're not telling me about, do you?" He looked so damn serious as he stared at her.

"No, hell no. I'm not popping out no babies. Kimmy's having all my kids." She claimed, smiling while staring at my stomach.

"Kimmy, you got any more?" He asked me.

"Yeah, a boy, Malik." Mya and I spoke at once. Looking at each other, we rolled our eyes at one another.

"Damn. How old?"

"Twelve." Mya and I again answered.

"Thank you, Kimmy." I glared at her before laughing. "Anyways, his name is Malik, and he's twelve."

"Twelve?" His brows shot up as his eyes rolled up in thought.

"Daddy, are you counting?" Mya asked the question I was thinking. He definitely looked like he was counting.

"Damn, I've missed everything." Once again, his brows furrowed. He looked back. "I thought I saw y'all's crazy ass momma in here." From the harshness in his tone and the pure rage on his face, he hated her. "Because of your crazy ass, I missed every fucking thing."

Kareem blaming Cassie for not coming around, I found that a bit farfetched, to be honest. "Daddy, you can't blame her for you missing anything—"

"The fuck I can. Once I left yo' momma psychotic ass, she practically held y'all hostage. Every time I tried to see y'all or pick the two of you up, that crazy bitch would call the damn police on my ass. Claiming I threatened to kill her and y'all. Every single fucking time and because of those gotdamn reports and the cop she was fucking, the crazy bitch got a restraining order on me. So, I couldn't come nowhere near y'all, or my ass was going to jail." He went off before he snatched Cassie up by the front of her shirt, jerking her to him. "Bitch, I should kill you—"

"Let me the hell go, Kareem!" Cassie hollered, fearful.

Mya and I quickly pushed ourselves between the pair. "Woah, Woah, Woah! Not in our store, you won't." I snapped at him before I shot a glare at Cassie. I knew that bitch was low down, but I didn't think her ass was that dirty to do something like that. Then again, knowing her, I shouldn't have been surprised.

"Daddy, I'mma need you to calm down, please. First off, you just got out—what? Two months ago? We don't need you going away again when we just got you back." I glanced back to see that Mya had begun attending to the nosey customers. "This is our place of business. We can't have that in here." Although I addressed them both, I spoke directly to my daddy.

"Kimmy!" Mike's loud pissed off voice immediately grabbed my attention.

My eyes found him instantly. My brows furrowed at the stressed outlook that covered his features. "Babe, what's wrong? Is Malik alright?" From the look on his face, I became scared something had happened.

His glare deepened. "Yeah, he's good. Where the fuck is your damn phone? I done called yo' ass damn near a hundred gotdamn times and texted you the same. Where the fuck is the work phone?"

My mouth opened, then closed, realizing I was the cause for his stress. "Oh—"

"Oh? I'm thinking something happened, and all you can think to say is, oh? Man…" Mike let out a long exhale.

Without meaning to, I started laughing. "Baby, I'm sorry. My phone is in the office. When we came back from lunch—it's just been a lot going on since then—"

"What the fuck is that bitch doing here?" Mike damn near growled as he glared at Cassie.

"Apparently about to die twice." My dad chimed in, mugging Cassie just as harshly.

Grabbing Mike's arm, I dragged him off toward the side. "Mya." I pointed to our dad for her to watch him. "First off, I'm going to need you to calm down. Like I told you, after lunch, it's just been a lot. Cassie popped up here talking about making shit right with us and wanting to be a damn family. Just a bunch of bullshit. Then my daddy popped up—" I pointed to my dad, who was still mugging Cassie. "—as you can see." My arms went around his waist, and I lay my head against his chest, finally exhaling from seeing my dad. "I'm sorry I made you worry."

Mike's fingers laced through my hair, and he pulled my head back. "You're cool with him being here? I can make his ass leave. All you have to do is say the word."

I opened my eyes and looked into his beautiful blues, which I loved so much. "No, you don't have to put him out. I want him here. This whole time we thought he just took off because he had the opportunity to do so and start over. Babe, that wasn't the case. She kept him away." I ran down everything my dad said.

"That's a low down dirty bitch. G, I will kill the fuck out that triflin' hoe, Kimmy." From the pure aggression in his tone, I knew Mike meant that sincerely. Not only that, but his hold on my hair also became tight. "Just blink, and it's done. I'll walk her ass out, and it's over with. Just blink both eyes right now."

Laughing, I looked away from him because I knew that blink was all he wanted to see so he could have a reason to kill that woman. Mike hated Cassie with a damn passion. That man has wanted to take her ass out since he discovered what happened to me. Honestly, death for Cassie would've been too easy.

Why should she be allowed an easy way out when I couldn't have that? Hell, if I had to live through her neglect and the pain of my constant rape, without an easy way out of that, why should she be able to rest freely? Mike didn't understand that at first. He just wanted to hurt her because she had hurt me.

Yet, a moment of pain before death would never suffice in my eyes. I wanted her to live with how terrible of a parent she was and what all she allowed to happen to me.

Now that it was nearly seventeen years later, she wanted to make things right for what she's done? In my eyes, at that moment, Cassie's loss was far greater than my past suffering.

"Did you just blink?" Mike's face was suddenly in front of mine.

Biting my lips, I tried to hold in my laughter until I saw that he was serious. I broke out laughing. "Dude, don't make me laugh. I'm being serious right now. Mike, my daddy's here." I sounded like a gotdamn kid, and I didn't like it. Yet, I felt so many emotions seeing Kareem—which caught me entirely off guard.

"I see his big ass." Mike glanced at my dad at the same time he looked our way. "Y'all look just like that nigga."

I tugged on Mike's hand and pulled him over to Kareem and Mya. My head shook at Cassie as I bypassed her. I didn't understand why she was still there.

"Mya, Kim, can I talk to the two of you for a minute, please?" The pleading in her voice caused me to look at her. Cassie's eyes held so much desperation in them.

"No, you can't. There's nothing you have to say to me." I pointed to the entrance. "But you can leave before I have security remove you from my establishment." Mike moved from my side, and instinctively I grabbed his wrist, stopping him. "What are you doing?"

His finger ran across the front of his shirt. "I'm security. I'm about to remove this bitch."

"Michael..." was all I could say as my fingers rubbed into my forehead. "Mya, please do something with Cassie. Call security if you need to." I was done dealing with her.

"Kimberly, please, just talk to me. Baby girl, I'm sorry. Tell me what I have to do to make things right. I know I've made some horrible mistakes with you and Mya. I wasn't the best parent. I know this, but please, let me make things right. I want to get to know this woman you've become. You have a son that's twelve that I never knew you had. I want to get to know my grandson—"

"Bitch, if you come near my fucking son, I'll murder yo' ass. Kimmy might've spared you, but I've been itching to kill you. Coming near my son will automatically give you a oneway ticket to hell—" Mike's words trailed off as if he realized something. "You know what? You can meet him—"

"Ha!" My dad barked out a hard, bellyful laugh.

Without thinking, I hit my daddy in his stomach. "Don't laugh at him. Mike, stop threatening that gotdamn woman. She's not worth the threat. And you know she'll never come near any of our kids. Now stop so I can introduce you to my daddy properly."

"Kimberly..."

I began talking over Cassie's sad tone. "Daddy, this is my crazy ass man, Mike. Babe, meet Kareem, my daddy."

The pair shook up in greeting. "What's up."

I glanced back just in time to see Cassie's tear streaked face staring at us. Catching my gaze, I rolled my eyes at her while shaking my head. Finally getting the hint, she left out the store looking pained. Yet, I didn't care.

My dad pulled me from Mike, and once again, his arms were wrapped around me. "Damn, I missed you, baby girl." His other arm opened, and Mya was pulled into the tight embrace.

"Kimmy, I'll be right back," Mike told me.

That got my attention, and I pulled from my dad. I was not about to let that man leave, especially not behind Cassie. He probably would murder her ass. My baby hated her with a passion so strong and deep, I'm shocked he hadn't killed her by now. Then again, he probably hadn't because of me. Plus, we hadn't seen her since I moved in with Mya.

"No, you're not about to leave, Mike. Babe, no, I don't want you to do anything stupid. Do you want me to go into premature labor?"

Mya broke out laughing. "Bitch, you're about to stop using that shit. I can't wait until you have my twins because you're working my damn nerves talking about some premature labor."

I was going to use the hell out of that until I delivered my damn babies.

"Your having twins?" My dad asked, and I nodded. "Wow. Three kids." He said, surprised.

The bell at the register started ringing, informing us that a customer was ready to check out. "I got it," I told Mya as she went to assist the customer. "Y'all, we really do have a store to run. We've given our customers more than enough excitement for the day." I informed them while making my way to the register. The lady at the front chuckled at that in agreement. "I'm sorry about all the family mess. Some folks just don't know how to act." I sighed while glancing over to Kareem, who was talking to Mya and looking around the store.

Mike came behind the counter, opened a clothing bag, and put the woman's items inside it. Taking the receipt from me, he put it in the bag. "You been on your damn feet all day, haven't you?"

Smiling at the woman, I proceeded to tell her to *have a blessed day* before glaring at Mike. "Babe, don't start. I'm working."

"Mya! Kimmy been on her damn feet since I dropped her off?" He questioned.

Mya's head instantly started bobbing, "Yup. I

told her to go home. But she had to check inventory, place orders, clean up the store. She acted like I wasn't here and couldn't do anything. I even tried to get her little friends to come and get her ass."

I just stared at her, not believing she actually told everything. Mike glared at me. "Don't look at me like that. I'm going on bed rest as soon as we get home, I promise." Mike's head shook, and he pointed to the stool for me to sit down. Chuckling, I did as he asked.

"So, y'all really own a store." Our dad questioned, still looking around the store as if amazed.

Chuckling, I nodded. "Yup. It was something I decided to do a couple of years ago. I got tired of working at that bank, plus I love clothes. Mya pretty much didn't want to work for anybody else and jumped on board. It started out as an online store. Now, here we are. Best decision we've ever made." I smiled at Mike because he was why we had a physical store. "What about you? Have you found work since you've been home?"

"Of course, a man that doesn't work, don't eat." He made a point to say. "I'm working at a garage right on Broadway..." he said while pulling out his phone. "Where I need to be getting back too. I had an hour break and decided to stop by here." He exclaimed. "Oh, here, before I forget. Give me your number, and I'll give you mine." He said, handing me his phone. Taking it, I quickly added my number, then opened a new text box and texted myself to save the number in my phone later. "We're still on for this Friday, right?" He asked.

Mya nodded. "Of course, we are." His eyes fell on me. "Oh, she's coming too."

"Okay, okay, it's a date. I have so much shit to catch up on." He repeated, staring between us before his eyes went to my stomach. "And I'm about to be a granddaddy." My dad's head just shook. "You don't seem old enough to have kids. And a twelve-year-old, damn." He exclaimed with a heavy breath.

I couldn't help but laugh at that. I would tell him later that Malik wasn't biologically mine. Even so, he was still my son in every sense.

"Bring him to dinner if you want. Mike can come too." He said, extending the invitation.

Mike nodded. "A'ight, that's cool." My hand slid into his, entwining our fingers. I knew how he was about Malik, so accepting the invite and thinking about letting Malik come to meet my dad meant so much to me. "I need to get you home," Mike said, pulling me up.

"Yeah, I need to be going too. I get off at Five. I'll call y'all a little after that. We could probably even meet up later." He suggested.

"That sounds like a plan." Mya and I told him.

He seemed excited about that as he pulled us into another tight embrace. "I love y'all." He whispered against our heads as he kissed us. I felt the emotions he was giving off couldn't have been faked. I knew he missed us just as much as we missed him.

After saying our goodbyes for the tenth time, our daddy finally left. Once he did, I felt beyond exhausted as the half-day I've worked caught up with me.

Who knew an unexpected family reunion could be so gotdamn exhausting?

Chapter Thirteen

Kimmy

Nameless Babies

Gripping the pillow, I bit into it as my nails dug into my hip. "Oh, my God." I moaned before biting into the pillow once again. "Mike, baby." I cried breathlessly.

"Fuck!" He grunted while stroking deeply into my body. My inner walls seemed to be working overtime as they milked him following my orgasm. "Shit!" Mike's hips pushed into me as he found his release. "Gotdamn." He panted while kissing my calf. Mike then rolled over on the side of me all the while, squeezing my thigh. "Fuck, Kimmy."

All I could do was nod, knowing exactly how he was feeling. It seemed like the moment Mike and I were on the same page, our sex life seemed to have gotten a hundred times better. Then again, maybe it was the damn pregnancy hormones—hell, I didn't know, but whichever it was, I didn't want it to stop.

A moan left my mouth, my body began to rock as my hand went to my lower back. Once Mike saw what I was doing, he moved my hand and massaged the area.

"What? It hurt?" He asked.

I nodded as his fingers dug into my flesh. "Yeah, I keep getting these cramps. They'll last for several seconds then pass. They've been happening on and off for the past hour or so." I explained after the cramp eased.

Grunting, Mike got out the bed and went into the bathroom. Several seconds later, I heard the water come on. Sliding back in the bed behind me, his hand came to my stomach, and he rubbed my huge belly. I said nothing because although the cramp had subsided, it was like I still felt an ache in its place. We lay in a peaceful silence for fifteen minutes as Mike continued to stroke along my stomach.

"Babe, we still haven't come up with names for the babies," I mumbled, exhausted.

Mike grunted out a chuckle. "I've been thinking about some. But none I'm in love with."

My eyes opened, and I started laughing. "Why I wanna look at you but don't feel like rolling over. Mike, come around to my front."

"Man, yo' lazy ass. You might as well sit up. We're about to get in the tub." I groaned, and Mike popped my ass. "Kimmy, come on. You said the jacuzzi help with the cramps."

My lips popped because I knew I didn't say

that. "I said it relaxed me when the babies were moving like crazy."

"Kim, get up." Whining, I grabbed his hands, letting him pull me up.

Once I sat upright, another cramp hit. "Mm…" Moaning, I rocked while rubbing my lower back.

"Another cramp?" He questioned.

All I could do was nod and rock until the ache subsided. After a minute, the pain eased, and I let out a breath. Maybe the warm water would help. "Okay, I'm alright." Grabbing Mike's hand, he helped me up, then led us to the bathroom. Once I sunk into the deep tub, a sigh left my mouth as the warm water felt good against my skin. Mike got in and sat in front of me. My eyes closed as I smiled at Mike. The water felt amazing. "Names you thought of; what are they?"

"As I told you, there's none that I love. A'ight, so, Kentrell and Montrell, Marshawn and Kashawn —"

"Baby…" Seeing that he was being one hundred percent serious and about the damn M and K names did it for me. I broke the fuck out laughing. "Michael, we are not doing the whole first letter of our name bit. Like, baby, just no. That's why you can't think of anything because it's hard to match K and M names together. Kentrell is really cute, but I don't like Montrell or Marshawn. Kashawn is also cute and different. But, yeah, I'm not in love with either of them. Kentrell and Kashawn can go in the maybe pile."

"Man, the names have to match, though. They're twins, Kimmy. You can't fuck up tradition." Mike's head shook as he stared at me disappointedly.

"Oh, my God! Dude!" All I could do was laugh at his silly ass. "Baby, tradition would be giving one of the twins your name. Michael Dontavious Payne the third."

Mike groaned at that. "Yeah, we ain't doing no juniors." He shut down once again.

"I really like Dontavious."

Mike hummed at that. "Yeah, but that's a single child's name. Not for no twins."

Once again, I broke out laughing at a single child. "A single damn child, though, babe? I'm quite sure we can find something to go with Dontavious." I told him, thinking about what could go with that. "Montavious Kentavious—"

"Nah, we'll keep Dontavious for a single kid. Hell, it's going to take one kid a long ass time to learn how to spell that shit. I'm not doing that shit to two. My granny was tripping when she named my pops." He laughed.

"How about we pull names. We'll write down all the names we like, put it into a bowl, shake it up, and the first one either of us grabs is what we name the babies?" I suggested. I couldn't believe how hard it was to come up with names. "Mm..." a moan left my mouth as another cramp hit, yet it wasn't as bad as the others had been.

"Another cramp?"

Licking my lips, I nodded. "Yeah, it's not as bad, though."

Staring at me, Mike started grinning as he pushed himself over to me. "So, the bath worked, huh?" His lips came down on mine.

My arms went around his neck as I kissed him. "Yes, Michael, it worked. I guess sometimes you know what you're doing. Although you suck at picking names."

"Yo, fuck you. At least I thought of something. You haven't come up with shit." Pulling my arms from his neck, he stood up. Mike's whole damn body was a gotdamn sin. My baby was ripped, and the tattoos on his chest only added to his damn appeal. I loved his body. The thick and long one-eyed snake that stood in my face knew he was the damn devil himself. "What you tryna do? I mean, you're staring hard as hell. Just tell me what's up."

My hand motioned over his physique. "Just damn sinful is what I'm thinking. Baby, I'm tapped for the day. You done jumped on me twice."

Mike's brow shot up at that. "You started that shit both times, though." Getting out of the tub, he went and turned on the shower.

"So. That's different, though."

Mike's head shook, and he ignored me as

he got into the shower and started washing up. Sighing, I made myself comfortable, allowing the heated water to soothe my body.

∞ ∞ ∞

Mike walked out of the closet fully dressed, looking good as hell. I watched as he hooked two holsters on his hip before putting his guns into them. I sat there silently, waiting to see if Mike would say anything to me. Once I saw him grab his keys and phone, I didn't think he was.

"Where are you about to go?" Speaking seemed to have made him remember I was in the room.

"Oh, shit, I have some business to do. I'll be back in a couple of hours. If you need anything, call me. If I don't answer the first time and it's important, call back and let the voicemail pick up. Bet? Do not text me because I'm not going to be checking them. Call me." He stressed that fact.

"Okay. If I don't, then call me on your way home. I might want something."

"A'ight." Kissing me, he stood up as there was a knock on the bedroom door. "Come in." He called, and Malik walked in with food, snacks, and drinks.

"So, you told Malik you were leaving but not me?" That was some Mike shit to do. My head shook, realizing he had everything set up. "I love you."

Nodding, he waved Malik to the bed. "I love you too, and yeah, he's your babysitter until I get back. Malik, call me if you think something's wrong with her."

After sitting the food and stuff at the foot of the bed, he shook up with his daddy. "You know I will. I got this. You don't have to worry about us."

Pulling Malik to him, he kissed the top of his head. "A'ight." Kissing me once more, he left out the room.

Malik hopped on the bed beside me and grabbed the remote. "What are we doing? Scary or stuff getting blown up?"

As I grabbed my food and drink, I hummed in thought. "Hmm…" Opening the container, I grabbed a piece of chicken. "Scary," I said as he turned on Candyman. I stopped mid-bite. "Malik, if you don't turn. I'm not watching this shit." I was not about to watch no damn Candyman. I didn't care how old I got; that movie will forever terrify me. "Put on Child's Play Three."

He glared at me. "That's not even scary, though. A'ight, I'll find something else that's not Candyman."

"Fine. Nothing with Clowns or damn Zombies either, Malik." I warned as I went back to eating my food.

Chapter Fourteen

Mike

Deeper Than I knew

"You niggas been putting those fucking miles in, haven't you?" My fist hit Don's as he walked into the Payne's Firearms & Range.

He chuckled from the door. After taking a pull from his cigarette, he tossed it, then came fully into the store along with two other dudes I didn't know.

"Shid, trying to get everything together for this big ass move back. I didn't think it would've taken this long to get everything down south situated. Nigga, I hate moving." He complained, referring to the past few months he's been in the south. Don's demeanor soon changed as he grinned and rubbed his hands together. He then motioned to the closed door. "Are my babies back there?" Don's diamond teeth were on full display, showing his excitement.

"Bring yo' goofy ass on." I led him to the indoor shooting range, where six gun cases lay.

Opening the first was a gold Desert Eagle sat inside in parts. On the barrel in black letters read, *I Plead The Fifth*. The slide was decorated with smaller skulls. Either side of the black grip was designed with a larger half-faced skull.

Don glanced back at me as if asking could he touch it. My hand waved out, giving him the go ahead. "Damn this bitch sexy." He mumbled while putting it together. Dude looked to be in awe with the gun. Seeing the ammo on the side, he loaded the magazine. Aiming, he started shooting his target sheet. "Oh, yeah, this my favorite new bitch." He gloated excitedly. "And this bitch is beautiful as fuck. Damn. Let me look at these other bitches." From the way he spoke, I knew he was excited.

I moved the desert eagle case and gun out of the way. Just like the first desert eagle, that one was in parts too. But unlike that one, it was rose gold with a white pearl grip.

One of the dudes he was with moved closer to him, looking at the gun. I stepped back, giving him space. Once Don put the gun together, he sat it down to load the clip.

His boy picked up the weapon, examining it. "This baby is beautiful."

Don seemed to have frozen as he looked at his boy. "Mike, you still have that no fighting, no shooting niggas rule in this bitch?"

"Of course—"

Don hauled off and knocked the shit out of

his homeboy. "Nigga, what the fuck are you doing? Did you pay for that bitch? If you didn't, yo' ass shouldn't be touching my shit."

His dude touched his mouth, seeing blood on his hand, he jumped for Don. Quickly jumping between the pair, I pushed his homeboy back. "Yo, you niggas better chill the fuck out. Ain't none of that shit in here. You wanna fight his ass, that's yo' right, but don't do that shit here. Nor in the parking lot."

Don started laughing. "Ain't no fighting in here, baby. Did you not just hear that man say that? Don't touch my shit again without asking." With that, he started shooting.

I couldn't do shit but laugh at that nigga. If Don's family wasn't so gotdamn twisted, I would no doubt maybe probably like his ass a little bit.

He went through the same process with the other four guns he ordered from me. With each case he opened, the nigga seemed to fall in love with every weapon. Once he finished testing each one, he put them up.

"You did your shit with these bitches, for real, Mike. Shid, I don't even know which one I wanna play with first." He chuckled, looking at the closed cases. He waved his two boys over. "Come on, so you can give me my receipt. Y'all can take my babies to the truck while I finish up with him." He instructed. Once they came over, his hand started waving. "If y'all drop my shit, I'm fucking y'all up as soon as we get off this property." He warned them.

"You a dramatic ass mothafucka, ain't you?" He was doing way too much with threatening them about guns that couldn't get messed up inside the case. The red light in the range came on, letting me know that someone had come into the store. "I'll leave y'all to this. I'll draw up that receipt."

When I did private business, the indoor range was closed for their privacy until we were done. After flipping off the *In-Use* light sign, I closed the door.

Once I made it to the front, I wasn't expecting to see Parker, Chris, or Mane in the store.

The trio stopped their glancing around as they heard the door close. They glanced my way for a short second before their attention returned to the guns. After several moments all gazes came back to me. I knew they weren't expecting to see me either from their expressions.

Ignoring them, I went behind the counter, finding the receipt for Don's six modified guns.

"What the fuck are you doing here?" Chris asked me as Don, and his boys came from the back.

My brows rose at the question as Don came to the counter. I handed him the receipt, and he let out a whistle. Turning my attention to Chris, I addressed him. "You're asking me what I'm doing in my own store?" I questioned as my phone started ringing.

"I didn't know this spot was yours." He

claimed, seeming to mean that.

Once again, my brows furrowed in confusion. They knew I dealt with guns, which was all they needed to know. The four of us never really conversed about our business. Hell, they didn't know if what I did was legal or not. "Why the fuck would you? We don't do business." I was saying as Don sat sixty thousand in front of me.

"Keep the change. You deserve that shit, dead ass." Folding up the receipt, he put it in his backpack. "About those big toys, we're gonna get up with you this weekend to set shit up, for real."

Nodding, I put the money up. "A'ight." My attention went back to the trio that still stood there. "Was y'all looking for something in particular?" I asked them.

Chris pointed to the range while glancing at Don. "We wanted to use the range." I pointed to the sign with the prices on it.

Don suddenly hummed before a look of confusion came to his face. "Chris?" He asked before finally turning and looking at them. "I thought that was yo' bitch ass, but I wasn't sure." I moved from behind the counter, I didn't know Parker and his boys like that, but I knew Don's ass. The mothafucka was crazy and would provoke some shit. From the underline hostility in his voice, I knew that was what he wanted to do.

"You mothafuckas out here hiding in different gotdamn states, but you wanna call me a bitch? Come on, baby, what sense does that make? I mean, you niggas turned into some straight ghost, that's how shook we got you niggas out here, but I'm a bitch? You bitches disappeared for fucking years." Chris told him, laughing.

Although Chris was talking, Parker was the one that stood out to me. "Yo, if you mothafuckas have problems, y'all take this shit from my establishment. If y'all wanna argue like some bitches, go the fuck outside and do that shit. If you mothafuckas can read, that sign clearly states, no fighting, or shooting mothafuckas for dumb shit in here." I pointed to the signs that hung on three different walls.

Parker's hand moved, his gun coming up, aimed straight at Don. My gun was pulled and aimed at him a moment later. "As I said, ain't none of that bullshit in here. If anybody is going to be bleeding or end up dead, it's gon' be because I shot the mothafucka. So, be smart and put yo' fuckin' gun away." I warned him.

"If you don't get that fucking gun out my face. Yo' fucking skull gonna find a bullet quick." Parker threatened.

I shrugged. "G, I'm not shook by your threat nor yo' niggas. But best believe I don't have a fucking problem with shooting you. So be smart because if I even think you're going to try and turn that bitch toward me, I'm shooting."

"Then, my clip gonna empty into yo' fucking head." Chris threatened as his gun was drawn.

The steel shutters soon came down, covering the windows and the door. "Then we're all gonna be in this bitch having fun." My pops spat out murderously. "You good baby boy?" I glanced over to see my dad holding his favorite toy, the MP5K.

Chuckling, I nodded. "I'm good, pops. I'm just running down the rules to everybody." Once again, my phone started ringing, and I clicked the side button, shutting it off.

"Woo!" Don suddenly hollered excitedly. "This is why I love doing fucking business here. You mothafuckas are upstanding with the rules in this bitch." He laughed. "We're all good, though, pops." He addressed my dad. "Wasn't shit gonna happen. Just a couple of old friends showing love is all." He informed him before he came beside me.

"Yo' ass still dramatic as fuck. Mook was the same gotdamn way." Parker and Chris laughed at Mane's joke.

Don laughed at that. "And we all know how that ended, huh?" His shoulder nudged mine. "These niggas killed my brother, and the mothafuckas wanna joke about it." He cracked up. "Cool, cool." He mumbled, nodding. "Pops, can you let me up out this bitch? Before I get stupid, and I'm really not tryna die by yo' gun." He told my dad before he started walking to the door.

Don suddenly stopped, but he didn't turn around. "As entertaining as this has been, I got shit to do. Don't pout, baby. We'll be seeing each other soon, I promise." He swore as he winked at the trio. As if a thought came to him, his fingers snapped. "Oh, wait, I need to know something. It was never clear which one of you bitches killed my brother."

Chris let out a groan at the question. "A couple of us was shooting, but I think it was my gun that fucked his ass real nasty, though. Mouth fucked that bitch disgustingly." Chris' hand went to his stomach as he once again grunted.

"Pops, open the door, so he can go." From how they were going, I knew shit would turn ugly quickly. My dad went to the keypad mounted on the wall and pushed in the code, causing the shutters to start raising.

Don nodded at what Chris said as he went to the door. However, he stopped before opening it fully and stood on the threshold. "If it was by yo' gun, I guess Mook deserved that given his actions. I mean, he did fuck yo' bitch, tore her ass apart. So, it was fair how you did him. Couldn't even recognize my brother. Had to have a closed casket. But it was the same with your wife. So, it was fair."

I didn't know how deep things really were between the men, from the sound of it, though shit was hella personal. I didn't even know Chris was married. Hearing what was coming out of Don's mouth, though, wasn't cool. I grabbed the muzzle of my dad's still raised gun and lowered it.

From Don's posture and the fact he kept on laughing, I knew then his ass was literally trying to rile them up for some reason. I didn't like it, but

I didn't say anything because I was curious about what he wanted to do.

Yet from the look on Chris' face, I saw he was about to snap. Mane and Parker had already closed in around dude, whispering to him.

"This is what that bitch wants. You know, once he leaves here, that bitch going back into hiding. Those bitches want us mad so they can hide." Mane was telling Chris.

"Get the fuck out of here, Don!" My dad growled at him.

Don's hands raised, and he looked at Chris, grinning. "I guess you're coming for me next, huh. Shid, it's only fair. I mean, I played my part. My brother might've fucked that bitch, but I emptied my clips into her fucking face and chest. Face fucked that bitch real disgustingly." Still grinning, he kissed at Chris.

Chris snapped, and Don quickly left out. The pair tried to hold Chris, but dude clicked the fuck out. Knocking Mane down, he punched Parker in the face.

Learning what Don and Mook did to Chris' wife didn't surprise me in the least bit. That was shit the niggas did. That was what I didn't want to happen to Angel. Those niggas were ruthless.

Discovering what Chris just had, I had every mind to let his ass go crazy, because had it been me. I couldn't have been stopped. Pops and I stood back, watching as Mane and Parker struggled to get Chris under control.

Parker finally got Chris in a sleeper hold, choking him out. Still, before he went out, dude put up a damn fight. Once he had Chris down, Parker's glare turned on me. "I'm not cool with niggas pulling guns on me. I'd be careful if I was you."

I shrugged at him. "As I said, it's a no fight or shooting niggas rule in this bitch. Either you follow the rules, or my gun goes in your face. It's that simple. Whatever outside beef you have with those mothafuckas don't need to be brought here. This isn't some small ass business. We have a fucking reputation. Y'all not about to fuck our shit up off some gotdamn street beef. So, nigga fuck you and yo' gotdamn threats. And I'm not cool with niggas threatening me either." I finished saying as my phone went off again.

Remembering the two times it rang previous, I grabbed it just as the call from King ended. I groaned, seeing I had two missed calls from Kimmy and a voicemail. "Shit..." I quickly called her back but didn't get a response. "It's Kimmy—"

"Go, I'm good here." My dad rushed me off. "Y'all might as well drag him to the side and start cleaning up this mess his ass made." He was telling them as I pushed through the doors.

Once I hopped in my truck, I took off toward the house, flooring it all the way there. My damn nerves were bad the entire drive. With Kimmy being eight months pregnant, I knew she could go into labor at any time. I didn't want her to go through that shit without me.

"Why the fuck you're not answering, sweetheart? Damn." I hung up as the voicemail picked up again. Calling Malik, he picked up after the third ring. "Malik—"

"Yeah. Man, why are you yelling?" He groaned out groggily, sleep still thick in his voice.

"What yo' momma doing? She called me." I told him.

He let out a heavy breath before I heard him moving. "I called you. She was doing a lot of moaning, rocking, and stuff. She said they were just cramps. But she's been having them a lot—she's having one now."

Kim's soft moans could be heard through the line. "What she's doing?"

"She's still sleeping, just rocking and moaning." He explained.

"A'ight, I'm on my way there now."

"Okay, dad. I'm going back to sleep."

Once I finally got home, I found Malik at the foot of the bed, hugging a pillow. Kimmy was on her side, knocked out. Kim suddenly started moaning as her body began rocking slowly before it picked up in pace. She swayed for a good two to three minutes before her body relaxed. She had been cramping on and off the majority of the day. I didn't know if that shit was normal or not, but since Kimmy wasn't worried eased my mind a bit.

I had just kicked off my shoes and removed my shirt when the phone I had for Don started ringing. Not recognizing the number on the screen. The only person who had that number was Don, so I knew it had to be one of them.

Leaving the room, I answered the call. "What's up?"

"Mike, this Martell." He announced.

"Okay...what's up?"

"Don told me what popped off at yo' spot. I just wanted to say good-looking. Those mothafuckas would've killed that nigga if you didn't help him out." He said, sounding appreciative.

All the while he talked, my head just shook. "Shid, I wasn't looking out for him to be real with you. What those niggas got going on with Don, or you for that matter, is y'all bullshit. I only stepped in because they were in my range. That's the only reason. So, ain't no need to thank me for shit."

Martell started laughing hard. "Damn nigga, we know yo' reason for doing the shit. Just take the fucking thanks damn, man. Point is, shid, you could've let shit go down because of yo' girl's relationship with his—"

"Man, that ain't got shit to do with me and mine. As long as we're not dragged into y'all shit, I don't give a fuck what y'all do." I was tired of telling folks that. I was starting to sound like a tape.

Again, Martell laughed. "I feel you, Mike. Still, good looking out. My other reason for calling was to set up that meeting. Don said he told you this week. We can do it Saturday night, say eight?"

"Let me see, hold on." Taking out my other phone, I pulled up the Calendar. "This weekend is taken. We can do it the following week, though. Or that Wednesday."

"A'ight, that Saturday good." Humming, I started to end the call. "Aye!" He suddenly called.

"What's up?" I questioned.

"It's good to see yo' ass ain't changed. Most niggas don't know how to stay authentic. It's good to know you haven't been corrupted, dead ass. That's what makes you a good businessman. That's reason niggas really fuck with you and pops tough."

I had to laugh at that. Martell must have been really grateful for me stopping Parker and his boy from killing his cousin. "Most definitely. Aye, I'm telling yo' ass now. If you don't make that meet Saturday, I'm canceling y'all shit and selling those bitches. I got a couple niggas trying to get those damn machine guns y'all got. But come Sunday, if I still have them, they're gone."

"Nah, don't do that. I'll be there, dead ass. If

something comes up though—"

"The reason doesn't matter. Those bitches gonna be gone come that Sunday, and I'm done fucking with y'all. I've been holding those damn guns for to gotdamn long for you bitches—"

"Nigga, yo' ass done racked up a fucking storage fee of thirty thousand. Fuck are you talking about? Mothafucka we're paying yo' ass for holding those gotdamn guns for us." He snapped.

Once again, I laughed while shrugging. "I don't care. Those bitches got to go. Then you niggas wanna add onto that shit every other week—"

"Mike, we're paying you for all that shit, fuck are you talking about? Man, is yo' ass high? You're talking straight bullshit right now. Man, regardless, I'mma be there Saturday."

"A'ight. I'll get up with you." With that, I ended the call then went back into the room. Kimmy was sitting up on the bed, rubbing her stomach. "You alright?"

Inhaling, she nodded. "Yeah, just another cramp is all."

I went over and sat beside her, leaning into the headboard. "You've been cramping all day. You're sure you don't wanna call the doctor?"

Kimmy's lips pursed, and she rolled her eyes at me. "That's a bit dramatic. No, I'm fine, though. If I start to hurt, then I'll call the doctor. These are just cramps...mmm." She moaned as she started rubbing her side. "Who are you calling?" She asked as I picked up my phone.

"Aye, Tasha. When you were eight, almost nine months pregnant, were you having cramps like most of the day?"

Kim pushed me. "You did not just call and ask her that shit." Laughing, she pushed me again. "You're so stupid."

"Hello, Mike?" Tasha called into the line.

"Yeah, what you say?"

She let out a breath. "I didn't have cramps at eight months—is Kim cramping?" I hummed in response. "Mike, she might be having contractions. When did she start having cramps?" She questioned.

"Shid, most of the day—"

"Mike! Most of the day? It sounds like she's having contractions. As in, her ass is in labor, and she should get to the hospital now. How far apart are the contractions, and how long are they?"

Kimmy let out another moan, and she began rocking. "Earlier, they were coming every fifteen minutes or so, shid, I don't even know for real. Now, though they seem to be five or six minutes apart and lasting for about...shid, I don't know seconds, a minute, something like that."

Tasha started laughing. "Oh, my God! Mike, take that damn girl to the hospital. She's in labor, man. What the fuck? Text me the hospital y'all

going to so I can come up there to be with Malik. He won't be able to go in there with y'all."
She explained.

"A'ight, I'll call you once we get to the hospital. Thanks, Tash."

"No problem. Make sure you call me, Mike."

Humming, I ended the call. "Come on, Kimmy, so I can take you to the hospital." Going into the closet, I grabbed the first dress I saw. When I went back in there, she looked bored. "Why the fuck you sitting there looking crazy for? Get up." I handed her the dress.

She motioned to herself. "Mike, there's nothing wrong with what I have on. Plus, I don't need to go to the hospital yet. I'm alright. How are you going to go by what Tasha said? That girl had one baby, twelve years ago..." Her words trailed off as she started rocking.

"Man, yo' ass going to the hospital. Malik." Shaking my son, I woke him up. "Come on, we're taking yo' moms to the hospital." Once those words left my mouth, he was up and out of the room, getting his shoes.

"I guess I'm coming since I don't have a say in the matter," Kimmy mumbled, getting up and grabbing her stuff.

Once we were in the truck, I sped to the hospital.

Chapter Fifteen

Mike

A Heart so Full

"Baby, you got this." I coached, kissing Kimmy's sweaty forehead while holding her hand as she pushed.

Once we made it to the hospital, everything seemed to go fast. Kimmy was having contractions and didn't know it. Not only that, but her water bag was leaking, which she didn't think much of. Shorty simply thought the babies were on her bladder. She figured that was the cause for her being moist and going to the damn bathroom frequently.

I wanted to choke the hell out of her crazy ass.

The cramps that she claimed weren't bad actually were. By the time we made it to the hospital, she was dilated to 8cm. Ironically, Kimmy continued to insist the cramping wasn't bad.

Kimmy wasn't shit how Tasha was when she went into labor. With all the damn crying and hollering that babe did, I thought her crazy ass would die from the yelling alone.

Kim wasn't screaming or doing any of that with her contractions. The pushing, however, was tiring her out.

"I can't." She panted out, shaking her head.

"Yes, you can, Kim. You got this, sweetheart. They're almost here. You just have to keep pushing." Mya said, wiping her forehead with a towel.

"Come on, Kimmy, I need you to give me another big push." The doctor instructed.

Once again, her head shook. "I can't. It's like he's not coming out."

"Kimberly, he's coming. You just have to push. I can see his head." The doctor told her. "Come on, push for me."

"Come on, baby, push." Staring at me, she nodded.

Kimmy's grip on my hand tightened as she leaned forward. A loud grunt left her mouth as she pushed hard. Kim fell back on the bed, panting. A second later, we heard the baby crying.

"You did good, baby. One more to go, and you're done." Mya grinned, comforting Kim. It seemed to be working as she began relaxing.

"Daddy, you want to cut the umbilical cord?" The doctor questioned.

"Yeah." I was too damn excited as I let Kim go, then went and cut the cord. After I did, the nurse took him, doing everything she was supposed to before handing him to me. I had just leaned the baby down for Kimmy to see him when she began moaning.

"Ooh, I think the other one's coming," Kimmy whined while grabbing my shirt.

"I'll take him." Mya quickly took the baby from me.

The second time was better and smoother than the first. After two big pushes, there was a second cry. Grabbing the cup of water on the side table, I brought the straw to her dry lips.

"Thank you." Kim panted out after drinking the iced cold water. "I want my babies." She breathed out as the doctor was talking.

"Congrats, you have two beautiful baby boys." The doctor told us, smiling. After cutting the second umbilical cord, the nurse cleaned him off. "You ready for babies?" She questioned, glancing from me to Kim.

"Yes. I want my babies." Kim's arms were out, and the nurse placed the babies in them.

I expected to see them looking about, taking in everything, but the twin's eyes were closed. Taking my phone out, I began recording them.

"They're so beautiful." She mumbled, kissing the tops of their head. "God, they look just like Malik when he was born." She cooed with a smile. Kimmy must've been too loud as the first baby's face turned up into a mean mug, and his eyes slowly blinked open.

I couldn't help but start laughing. "Kim, you done pissed him off already."

"I swear he's ready to fight." Mya chuckled before her laughter died down.

"Mike, his eyes." Kimmy's tone was a mixture of surprise and concern as one blue eye, and a light brown eye stared back at us.

∞ ∞ ∞

"Heterochromia Iridium or Complete Heterochromia is what the babies have. Majority of the time, it doesn't affect the babies' eyesight, so there's no cause for concern. The condition is usually passed down through genetics." She pointed to me then motioned to my eyes. "Your eyes are blue, but there are specks of brown in them, which is called Central Heterochromia. Am I right to assume that the condition runs in your family?"

Not only did Malik share my eye color, so did my dad and grandfather. I never knew the color of my eyes was considered a condition. I thought they were normal. I've never been told differently. "It does."

"So, I'm going to say it's hereditary." She stated, trying to ease Kimmy's worry. "Mom, as I stated, usually, there's no cause for concern. Only time will confirm that." The doctor went on to tell us how rare it was for both babies to have complete heterochromia.

After hearing the doctor talk, I could see the tension in Kimmy's body leave as she relaxed. All the while, she did her Google search on the condition.

"I don't care what color their eyes are. As long as they're healthy, then I'm happy." She told her before looking at me.

I nodded in agreement with her. "Shid, their eyes look dope as fuck to me." Kim glared at me, and I laughed. "Shid, they are. My little dudes look good as fuck. They gonna be some little heartbreakers." Grabbing the twins from Kimmy and Mya, I started rocking them. "Ain't that right."

Their eyes were crazy, but it was beautiful as hell. It was ironic how they both had heterochromia, but the colors were reversed in different eyes.

"I'mma have to lock y'all down early. I can see now that you two gonna be trouble." I talked to my boys, chuckling and kissing the top of their heads. "Y'all some handsome little dudes already, and y'all looks ain't even came in yet."

"Girl, he took those babies and forgot all about us." Mya laughed along with Kim.

"He's irritating. Michael," Kimmy's loud voice grabbed my attention.

"What's up?"

"Milly is calling." She informed me. "They want to see the babies. Now that I know they're alright, we can let them come in."

After seeing the babies' eyes, Kimmy didn't want anyone to come into the room to see them because she didn't know if it was something wrong or not. Now that she knew it wasn't, her ass wanted my momma to come in.

I wasn't trying to hear anything she was saying. The truth was, I didn't feel like fighting with my momma over my damn sons. Once she came into the room, I already knew she was coming straight for them.

"Kim, I'll be back in a minute. Daddy's here." Mya told her, then came over and kissed the boys covered arms. "Y'all are so gorgeous. T-Mya will be back in a bit." She whispered, then left out the room.

"Babe, I'm about to tell her and Poppa to come in," Kimmy said while laughing at my irritable growl. "They're worried about the babies. Even though I told them they're fine, Milly isn't listening to me."

"Man, I don't care. She can wait." Going over to Kimmy, I leaned down and kissed her. "Just so you know, I'm fucking you up. With your—*I'm alright*—ass."

Kimmy let out a whine before laughing. "I was alright. I told you those contractions weren't bad to me. Hell, if anything, the pushing was the hard part." Looking down at the twins, she smiled. "Babe, they are so beautiful. I'm going to spank that one already." She pointed to our firstborn, who seemed to have a permanent scowl on his face. Laughing, Kimmy took him from me. "He was not ready to come out. He's mugging like he wants us to shut up." She chuckled while kissing his nose. "You are so handsome...Montavious..." Kimmy called him, then looked at me.

"Hell nah, man. We already said that wasn't happening." We weren't naming our son Montavious, Kimmy ass was crazy. "We'll come up with something. But that shit ain't it." I didn't like that damn name at all.

The slight tap on the door grabbed our attention. "That's probably Milly and Poppa," Kimmy said as the door was pushed open. I glared at Kim as my parents and Malik walked into the room. "They were worried." She whispered.

"Malik, come meet your brothers." I waved him over to me.

"Are they okay? Nana was worried something was wrong when we couldn't come back here." Malik was saying as he walked to me.

"Yeah, they're cool, healthy. The babies' eyes are different, though." Saying that got my mom's and dad's attention.

"Different? Different how?" They asked. I quickly ran down to them what the doctor told us.

My momma walked over to us, and I turned away from her slightly.

"Oh, that's what you meant. They have your great-great grandfather's eyes." My pops said, grinning.

That was news to me. I've never met my great-great grandad. He had passed on before I was born. "The doctor said it was hereditary," I told him, and he agreed.

"It is. Our damn eye color is dominant in our bloodline, which is rare as hell. Yet, look at us." He motioned between himself, Malik then me.

"So, they can see and everything?" Malik asked, staring at the babies.

Pulling him into my side, I kissed the top of his head. "Yeah, they can see. He's looking at you, ain't he?"

Malik laughed at that. "Yeah. Their eyes tight, though. One blue and one light brown. It looks dope."

Kimmy and my momma suddenly broke out laughing. My mom's hit me in the back as I kept turning away from her every time she tried getting close to the baby. "Mike, if you don't stop playing with me. I'm trying to hold my grandson." My moms grabbed our youngest, hugging him to her cheek. "You are such a cutie." She cooed him. "Sitting over here looking just like your daddy."

"Have you named them yet?" My dad asked

while taking the oldest from Kim.

My head shook. "Nope. Still don't have names yet."

"Good thing Nana's been thinking." My momma claimed as she began looking between the babies. "He's the oldest?" She motioned to the baby my dad held, and Kimmy nodded. "I can tell from how he's sitting there glaring." She laughed, kissing his hand.

"Little dude has been mugging since he got here," I told her while taking him from my dad. "So, what are these names you got?"

"Let me look at them." She glanced between the two. She pointed to the baby I held. "Millian—"

"I like that." Kimmy and I said at the same time.

She pointed to me. "The first name we'd agreed on." She laughed. "What's the other name, Milly?"

My momma smiled at the twin she was holding. "Killian. That's their name, Millian and Killian Payne."

"I like them. Mike, what do you think? Are these good, or do we need to pull from a hat?" Kimmy stared at me, nodding her head as if she wanted me to mimic her.

"You got no argument out of me, sweetheart. That's their names." My gaze settled on my sons. "What y'all think? Do you like Millian? What about you, Killian?" I asked them, making Kimmy laugh. Millian's mug didn't change. He looked like all he wanted was sleep, but we were stopping him from doing that. Whereas Killian was looking around, taking everything in.

"You were determined to use those names." My dad laughed, making my momma glare at him.

She snapped her fingers at him. "Shut up, Big Mike. Nobody asked you."

"What's that about, Milly?" Kim asked, looking between my folks.

My momma shot my dad another glare. "The boy's names are a few I picked out a while ago, just in case Mike ever had twins."

I had to laugh at that. I wasn't surprised, given she named Malik. She wouldn't be my momma if she didn't do that.

"How are we gonna know which is who?" Malik asked, rubbing Millian's arm. He then looked at Killian. "Yeah, how we gonna tell them apart?"

I pointed to Millian. "Little dude gonna make sure you know who he is. Look at how he's looking at you. That glare is permanent." I told him. "Besides, just look at their eyes. Millian's right eye is blue, and his left is brown. Killian's right is brown, and the left is blue. You'll catch on."

He nodded in understanding. "Y'all some handsome little dudes. Oh, let me take a picture of them. My momma wanna see them." Taking out his phone, he took some pictures.

There was another knock on the door before it was pushed open. Angel's head popped into the room. "We're coming in." She announced, walking into the room with the other three girls behind her.

"Hey, Milly, Big Mike," Angel spoke, giving them quick hugs. "Ooh, can I hold him? I promise I just washed my hands." She told my momma before taking Killian from her before she could say anything. "Oh, my God, you're so freaking cute. Y'all look at him." She said, showing him to the girls. "Ooh, I want him. You are so freaking handsome."

"Let me see him." Peaches tried to grab the baby from her, but Angel moved out of her reach.

"Girl, I just got him. You better ask Mike." Angel looked at me and started laughing. "That's why I got the baby from Milly. He looks like he's not sharing." Coming over to me, she looked down at Millian. "Oh, my God. Y'all, they really are twins. They are so cute—ooh, he's smiling at me." Angel gushed as Millian's mouth opened, forming into a smile.

"Ain't that some shit. Homie has been mugging since he's got here, now he wanna smile at you—what are you doing?" Angel grabbed the baby from me while I was talking.

"He wants me." She claimed, taking him over to the girls, showing him off.

"I feel so damn neglected. I can't get any type of love. You hoes didn't even say hey to me."

Kimmy glared at her girls hard before she broke out laughing. "Give me my damn babies."

"We're sorry, but we've been waiting on them forever." Missy chuckled, going over to Kimmy and hugging her. "Kim, Mike, they are so handsome."

"I know, I did my thing with them—"

Kimmy hit me in the stomach, laughing. "Shut up, you damn fool."

"Their eyes, is that normal? Did the doctor say anything?" Missy's gaze fell on the babies then back on us.

I noted the girls were paying attention, looking for the answer to that question. "It's rare, but it's something that happens. The doctor says there's no cause for concern yet, if ever for that matter. Y'all give me my babies. Mike's been hogging them since they came out. I held them twice." Kim complained, making me laugh.

"Man, yo' ass was tired. I was giving you a break." Taking my babies from Missy and Angel, I went over to Kim, giving her Millian. "Happy?"

She nodded, looking down at him. "Yes. Give me him too."

"Wait, what's their names?" Ebony asked, rubbing Killian's head.

"This mean one is Millian Royal Payne, and Mr. Wonderer here is Killian Loyal Payne. Babies, these are y'all, insane aunties." Kim introduced them, making her girls laugh.

"That's cute, and it matches. Millian, Killian. Oh, shit, they're about to be trouble." Peaches groan out before chuckling.

"Oh, most definitely, they are. So gone head and hide y'all daughters." Malik gloated, grinning hard as hell.

I broke out laughing. "On what you ain't lying though, G."

"I know you bet not be around nobody's daughter." Kimmy glared at Malik.

Malik rubbed his mouth while grinning. "Momma, what you mean? I don't go around nobody's daughters. Their daughters come around me. You can't blame them, I'm a handsome dude, and I play football. Momma, I'm cursed. The twins are too. All the girls have to do is look into their eyes, and it's over."

My pops fell out laughing as he grabbed Malik to him. "That's it! Y'all definitely can't help that you're cursed with looks and brains." His fist bumped with mine as I agreed.

"Oh, lord! We're keeping the twins away from these three. Malik, you're helpless at this point. We don't need y'all rubbing off on them." Kimmy laughed, hitting me.

"I swear they're crazy. Still, they're not lying, though." Angel agreed. "They are going to be trouble. Y'all, I want twins. Bitch, I want them." Angel whined while rubbing their feet. "I really want them, y'all, like for real, I do."

I ignored Angel's crazy ass and brought my attention to Kim. "Royal and Loyal?" Those names were new to me.

"They didn't have middle names, and I just thought of those while looking at them." She explained while looking down at our babies. "You don't like them?"

"Royal and Loyal..." I spoke out loud, trying them out. "Millian Royal and Killian Loyal Payne." Nodding, I shrugged. "The names sound right together. I like it." Leaning over Kim, I kissed her. "You done gave me two beautiful ass boys. Thank you."

"You're welcome." She kissed me back.

My gaze fell on my sons, and my damn heart was filled with so many emotions. Given how things were between us several months ago and how I felt during that time, I didn't think I could ever love shorty more than I already did. Just looking at her holding my sons at that moment, the boys she'd given birth to, proved me wrong.

My damn heart was fucking full.

All the previous bullshit didn't matter anymore, given what it brought us. Hell, had she not confessed any of that bullshit to me. I would've never slipped up, and we wouldn't be here.

Child's play was how I now saw the situation only because of the ending outcome.

"Babe, what's wrong?" Kimmy's face came into my view.

My head shook. "Nothing." Grabbing hold of the nape of her neck, I kissed her. "Ain't shit wrong, we're good, sweetheart." My lips pressed into hers once more before my eyes fell on my twins, then Malik, who stood beside me. Pulling him into my side, I kissed the top of his head.

My heart was so gotdamn full, and I wouldn't have wanted it any other way.

Chapter Sixteen

Kimmy

Houseguest...Maybe? I Think The Fuck Not...

My hand moved hastily, ushering Mya inside with her bags. "Hurry up." I whispered-shouted for her slow ass to get in the damn house. I wanted all her damn luggage put up before Mike saw it.

Since I had the babies a week ago, Mike hadn't left my side, which I was beyond thankful for. I knew having twin babies would be tough, so mentally, I was prepared, physically; however, not so much. Having two six-pound babies definitely took its toll on my body. Mike being home with me during that entire time was so much help.

Now that he had to get back to work, I knew handling two boys on my own would take more of a toll. I got my first taste the day before—which was my first time with the boys on my own. The shit wasn't pretty.

They were on two different feeding schedules, which was weird to me, yet it was easier to handle one at a time.

Until I realized once I've finished taking care of one and getting him back to sleep. The other woke up, and I had to do the same routine again. The thing I found crazy was they didn't sleep how newborn babies should have. With Malik, all he did was eat, poop and sleep. The twins didn't, however. They seemed too curious about what was going on around them to sleep. They were constantly taking everything in.

It was their curiosity that wouldn't allow me to sleep. I couldn't pass out with either one still awake.

"I'm coming." She whispered, dragging her suitcase into the house. "Where's Mike?"

I motioned to the stairs. "He's feeding Millian. So, he'll be occupied for a minute."

"Okay, I got like two more bags in the car." She said, giving me her suitcase.

I glared at her. I didn't know why she had to pack so gotdamn much. "Girl, you can bring that shit in tomorrow when he goes to work."

"So, what are you going to tell him when day five hit, and he wonders why I'm still here?" Mya questioned.

I didn't know what I was going to tell him. I knew he was going to be pissed.

"Why are you here now?" Mike asked, walking into the kitchen with both babies in his arms. Mya quickly pushed her suitcase under the counter.

"I asked her to come over and help with the twins. With you going back to work and all. Here, give me him." I grabbed Killian from him. Smiling down at my handsome little man, I kissed his spitty mouth.

Mike hummed at that. "At six o'clock, though? And while I'm here? What kind of help is she gonna be?" He asked.

My mouth opened, then closed as I thought about how to respond. I wanted to slap the hell out of Mya's tack-headed ass. I told her to come earlier that day while Mike was actually at work.

I couldn't really complain because I knew she had to get things in order before moving in with us for a few weeks.

"A lot of help." It was my only defense. "Plus, she wanted to see her nephews—"

"I got them some stuff that I wanted to bring by." Mya chimed in, helping me out.

Mike glanced between the two of us and shook his head. "Whatever the fuck it is, no. I don't know what the fuck y'all up to, and I don't care. But no." Grabbing the front of my shirt, he kissed me, then took the two bottles from the warmer. "Get that damn girl out of here. Give me him. Finish doing whatever the fuck it is y'all doing." He kissed me once more, then took the baby from me. "Bye, Mya." He called over his shoulder as he left the kitchen.

"I can't stand him. That nigga do know we're family, right? Like, I should be able to come and go as I please with no complaints from him. You need to check his ass." Mya glared at the hallway that Mike went down, making me laugh.

Everything she said, I felt, was true. However, Mike just didn't care for people to come to the house.

"Girl, I'm not about to check shit. You just go bring your things in while I keep him occupied. Mya, I hope you don't have a shit load of stuff." Grabbing my cranberry juice from the fridge. I kissed my sister on the cheek. "Thanks for coming, baby."

"Of course, I was coming. You know I'm always here when you need me." She returned my kiss then gave me a little shove. "Now, gon' go suck up to that man."

Laughing, I left the kitchen, going upstairs to our bedroom. Mike lay on the bed talking to the twins like he'd done since they were in my womb. I didn't say anything at first, just watched him interact with his boys. Mike was nothing shy of amazing when it came to taking care of our kids. I loved how he loved our boys, and he wasn't afraid of showing it either.

"I'mma need y'all to take it easy on your momma. I mean, give her a little hard time but not too much. Because if y'all start acting the fuck up too much, I'mma get punished for that shit. Then she gonna want to invite mothafuckas here for help. She already got her worrisome ass sister here. So, I'mma need y'all to chill out." Mike whispered to them. I wanted so badly to smack him upside the head for telling the boys some mess like that. "Y'all do this for me, and y'all gonna be straight. Otherwise, I'm shipping y'all asses off to Nana and Pop's."

I couldn't hold it in as I broke out laughing. "Why are you telling them some mess like that, Michael. If anything, you're the one who's going to be shipped off to your folk's house, not them. Something is seriously wrong with you." Kissing my babies, I pushed Mike out of the way. "Don't listen to your daddy. He doesn't know what he's talking about." I kissed the pair once more before looking at Mike. "You need to stop being so mean. If Mya wants to come over and visit us, she can."

Mike shrugged. "I'm not mean. I just don't like my space to be invaded. Ain't shit wrong with me wanting my damn privacy. And I don't mind your people coming over here for a couple of hours. As long as they know when it's time to go home." His explanation had my eyes rolling. "Is that girl gone?"

I hit him in the chest. "No, she's not. I told Mya she could spend the night here. I mean, she just got here, plus it's getting dark outside, and I don't want her driving home alone."

"Kim, she drove here in the damn dark. What the fuck are you talking about?" Taking in my glaring face, he shook his head. "A'ight man, whatever—why the fuck you smiling for?"

"Because I love you. Give me a kiss." My lips puckered up.

Shaking his head, he pressed his lips into mine. "Kim, yo' ass ain't slick. I know you up to something with Mya's ass, and the answer is no."

A groan left my mouth as he went to pull away. Grabbing the front of his shirt, I brought him back on the bed. "Okay, whatever we have going on, we'll leave you out of it, I promise. Now kiss me."

Shaking his head, Mike looked at the twins. "Y'all momma nasty, she better chill out before I have her ass folded the fuck up, knowing she's not healed yet—"

"Oh, my God!" I broke out laughing. "Why would you say that to them? What is wrong with you, Mike? Oh, my God, dude, why?"

"I'm just saying, shid, I'm sex-deprived like a mothafucka. Then you wanna sleep with yo' ass all on me." He complained, making me laugh. "Shid, I'm dead serious."

Laughing, I kissed him. "Mike, we always sleep like that, though. So, because we can't have sex right now, you don't want my ass all on you?"

He started nodding. "That's exactly what I'm

saying. You need to keep your ass off of me. I can see if I could still fuck your mouth, but since you wanna breastfeed, that's out of the question."

My hand covered my face as I hollered out laughing. The man had gone a week without sex and didn't know how to handle that shit. It was so damn funny hearing him complain about it, however.

"You're so damn irritating. Baby, I'm sorry, but you knew this would happen after I had the babies. So, you should've been preparing yourself for this drought." I laughed at his glare. "When the babies go to sleep, I can play with it."

"If you ain't talking about letting my dick play with your tonsils—"

Laughing, I hit him. "I'm not talking about that. Now give me a kiss. And none of that little pecking shit you've been giving me either." My tongue ran over his bottom then top lip before I sucked on it. Mike let out a groan, kissing me back. A groan soon left my mouth as one of the twins started crying. "I'll get him."

Rolling off my side, I glanced at the twins. Killian was crying as Millian's eyes furrowed into a little tired glare. "Come on, momma's Buddha baby." Kissing his head, I picked him up. "Babe, Millian's ass is going to be mean as hell. It doesn't make sense how he's always glaring. He didn't even have to mug Killian like that." My baby was going to be mean for no reason.

Mike pointed to me as he picked Millian up. "All this is your damn fault. Yo ass used to jap the fuck out for no damn reason."

My eyes rolled at him as I grabbed a pamper. "Stop lying, no, I wasn't. I only snapped when somebody pissed me off. So, don't even do that. If anything, he gets it from you. Mike, you're mean as hell to everybody except for Malik, Milly, and Poppa."

"So, what. Plus, I'm nice to your mean ass... get that." He motioned to his phone.

I glared at him as I held the folded shitty diaper in my hand. Rolling my eyes at him, I grabbed his phone. Seeing Tasha's name on the screen, I sighed. "It's Tasha."

His hand waved. "She don't want shit. I'll call her back."

I tossed his phone to the side. I didn't know what was going on with her, but she had been blowing him up a lot lately. Mike's phone chimed with a text. Tasha's name popped up on the screen once more. Unlocking the phone, I read the message.

Tasha: *Hey Mike, I know it's late but can you call me back so we can talk.*

I read out loud. I continued to read the previous messages as well.

Tasha: *Mike, please answer the phone. You didn't have to leave.*

Tasha: *I wasn't expecting that to happen. It just did. Mike, it doesn't have to be made into something bad. We do have a child together.*

I read the first message that came in two days ago, then the second one. I looked at Mike, waiting on him to respond to the texts I'd read.

Mike kissed Millian's nose, laughing. "Don't have drunk sex with crazy bitches without strapping up. Those mothafuckas will turn into clingy ass baby momma's. Bitches you can't get rid of."

My eyes closed as I rubbed my forehead. Was I surprised by what was leaving his mouth? Yes. Should I have been? Hell no, because he talked to Malik the same way when he was a baby.

"Michael…" I laughed, remembering feeling that same way twelve years ago. "Babe, stop talking to him like that. He has one time to cuss, and I'm whooping your ass. Think I'm playing."

Reaching over, he took Killian from me. "Don't have crazy ass girlfriends either. I don't care how much you love them. Leave those mothafuckas alone. They'll drive yo' ass insane. Like y'all gotdamn momma does me. Shorty worrisome as hell."

"You gonna make me hurt you, watch. Anyways, what is Tasha talking about?" I questioned, pointing to the phone.

"It wasn't shit. Tasha's crazy ass tried to fuck

me the other day. Shorty figured since yo' ass out of commission, then I'll fuck her."

My hands covered my face at his terminology of why we weren't having sex. Did I think he messed around with that damn woman? No. From how Tasha tried to vaguely imply that they messed around flung that thought right out my mind. Now, I might've believed it had she outright said the shit.

"Something is really wrong with you. I'm out of commission, Michael?" He got on my damn nerves, I swear.

He shrugged at that. "Shid, you are. But her ass called me about Malik, and since I was out that way, I stopped over. Shorty started off talking about Malik but then tried to fuck. Baby was trying hard as hell, too; I mean desperate as fuck. She had on these little tight-ass lace shorts." Mike let out a loud groan. "My ass damn near gave in. You should've seen me running out that damn house." Mike quickly jumped off the bed as I went to smack the shit out of his ass. "I know damn well yo' ass wasn't about to hit me."

"Yes, the fuck I was and still am while your stupid ass playing. That shit ain't even funny. Mike, I'll kill the fuck out of you. Don't play with me."

Mike grabbed my wrist, stopping me from hitting him. He thought the shit was funny when I was really about to try and knock his damn head off.

"Man, calm yo' ass down. You know damn well I wasn't even tempted to fuck her crazy ass."

Jerking me to him, he trapped my arms at my side. "You know I was just fucking with you. My dick won't even move for Tasha, dead ass." He really thought the shit was funny.

Nodding, my eyes rolled at him. "You think your ugly ass cute when you're not. I'll beat yo' ass, Mike."

"Baby, I know you will—"

I broke out laughing. "You're not funny, for real. Let me go." Biting at his bottom lip, I kissed him. "Irritating ass."

"I wouldn't fuck her, though. I won't feel right, knowing I got a nut off and you can't. I'mma wait this shit out with you. We're both out of commission."

All I could do was laugh at his ass. "You're so stupid. But I appreciate your thoughtfulness." Standing on my tiptoes, I kissed him. "I love you."

"I know you do." My lips popped, and he kissed me again. "I love you too, Kimberly." His arms tightened around my waist as he walked me to the bed. "Now, can we go to sleep?"

Pecking his lips, I pulled away from him. "We can go to bed. I'm tired, honestly. Your son's kept me up all day." I told him while pulling off my shirt. Getting on the bed, I pulled my sleeping babies onto my chest. That was how Mike and I slept since the babies came home. The twins took turns sleeping on us. I wasn't ready for them to sleep in their bed or bassinet. I wanted them close to me, and apparently, Mike felt the same way because he didn't complain about them being in our room, not once.

∞∞∞

The constant blurring ringtone woke me out of my sleep. Seeing that it was Mike's phone, I rejected the call, only to have it start ringing once again. Tasha's name flashed on the screen. Denying the call once more, I looked at the time to see that it was two in the damn morning. Mike's phone pinged with a text from Tasha.

Tasha: *Please call me it's important.*

The phone started ringing once again. Growling, I answered the call. "Girl, why the fuck are you calling us at two in the fucking morning. We have two newborns that are fucking sleeping." I was pissed off that the bitch kept blowing his fucking phone up.

"Kim, I'm sorry for calling this late, but I really need to speak with Mike. It's important." She insisted.

Sighing, I laid back down, ready to hang up on her. "Look, we're sleeping. He'll call you in the morning—"

"Kim, I need to talk to him now. The house caught fire." She blurted out before breaking into sobs.

"Wait, what?" I knew I heard her wrong. I had to have because if I didn't. Why the hell didn't she lead with that?

"The house caught fire. I almost didn't make it out." She cried hard. "I had just woken up in time to get out. Oh, God, my house." Tasha bawled. The blurring sirens in the background let me know it was real.

"Babe…" I shook Mike, who had the twins on his bare chest, sleeping. Mike was out of it. I made a grab for the baby closest to me, and Mike quickly grabbed my wrist. Glancing at me through sleepy eyes, he let my wrist go. "Babe, Tasha's on the phone. She said the house caught fire."

Mike stared at me for a long while before his eyes closed, and he fell back to sleep. I shook him. A glare formed on his face, and the stare he gave said so much. "Man, what?"

"Tasha said the house caught fire. The firemen are there. I can hear them in the background." I explained to him.

A breath left his mouth as a hand ran over his face. "Is she hurt?" He asked.

"Are you hurt?" I repeated his question.

"No, I'm not. I got out before the fire could reach me." She explained.

I relayed what she said.

Mike glared at me. "She ain't hurt, and Malik isn't there. What the fuck does she want me to do?

If the firemen are there, they'll take care of it. That's their fucking job, not mine. I don't know why she's calling me like I can do something." He snapped, pissed.

He could be so gotdamn mean and insensitive as hell at times. Although he was harsh, I had to agree with him. I didn't know why she called us at two in the morning. Especially when she had already called the police and fire department. What was she really expecting Mike to do? Go get her? If Malik was at home, Mike would've flown his ass to that house to get his son. He wasn't moving for Tasha, however.

After Mike said all of that, I didn't know what to say to the girl. "Look, Tasha, the police and fire department is there. I don't know what you're expecting Mike to do exactly."

"I need him to come and get me. That's the least he could fucking do considering we just lost mostly every fucking thing." She yelled, sounding pissed off. "Kim, put my baby daddy on the fucking phone." She snapped at me.

Pulling the phone from my ear, I looked at it. "Bitch…" I caught my tongue before I could go off on her ass. It was too gotdamn early. I was exhausted and still sleepy. "Look, Mike isn't coming to pick you up. He's asleep with the twins. If you can't go back into the house, get yourself a room for the night. We'll call and check on you in the morning."

"Bitch, put Mike on the fucking phone—"

I hung up on her. What that bitch wasn't going to do was be disrespectful when she was calling us for help. After turning off his phone, I rolled over and went back to sleep.

∞∞∞

The continuous blurring of the doorbell woke the twins up, making them cry. "I got it." Mike let out an irritable growl. "Who the fuck is here at three in the fucking morning." Pissed, he snatched open the nightstand and grabbed his gun as well as the tablet. "What?" He barked at the knocking on our room door.

Seeing Mya's head pop into the room had me sitting up. "Tasha's at the door. She's on the porch crying."

Mike looked at the camera screen and sighed. "What the fuck does she want?"

Pulling down my bra, I started feeding the babies, and immediately the pair's crying stopped. "Probably because you didn't go pick her ass up when she called about the house."

Mike glanced at me tiredly. "What about the house?"

My eyes rolled at him. "Remember she called because the house caught fire?"

Sighing, he began tapping on the screen, and a few seconds later, the doorbell stopped ringing.

Mike sat the tablet on the nightstand, then laid back down. "Mya, take yo' ass back to bed." He instructed as his arm went over his eyes.

Looking at him, I laughed. "Babe, go to the door. Otherwise, she's going to be banging all gotdamn morning. She's not going to leave." I knew for sure if Mike didn't open the door, homegirl would stay outside all damn morning. Mike's low snores had my brows furrowing. It wasn't even a whole damn minute before he told Mya to go back to bed and his ass was out of it. My baby was exhausted.

Although it had only been two days since Mike went back to work, I believed he really was tired. The moment he stepped through those doors, he was in full daddy mode, doing his part. The man didn't go to sleep until we did.

"Babe—"

"Kim, feed the babies and leave me the fuck alone." Grabbing the pillow, he pulled it over his face. Shaking my head at him, I left him alone as I continued feeding my babies.

I had just nodded off when my back hit the headboard hard, as I was jerked awake from the sudden blurring of my ringtone. The tune sounded louder than it actually was. Sighing, I looked down at the twins to see my nipples sitting on their bottom lips. Their mouths were parted wide, and they were out, just like their daddy.

I began dozing off when my phone started

ringing again. Laying the twins down, I reached over and grabbed my phone. Seeing Malik's name, I quickly answered it.

"Hey, babe, what's up? Is something wrong?" I immediately became worried, thinking something happened, given he was calling at damn near four in the morning.

"Hey, momma, I'm sorry for waking you up. My mom just called me crying, saying the house had caught fire. She says she's outside, but nobody's answering the door. Momma, she's crying bad. Can you make sure she's not hurt or anything? I was going to wake Jerron up and see if he'll bring me home—"

"No, baby, don't wake Ron up. I want you to go back to sleep and not to worry. I spoke with your mom, and she told me she wasn't hurt—"

"Are you sure? She's crying hard like she's hurt or something." Malik questioned, concerned.

I couldn't stop the fucking glare from coming to my face. Tasha was a twisted ass bitch. I didn't understand why the fuck she would even call Malik, worrying him with that bullshit, especially when her dumb ass wasn't hurt. "Baby, I'm positive she's alright. Now go back to sleep. I'll call you in the morning, okay."

He let out a heavy breath. "Alright. Are you going to let her in the house?"

My vision went black as my eyes rolled hard and long. "Yes, Malik. I'm going to open the door.

Now, go to bed. Love you."

Once again, he sighed worriedly into the line. "Alright, I love you too, momma."

After hanging up the phone, I reached over and slapped the shit out of Mike. He jumped up out of his sleep so fast, looking murderous, and had I not been pissed off, I probably would've been scared.

"Bitch, you done lost yo' mothafuckin' mind slapping me like you're fucking stupid—"

My finger jabbed in his face. "First off, lower your fuckin' voice before you wake up the babies. Secondly, you better go to the fuckin' door before I do, and I beat Tasha's trifling ass. The bitch called, waking Malik up, crying about the damn fire. Now, he's worried and calling, thinking her stupid ass hurt. When she's not, the dumb hoe told me she wasn't." I was pissed off yet wasn't surprised that Tasha called Malik. She knew that was her only way to get Mike to do shit for her.

"Dumb ass bitch coming over beating down the bell, like she's fucking stupid. Stupid, trifling ass bitch." Still fussing, I snatched the blanket up to my shoulder, covering myself and my babies.

"Kimmy, if yo' dumb ass hit me like that again, I'm beating the fuck out of you." He threatened.

I shrugged. "Then we're going to be some fighting bitches. Now, get rid of the hoe before she calls Malik again." The entire time I spoke, Mike was mugging the hell out of me. "Go—ow!"

"Stupid ass mothafucka!" He pushed my head into the pillow before, letting my hair go.

Grabbing his pillow, I threw it at him. However, I broke out laughing. "Dumb ass gonna pull my damn hair." Mike jerked the shit out of my head by snatching my hair. Looking at the empty spot behind the twins, I groaned out a chuckle. "Ignorant ass gonna hurt my damn head." I fussed while making myself comfortable once again.

Glancing down at my babies to check on them, I laughed, seeing them both awake, staring at me with those beautiful, curious mismatched eyes of theirs. "I swear y'all daddy is a damn punk." Sighing, I pulled them closer to me as I tried to fall back to sleep. After a while, I threw the covers from my body then got up. I knew I wasn't going to be able to fall asleep again. "Come on, let's go see what's going on downstairs." After pulling on my shirt, we left the room once I had the babies securely in my arms.

"Yo' ass shouldn't have called Malik with that bullshit, Tasha." Mike was fussing at her as we made it to the bottom of the stairs. "You got to be the stupidest mothafucka in the world, man. Why would you want to worry him like that? Especially when yo' ass ain't even fucking hurt. Then you bring yo' ass here, waking us the fuck up. What the fuck are you looking for me to do?"

Once I heard him going off, I stopped on the stairs and sat down to see how Mike would handle the situation. Also, I wanted to know what she would say to him.

Tasha sat on the couch sobbing as Mike fussed at her. "What do I expect you to do? What do you mean, Mike?"

"Just how it sounds, Tash." My eyes rolled at the pet name he used.

She sniffled, trying to calm herself down. "I figured you'd at least let me stay here until I found something else. Do you not understand that the house our son lives in is now destroyed? We don't have anywhere to stay, Mike." She cried to him.

Mike let out a heavy sigh. "Tasha, Malik's gonna always have somewhere to go. Shid, this is his crib too. Yo' place wasn't his only home. As far as you, sweetheart, yo' ass can't stay here. You already know that, though, not after that bullshit you pulled the other day with trying to fuck me." He told her, and I couldn't help but glare at the living room entrance. I wanted to go in there and slap her ass so bad.

"Mike, I don't care about what happened between us. I don't have anywhere else to go." She cried.

"You got places to go. Yo' ass just wanna come stay here, and you're not, Tasha. Shid, you might not care that you just tried to fuck me, but I do."

"Wow, Mike, seriously? How the hell you're going to assume I have somewhere else to go? If I did, do you think this would've been the first place I'd come to?" She questioned, and I nodded instantly, knowing for a fact that Mike would always be the first person she ran to.

I don't know why she thought Mike was responsible for taking care of her because they had a child together. If Tasha didn't have feelings for Mike still, I wouldn't even mind her staying at the house. Yet after learning what she tried with him the other day, I didn't want her ass under the same roof with me. And it wasn't because I didn't trust Mike not to fuck her, but simply because of her ass.

"This is beyond fucked up, Mike. How do you think Malik is going to feel when he finds out you put his momma out on the streets?" She continued to bawl.

My vision went black as I rolled my eyes hard as hell. Of course, she was going to bring Malik into the mix. She used his name for everything to get what she wanted from Mike's ass.

"I don't give a fuck what he gonna think. I've already told yo' ass that shit you do by using Malik to get what you want from me is done with. I'm not responsible for you, Tasha. I don't know why I have to keep telling yo' ass that shit." He told her, and I could imagine him shrugging nonchalantly. "You got your folks crib and yo' homegirls who you can stay with. Those the mothafuckas who's houses you should be at, not mine." My head was nodding vigorously in agreement with everything he said.

"Mike, I know that. I'm not asking you to take care of me. I'm simply asking you to let me stay here until I get back on my feet. I don't want to be separated from Malik. Plus, I don't want to go to my parents' house because we barely get along. And my homegirls have kids. I can't go invading their damn spaces with Malik and me."

Once again, my eyes rolled hard at the reasons she gave. Even so, I shrugged. As much as her friends and their gotdamn kids stay with her, breaking up mostly everything of Malik's. They should welcome her ass in with opened arms.

"Malik's not staying with yo' people. He can live with me until you get back on your feet. So, call whoever you need to and set something up."

"No, Mike—"

"Tasha, shut the fuck up, damn. We're not about to go back and forth on this bullshit. Yo' ass ain't staying here. It's that fuckin' simple. Malik is, though—stop all that fucking crying." He snapped, pissed off. "Man, it's too gotdamn early for this bullshit. You can sleep here tonight but in the morning, call yo' people. You can take the guest room next to Mya's. And don't be roaming all through my fucking house."

"Let me talk to Kim about staying here—" She started saying, but he quickly cut her off.

"I just told yo' ass you weren't staying here. Kimmy can't say if you can live here or not. The fuck? She most definitely ain't about to agree with the shit now that she knows yo' ass tried to fuck me —"

"You told her that? Why would you even do

that?" Tasha's words trailed off as Killian started to whine.

My arm started to bounce as I shushed him. Mike soon appeared at the living room entrance. Once he saw me on the stairs, his head shook.

"Don't say anything. Let's just go back to bed." I told him, and he came over and grabbed the babies from me. Glancing over him, Tasha stood there looking at us. My eyes rolled hard as hell at her before I turned and went back upstairs. It took everything in me not to go down there and knock Tasha dead in her shit. All because her simple-minded ass called Malik.

Once we made it into the room, I got in the bed. "You already know she's going to call Malik crying about not having anywhere to stay."

"I don't give a fuck what she does. That crazy mothafucka ain't staying here. Now, take yo' nosy ass back to bed. The three of y'all go to sleep." I turned to see him laying the babies in their bassinets before he got in behind me. I said nothing else as his arms went around my waist, and I slowly fell asleep.

Chapter Seventeen

Kimmy

Lying Ass Insane Baby Momma

"Baby, if Mike talked to me like he did her, everything in that damn living room would've been broken because we would've been banging," Mya exclaimed before looking down the hallway. "Tink would beat your daddy's ass. Yes, I will." She cooed to the twins.

I had to agree with her. Although I wasn't there from the start of their conversation, I knew how Mike's mouth was. He would definitely make you want to fight him. Still, Tasha wasn't stupid enough to try that hitting shit with Mike. Homeboy hit back and hard, plus I'd drag her if she tried.

I laughed at Mya as she checked to make sure Mike wasn't coming down the hall. "Scary ass. But shit, that's her own fault. I don't even know why she brought her ass here, to begin with. Then she had the nerve to think he would let her stay here. But check this. He tells her ass no, and she says—*well, let me talk to Kim about it.*" The irony of her audacity had me laughing. "Like, bitch, you just tried to fuck him. Hoe, I'm not even about to let your tack-headed ass live here, the fuck. Something is wrong with her ass. Homegirl needs to find herself a man and let go of that hope of them being together. Shid, I don't understand why she wants his dirty ass to begin with."

Mya's face changed from goofy to completely blank in seconds. "The same damn reason you're still with his ass."

My eyes rolled at that. "What Mike and I have, they never had ever. So, our reason is completely different. Besides, they don't have a relationship aside from co-parenting. Either way, she needs to find her a damn man..." my words trailed off as I stared at my sister, who was smiling at her nephews.

Mya glanced at me, then did a double-take. "What?"

I pointed to the hallway. "Maybe you should try to get with her—"

"Ha!" She hollered out loudly. "Y'all momma's a damn fool. Yes, she is. Shorty done lost her whole gotdamn mind." She told the twins, still laughing. "I don't wanna be with nobody who y'all daddy slept with. That's trifling."

Grabbing a piece of sausage, I threw it at her. "Bitch, don't do that. Mike slept with her ass over twelve years ago and never again." Although I defended my baby, I couldn't help but laugh. "Mya, I'm being dead serious, for real. Make her one of your girlfriends."

Mya shook her head. "No. She's not my type. I don't like crazy chicks—"

"Hoe, stop lying. Did you forget yo' ass was messing around with one of my best friends, who I know for a fact is crazy as hell?" I pointed out, and she waved me off.

"Missy was different, though, plus I knew how she was before I started messing with her. Tasha's ass is on a whole other level of crazy. She's the type of mothafucka you'll have to shoot, and I'm not trying to go to jail." She chuckled while kissing the baby's feet. "Anyways, you talked to daddy?"

I nodded as I tasted the fried potatoes. "Mmhm. We talked last night. He wants to see the twins. I told him I'll bring them by later." After reuniting with my father, we talked nonstop. I was really enjoying talking to him again. "I was going to have him meet us at my house." I glanced at her to see how she was going to react.

"Okay. I'll come with you. Just let me know what time y'all meeting up."

"So..." I began saying. "I was thinking of letting him move in there. I mean, I'm not living there, and it's just sitting up empty and fully furnished. He could look after the place, plus he'll have his own space. What do you think?"

"What she thinks about what?" Mike asked, coming into the kitchen. Kissing the side of my head, he reached over and grabbed a piece of bacon.

"About Kareem moving into my house," I informed him. "What do you think about that?"

He shrugged. "Shid, I don't care what you do with that house." He took another piece of bacon then turned his attention to Mya. "Get out their damn faces." He glared at her, making me laugh. He couldn't help but fuck with Mya.

"Babies, Tinka here!" Missy's loud voice came from the hallway.

Mike glanced down the hall, then at me. "I know that mothafucka don't have a gotdamn key to my crib, Kimberly." He fussed, sounding pissed.

My hand flicked at him. "No, Michael, she doesn't. I left the door unlocked for her. And if she did, so what? I mean, it'll be fair if all my girls have a key, seeing as I have keys to their houses. Besides, this is my house just as much as it is yours."

"Ha!" Missy laughed, coming into the kitchen. "Mikey, I don't know why you wanna start with me this morning." Missy bumped into him before dropping a bunch of damn bags. She then went to the sink and washed her hands. "Come here, Tinka babies." She cooed, sliding in front of Mya without acknowledging her.

The head that popped into the hallway had me doing a double-take. "Ah!" I hollered as my arms went out. "Ang!" Meeting her halfway, I hugged her tightly. "When did you get in?" Although I saw Angel every other couple of weeks, that didn't change the fact I missed her like crazy.

"We got in late last night. After we dropped the kids off at Mom B's house, we went home and passed out." She explained while hugging Mike. "Hey, Mikey. Let me see my nephews with them handsome selves." She moved around him before looking at me. "But, yeah, we got in late as hell."

"They did, though. She was tired too because she passed out in my bed, and we cuddled all night. Until Parker's ol' horny ass came in and took her from me." Missy chimed in as Angel moved over to her. Like Missy had done, Angel slid in front of Mya without acknowledging her. The action caused my sister to roll her eyes and laugh, but she didn't say anything.

"Y'all childish. Get the fuck off of my damn sister. Irritating asses." Looking at Mya, I laughed, seeing that she was staring at Missy's ass. Turning off the stove, I made Mike's plate, then Mya's. After getting them together, I fixed my own, then sat beside Mike.

"Good morning," Tasha spoke, walking into the kitchen.

My two best friends glanced at her, then did a double-take before their gaze fell on me. "What the fuck is she doing here?" The pair asked in unison.

After eating a fork full of eggs, I pointed the

utensil at Tasha. "Somehow, her house caught fire, and she came here at damn three, almost four in the morning for some reason."

"She's staying here?" They once again spoke at once.

My head shook. "Not at all. Homegirl to gotdamn messy for all that. And I'm not about to let my peace be invaded with her energy. It's bad enough Mike invading my shit—"

"Don't be lying. I haven't invaded yo' ass for a good week, and I'm having withdrawals." Of course, he would twist my meaning around and make it about sex.

I ignored him and continued talking to my girls. "Y'all have to excuse him. This is the longest he's ever been without sex. So, he's really going through it." Laughing, I kissed the side of his head. "He knows I'mma make it up to him once I'm all better."

Grabbing my chin, he turned my face toward his. Mike kissed me full on, yet he pulled away before I could get into the kiss. "Oh, you most definitely are." He claimed while rubbing my ass. His attention then went across the island. "Don't sit at that fucking table. You see all this space here." He told Tasha, motioning to the counter.

Angel broke out laughing. "Mike's ass don't play about his damn sex table. Y'all know I still can't get that image out my head." She hit Missy. "Bitch, if only you saw how he had her ass. He was laying that shit into Kim's ass. But the fact his ass didn't stop when I walked in." She broke out laughing, causing Mike to do the same thing.

All the while, I groaned. I loved my best friends so much, yet there were parts of my life I didn't think I had to share with them. My sex life was one of the aspects I wanted to keep private. Although they were cool and open about putting their shit out to us—which I was all ears for— I didn't want my shit out. And it wasn't out of embarrassment or shame. I just didn't think that every single thing that went on in our lives needed to be shared.

"Ang, shut up. Yo' ass is not gonna bring that up every time we're together. Irritating ass." I hit Mike as his shoulders shook. "Shut up because this your damn fault. If you would've left me alone or taken me to our room, she wouldn't know shit."

"Okay, I'm sorry. I'm not going to say anything else about it, promise." Angel swore, yet still, she chuckled.

My lips twisted, not believing her. I knew my best friend all too well. She'll let it go for a time but would bring it back up. She couldn't help herself. That was why I didn't acknowledge what she said. Instead, I went back to eating my breakfast.

"Tasha, you talked to yo' people yet?" Mike questioned, finishing off his food.

She shot a glare at him. "No, I haven't. I just got up, Mike. Plus, I was hoping you might've slept on it and thought about me staying here." She put it out there, looking at me. "I mean, with Kim being present, we can talk about me staying here until I get on my feet."

"I already told you no, so there's nothing to talk about." He told her.

That woman had some damn balls on her. "Okay, let's talk about it, Tasha. No, you can't live here. You have family and friends you can stay with until you get back on your feet. Doing that shouldn't take longer than a month or two, seeing as you do work, and I know you have money saved up given all the money Mike has been giving you through the years. Now, if you don't have anything saved," I shrugged. "I don't know what to tell you. But, you're not living with us."

"First off, all the money he's given me has gone toward our son's needs, every damn penny." She had the nerve to say that with an attitude while trying to get me to let her stay with us. "But what's the real issue with me staying here, Kim, if you don't mind me asking?"

That babe was fucking insane. The nerve of her to even ask that question told how looney she was. "Are you fucking serious? You dead asking me that dumb ass question?" I looked at Mike to see if he was hearing her simple ass. He just shrugged. "Is she dead ass, right now?" I asked him.

Mike looked in Tasha's face, then back to me. "Oh, she's serious as fuck, sweetheart."

"From your reaction, I know it's something. So, what's the issue?" With a straight ass fucking face, she asked me that question.

I laughed. I couldn't help it. Tasha's ass was something crazy for real. "Bitch, you just tried to fuck my man the other day. That's one of the main reasons right there." Tasha's eyes snapped to Mike's, and homegirl genuinely seemed surprised that I knew. "And, no, he didn't tell me right off bat. You did with your text messages last night—which implied y'all did something. But I knew better because if the two of you fucked, your messy ass would've said it outright instead of insinuating y'all did. Bitch, you're catty as fuck for no reason.

"On top of that, I don't like you, Tasha. I deal with you because of Malik. So, there's your reason as to why. Mike told you that last night, so I don't know what you thought asking me would do."

"Well, like I told Mike last night. Malik and I aren't going to be separated. We're staying together." She stated factually, sounding as if it was final.

I nodded in agreement. "I completely understand where you're coming from. If your parents or friends have enough room for the both of you, that's absolutely fine. However, if they don't, Malik can stay here with us, as we said. Malik knows this is his home, and he's welcome to it at any time. But you living here is not going to happen no matter what. We'll be sure to let Malik know this just in case you forget too. I'll also tell him why you can't live here with him." I explained while grabbing our dishes and putting them in the sink. "You know what's funny, though. After your messages last night, your house mysteriously catches fire. What part caught fire anyways?" I addressed that last bit to Mike.

"Shid, I don't know. She didn't say, and I ain't ask. I don't wanna know either. Tasha, you can take off." He exclaimed while getting up. Tasha's mouth opened, but his waved hand shut her up. "You don't need to say shit. The conversation's dead. So, gon' 'head and get out of here." I could tell his words pissed her off from the harsh scowl on her face. Even so, she didn't say anything, just remained seated. "I have to go. I'll be in late, so don't wait up." He kissed me, then went over to the twins, kissing the pair.

"Why are you gonna be late, and how late is late?"

Mike glanced around the room, then back to me. "It's none of your business, Kimmy. I'll be back." With that, he left the kitchen. It took me a second to guess what was probably going on.

"I'll be back, y'all. Tasha, you heard him. You should take off. There's no reason for you to lounge around here." I told her while heading out of the kitchen. "Y'all can go in the living room or the game room," I called out while trying to catch up to Mike. But his ass had already bolted up the stairs. Making my way up to our room, I walked in just as Mike was getting dressed. "You wanna tell me what's going on?" I knew whatever it was had to do with Martell.

His head shook. "I already told you, it's none of your business." He reminded me.

My eyes rolled at that. "I know it's not, but can you at least tell me something?"

"It's nothing to tell." He claimed, putting on his shirt.

I stared at him hard, trying to see if he was lying or not. I couldn't tell, however. "So, Angel and Parker being here don't have anything to do with you?"

His brows furrowed as he looped the belt through his jeans. "Does it ever, Kimmy?"

My mouth opened but closed right back, realizing what I was asking. Of course, it wouldn't make sense. "Okay, no. But if it doesn't have anything to do with them, why are you going to be late then?"

Grabbing his shirt, he pulled it on, then looked at me. I could see that he was frustrated with my questions. I didn't care, though. If he had something going on that involved Martell, then I needed to know. Just in case something happened to him, I knew who the fuck I was going after. It was that simple.

"It's a weapons deal, that's all. I don't know how long that's gonna take. That's why I'm warning you about me being late." He explained.

I pushed him. "How come you just couldn't

say that? You just had to have me thinking the worse."

Mike laughed as he sat on the bed, pulling me between his legs. "Because it's none of your business, that's why." My eyes rolled at that, and he pinched my thigh. "I'mma need you to stop worrying so damn much. When I start to worry is the only time you need to be concerned. Alright?"

I sighed, knowing he was right. "I mean, knowing who you're dealing with, I can't help it. I don't like this shit, Mike. Those mothafuckas crazy, and you're not like them—babe, don't laugh when I'm being so damn serious, Michael."

Mike stood, snaking his arm around my waist and holding me to him. "I don't have to be like them to know how to handle shit."

"I know—"

Mike's lips covered mine as his arm tightened around my waist. Biting at my top lip, he sucked it into his mouth before biting into the bottom. Instantly I melted into his body as his tongue began dancing sexually with mine. My arms went around his neck as I moaned.

After giving birth, thinking about sex made my damn coochie ache. Yet, the moment Mike kissed me, all that went out the window as my body began craving him.

Mike knew what he was doing by kissing me in that nasty, all tongue and hungry way I loved. I was about to say fuck the six weeks and give in. My damn body was hurting for it. I felt like a gotdamn addict.

With a groan, Mike broke the kiss. "Fuck, sweetheart, you're leaking."

I whined at his words. He wasn't even touching me, yet he knew my pussy was aching for him. "How'd you know?" I couldn't explain why, but I felt embarrassed by him knowing that.

Mike laughed and pulled back. "Baby, I'm not talking about your pussy. Your titties spilling." He pointed down at his shirt, which had two wet stains on it. I couldn't do anything but laugh. I went to walk away, but Mike stopped me. "I didn't tell you to go nowhere. Kim, I wouldn't do shit if I thought it would put you at risk or take me from my boys. I don't have to be like them, but I'm insane about my family." He kissed me again, then moved back. "Now, it's something I want you to do for me. It's important, so don't argue with me about it. Bet?"

Hearing how serious his tone had gotten, I became worried. Yet, I nodded in agreement to do whatever it was. "Okay. What do you need me to do?"

"Really listen to what I'm about to tell you. I'm serious, Kimmy—"

"Babe, I'm listening, I promise." I would do anything he needed, especially to help him with Martell.

"This is what I want you to do. Pack up some of your stuff and go stay at your crib with yo' pops for a few weeks—"

"What? Why? I thought you just said everything was going to be alright." I was beyond confused by why he was asking me to leave. Yet, I noted he only said for me to pack and go. "And what about the boys?"

"Don't worry about them. You can keep the kids while I'm at work, and when I get off, I'll bring them back home—"

My hands waved, cutting him off as I moved further away from him. "Okay, I'm confused. You want me to move back to the house, but my babies will stay here. No, babe, you need to explain to me why."

Sighing, he rubbed a hand over his mouth. "This isn't working for me, Kimmy. We need some space until you're healed—"

Grabbing the shoe off the floor, I threw it at his damn head. Mike ducked down just in time, causing the shoe to hit the wall.

"You're an irritating sonofabitch! I'm thinking—I don't even know for real, but I was confused as hell. Ugh, you get on my damn nerves. Get the fuck out, Michael!" There I was, seconds away from getting scared about some unknown danger, and his ass was saying the shit because of sex the whole time. I broke out laughing, not being able to help it. "Something is seriously wrong with you."

"G, I'm being dead serious. Make sure you

take yo' damn sister with yo' ass too, along with all her suitcases. She ain't staying here, Kimmy. Don't stand yo' ass there looking confused because I saw her shit in the room this morning. Sweetheart, I'm not dumb. Now, get her ass and Tasha out our shit." His hand waved toward the door as if shooing me out of the room.

I wasn't about to argue with him nor lie about the reason for Mya being there. Hell, it would've been pointless. Once Mike's shirt came off, I went behind him, wrapping my arms around his waist.

"This is why I'm putting yo' ass out now. You wanna slob and kiss on a mothafucka skin, knowing we can't do shit." He complained.

Biting into his back, I kissed the skin, then moved up to his neck, placing kisses along his flesh.

Mike let out a hard laugh as my lips continued their assault on his skin. "What do you want, Kimmy?"

Kissing along his jawline, I moved to his mouth, pecking his lips twice. "I did ask Mya to come and stay with us for a few weeks when you went back to work. Babe, dealing with two babies on my own is entirely new and a learning experience. It's different from when Malik was a baby. For one, I didn't keep him twenty-four-seven, and on days when I did have him by myself, I was tired once you got back home.

"You remember how it was. Now it's Malik times two. I really do need Mya here with me. At least until I can handle it on my own. But I don't wanna get too worn out then become stressed, depressed, just overwhelmed from doing this on my own while you're working."

I wasn't new to dealing with a newborn. Even so, the first two days I've had them on my own, I saw how overwhelming it would become. So, asking for help when I knew I had it was the best option.

Mike's head shook, and he rubbed the nape of his neck. "Alright, Kimmy, she can stay. But I don't want none of her damn girlfriends over here. The first time I see one of Mya's chicks here, her ass gone."

Grabbing his chin, I kissed him while grinning hard. "I love you."

"I love you, too. Now gone downstairs with those worrisome ass girls of yours." He kissed me once more and then grabbed his ringing phone.

I left the room, going to the living room where the girls now sat. Sitting on the chaise, I reached for my babies, who Angel and Missy still held, rocking. The pair looked at each other, pretending they didn't see me.

"Y'all hoes irritating." My eyes rolled at them as I chuckled. Mya came over and sat at my feet. "Oh, Mya, Mike said you can stay, but none of your little girlfriends can come over. Otherwise, you're gone." Usually, I'd tell her to ignore Mike's mean ass. However, I agreed with him on that. Mya's girls were ghetto and ratchet as hell. "You can only invite one damn girl here, and that's it. But the bitch can't be a hoodrat." I was saying as Malik barged into the house. I sat up straight, surprised to see him there. "Hey, babe, what are you doing here?"

"Hey, momma. I had Ron bring me home. He was cool with it after I told him what happened." He explained as he walked into the living room, looking around at everyone. "The house isn't bad. I thought it was burnt to the ground from how my mom was crying. It was only the kitchen counter and the cabinets above the stove that got burnt." He further explained, still confusing me.

After what he said dawned on me, my finger threaded against my forehead. "Malik, please don't tell me you went to that house and took your ass inside it—"

"I asked Ron to take me by there. I had to see how bad the house was. And I only went inside after Jerron checked everything out first." He stated as if that was fine. "So, my moms staying here with us until the kitchen gets fixed?" He questioned as Tasha walked into the living room. "Hey, Ma." He hugged her. "I went by the house. Man, I thought you almost died with the way you called crying. The house ain't bad. It's just the kitchen."

If Malik wasn't Mike's damn son through and through with that mouth. Yet, I was glad he had begun noticing just how dramatic Tasha's ass was.

"Boy, what do you know? The house is bad. I was stuck inside it while the damn thing was on fire." Tasha fussed, glaring at him.

My eyes rolled at her because I knew she was trying to downplay what Malik said. Still, I knew what Malik said was true because he had no reason to lie.

"And I'm not staying here. Your dad and Kim said I couldn't. Although I explained to them we weren't going to be separated. That obviously doesn't matter to them." She went on to tell him as if that would change anything.

I shrugged, noting the pair's glances. "As we told her, Malik, this is your home which you're welcome to live in for however long you want," I explained before pointing to her crazy ass. "Tasha can't, though. We're not responsible for her. She has friends and family to live with until the kitchen is fixed up or until she finds another house. Whichever she decides to do, is her choice and isn't our business."

My eyes rolled at Tasha, already knowing what her plan was. She figured saying something in front of Malik would probably change our minds for his sake. "Tasha, you can leave now." I motioned to the front door. "Malik, go wash up. It's breakfast in the kitchen if you're hungry." I instructed, waving the pair off.

"Okay. But am I staying here with you and dad?" Malik asked.

"Baby, if you want to. As I said, this is your home." I pointed to Tasha. "You have to talk with her. Y'all can do so in the room." I once again waved the pair off. That time they left out the living room.

Missy and Angel looked at me then started laughing. "That damn woman is a piece of work." They said in agreement.

With pursed lips, I nodded. "I swear she is. Anyways, why did Mike just say he wants me to move back home until I'm healed up. Say, the twins can stay, but I have to go." I started laughing, thinking about the seriousness his voice took on. "That man's a damn fool."

"Girl, Parker was the same damn way. After Ant and Pixie, I had to put his ass out of my room. He would not leave me alone, then wanna say it's my fault. Like, dude, if you don't leave me the fuck alone. His ass was pissy when I got on birth control too." She laughed while smiling at Millian. "Mike's ass is gonna wanna keep you pregnant, especially if you're popping out twins. Beautiful ass twins at that, hell, I know if it was me, I'm unloading in you every time—"

The fact she said it so damn seriously had us cracking the fuck up. "Girl, give me my damn son because he's clearly making you deranged. Girl, I'm done with kids. We have three beautiful boys. That's all we need. I can't deal with all the pushing. It's so damn dramatic." The girls broke out laughing at that. I didn't find anything funny I was beyond serious.

"Not it's dramatic, though." Angel laughed. "I can do the pushing, those damn contractions, though. No ma'am. They had a bitch feeling like she was dying." She claimed with a shake of her head from that memory. "Nope, my body is still in recovery, and it's been what? Three years. Pixie will be four this year, so yeah. Y'all, my body starts to ache as soon as Parker says, baby. I instantly start having contractions." Angel claimed, making us laugh.

"You're so damn stupid." I cracked up at how dramatic she was being. "Girl, stop playing and give him some more babies."

I knew Parker wanted more kids; hell, Angel complained about him asking her for the past three years. Parker ass was determined to keep her pregnant if she'd let him. He wasn't trying to give my girl no breaks. Hell, their first three kids were back to back. So, to be honest, I didn't blame her for saying no. Shit, her body needed a ten-year break if anyone asked me.

Angel shook her head. "Nope, not right now. I need a few more years, hell, several more before I can even start thinking about babies for real." A laugh suddenly burst from her mouth, and she pointed to Missy. "Girl, he's ready for her ass to have some kids now. Meka and Missy. Parker ass just wants some kids to take care of. Like dude, at this point, let's adopt. He even asked Chris about having more kids. Hell, Christiana has practically moved in with us."

All I could do was laugh. Hell, Parker's ass was fucking rich. His wealth could last for generations. So, it didn't surprise me that he wanted a shit load of kids to share it all with.

"Kimmy!" Mike called out.

"I'm in the living room!"

Mike appeared at the entrance a few seconds later with Malik beside him. "I'm about to head out." After kissing me, he took the babies from Angel and Missy, making them complain. "Shut the fuck up." He snapped at the pair. "Kim, don't be letting them hold my damn sons all day either. We ain't even about to start that bullshit with them. And don't be having them all in their faces either. I know they some handsome ass dudes—"

"Mike, shut up," I swear the man couldn't help but talk shit. "You're not going to be satisfied until they jump your ass."

He looked the girls up and started laughing. "I'll let you know when I'm worried about them." With the babies tucked in his arms, he walked away from us while whispering to them.

"I can't stand him." Missy laughed with a roll of her eyes. "Mike, give me my babies and take your ass off to work." Her arms went out, urging him to give the babies up.

Mike glanced at her, then tilted the babies in her direction and whispered to them once again. "Cry, spit-up, do whatever but give shorty the works. Understand me?"

"Mike, get out. You're so damn irritating, I promise." I held my arms out for him to give me the twins.

Instead of giving me our sons, he lay them in their swings. "Man, y'all ain't about to be holding them all damn day. Don't be picking them up if you're not feeding them or no shit like that."

My brows raised at that. I didn't know who Mike thought he was talking to, but I wasn't hearing a damn thing he said. If I wanted to hold my boys, I would be doing that. My eyes rolled at him, yet I said nothing in response. Noticing that, his eyes came to me.

"Don't make me call my momma over here—"

The fact he wanted to threaten me with Milly had me cracking up. "Michael Dontavious Payne, if you don't get your ass out this house, I'mma call the damn police on you for harassment." I threatened jokingly while pointing to the front hallway.

"I'm serious, Kimmy." Coming to me, he grabbed my chin, and instantly my lips puckered. He pushed my head back. "I ain't about to kiss yo' ass."

Glaring at him, I slapped at his hand. "Mike, kiss me, then get out my damn house." Stretching my neck up, I pressed my lips to his. "Now, go. And call me on your way back."

Mike pecked my lips twice. "A'ight, don't leave this house. Call your pops and let him know you'll meet up with him tomorrow. That way, I can go with you."

Sighing, I nodded. "Okay." I wasn't going to argue because I knew why he told me that. I just hoped like hell that everything he had going on with Martell and Parker went according to plan. "Call me on your way back just in case I need something."

"Yeah, I ain't doing that shit. I'll be back. Malik, look after yo' momma and brothers. Make sure those mothafuckas ain't holding them all day either. You have my permission to slap fire from all three of those mothafuckas if they give you mouth. So, we're clear on who you're slapping..." he turned to face us. "Yo' aunties Mya, Angel, and Missy's ass. Don't hit yo' momma because then I'mma have to fuck you up after she beats yo' ass—"

Grabbing the couch pillow, I threw it at him. "Michael, get the hell out!" I couldn't stand his ass at times.

The girls looked at me then broke out laughing. Even so, the trio didn't say anything about what Mike had said.

"A'ight, I'm gone." He announced, kissing me once more. "Come on, Tasha, so we can walk you out. Malik, come on so you can say bye to your mom's." With that, Mike and Malik left the living room.

A few seconds later, Tasha came stomping down the hallway. From the glare on her face, I knew she was pissed off. Still, I didn't care. I refused to let her invade my peaceful place.

The hilarious part was that Tasha thought she would actually stay with us. Tasha's damn audacity was out of this world. Homegirl had massive balls on her insane ass.

Chapter Eighteen

Mike

According To Plan

*A*fter hours of working in our factory, I was exhausted, but I couldn't complain because I loved making guns and custom designing them. I couldn't pretend like I didn't get completely lost in my work. No matter the years I've been honing my craft, I was still in love with my work.

Once showered and changed, I went back into the plant, checking out the beautiful purple and black Sig Sauer P238 with the marbled purple and white handle. The gun was a small toy for a female. I had done three of the same guns but different colors. One was purple, another was red, and the last was pink. They were all beautiful little pieces.

After locking the guns away, I grabbed my stuff then left the factory, hopping into my car and leaving. Fifteen minutes later, I pulled into the warehouse, only to swap vehicles. I jumped into the truck that had all the guns Martell ordered.

Shooting Martell a text, I let him know where the meeting would take place. Given the machine guns ordered, I was taking them to our more extensive and secluded gun range surrounded by nothing but a woodland area.

After the message was sent, I headed toward the range just as my phone went off. Seeing Martell's number, my brows furrowed in confusion. Still, I answered.

"Nigga, if you're calling to cancel this fucking meeting—"

"Nah, it ain't shit like that, so calm down. It's the spot you wanna meet at. You don't have nowhere local?" His question confused me further.

I did, but with them testing the guns out, that was the only place we did it. "If you plan on shooting them, no, I don't. If you just wanna pick them up, then shit, yeah." He grunted into the line. "You already know this, though, so, what's up?"

The line was quiet for a long while, causing me to get frustrated, so I pulled to the side of the road. I wasn't about to make that long ass drive if that mothafucka wasn't going to show up.

"Martell, what the fuck is up? Are we doing this shit or not? If you don't wanna go out there, I can drop the guns off to you—"

"It ain't shit like that. Yeah, we wanna test those babies out." His words trailed off as someone in his background started talking. "A'ight...Mike,

I'mma be straight up with you. You know we got a lot going on right now. Dead ass, I ain't tryna drag you into our shit with Parker and his niggas. I just got word that they're back in town. My nigga ran into them earlier—"

"Okay, I'm confused. So are they following y'all or some shit?" I didn't lie about being confused. Hell, I didn't tell Parker shit about meeting up with Martell. I was by far a businessman first. All the other bullshit was going to come after our dealings were done.

The sigh that came through the line had my head shaking. At that moment, I realized Martell didn't want to run into Parker at all. Hell, dude moved across fucking states for years just to avoid him.

"Nah, I don't think we're being followed, but I don't know either. I'm not trying to have those mothafuckas messing up this shit—you know what? Why don't you come swoop us up real quick."

"If those mothafuckas are following you niggas, I'm not about to have my fucking truck shot at. Fuck no. Especially not after that bullshit Don ass was spitting at that nigga Chris. I saw it on homeboy's face. If he sees yo' cousin, it's over with. He's unloading a clip without talking. So, nah, I'm not picking y'all up. This is a business transaction only, meaning I'm not transporting shit but these guns. You niggas better make y'all fucking way to the range or give me a drop-off location. So, what we're doing?"

I wasn't protecting or helping those mothafuckas, and I didn't want them to think I was either just because we were doing business together.

After some mumbling in his background and Don's sudden laughter, Martell came back to the line. "A'ight, we'll meet you there in about fifteen/twenty minutes. Oh, Don said you ain't shit. You could at least give us transportation seeing that you're having us drive out to the middle of nowhere." He laughed, no longer seeming worried about Parker.

I brushed that off, not bothering to bring up the sudden mood change. "Tell Don to suck my dick. The both of you knew where we'd be going. The location hasn't changed. This is where we always go when y'all buy big shit. Now hurry the fuck up. I'm trying to get to the crib." Ending the call, I made my way to the range.

"Nigga, who the fuck is blowing you down?" Martell questioned, glancing at my ringing phone.

To say Martell was paranoid would've been an understatement. He had been on edge since they showed up at the range. Not only that, dude brought damn near fifteen other mothafuckas with him. He had at least five on his ass while the others stayed out front.

After ignoring Kimmy's third damn call, I went to slide the phone back in my pocket but stopped as I noted Martell's eyes on the device. Laughing, I unlocked the phone then tossed the device to him.

"It's my girl, nigga, damn. Yo' ass need to relax. Look at it—as a matter of fact, call her back if it'll calm yo' damn nerves."

Don instantly snatched the phone from Martell and pressed on the screen before bringing it to his ear. Glaring at him, I snatched my damn phone from his dumb ass.

"What the fuck are you doing? You said to call her. I'm just trying to make sure it's yo' girl." My brows shot up from his seriousness. Dude was mad that I took my phone from his ass.

"Helloooo? Mike? Michael? Hello?" Kimmy's voice sounded muffled. Even so, she could still be heard.

I pointed to Don. "Yo' ass gonna make me kill you. Keep on." My attention went to Martell. "When I kill his ass, don't get mad," I told him while putting the phone on speaker. "What's up, sweetheart?"

The line was quiet for a second before she hummed. "Nothing, feeding your greedy ass boys." She explained, sounding relaxed. Kim sighed softly into the line. "You're done doing your business already?" She asked, seeming confused.

My head shook, although she couldn't see me.

"No, but yo' ass done called me three damn times. You got these niggas paranoid. So, what's up?"

Once again, the line went silent. "Babe, I didn't call you—" Kimmy's lips smacking came through the speaker. "Hold on...Malik!" She hollered, and instantly the babies started crying.

"Damn, shorty had the baby already," Don stated, making me look at him. "What? Man, I could tell shorty was pregnant when we met, so don't be mugging me. I'm observant when I'm interested."

"Did you call your daddy from my phone?" Kim questioned.

"Oh yeah, let me talk to him." Malik was saying until Kim cut him off.

"Hey, babe, Malik called you. He doesn't want anything, just wannabe worrisome. Gone head and finish up, so you can get back and rub me down—"

"Bye, Kimmy." Shorty was stressing me the fuck out. She didn't know I was serious about her leaving the crib. We couldn't be in the same house, let alone the same bed, and not be intimate. It had only been a week, and I felt like a gotdamn fiend.

The ripple of the semi-automatic pistol muffled Kimmy's laughter and reply. Looking at Don, he held the Draco, letting that bitch go as he shot into the wooden board.

I couldn't help myself as I started laughing. "You shot that bitch like you're mad. You angry, baby?" The mug Don wore said it all. Homeboy was pissed.

"Mike, who are you talking shit to now?" Kimmy asked, sounding irritated.

"Nobody important. I'll call you back when I'm finished up here."

"Alright, babe. Hurry up so you can rub me down." She stated, chuckling. "Love you, bye." She ended the call with that.

Seeing Don mad was comical as hell to me. Buddy had no reason to feel any type of way about me talking to Kim.

"That fascination you feel toward my girl, yo' ass need to lose it quick. That mothafucka will get you killed if you keep it up." That threat I meant wholeheartedly. I would kill the fuck out of Don if he went near Kimmy. Only because I knew he wasn't all the way together in the head. The mothafucka was twisted just like the rest of his people.

After reloading the Draco, he started shooting again. Once he finished, his eyes fell on me before he started smiling. "Shorty beautiful, though. She's too good for you." Don claimed before his attention returned to the field, and he started shooting again.

"Ignore his dumb ass. He just fucking with you—well, not really, but still, ignore his ass. He knows to stay away from yo' lady. So, yo' girl done popped out a little shorty? I ain't even know baby was pregnant." Martell glanced at his cousin and laughed. "How the fuck did you notice that shit when I didn't, and I saw baby when you did?"

Don looked to me then at his cousin. His gaze settled on me again, and he smiled. "I saw shorty around the way a few times when we got back. The club was the first time I approached baby, though. But from the dress she had on, you couldn't help but tell she was pregnant. Real shit, though, I didn't know she was yours. I thought homeboy she was talking to was her nigga, dead ass." He claimed, staring at me as if waiting for a certain reaction.

"I ain't talking about yo' boy King either." He further explained. Still, I didn't react to what he said. It was obvious that he wanted a different type of reaction. Even so, I wasn't giving it to him. "Shid, I wouldn't have minded playing step-daddy —yo' calm down. I said *wouldn't have minded*. Chill, damn, I know baby is off-limits. So, put yo' gun away. I'm not that damn disrespectful. But know, if you fuck up, I'mma slide right on in." Dude grinned, showing off the diamond grill in his mouth. "Please fuck up." He begged.

I wanted to shoot the fuck out of him. Instead, I continued to ignore him. "Finish testing these bitches out before I purposely shoot that mothafucka in the mouth," I told Martell, waving for him to continue.

Martell pushed his cousin, laughing. "What the fuck I tell yo' ass? Man, stop talking about that damn babe. That nigga stupid behind shorty." Grabbing the B&T TP9, he went to his lane and started shooting the target board.

Moving back, I leaned against the wooden pole as I watched the pair test each gun out.

∞∞∞

"As always, it's good doing business with you," Martell said, walking with me to my truck. "I'mma be bringing some business your way in a few weeks. Aye, if you and pops are looking for a business partner to deal with streets or a nigga to travel with shipments. I got this shipping company I'm about to start up with my people." He said as I tossed the backpack of money into my passenger seat.

My brows furrowed hearing what he was saying. "Nah, we ain't looking to venture out with nobody new. We got shipping and all that, baby, which you already know. Our shit is strictly family, no outsiders. Doing business with you would mean getting rid of family. You know that ain't happening. But if you got business coming our way, good looking."

He laughed at that. "A'ight, I feel you. Don't brush the idea off, though. Think about it, and in a couple of months when we're up and running, I'mma come at you to see if you've changed your mind."

Humming, I nodded. "A'ight, I'm out." Tossing up two fingers, I hopped in my truck. Martell knocked on the hood and started walking off as shots rang out. My back door was jerked open, and Martell jumped in. "What the fuck?" I yelled, pissed.

"It's that mothafucka, Parker. Fuck!" He yelled, sounding just as angry as I did.

"Nigga you better shoot the fuck back!" I ordered ass bullets hit my truck. "That stupid mothafucka!" I was glad for bulletproof windows, or my ass would've been shot, no doubt.

"The fucking guns in the truck! Fuck! Yo' Don! Fuck!" The back door was thrust open, and Martell started yelling. "Don! Get over here! Mike, grab that nigga and get us the fuck out of here. If you don't, those niggas gonna kill yo' ass too for being with us. Now go!" He demanded, hitting the back of my seat with urgency.

Throwing the truck into reverse, I moved back, swiftly turning and shielding Don. "Get the fuck in!" I shouted as Martell pushed the door open. Don didn't hesitate to jump into the back seat. Once he was in, my tires kicked up dirt as I sped off.

"Yo! Fuck! We left all the gotdamn guns back there. Mike, turn the fuck around!" Don demanded, enraged.

"Man, fuck those guns, I'm not about to die while trying to get those bitches—" Martell began saying, which pissed Don off even more.

"Bitch, if those mothafuckas get the guns, they'll try to kill us with our own shit. Do you hear yo' fuckin' self right now? Man, turn this bitch around so I can go get our shit." He once again demanded.

My brows raised as I stared at him through the rear-view mirror. "I'm not turning shit around. I ain't about to get shot behind y'all fucking bullshit. Now, I'll pull this bitch over and let you mothafuckas out. That's the only stopping I'm doing." From the mug Martell gave his cousin, I knew he wanted him to shut up. He didn't give a damn about those gotdamn guns. He was trying to put as much distance between them as possible. "So, what I'm doing?"

"Driving," Martell responded. "We can always get new fucking guns. Fuck!" He yelled. "I knew I should've canceled this damn meeting when I heard those mothafuckas was in town. Fuck, man, damn!" He growled, pissed off. "We need to quit playing and kill those mothafuckas."

"Bitch, shut the fuck up!" Don snapped at him. "You don't want that mothafucka dead for real. If you did, then yo' ass would've been gunning for his gotdamn head, not doing all this fucking hiding out. Those bitches killed my fucking brother, but we're hiding the fuck out. What type of sense is that? Now, we've let those niggas take our fucking guns!" He raged on. "If you wanted to kill that bitch, you could've easily killed that nigga sister and nephew—"

"Just because we've been laying low doesn't mean I don't want that bitch dead! I'm just not fucking stupid to do no dumb ass shit like that.

Now, if I killed that nigga's sister or nephew, what the fuck do you think he would've done? Huh?" Martell yelled at him. "That bitch would've came for my damn momma—"

"So fucking what—"

Martell punched Don hard as hell in the face. "Nigga, you might not give a fuck about yo' bitch ass momma, but I'm not about to get mine killed behind my bullshit. Killing Parker's sister would've caused way more fucking bloodshed—"

Don knocked Martell right back in the jaw. "Bitch, that's part of the fucking game. Family isn't off fucking limits because you're scared of yours getting hurt. What the fuck do you think he's going to do when you kill his bitch. You don't think he'll start a fucking war behind her ass?"

"After I had him, that was when I would've snatched her ass up, but never before that, though. Nigga, I'm not fucking stupid. I know how that mothafucka thinks. That's why I move the way I do. I done planned all this shit out." Martell explained.

I was tired of those two mothafuckas and was ready to get rid of them. After driving down the dirt road for several minutes, I turned off, going up to our warehouse where our more expensive rifles and machine guns were stored.

"Where the fuck are we?" Don asked.

Ignoring him, I reached into the glove compartment, grabbed a set of keys, and then got out of the truck. Once inside the building, I went straight to my office and grabbed the keys to the Yukon parked out front.

Quickly heading back outside, I locked up the warehouse then made my way to the truck the pair occupied. "Here, y'all can take this bitch. I ain't fawn of niggas shooting at me behind somebody else's bullshit. What happens to you mothafuckas from this point forth is on you bitches." I snatched the backpack from the front seat then slammed the door shut.

"That's real fucked up, yo' ass gonna leave us out here like this. It's about ten of those mothafuckas." Don yelled as he got out of the truck.

I shrugged. "I don't give a fuck how many mothafuckas there are. That's still y'all bullshit, not mine. In truth, that mothafucka Chris needs to kill yo' ass for the shit you did to his wife. Had it been me," I pointed to Martell, "as he said, I would've killed yo' whole gotdamn family, momma, daddy, kids and all." My finger then jabbed back to Don.

"Just like you said, family ain't off-limits. It's all part of the game you choose to play. So, don't bitch up and complain about those ten niggas coming after you. Real shit though, I hope that mothafucka torture the fuck out of you, dead ass." Tossing up two fingers, I jogged to the Yukon. Once inside, I started up the truck and pulled off.

Don walked in front of my truck, his gun drawn. "Now, It'll be fucked up if I shot yo' ass for that bullshit you just said, wouldn't it?"

I tapped on the windshield, then the window. "Baby, it's bulletproof." Letting the window down, I stuck my head out of it. "You can do what you feel you need to. But those little bullets are all you have." Shaking my head, I pulled out my gun. "See, I threw you bitches a lifejacket so that you mothafuckas had a chance. But yo' simple-minded ass done fucked that up. Now, I'mma let you bitches drown." Looking at Martell, I pointed to his cousin. "Thank him. I don't take threats easily. You know that." Shooting out the front tire, I quickly rolled up my window before either one of those niggas could let off a shot. "I only let you stop me because I forgot to give y'all the fucking keys. You fucked up." I showed them the keys to the truck that I had taken out.

When the pair noticed Don's fuck up, they quickly ran to my truck, just as I pulled off.

Once I did, two trucks pulled in front of me. Immediately my gaze locked on Chris' murderous stare then with Parker's. My index and middle finger waved to the side, motioning for them to get out my damn way. The two trucks turned, speeding toward the warehouse.

I didn't look back, nor was I curious about how they would kill those two mothafuckas. Getting Don and Martell separated from their boys —who I knew they would bell on—and leaving them at the warehouse was as far as my involvement included.

I gave them those two mothafuckas on a silver platter. Whatever they did to them from that point was on them.

Chris and Parker were constantly on me about when everything would be going down and what I had planned. I didn't tell them shit until after I talked to Martell when I knew for sure he wasn't going to cancel.

On my way to the meeting, I sent the location of the range and warehouse to Chris. I've done business with Martell plenty of times before, so I knew how things would go.

After running things down, I told Chris they weren't to start shooting until after I was near my truck, and they were to kill off Martell boys first. From the way Martell had been acting, I knew he would take off before trying to help his boys. In Martell's eyes, they were there for his protection. So, while he got away, they were to kill everyone who came with them.

Martell did what I expected he would, and leaving his cousin behind wasn't an option, which I also knew.

The fact that they weren't expecting Parker and his boys was perfect. Not only that, those mothafuckas were deep as hell. I wasn't expecting that, to be honest. They rolled up five trucks deep, and those mothafuckas started shooting as soon as they hit the parking lot.

As the events replayed in my mind, I started laughing. The shit was funny as hell. Martell was fucking terrified.

Grabbing a blunt from my case, I lit it, still laughing. Everything definitely went according to plan, with no fuck ups.

Chapter Nineteen

Mike

Are We Unbreakable?

Once I got home, I hopped in the shower, washing the day's events from me. Kim and her girls were all in the living room when I came in—which wasn't surprising. Whenever Angel came down to visit, they got together and chilled for hours at each other's crib.

I pulled on a pair of sweats when the bedroom door came open. Kimmy walked in with my sons in her arms. Going to her, I took them and then sat on the bed.

"Y'all missed me?" I was asking as the pair started sucking on my bare tattooed chest. "Yo, what y'all doing? You ain't getting no damn drink up out of me."

Kimmy laughed, hitting me. "Shut up, fool. They just ate, so they're not hungry. They've missed you and want that skin-to-skin contact." Sitting beside us, Kim leaned over and kissed me before righting herself. "So, what happened? Did everything go good?"

Kimmy couldn't help how damn nosy she was. "Yeah, Kim, it did."

"So, they killed them?" She continued with her questions.

I shrugged. "I'm assuming they did."

Instantly her brows furrowed. "You assume? Why would you assume they did? Where you not there—"

"No, I didn't stay there to watch and see what they did or how they may have done it, Kimmy. I'm sure Parker will tell Angel about it, and then she'll tell you and the girls. So, calm yourself."

Kimmy glared at me, and I knew she wanted to hit me from that stare. "If you weren't holding my damn babies, I'll knock you out. Yo' big-headed ass didn't even have to say it like that. Babe, why wouldn't you stay back and watch what happens? You knew I was going to want damn details—" she punched me in the leg. "—that shit is not funny, Michael. I've been waiting for them to die for fucking years. And now that it happened, I don't know shit because of your ass. Damn, I hope they killed that mothafucka painfully. Ugh, why wouldn't you stay and watch for me?"

I just stared at her because she was so damn serious. I broke out laughing as I looked down at my boys. "Yo! Y'all fucking momma is insane. Do y'all hear her crazy ass? Man, you two gonna be fucked up because of her ass. Damn, I hope y'all don't take no parts of her fucking crazy." Looking back at Kimmy's glaring face, I started laughing again.

She chuckled as well while hitting me. "That's not funny, Mike. I was so serious. You just don't understand the shit he put them through. Martell and his crazy ass ex. I really wished you would've stayed and told me how they killed them, at least. Ugh, I hate I missed it." Kim hit my legs. "Stop laughing at me."

"Yo' ass is insane. But what do I look like standing around watching a nigga get tortured when I don't have shit to do with it? Their death doesn't benefit me none." Looking at my boys, I kissed their heads. "Y'all momma sick. Look, the first sign y'all show of being insane like that mothafucka, I'm going to have you two committed to somebody's insane asylum with her ass." The pair gave unaware smiles as they began falling asleep. "Look, at that. They already know what's inside them."

"Dude, shut up. We're both insane, so they're cursed from both genes." Leaning into me, her lips pressed into mine. "I'm glad you're alright, though. I was going a little crazy, not knowing what was happening. I let out the biggest breath of relief when you walked in." She kissed me again. "I love you so much more for doing this. Thank you, babe." Kim pecked my lips, then bit the bottom. "Once these five weeks are up, I promise, I'mma thank you properly."

My head just shook at her. I didn't even have to question it because I knew she was serious. "Let me ask you this." Once the sentence left my mouth, I could see the confusion in her features.

"Okay, what's up?"

"The night you saw Martell, who was you with?" I didn't know why, but what Don said came to mind at that moment.

Kimmy's eyes moved up thoughtfully as she hummed. "Nobody aside from Nya." She spoke slowly as if not understanding why I was asking the question.

"Not her. What nigga were you with?"

Again, she looked lost. "Aside from you?" I nodded. She shrugged. "Babe, I don't understand. Like, with how? Because I wasn't with anybody but you until y'all went into the private room—oh—you mean King?"

"Nah, not King. You were with somebody else. Who?" A groan suddenly left her mouth, and I nodded. "Yeah, who were you with?"

Kimmy's fingers massaged her forehead. "I ran into Bell, but nothing happened, I swear. He saw me and wanted to know how I was doing, that's it. Look, before I knew I was pregnant, my emotions were all over the place, I wasn't myself and acted crazy—which he noticed. But that's it, he asked how I was and wanted to know if I still had him blocked —" Kimmy grabbed her phone from her pocket, she did it as if unaware of the action. "—which I do. Nothing happened. We didn't even talk long, I promise—"

"Shorty, calm down." I believed nothing happened between them from the way she was ranting on. "I'm not accusing you of doing shit. Don told me earlier that he saw you and some nigga together. He said it wasn't King, just trying to make it seem like there was more to it. I'm asking because I don't remember you saying you saw anyone else. So, ain't no need to be scared and think I'mma put yo' ass out for having a conversation with a mothafucka."

Kim's brows furrowed at that as she took me in. After a while, her eyes rolled. "First off, I wasn't scared. Secondly, I didn't think you were going to put me out. As if you could, though, this is our home—"

"Man, get yo' ass away from me." I continued to rock my baby boys to sleep as I noted Kimmy still watching me.

"So, you're not mad that I was talking to Bell? Because it really wasn't anything, I promise." She once again assured me, which I believed.

I shrugged. "I don't think shit happened. Do I want yo' ass talking to that mothafucka? Hell nah. But I know it's a given that y'all will converse at some point. Conversation ain't shit to me, Kimmy. Now, if you start fucking that nigga, that's when we'll have a problem. So, nah, I ain't fucked up about no talking." Which wasn't a lie. I knew I couldn't keep her from not talking to dude or running into him. That would've been impossible given who they're associated with. Another reason was because of Tasha's ass. If Kimmy had to deal with that crazy-ass chick daily without complaining. I can handle her conversing with a mothafucka.

Even though I felt that way wholeheartedly, I knew that I would kill them if those two had another affair.

"That's never going to happen again, Mike. I know I keep saying that, but I really mean it, and I want you to trust me fully. These past several months have been a damn roller coaster for me emotionally. Hell, in the beginning, I wasn't sure that I even wanted this relationship to continue. I honestly thought I was still with you because of everything you've done for me and helped me get through." A laugh suddenly left her mouth.

"Until I confessed everything and actually knew I was about to lose you. Like, I saw it all in your face that day. Knowing you were about to end our everything scared the hell out of me. I knew losing you—us—wasn't an option at all. Yeah, I made mistakes and showed my ass—which I'm going to blame on being pregnant—during that time, but you were always it for me, no one else, I swear. You're probably tired of me saying the same thing over and repeating my promises. I just want you to know how serious I am about us. Regardless of the bullshit we might go through, we're in this forever. We're unbreakable. We can talk it out, fight the shit out, but we're stuck together until one of us dies—"

I broke the fuck out laughing. Although shorty was being serious as hell, I couldn't stop myself.

Kimmy hit me. "Dude, why would you laugh in my face like that. I'm being so damn serious, Michael, while your ugly ass sitting there laughing. You're so damn irritating." She hit me in my legs again.

"Sweetheart, I know you're serious as fuck. Kimmy, I trust you to do exactly what you're going to do. Shorty, I might have slipped up these past few years, but baby, I know you. Shit, probably better than you know yo' damn self. Before, I was too stuck on my own thing to pay your actions much attention. That's not going to happen again. None of the bullshit that happened with either of us will be repeated.

"I'll say this, yeah, we're bonded for life, Kimmy, you got my heart no doubt about that. We're breakable, though, sweetheart. Believe me when I say that. You're my weak spot, and I don't like that, nor can I change it. But I'd rather leave this relationship than lose myself or my sons." I told her while looking down at my boys.

My gaze fell on her. "Kimmy, I don't wanna kill yo' ass, but I will if you ever do that bullshit to me again. So, if you feel the need to go fuck on that nigga or any other mothafucka, end this relationship with me."

Kimmy wasn't a cheater, which I knew. The shit with Bellow was something that went too far.

"If you loved me as you've claimed. You won't let that heart of yours be so selfish with me."

"It's because I love you that my heart will forever be selfish with you, Michael. I'd rather have you lose yourself than for me to lose you. I know how that sounds and what it would mean, but losing you isn't an option for me. That's how I know I will never do anything to risk losing you again."

Baby was dead serious, and that further let me know how insane her ass really was. There I was, threatening to kill her ass, yet, she wasn't concerned with that threat, which I meant whole gotdamn heartedly.

Kimmy was gotdamn insane.

Hearing how selfish she was willing to be just to keep me probably should've pissed me off. Yet, it didn't. If anything, it just made me love her ass more.

Kimmy was poison to me, always have been. Any sane person would've said, fuck it, and walked away for their own sake, especially knowing shit could turn dangerous with us. Ironically, I wasn't the sane one to do it. And the fact she was now the mother of my twins, wasn't cause for me to walk away knowing what was at stake.

I guess that made me just as selfish as she was.

"That's fucking terrible, Kimmy, dead ass."

Leaning into my body, Kimmy cut my words off by kissing me. "True...still, you love me and all my selfishness anyway." Her tongue came out, and she licked from the rim of my bottom lip to the top of it. Kim's eyes jumped to mine, and she smiled.

"Yo' get the fuck away from me." Kimmy knew she was gotdamn poison. She licked my top lip then kissed me once more.

"Now lie and tell me we're not forever? We've both done some fucked up shit. You learned and grew from yours. I've learned from mine, and I'm growing. My growth is why we'll be forever and unbreakable. Now tell me, I'm right, you love me, then kiss me." She sat back and stared down at me expectingly.

My brows raised at that. Nodding, I lay the twins in their bassinets. Once I sat back down, Kimmy leaned into me again with that same expecting gaze in her eyes.

"I'mma give it to you. You're right about me. I learned and grew from my mistake. We'll see how you'll be in a year or two." Grabbing the nape of Kim's neck, I jerked her to me. My lips pressed against hers. "I love you."

"You're so damn irritating." She laughed, wrapping her arms around my neck. "I really do love you."

Nodding, I kissed her again. "I know you

really do." My hand slid around to her throat, squeezing, instantly her lips parted as she sucked in the breath I released. My tongue came out, and she grabbed it, sucking on the long pink flesh. The moan that left her mouth was followed by the twins crying. Kim groaned disappointedly. I was glad for the interruption. Kimmy loved starting shit when she knew we couldn't do anything. Those five weeks were going to kill me.

"I got them." I quickly hopped off the bed, getting away from her ass. As I stood over the twin's bed, rocking them back to sleep, I looked at Kimmy. "You keep on playing with me, yo' ass gonna get pregnant as soon as we fuck, I promise. I'm telling you. If you don't want that to happen, yo' ass better find some type of birth control, asap and condoms ain't an option no more—" Kimmy broke out laughing, "Shorty, I'm being serious as fuck."

"I know, and I believe you. That's why I'm laughing." Coming up behind me, Kimmy wrapped her arms around my waist while looking down at our sons. "If our babies will come out as beautiful as all three of our boys, I'll give you more." As she kissed my arm, her hand slid into my sweats and shorty took hold of my dick, stroking it. "And trust, you're not the only one going through withdrawals."

Grabbing the nape of my neck, she pulled my head down and kissed me. "I'm ready to say fuck that one stitch and few weeks and just let you tie me up and fuck me roughly...as only you do..." she bit my bottom lip. "Giving me back-to-back orgasms..."

she squeezed my dick, then bit my bottom lip again. "What you think…" she mumbled, kissing me.

Kimmy was sexy as fuck naturally, but shorty knew how to turn that shit up to a thousand. "Fuck it." I pushed Kim down on the bed. I was about to fold her up and fuck the shit out of her. My damn nuts were tight, and my dick was stiff, begging to be buried inside her.

"Ah!" Kimmy hollered out a laugh.

"Kimmy! Did you forget we were here?" One of her damn friends asked from behind the closed door.

"Yo! Get the fuck away from my door—"

Laughing, Kimmy hit me. "Don't talk to her like that. Nah, babe, I didn't forget y'all. I was on my way back down now." She told whoever. Taking in my glare, she smiled at me.

I smacked her thigh hard. "Why the fuck are you playing with me like that?"

"I wasn't playing. I was so serious in that moment…" she groaned. "You're gonna have to move into the guest room. This not gon' work for me. You're too fucking tempting." She ran her hand down my chest, then grabbed my dick.

She had me fucked up. "Hell nah, you ain't even about to play with me like that." I grabbed the hem of her sweats.

Again, Kimmy broke out laughing. "Mike, stop! You're making my stomach hurt. Ang! Come here!" She hollered, cracking up. I didn't find shit funny. I was about to choke her ass. "Babe, stop for real. I'm sorry. I was dead serious for real until Angel knocked on the door. We can't take the risk of me getting an infection or damaging—"

Groaning irritably, I pointed to the door. "Get the fuck out now. Don't bring yo' ass back in here either." I pushed away from her. I knew what she said was true, but I didn't want to hear that bullshit. "Matter fact." She wasn't even about to play with me like that. Grabbing a handful of her hair, I brought her face to my dick. Kimmy chuckled once again. "Ain't shit funny."

Kim's hands covered her face. "I'm sorry, you're right, it's not even funny. Okay, I'll suck your dick, but later tonight. Let me pump enough milk for them, and I got you. I promise." Standing, she went to kiss me, but I pulled back.

"Get the fuck out." I pointed to the door. Chuckling, she pressed her lips to mine, kissed the boys, and left the room. "Y'all fucking momma a gotdamn tease. She gets on my gotdamn nerves." Picking my boys up, I got back in the bed, lying against the headboard. My head fell back, and my eyes landed on the mirror built into the ceiling. I started laughing.

"That mothafucka was a gotdamn tease. I ain't even gonna trip about her little child's play. I'mma have her ass crying and begging—" Realizing I was talking to the twins who were staring at me unaware, I started laughing.

J PEACH

I was going to fuck Kimmy's ass up.

Chapter Twenty

Mike

A New Family

wo days had gone by since the whole thing with Martell and Don happened. During that time, my phone rang with calls from Martell and Don's uncle Pooh. I knew that because dude left about four voicemails, asking me to call him.

"Yeah?" I finally answered his call.

"Damn, nigga, yo' ass don't know how to answer the fucking phone or return a gotdamn call? Shit." He snapped, pissed off.

My brow raised, and I looked at the phone before hanging up. After a few seconds, the phone went off again. I answered it. "Yeah?"

"Did you just hang up on me?" He questioned.

"I did. Nigga, when you call my fuckin' phone, have yo' gotdamn mind right. All that growling and barking bullshit you doing, ain't it. I don't have to answer this bitch if I don't wanna." I wasn't avoiding Pooh's calls. The only reason I hadn't hit his line was that work had been hectic. With me just coming back after a week of being off, I had to play catch up with custom orders.

"Man, look, I'm just trying to see if you heard from my nephews. I know y'all had that meeting, but I haven't heard from them since then."

Although he couldn't see me, I shrugged. "Nah, I haven't seen them since the meeting."

The line fell silent, and I could hear a slight tapping coming from his end. "Ain't shit happen with y'all, did they seem cool to you?"

Again, I shrugged. "Yeah, they were when I left—"

"Fuck! So ain't shit happen while y'all were out at the range?" He repeated.

My brow raised at that. "Aside from them testing out the guns, what the fuck else was supposed to happen?"

"Nothing else, just that meeting. I'm just asking because I haven't heard from Don or Martell. I know Martell told me Parker and his boys were in town. Man, fuck. I'm trying to make sure they ain't run into them niggas—"

"When I left yo' people, they were breathing and standing by a truck. That's all I can tell you. If you wanna ride out to the range, aye gon' head—"

"I did that yesterday and wasn't shit there, aside from yo' pops and some other mothafuckas. But yo' old dude said he ain't seen them since the meeting. He says they left shortly after you—"

"Hold the fuck up. If you talked to my pops yesterday, why the fuck are you calling me about yo' fucking people?" Realizing he was playing some type of fucking game pissed me off. Shid, I didn't know my dad even talked to Pooh. His ass didn't tell me shit.

Of course, my dad would've known what happened at the range because one, I told him what was going down, and two, he would've seen the security footage, which he'd no doubt altered after watching what happened. I wouldn't have been surprised if he helped Parker and them clean up their mess.

"Man, calm down. I just wanted to see if you remembered something yo' pops didn't. So ain't no need for you to get rowdy. Mike, you know me, if I thought you did something to my nephews, we wouldn't even be talking, dead ass. We know you don't play sides or get involved with niggas bullshit. By the way, I heard how you looked out for Don at your spot that day—"

"Man, like I told Martell, the only reason I stepped in is because it was at my range—"

Pooh laughed, cutting me off. "We know why you did it. As I said, we know where you stand with other folk's shit. A'ight, look if you hear something, do me a solid and send word. Bet?"

"Nah, I ain't no messenger, baby. A'ight." I ended the call, tossing my phone into the cup holder.

"Who was that?" Kimmy questioned curiously.

I muffed her head to the side. "It was none of your damn business, that's who. Yo' ass nosy as hell." The entire time I was on the phone, I could feel Kimmy staring at me hard. Shorty definitely couldn't help herself with being in my damn business.

"Just tell me if it was about Martell—"

I pointed to the house we were parked outside of. "Get the fuck out of my truck and go inside before yo' girls come out here."

She glared at me. "You really get on my damn nerves..." she stopped speaking and glanced in the backseat. "Malik, you can go inside. Blake's waiting for you." She pointed to the house where Blake and another little boy stood on the front porch. Malik didn't hesitate to jump out of the truck and run to the house. Once he was gone, Kimmy's eyes fell on me again. When I saw her mouth open, I got out of the truck. Doing that made her laugh. "You're so damn childish. You remember this, Michael!"

I didn't even respond as I opened the back door and grabbed the babies'. Kimmy came over to me, making a grab for Millian. "I got it. You just go open the door."

Coming to the door, she stood in front of it, facing me. "Just tell me everything is okay. Let me hear you say that."

Sighing, I had the urge to rub my forehead. The only reason I didn't was because of the seats I held. "Sweetheart, everything is cool. I don't know why yo' ass is always worrying. If I don't tell you to be concerned about shit, you don't need to be. I wouldn't have you out here blind to shit if I was at risk."

Kimmy let out a breath. "I know, you wouldn't. So, what was the call about—"

I glared at her. "Get the fuck away from the door, Kimmy. Ol' nosey ass mothafucka." Laughing, Kimmy opened the front door, letting us in. The moment we walked in, all you could smell was food. "It's smelling good as fuck."

"Thank you," Angel said, coming from the living room. "My baby can cook his ass off." She told me while forcing me to stop in the hallway. "Hey, Tinka's handsome little babies." She cooed, coming to a squat in front of us. "Tink, don't even know which to grab first. I'll just get the both of you handsome little fellas..." she continued to coo at them.

My brow raised at Kim, but she shook her head and walked into the living room. Angel wasn't wasting no time as she tried taking them from the car seat.

"Can we at least get into the damn house first?"

"Okay, fine. Go to the living room, and I'll get them from there, hurry up." She rushed me.

"Syn, who's that?" Parker yelled from somewhere in the house.

"Kim and Mike!" She yelled back as we walked into the living room fully. Once I sat the seats down, Angel started taking them out. I didn't even say shit to her. After undoing the seats, she pointed toward the hallway. "The men are in the kitchen. Gone head. I know Parker's been waiting for y'all to get here. So, go." She shooed me off.

I didn't say anything as I followed the directions she gave me. She wasn't lying. Parker, Chris, Mane, their other boy Jason, King, and Blaze all sat around the large island.

"What's up, baby," King spoke once I walked in. Standing, he shook up with me. "You bring the babies over?" He asked, excited.

Once the twins were born, King had been to the house daily to see them. Which wasn't surprising because I was the same damn way when he had Keema. Not only was his presence known, so were the tons of matching clothes, shoes, and baby toys he bought them. The boys had way too much shit because of King, Leon, and Ron's asses.

"Yeah, Angel ass took them once we walked in." King got up, but I stopped him, shaking my head. "Don't even go in there. She just got them, and I don't wanna hear her ass complaining." I warned him.

"I'll give her ass a minute." He claimed, sitting down and making me laugh.

Chris, Parker, Mane, and Jason were next to speak as they shook up with me. Blaze tossed up two fingers which I gave a head nod to.

"It took y'all mothafuckas long enough to get here," Chris claimed before nodding to the side. "Let me holler at you real quick." He insisted, his head once again motioned to the side. Without another word, Chris went to a door that I overlooked before. Opening it, I could hear him going down some stairs.

I went to follow but stopped once I saw King get up. "Man, sit yo' ass down." Hitting his shoulder, I pushed him back into the chair. I then followed Chris and bounced down the stairs. Hearing movement behind me, I saw Parker, Mane, and Jason following.

"What's up?" I asked once we all made it to the basement.

Chris came into view with a little backpack in hand. He tossed it to me. "Just a little something to show our appreciation for what you've done. It hasn't been easy trying to find that bitch ass nigga, Martell, and had you not reached out, I'm sure shit wouldn't have gone this smoothly."

Looking into the bag of money. I zipped it back up and tossed it to him. "I don't want your money. In fact, I don't know what the fuck you're talking about or why you're giving me this." I didn't want their money because it wasn't why I got involved.

Them trying to give me money was a thank you, and thanks wasn't needed. As long as Angel and Missy were good, so were we. "We're good," I assured them before going back up the stairs.

Once I made it back to the kitchen, the girls came in with Keema right on their heels. Shorty looked pissed too. "What the fuck wrong with you?" I questioned.

Once Keema saw me, her eyes lit up. "Uncle Mike!" She ran and jumped on me. That excitement immediately left after she hugged me. Keema's eyes cut to the side as she glared at Angel and her momma.

"Girl, look at me like that again, and I'll whoop your ass, Sha'Keema." Angel threatened, laughing.

Keema wasn't fazed as she rolled her eyes. "Take your babies from them. They won't let me hold my baby cousins. Get your babies back." She damn near demanded, making me laugh.

"Sha'Keema, go sit yo' little ass down somewhere before you get hurt," Ebony warned her.

"So, you not going to get your babies back?" She asked, ignoring them.

I couldn't do shit but laugh at her grown ass. "You can come over later and hold them all you want. Bet?"

She let out a dramatic sigh. "Okay, fine. I guess that'll have to do. Can I spend the night?" She asked.

The movement in the corner grabbed my attention. Kimmy stood there shaking her head.

Grabbing my face, Keema brought my attention back to her. "Can I spend the night?" She repeated.

"Yeah, Keema, you can stay the night." Of course, I was going to tell her little spoiled ass yes.

Keema kissed my cheek. "Thanks, Uncle Mike." She got off me then turned to her momma and Angel. "That's why I'm spending a night with the babies." She told them before running to her daddy. "Can I sleep at Uncle Mike's house? He wants me to help with my baby cousins."

I broke out laughing at her lying ass. King looked at me, and once again, Kimmy grabbed our attention as she continued to shake her head no. Grabbing her arm, I pulled her into my side. "Man, leave Keema alone. She can come over."

"Keema ass is bad—"

"No, I'm not, Auntie Kimmy. I'll be good, promise, watch." She swore. Getting out of King's arms, she took off running outside. "Peewee! Come here!" She hollered.

"I don't know what the fuck y'all gonna do with that damn girl," I told them. Keema's ass was to gotdamn grown.

"Let me see these gotdamn babies." Parker was saying until Angel cut in.

"Babe, they're so beautiful too. I want twins now, but I want them." She cooed, taking Killian from Ebony, who pulled back. "Girl, give me this damn baby, so Parker can see him." She fussed at her. The shit was ironic because she was holding a damn baby herself. "Like how you gonna be stingy with him." She made a point to say, making me laugh because Ebony gave her the baby without much fight.

"Ang, you have a whole baby in your arms. You could've given Millian to Parker." Kimmy told her, laughing.

"Bitch!" Ebony said as if that just dawned on her. "Girl, give me my gotdamn baby back." Although she said that, Ebony didn't grab him as Parker took him from Angel.

"Syn been talking about gotdamn twins since she's seen y'all's—oh damn, that's a look," Parker stated before his gaze fell on me, then to Kimmy. "You didn't tell me one had mismatch eyes."

"Babe, both of them do. Look." Angel was gushing over the boys as she put them side by side. "I want them." She cooed.

Parker laughed at that. "I'm starting to believe you really do for real."

I was starting to think that bullshit too.

"Their eyes are so beautiful. It's one light brown then that vibrant bright blue." Angel groaned, excited.

"Let me see this shit." Chris pushed his way between Angel and Parker. He stared at the babies, then between Kimmy and me. "Oh yeah, these mothafuckas gonna be trouble." His words trailed off as Millian face twisted up. "Oh, this little dude gon' be mean. Look how his little ass is mugging already."

Angel pulled Millian away from Chris' view. "He doesn't like loud talking. Ain't that right, Tinka stink-stink man." She cooed, kissing his gloved hand. "Aren't they so handsome, babe?"

Parker laughed at Angel and nodded no less. "Yeah, Syn, they are. I agree with Chris. They're gonna be hell when they get older."

"Seeing them on a picture is completely different face to face. Their eyes gonna have those little girls going crazy." Blaze chimed in.

Chris took Millian from Angel, and shorty was pissed off about it. Chris didn't pay her attitude no attention as he walked into the backyard.

My arms went around Kimmy as we followed him. "Next time, the twins are going to my folk's crib," I told her as I watched Angel try to get the baby back from Chris, but he wasn't giving him away.

We had just sat down when Mane walked over to us. He kneeled beside Kimmy. "Here, this for the babies. Just a little something to welcome them into the family." He claimed, giving her the same bookbag I had given back to them.

I glared at him only to have his ass grin back. My sights drifted to Chris, Parker, and Jason only to find them wearing the same gotdamn smirk.

"What's that?" The girls asked her.

She looked at them and laughed. "How the hell am I supposed to know?"

Angel glanced at Parker and his friends, confused. I could see her whispering to him, but I couldn't hear what was said. However, Parker's head shook in response.

Kimmy opened the bag, and her eyes damn near bucked out of their sockets as she saw the money. "What?" She looked at Mane as if asking was he serious? "Nah, I can't take this."

"You can, and you are. We ain't taking it back." Chris told her. "It's a welcoming gift. As he said, they're family and forever will be." He explained, yet his gaze fell on me.

I knew Kimmy caught the action because her sights fell on me. Her mouth opened and closed before she nodded in understanding. "Thank y'all. I don't even know what else to say for real."

"You don't have to say shit. Just know y'all family and forever will be." Parker told her.

"Okay, okay, I feel some type of way." Peaches speaking brought our attention to her. I didn't even know shorty was there. She held her baby girl Brianna in her arms while the little boy pulled to get free. Once he was loose, he wobbled over to Blaze.

"What got you feeling some type of way, sweetheart?" Chris asked her.

She pointed to Kimmy, then our twins. "How come they get welcomed into y'all family, but I don't? I don't think E's been welcomed into the damn family yet. Like what the fuck?" She questioned before looking at Angel. "I told you, his ass doesn't like me after what happened at your party." Peaches claimed, slickly glancing over at Parker.

"Peaches, don't start that, okay. I already told you we've been over that." Although that's what left her mouth, Angel's eyes told Peaches to shut up.

I've been around those girls long enough to learn their silent eye motions and gestures.

Peaches got it. Even so, she glanced at Parker as if wanting him to clarify what Angel said.

Parker caught it and laughed. "Real shit, you're right. Personally, I don't care for you. Yeah, Syn's over it, but because of how you acted toward *your supposed sister*, won't ever sit right with me." He shrugged uncaringly. "But that's just *me*. Syn loves the fuck out of you, so you'll always be her family to me. For that reason alone, I'll forever tolerate you until she says otherwise. That's how I feel when it comes to just you." He explained further. "This shit right here though—" he motioned from the bag of money to us, "—don't have shit to do with how I feel about either of you. This shit is simply between us." He motioned between his boys and me.

The girls looked at Angel, whose hands covered her face. "Babe, you didn't even have to say all that. The party was years ago. Like the shit is dead, leave it buried." She said, looking at Parker as if asking him—what the fuck?

He shrugged and pointed to Peaches. "She asked me how I felt about her. I wasn't about to lie to the damn girl."

I wasn't at Angel's party when everything came out. Of course, Kimmy later told me what went down. I wasn't surprised by Peaches' reaction. That was just her, but I agreed that the shit should've been handled privately, especially given what was later exposed. I knew that made Peaches feel like shit.

Yet, I couldn't blame Parker either. Had it been Kimmy, I would've felt the same way without a doubt.

"Y'all mothafuckas funny as fuck." The way he laid the shit out was hilarious to me. I could tell dude was a straight shooter and spoke what he thought or felt without regard to anybody's feelings.

Kimmy turned to face me. "That's not funny —"

"The fuck if it ain't. Angel told her ass to shut the fuck up. But Peaches hardheaded ass didn't listen." Kimmy hit me in the stomach, mouthing for me to shut up.

"Bitches...or not," Missy said, reaching us. "Why you hoes looking so damn...I don't even know what this look is. What happened?" Missy walked into the circle and glanced around for an empty chair before going over and sitting in Angel's lap. "What we miss? Y'all, we missed something! We might have to beat some ass!" She yelled while waving her hands.

I glanced in the direction she was motioning in. Two females were coming our way.

"Damn."

"Same shit I be saying," King grunted from beside me.

The hard whack to the back of my head had me looking at Kimmy like she was stupid. "Why the fuck you just hit me for?"

She hit me again. "Make me beat yo' mothafuckin' ass, Michael."

"What the fuck did he even do?" King and Blaze asked, laughing.

"That's what the fuck I'm trying to figure out before I beat her ass." She had slapped the shit out of me.

"The man ain't even said shit." Chris chimed in, laughing while looking between us.

Kimmy's ass wasn't paying them no attention as she glared at me. "You better watch yo' fucking eyes before I beat the fuck out of you." She claimed before pointing to the chick who went and sat beside Mane.

My brows furrowed before I laughed. "Man, get the fuck away from me. I just looked at that fuckin' babe when she walked out—"

"And yo' ass groaned. Don't play with me, Mike." Kim's glare deepened as if telling me to lie.

Shid, I didn't know if I groaned or not. The chick was cute, thick boned, and full in all the right places, just like Kimmy. I could admit I had a type, and that babe was it. But shorty wasn't touching Kim, in my opinion.

Grabbing a handful of Kim's hair, I jerked her crazy ass to me. My mouth went to her ear. "If yo' ass hit me like that again, I'mma beat the fuck out of you. I ain't checking that gotdamn babe out." I told her before looking back at ol' girl. "That's Mane's girl? Just say yes or no, don't do all that extra shit." She nodded in response. "Shid, now I see why he liked yo' ass. You and his shorty shaped the same. Your ass fatter, though." I held her head tighter to me as she tried to move back.

"Man, calm yo' ass down. That's the babe he wanted you to have a threesome with?" Again, she nodded. "See if she'll do a threesome with just us—" I grabbed Kimmy's arms. "I'm bullshitting. Calm yo' silly ass down. Now you see how I feel when you're playing about the shit with Missy and her nigga. Yo' ass bet not touch me, Kimmy." I let her go, and she jumped at me.

"What the fuck?" King asked.

I pointed to Mane's girl. "Kimmy dumb ass thought I was looking at her. Baby, cute, but I wasn't checking her ass out. Dead ass, I was looking at baby right there." I pointed to the chick sitting next to Jason. "Who is she?"

"My wife, that's who." Jason chimed in, glaring at me.

I nodded, then looked at Kimmy. "We can do a threesome with her if you wanna, and if she's down for it. She's the only exception. I'll even watch." I glanced back at ol' girl, then to Kimmy, and nodded. "Yeah, I'll watch. What you think?"

Kim's mouth opened, then closed, and she looked to Jason's wife. She started laughing. "I'm sorry, Meka, he's not serious—"

"The fuck I ain't. I'm dead fucking serious. If you wanna have a threesome—shid, it could just be the two of y'all for real." My hand went to my stomach, and I groaned. Although I was only joking initially. As I thought further on it, I wouldn't even mind watching Kim fuck that babe.

"Shid, if Jason's cool with it, I'm definitely down to fuck Kimmy." Meka jumped in, smiling. "I wouldn't even mind y'all watching either." She motioned between her dude and me.

"Meka!" Angel broke out laughing. "Girl, don't feed into his damn foolishness."

Meka waved her off. "Oh, I'm being dead ass serious. I'll fuck Kimmy. Lick her ass the fuck up—"

I fell the fuck out laughing at how serious she sounded. Kimmy's face was red as hell. "What the fuck is up with y'all wanting to fuck my shorty?" I looked from Delilah to Meka.

"Her ass." The pair chorused. "She's sexy as fuck too." They again said at once. Looking at each other, they broke out laughing.

"Kimmy, you stay away from them. I didn't even know Meka felt like that." Missy said, looking surprised. "You hoes, stay away from my best friend. She is mine only."

"Missy, shut up," Jason told her before looking at his girl. "Dead ass?" He asked her, and she nodded. His gaze fell on Kimmy. "What you think?"

Kimmy started laughing. "No, absolutely not. Y'all are so beautiful. I mean sexy as fuck, but women just don't move me sexually. Now that we have that cleared up, let's move on." Kimmy turned to me, glaring. "I'mma beat yo' ass for getting this shit started. Plus, no matter how much that damn thought might've played in your head, yo' ass won't even be cool with a damn threesome or watching, for that matter. You're to gotdamn possessive for that shit. Especially sexually. That's the only reason I'm not slapping your ass." Leaning into me, her lips pressed against mine.

Grabbing her arms, I pulled her into my lap. My hand slapped the side of her thigh. "Don't say shit."

"Okay, so now that shit has calmed down.

What did I walk in on?" Missy asked.

Ebony pointed to us. "Apparently, only the twins and them—" she flicked her hand in our direction dismissively. "—have officially been accepted into their—" her fingers wiggled at Parker, "—family or whatever."

Missy looked confused by that. "What? Why do you think that?"

Once again, Ebony's finger wiggled at the dudes. "Because Mane gave her a bag and said *this is something to welcome them into the family*." Ebony mimicked Mane's voice while pointing to the backpack. "We didn't get welcomed like that."

"Wait, he did what now?" Meka questioned, seeming confused. The girls nodded in response. She then looked at Kimmy and me. Shorty's lips started moving soundlessly before her sights soon fell on the bag. I could see the confusion all over her face. "P-Nut, what the fuck happened?" Meka asked, looking at Parker. "You don't just welcome anybody into the family. Why them?"

"Damn, Meka, just offend us," Kimmy told her.

Meka waved her off. "You know I don't mean it like that. We're all cool. And Y'all became family because of Angel, but to be with us is completely different." She explained before motioning from Parker, Chris, Mane, Delilah, and Jason.

I could tell she was deep with them from the way she talked. Jason's arm went around her shoulders, and he pulled Meka to him. He began whispering to her, and her mouth snapped shut. Meka's lips soon formed in the shape of an O, and she looked at me.

"What is the family? I'm so confused." Kimmy finally asked what I was sure the other girls were wondering.

When nobody said anything, Angel's lips smacked, and she rolled her eyes. "Basically, y'all will forever be looked out for. If you ever need anything, they're there no matter the time of day. If anything happens to either of y'all," she motioned between Kimmy and me. "The twins will forever be taken care of. Y'all are basically with them in a sense. It's more to it, but that's the basic." Angel explained as if it was nothing. "Wait..." She stated as her explanation hit her. "Wait, what I miss?" She turned to Parker, then looked back to us. "We'll be back. Come on."

What Angel did, by pulling Parker off to question him, is what I felt Meka should've done. At least that way, the shit would've been private without having anyone wondering. Especially if they didn't want everybody else to know why they welcomed us.

Parker didn't hesitate to get up and follow behind her. As they were walking off, Kimmy tried to stop them. "Parker, I can take Killian—"

"We got him; girl, sit down, damn." Angel waved her off and kept walking into the house.

"Syn wants these damn babies." Chris laughed. "They're all she's been talking about. She got baby fever but don't wanna pop no more out." He said while playing with Millian's covered hand. "Yo' auntie needs to quit playing and give us some more babies."

"Nigga, you talking about her. Yo' ass ain't tryna hand shorty over. You sat there and had a whole conversation with dude, and he doesn't even know what the fuck you're talking about or who you are." Mane told him, laughing.

Chris chuckled at that. "We're getting to know each other. He gonna know I'm Uncle Chris. Tell him to mind his fucking business." He held Millian up to face Mane. "These little mothafuckas tight, though. They're definitely gonna be kicking it with Unc when they get older. Ain't that right?" He cooed him.

"Nigga, at this point, you need to stop playing and gon' head and give Tiana a sibling," Jason told him.

Chris started smiling as he whispered something to Millian. He then addressed Jason. "Shid, I've been trying, but Missy's bullshitting."

"Oh my God!" Kimmy broke out laughing. "Boy, shut the fuck up." Chris looked at her, his brows furrowing, which caused Kimmy's laughter to stop instantly. "No, you're not serious, Chris?"

"How come I'm not?" He questioned.

Delilah started laughing. "I actually believe he asked her to have his baby. Missy, did he for real?"

Missy's eyes rolled. "No." Chris laughed, making her glare at him.

"Yo' Auntie on that bullshit. She knows she wanna carry my baby for me. But she's with that lame ass nigga, so now she doesn't want to have my baby. That's alright because she's gonna be jealous when I find somebody else to give birth to my shorty." He told Millian, who smiled.

Missy seeing that started laughing. "Man, give me my damn nephew. He don't need that type of foolery in his damn head." She tried to take Millian from Chris, but he pushed her back.

"Man, watch out. I got him." He turned so that Millian couldn't see Missy. She started laughing then sat on Chris' lap.

"Lord, let me see him," Mane asked, moving to the edge of his seat.

"No, I'm next," Missy told him.

Chris got up, forcing her off his lap. He went over to Mane and handed him the baby. "Oh, my God, he's so cute." Delilah gushed over him.

Missy, on the other hand, was mugging Chris.

"What's good with you, nephew?" Mane asked, making him smile. "Oh, you're definitely going to be a little heartbreaker," Mane told Millian before his gaze settled on us. "Y'all might as well get ready for problems.

"As long as they're not teen parents, we're good. The girls gonna come, though, we're cursed like that." I told him before motioning to my son. "Now, can I get my shorty back?"

"Man, y'all ain't getting them back until it's time for y'all to bounce," Mane claimed as he too began talking to Millian, ignoring us completely.

Kimmy turned in my arms, bringing her mouth to my ear. "Is the money and everything because of Martell?" I nodded in response. "So, you wouldn't take the money. That's why they gave it to me?" Once again, I nodded. "They don't know I'm aware of everything?" My head shook. "Why the fuck are they talking about the family like it's some type of mob shit?" She asked.

"What y'all two over there whispering about?" Ebony questioned.

"What we're whispering about that's what with yo' nosey ass," I told her.

Kimmy popped my chest as she chuckled. "It's nothing for real." She let Ebony know, then turned her attention to me, bringing her mouth to my ear. "You think Parker telling Angel?" I nodded in response.

I was surprised he hadn't told her after it happened.

"What is this?" Missy speaking grabbed my attention. I watched as she grabbed a chain from around Chris' neck. "Is that a grill?" She questioned, looking at the diamond mouthpiece. "Why do you have a grill as a charm?"

"It's my trophy." He smiled, fingering the diamond teeth. My brows furrowed, recognizing the grill Don was wearing.

I laughed at seeing Don's grill. That crazy mothafucka cleaned that bitch off and wore it around his neck. Chris called it right because that was a gotdamn trophy, and from the look on his face, he was excited about having it. Then again, I wouldn't expect him to feel any other way.

Hell, killing that nigga probably gave him peace of mind or the closure he needed for his wife. Given what Don said he and Mook did to Chris' lady, he no doubt needed that for his sanity and for him to let his shorty rest peacefully.

Chris' eyes met mine, and he nodded at me as he continued to stroke that grill. Instantly I regretted how I acted in the basement. Chris trying to show gratitude was because I gave him the closure he needed. It wasn't only because I helped them out. It was for him personally, too.

I returned his gesture, fully understanding why they felt grateful. I couldn't even imagine the head fuck he had gone through.

My eyes slid down to Kimmy, and I pulled her closer to me. I couldn't even imagine how I'd be mentally if some shit like that ever happened to her.

Just thinking about the possibilities of some shit like that occurring made me not want to let her out of my sight, hell, let her go period.

At that moment, I knew being without her was never going to be an option for me. I was to gotdamn protective and possessive of Kimmy. Regardless of what bullshit comes our way. I couldn't see my life without her.

Shorty was my future, my life, shit, my everything. She was right. No matter how bad we probably were for each other, we were forever.

Grabbing a handful of Kimmy's hair, I pulled her head back, kissing her just how she loved.

She was right. Because of how much we loved one another, we couldn't help but forever be selfish with each other.

Epilogue

Kimmy

A Forever Love

Four Years Later

"Millian, you better not!" I yelled at my four-year-old son, who was trying to push his four-wheeler into the pool.

"Baby, that damn Millian is fucking terrible." Peaches said, watching as he pretended not to hear me. "Like, Kimmy, I'm not even exaggerating, I mean, we all have bad kids, but Millian takes the cake. On top of that, his ass is mean."

I couldn't argue with her and defend my baby because he was damn Chucky in the making. "Peach, I know. Malik wasn't shit like that at his age. Even Killian, his damn twin, isn't anything like that. Girl, he's going to make me go to jail already—Millian Royal Payne, if you push that damn bike into that pool, I'm whooping your ass. I'm not playing with you!" I yelled as Killian ran out of the house with Mike behind him. A second later, Parker and Chris soon followed behind them. Seeing my babies, I smiled. My fingers started waving for them to come to me.

"Lil' Money!" Chris called to Millian, who ignored him too. "I know his ass hear me." He said, glaring at my baby. Since Millian was a baby, Chris gave him the nickname Money, saying his name meant that. Although his name was spelled MILLIAN, the pronunciation was Million. The nickname stuck, and everyone called him Money when he wasn't acting up.

Once Killian reached me, he rubbed his sweaty face against my shirt before he pulled back, smiling. "Gimme kiss." Grabbing my face, he kissed my lips. My baby was the sweetest child when he *wanted* to be. "I love you, sweetheart," Killian said, kissing me again.

Mike broke out laughing as he muffed Killian's head to the side. "Man, move yo' little ass out of the way."

My baby rubbed his head and glared at his daddy. "Dude, stop, irritating." He pushed Mike, making me laugh.

"You call that man irritating way too damn much." Peaches cracked up. "Can I get a hug?" She asked, holding her arms out. He didn't hesitate to go to his auntie and climb into her lap.

"Every single day, I'm calling that man irritating." I laughed while hitting Mike. "I know he better leave my baby alone before we have to jump him. Ain't that right, Buddha?"

Killian's head bobbed. "Yup!" He said, popping the p.

Leaning over to him, I kissed the top of his head. My sights soon landed on Parker, and I held my arms out.

"Man, I got him. Tell yo' moms to chill the fuck out, Kells." He told my two-year-old son, MyKell.

When Parker and his people said, we were part of the family. They meant that wholeheartedly. Neither of them ever missed a birthday party, a baby shower, or anything regarding the boys. Not only that, they all made a point to get to know my sons. The boys were out in Bloomingdale with them at least one week out of a month. Their visits only lasted a week because that was the longest I could go without seeing my babies.

"Can I at least give him a kiss? Like, you've had him all morning." I complained, glaring at Parker.

He shrugged. "Kells, you wanna go with yo' moms?" He asked him while giving MyKell a sucker.

"Dude, give me my damn son." Grabbing him from Parker, I kissed him. "You had fun with your Uncle Parker?"

He nodded before pulling the sucker out his mouth. "Yeah. Candy?" He said before pushing the sucker against my lips.

Laughing, I sucked on it. "Thank you."

"Thank you." He repeated before kissing me. "Daddy." He wiggled out of my arms and went to Mike, making me roll my eyes. MyKell was definitely a damn daddy's baby.

"Mommy, mommy!" The little voice that hollered from the back door caused a wide smile to grace my lips.

"Kimmy, bitch, I'm damn done!" Angel hollered, letting go of the jerking little boy trying to escape her grasp. Finally letting go, my baby took off.

I broke out laughing at the little bowlegs running toward us. Reaching me, he ran into my arms, cracking up. "Jaheem, you were working your Tink's nerves?" I kissed my baby boy's cheek.

"Kim, bitch! Get Chucky damn junior!" Missy yelled, coming into the backyard, looking stressed out.

"Man, y'all better quit playing with my damn sons like that." Mike snapped at them but chuckled no less. He knew just like I did that our sons were handfuls. "Come here, Kareem."

Missy and Angel looked at each other before they glared at us. "Those gotdamn boys are fucking bad!" They exclaimed at once.

My head shook when I glanced between my second set of twins, Jaheem and Kareem. "Y'all wasn't bad, were you?" I asked them.

Jaheem pointed to his twin. "Remmy was." He told, making me laugh. By Jah telling, I knew his ass was acting up as well. He always blamed Kareem when he didn't want to get in trouble.

At two, three, and four years old, my babies were so smart for their ages. Looking at my five babies, both sets of twins, Millian aka Money, Killian aka Buddha, Jaheem aka Jah or Jah-Jah, Kareem aka Remmy, and MyKell aka Kells, all I could do was smile at them.

Jaheem Kentaivous Payne and Kareem Jontaivous Payne, my second set of twins, were born eight months after I had Millian and Killian. After they were born, I gave birth to my youngest, MyKell Deontay Payne, literally eight months later.

Mike wasn't playing with me when he said I'd stay pregnant. Plus, my constant teasing throughout those weeks after every birth didn't help. When week six came, that man had my feet tied to my hands each damn time, and I ended up pregnant afterward. Although my kids were literally eight months apart, I loved that they were all close in age and had each other to grow with.

Mike's genes were strong as ever because not one of our children looked like me. They all took after him. It was like all my kids had been run through a damn copy machine. My boys had his eyes, except for MyKell, who had my light brown orbs. Jaheem and Kareem's eyes were blue with specks of brown.

"Jah-Jah—" I groaned as he pulled up my shirt and started kissing my swollen eight-month belly.

Since my due date was around the corner, Missy wanted to throw me a baby shower—which I didn't want, of course. I had been dodging having one for months simply because Malakai, my unborn son, already had more than enough stuff. Everything his brothers had was passed down to him. But of course, I didn't have a say in the matter. So, I agreed to show up to the baby shower only if it took place at my house. For one, I was pregnant as hell, my feet were swollen, and I didn't feel like lugging my five sons around. Missy agreed, of course.

Little spittle began hitting my stomach as Jaheem whispered unknown words to my belly. I looked at Mike and shook my head, laughing. "Love you." He kissed my stomach again.

"Aw." The girls cooed at him. "Mike must talk to your stomach a lot," Angel said, picking Jaheem up.

"Every damn day since he found out I was pregnant. He did the same thing with all of them." I motioned to my five kids. "Millian!" I yelled as he pushed the bike to the edge of the pool.

"Shh." Kareem's hand covered my mouth as he shushed me. Kareem, who I named after my daddy, was the youngest of him and Jaheem. Yet, he and Millian gave me the most gotdamn problems. Those two were so much alike that it was crazy to me. Whereas Killian and Jaheem were the calmest out of the two.

I glared at Mike. "I'm going to whoop his ass and Millian—if he don't get away from that pool!" I yelled just as he pushed the four-wheeler into the water.

"Oh, my God." The girls muttered.

Once the bike splashed, he fell on the ground and balled up.

The girls instantly became worried, whereas I just rubbed my forehead. Yup, that boy was going to have me locked the hell up for whooping his ass.

"Millian! Money!" Peaches and Missy hollered as they jumped out of their seats and ran to him. I glanced at Mike to see his face pressed into MyKell's back. Yet, the shaking of his shoulders told me his ass was laughing.

My gaze fell on Peaches and Missy, who kneeled beside Money. After a second, the pair looked at me.

"Is he alright? What even happened?" Angel, who stood with Jaheem in her arms, yelled, concerned.

"Bitch!" Missy hollered at us. Whereas Peaches picked him up laughing.

"What happened?" Angel asked once they reached us. Peaches held Millian out toward Angel as his soft snores could be heard. "Girl! I know damn well..." she glared at me before looking back to him.

"I'm about to whoop his ass."

Millian's eyes popped open then. "Nuh-uh, you not!" He stated, wiggling out of Peaches arms. "Uncle Chris!" He pushed away from Peaches and started to run off but stopped once he saw Mike. "Daddy, what's up." He went over and climbed into his dad's lap. He forced MyKell to move over as he hugged Mike.

"Why you push that gotdamn bike into that pool?" Mike fussed at him, and Millian's lip drooped as he started sniffling. "Boy, don't play that fake shit with me."

Millian's little head rolled around, and he exhaled a breath before he shrugged. I looked at Mike to see what he was going to do.

"Dude, go play and stay yo' ass away from the damn pool," Mike told him.

"A'ight." Millian's fist came out, and Mike bumped it. "Kells." He turned his fist to his baby brother, and MyKell gladly punched it. Once he did, homeboy took off running over to Chris and Parker.

"Kimmy, what the hell was that with him falling down?" Missy asked, laughing.

My head just shook before I chuckled lightly. "Girl, he'll do that shit and fake sleep so he won't get in trouble. Y'all, I don't know where he gets that shit from. But I swear he works my damn nerves doing it." I told them before I glared at Mike. "The way Mike just reacted, that's why his ass is like that now. He don't ever whoop him. Like, this shit is not cool,

Michael—"

"Ooh, you in trouble." Killian laughed before pushing Jaheem off me, making him fall to the ground. "Move, Jah-Jah." He said, then started rubbing my belly.

"Buddha, now why the fuck you push him—" Mike was fussing at him when Remmy came over and whacked the shit out of Killian in the back with his stainless steel insulated cup.

"Punk ass!" Kareem pushed Buddha down, then helped Jaheem off the ground. "Get up, bro." He told him, sounding like Malik.

Killian burst out crying, but he went to attack Kareem, no less.

"Yo!" Mike yanked the pair apart. All the while, Jaheem and Kells cracked up.

"Crybaby," MyKell taunted, laughing.

I looked at Mike, and he glared at me. "Don't say shit." He said, still holding Buddha and Remmy apart. "Jah, Kells, come on." He told them, and they took off behind him.

Looking at my five boys, I wanted to bawl and laugh simultaneously. They were so gotdamn bad when they wanted to be. Not only that, but they constantly fought, which I knew that was what siblings did. Yet the shit was daily and nonstop. Every day I was breaking up a fight with my boys.

"I swear this is my last damn child. Y'all, I'm getting my tubes tied, burnt, bitches, I'm getting the fucking works." I told them while shaking my head. "Like, I can't. We're about to have seven gotdamn boys. Malik's cool because he's older, but those five I can't." The girls broke out laughing at me. "Y'all, this is not even funny in real life."

"It's not at all, yet it is. Kimmy, you used to talk hella shit about my boys. Now, look at yours. Baby, yo' damn boys are terrors." She hollered out a laugh before pointing to Jaheem. "Girl, that one and Kareem went to the store with us, and those fucking boys took the fuck off on our ass. Bitch, had us running through the damn store looking damn crazy. Then they have the nerve to be fast as hell. Before you ask, they didn't want to get in the buggy. So, we let them walk. Never fucking again. Peewee and Ant's asses weren't no fucking help. All they did was laugh while we chased your damn kids." Angel explained.

Missy burst out laughing. "Bitch, Kareem looked at me and said—bye, then took the fuck off running. Like, he dead ass stared me in the face and told my ass *bye* before he ran."

That was precisely why I didn't bother taking those two to the store. They played entirely too much. My gaze settled on Mike, wrestling with Killian, Kareem, Jaheem, and MyKell. "That's why their asses bad now. Y'all, I'm about to pack myself and Malakai—" I pointed to my stomach, gesturing to my unborn son, "—up then runaway. They're not about to corrupt my baby boy." I chuckled while rubbing my stomach.

Missy chuckled as she rubbed my belly as well. "Girl, Mike said he wasn't having any girls, and his damn sperm agreed. He has kept your ass pregnant back to back with straight boys. Bitch, yo' coochie ain't tired? You have popped out five kids in the last four years. Now you're about to drop a sixth. Baby, my coochie is tired for you."

I laughed at that. "I'm so over being pregnant. Like, I'm done after this shit, I swear." Yet, I didn't know how true I was to that promise. Hell, I loved my babies and giving birth. I loved being a mom, to be honest. "I'm not having any more of Mike's badass babies!" I yelled over to him. Millian had joined in and was wrestling with them.

"Y'all, he's an amazing father, though, for real. I mean, he's always been a great dad, but everything just seemed to have amplified with him. Don't get me wrong, my ass is exhausted from being pregnant. Still, Mike makes me feel so damn good while I'm feeling huge. The way he caters to my body, I feel so damn sexy still." I told them without even intending to say all of that. The words just flowed out of my mouth as I stared at my man and our kids.

"Nah, her damn coochie ain't tired yet." Peaches claimed, causing a burst of laughter to leave my mouth.

"You're so damn irritating, I swear." I pushed her before laying my head on her shoulder. "My body is tired, but shit, I love being pregnant for real y'all—"

"Oh, we can tell. Hell, you don't complain nearly as much as I did." Angel chuckled.

"Mommy!" Millian yelled, running over to me. His sweaty face rubbed into my chest before he grabbed my cranberry juice off the table. "I'm hot." He expressed, breathing hard. Kissing his sweaty forehead, I opened the juice for him. After taking a long drink, he gave me the bottle back, breathing heavily. "Gimme kiss." Grabbing my face, he kissed my lips. He then grabbed the hem of my shirt.

"Gone now, Money—"

His hand raised at me. "Shorty, let me kiss my baby." He demanded as he pulled my shirt up. My eyes shifted to the girls. The trio was against each other, trying hard not to laugh. "Don't give yo' momma a hard time. Be good." He kissed my stomach again. Grabbing my face, he kissed me once more. "Bye." With that, he took off running.

"Bitch! No, he did not shorty you, though!" Missy hollered as the others fell out laughing. "Girl, that damn boy is too grown."

"Sounding just like Mike's ass. Y'all, I can't stand that little boy." I stared after Millian and broke out laughing. "His ass is Mike, through and through. My damn kids are cursed—"

"Shid, I told you that already." Mike grabbed a handful of my hair, pulled my head back, and kissed me. "What Money ass do now?"

After pecking his lips once more, I pointed to

Millian. "Yo' damn son is what happened. Why did he just shorty me? Talking about, let him kiss his baby."

Mike started cracking up. "Man, leave that boy alone. He wanted to kiss his baby brother."

"My girlfriend here!" Killian shouted and took off, running toward the back door.

Again, I looked at Mike. He just shook his head. "Look, I ain't got shit to do with that. That's all you, sweetheart. Plus, Keema started him with that shit." Mike said as Killian ran to Keema, and she picked him up, kissing all over his face.

"It's about time y'all got here," I told Ebony.

She pointed to Keema. "That was her ass. She's always trying to do extra shit." She complained. "We had to stop and get Linnea." She pointed to Sam's daughter, walking into the yard with King and Malik.

Seeing my oldest baby and the chick with him, I turned and glared at Mike. At sixteen years old, Malik was a handsome, 6'1 tall young man. He was the spitting image of his father at that age. On top of that, he's a straight A+ student, a football star, and my baby was driving. Which were all fantastic things in my eyes. Yet, the only downside of having a handsome son was that his appearance attracted hot ass girls.

"Mike, did you know he was bringing her over here?" I asked, pointing to Chyna, Malik's little friend as he calls her.

He nodded. "Yeah, he said she was coming over." He shrugged.

Malik started bringing her around about a year ago. Chyna was a gorgeous girl, but her attitude was horrible. Not only that, she was entirely too gotdamn whiny. If homegirl couldn't get ahold of him, she would call my gotdamn phone looking for his ass. Chyna was just too much for a fifteen-year-old.

"Hey, Mr. Payne." She waved at Mike. I couldn't help but laugh at her formality when she addressed him. Chyna ass was scared of him. She had called his damn phone one time looking for Malik. My baby went the fuck off. Never again had she redialed his line. "Hey, Mrs. Kim." She smiled, waving at me.

"Hey, Chyna." I returned the gesture.

"What's up, momma?" Malik's deep voice spoke as he leaned down and kissed my cheek. "I was going to tell you she was coming but forgot." He whispered into my ear. After kissing my cheek again, he stood up. Taking in my glare, he chuckled lightly. "I'm sorry." He apologized as his arm went around her shoulder.

"I brought a gift. Where should I put it?" Chyna was saying as Keema bumped into her, pushing between the pair.

"Probably on the table where all the other gifts are at. Maybe, you think?" Keema pointed to the area where tons of gifts sat, most of which came from damn Parker and his people.

Chyna's lips pursed together, and she waved her finger at Keema. I knew she wanted to say something slick from the harsh look on her face, but she decided not to. Whereas I looked at Ebony, who just shook her head.

At eleven, Sha'Keema was to gotdamn grown for her age. Homegirl did not like Chyna at all, and she made it known. Keema claimed her distaste for her was because the girl was tacky.

"Hey, auntie." She leaned down and hugged me. "Baby, you looking ready to pop." She laughed, rubbing my stomach. "Hey, Unc." She hugged Mike. Turning to Malik, she rolled her eyes before punching him in the chest. "What happened to yo' little ugly ass—butt coming to pick me up and taking me to the mall?" She fussed at him.

"Oop." My lips pursed together as she fussed at him. My hand covered my mouth so that I wouldn't laugh. Keema ass knew she ran the men, especially Mike and Malik. They did whatever her spoiled ass wanted. The shit was simply hilarious, especially with Malik.

Malik muffed the shit out of Keema before putting her into a headlock so she wouldn't hit him again. "Man, I told you I had something to do." He pushed her away from him and jumped back.

"Get off my girlfriend!" Killian ran up, pushing Malik back. "Punk ass!" He punched his big brother in the legs.

My hand covered my mouth as I leaned into Mike, trying not to laugh. "Oh, my God." Killian loved him some damn Keema. "Buddha, you better watch your mouth before I hit you in it," I warned. Looking at me, he took off running, cracking up as he ran over to Parker.

Keema rightened herself and hit Malik again. She pointed to her face. "Does it look like I care for what you had to do?" She asked before rolling her eyes at him. Grabbing his arm, she pulled him away from Chyna. "Come on so I can talk to you real quick." She said before jumping on his back.

Malik must have heard my laughter as his gaze landed on me. His head shook. "Man, this girl worrisome." He claimed before walking off, carrying her.

"Seriously, Malik?" Chyna called after him.

"Girl, we'll be back. Go find the gift table while we're gone!" Keema yelled at her.

I looked between Ebony and Peaches. "Bitch, y'all damn genes done messed her ass up. Ooh, she's a whole ass mess."

"And she is. That is Ha'Keem's child through and through." Ebony said, shaking her head with Peaches agreeing.

My attention went back to Chyna to see her glaring at Malik and Keema. "Thanks for the gift. You didn't have to bring anything." I told her, getting her attention.

"Of course I did. I couldn't come over here empty handed." She smiled at me then held up the gift bag. "I'mma go sit this down." She said before walking off.

"She seems like a sweet girl," Angel said, smiling after her.

"No, the fuck she ain't, though." Mike chimed in. "That damn girl always in some bullshit." He told her, shaking his head.

I agreed with Mike. "She really do. Every other day she's fighting some girl behind Malik. The bad thing about it, she knows they're not together, they're just friends—"

"Kimmy, we know what just friends mean—" Peaches started saying.

My hands quickly covered my ears. I knew what it meant, and I hated it. "Y'all, I don't wanna think about that shit for real. Like, I know what it means, and I don't condone that bullshit at all. But I know he's going to go out and have sex, though. So, we got him a box of condoms, but he's not allowed to have no girls here unsupervised." I explained to them.

The girls broke out laughing as they stared at me. "Bitch, why are you covering your ears?" They asked.

Moving my hands from my ears, I chuckled too. "I don't like talking about it. Y'all, I really hate that Malik's growing up and wanting to have sex.

Y'all hoes wanna laugh at me now but wait until, Peewee, Blake—hell, Keema's ass wants to start having sex. You bitches are going to be just like me. And knowing Peaches and E's dramatic ass, those bitches are going to cry."

Peaches nodded while still laughing. "Sure is. I don't care." She said, looking at her twins playing inside the bouncy house with Blake watching them.

Ebony, however, shook her head. "No, the fuck I'm not. Do you not know who Keema's daddy, uncles, and cousins are? Bitch, they're going to handle any nigga that tries her." She leaned forward, looking around me. "Am I wrong, Mike?"

I glanced at him only to see a mug on his face. "I don't know why she even brought Keema into that bullshit. Them damn boys going to be boys—"

"And girls are going to be girls. They wanna have sex too—"

His glare deepened. "What the fuck are you even talking about? Man, shut the fuck up, Kimmy." He snapped at me, causing the girls to burst out laughing.

"See. They will handle my light work. So, I'm not worried about shit." Ebony said, cracking up.

I laughed lightly before my attention went to Mike, who was rubbing my stomach. I leaned over to him. "Can I have a kiss?" MyKell grabbed my face and kissed me.

Mike's hand pressed into Kells face, pushing

him back. "Nah, she was talking to me, pimp, so watch back."

"Nah, Pimp." Kells hit Mike's hand then kissed me again.

Laughing, I pulled MyKell into my lap, then kissed the side of his head. "Can daddy give me kisses?" I asked him.

His head started moving fast, going from yes to no. "Nope, nope, nope." He chanted.

Millian soon ran over to us. "I got to pee." He said, pulling on my hand.

"I got it." Mike started getting up, but I stopped him.

"I'll take him. I have to use it anyway." Placing Kells down, I stood up. "Buddha, Remmy, Jah-Jah, let's go to the bathroom," I called to my boys. The trio quickly came running over, and I led my squad into the house.

In the first bathroom, Money ran in, going straight to the toilet, whereas MyKell went to the toilet-shaped potty, using it."

"I got to shit," Remmy called out.

I glared at him. "Kareem, get slapped in the mouth. Cuss again here. I'm not playing with you." I fussed and heard Mike laugh.

"I got him." Mike laughed, picking Kareem up. "What I tell you about yo' damn mouth? I'mma whoop yo' ass, Kareem. Jah, Killian, come on." He took the other boys to the half bathroom down the hall.

"I have to wash my hands," Millian said, grabbing his step stool and pushing it to the sink.

"Wash hands," MyKell exclaimed, trying to climb on the stool with Millian.

"Come on, Kells." Money helped him up, letting him wash his hands first.

I couldn't do anything but smile at Millian. Although bad as hell, he was a great big brother when he wanted to be.

"My turn." He said after helping MyKell wash his hands. "Here. Dry your hands." He told him, holding out a paper towel. MyKell took it, and he helped him off the stool. "Stay right there." He instructed, pointing to the door. Once he washed his hands, he got down and then left the bathroom, closing me in.

All I could do was laugh at him. He had watched me do that too many times. I wasn't complaining, his added help was needed.

Once I finished in the restroom, I made my way into the kitchen, where Mike stood, watching the kids run around in the yard. As if sensing me, he glanced behind him. Seeing me, his hand came out, touching my stomach. He rubbed my large belly then pulled me to his front.

We stood there silently for a long while, watching our kids, friends, and their children laugh and have fun together. The sight was an amazing one. Just seeing everyone so carefree without a single worry was incredible.

My smile grew wider as I watched my daddy talk with Mike's parents. I didn't know what they were talking about, but the trio was cracking up, which made me laugh.

Seeing Angel, Parker, Chris, and them all enjoying themselves freely without worrying about Martell was a fantastic sight, honestly. It had been four long years, and the calm that washed over them after his death was still felt.

"Chris asked if Malik can come down for the summer again," Mike spoke softly against my head.

With welcoming us into the family, that invite was extended to Malik. That would be the third summer Malik would be spending out there with them. My baby seemed to enjoy being out there, working with Parker and Chris at their Fast Line Shipping warehouse. That was his summer job, and he loved it and the money he made during that time. Which was way more than needed, I felt. But I learned not to complain or say anything to either of them about it because Parker, Chris, Mane, nor Jason listened to me. My words fell on deaf ears.

"I'll call Tasha and let her know. Which I know she won't have a problem with." I told him. After the whole ordeal with Tasha's kitchen catching on fire, I haven't had a problem with her. I don't know if it was because Mike didn't let her move in with us, but homegirl seemed to have come to her senses after that. She no longer tried demanding shit from Mike. Hell, Tasha hardly ever communicated with him. Whenever Malik needed anything, or if she had something to discuss regarding his schooling, she called or texted me.

When Malik turned fourteen, he decided to move in with us. Tasha damn near lost her mind when he sat us down, letting us know what he wanted. That was the only time I saw the old Tasha resurface.

After Malik broke down how he was becoming a man and needed his dad during this time. Saying Tasha was an amazing mother and had done great with taking care of him, yet, he felt it was time he moved with us, his daddy.

Tasha agreed after days of crying. It had been two years since then, and I could honestly say she didn't regret her decision. Baby girl was out living her best damn life like she was sixteen. Not only that, Tasha had her own man. I was happy for her.

Although it had been four years, and I was staring at my kids, the evidence of time passing, it didn't seem like that long ago.

I stood there staring at my family, with a full heart and not one single regret from my past. If it wasn't for my mistakes, I wouldn't be living such a wonderful life or staring at my growing family, my kids, my man.

The years had started off rocky as my affair with Bellow finally came to light. Even so, I didn't regret that. I couldn't. My time with Bellow was an amazing experience. Because of that, we would forever be bonded on a friend's level.

We still occasionally saw each other because of our friendship with Blaze and Peaches. So, I was happy for not only our maturity but our significant others as well. There was never any awkwardness or drama when we all got together.

Hell, I was happy for him and the family he was building with Sabrina. The pair now had two kids, a boy, and a girl.

After years, I finally understood that I loved Bellow, but I wasn't in love with him. I loved the emptiness he filled inside of me at that time. And I was afraid that if I let him go, that emptiness and loneliness I felt before would return, which I didn't want.

The feeling never returned.

Mike had changed over the years. Although he worked, his hours weren't crazy as before. Mike didn't allow himself to get lost entirely in the job. Not only that, but he was more attentive to me and catered to my mind, body, and soul like he had when we first got together. Yet, the feeling was far better. It made me feel like I was falling more in love with him every day.

Of course, it took me a while to realize it all. Yet, with the help of my remarkable therapist, Elizabeth, she made everything so much clearer.

So, no, I could never regret anything from my past mistakes.

"What are you thinking about?" Mike kissed the side of my head before taking hold of my thick red hair and pulling it back.

Smiling, I glanced up at him. Puckering up my lips, he kissed me. "Everything," I admitted before pointing out to the yard. "I'm really happy, babe. I love this right here." I motioned from our friends than to our boys. Remmy caught my eyes and came running toward us.

"Shorty, I think your hormones fucking with you." He chuckled as I smacked my lips.

"See, ugh. You're an asshole, Michael, I swear. I was being serious." My eyes rolled, and I laughed at him. That man couldn't help but ruin the insightful moment I was trying to have.

"You damn asshole," Kareem said, pushing at Mike's leg.

My hand covered my face as I tried not to laugh. My son had a terrible ass mouth, and it was our own fault. For that, it made disciplining him hard, simply because he only repeated what he heard us say constantly.

"Kareem, what the fuck I tell you about yo' gotdamn mouth?" Mike fussed at him, yet I knew he wasn't pissed off from his tone. He was just saying that for my benefit. Apparently, Remmy knew that as well because he broke out laughing.

"Michael, cussing at him isn't going to help. Ugh, I swear me and Malakai are running away. Y'all aren't corrupting him." If only I could run away from their craziness. Hell, given all the talking Mike has done with Malakai still in the womb. My poor baby was probably already influenced to be honest.

"So, you're thinking about taking off on us?" He questioned while biting my bottom lip. Smiling against his mouth, I nodded. "You think I'll let you take off?"

My head shook as I kissed him. "No, that's why it's called running away." I licked his bottom lip, then the top.

"That's why you stay pregnant now," King said, walking onto the porch. "You mothafuckas ain't tired yet?"

King's words had me cracking the hell up. "Babe, but why the girls were saying the same damn thing earlier, though?" Looking at King, I pointed to Mike. "Man, that's all his ass. He keeps on trapping me with these little monsters." I told him while pointing to Remmy, who was in the fridge looking for something.

"I'm trapping you?" He questioned, sounding offended, making me laugh.

Still, I nodded. "Yes, you are for real, Michael. After Kai, I'm done, I'm running away." I told him, trying to sound serious as possible.

"If you give me one more baby after Kai, we'll take a break for two years, dead ass." He bargained.

Looking into his smiling face, I broke out

laughing. "Yeah, right, Michael. You said that after we had Jah and Remmy. Now look, we have MyKell, and now Kai's coming."

Laughing, Mike rubbed my belly. "That was your fault. I'm serious this time, though. Give me one more, and we can take a break if you want." He tacked on. Biting into his bottom lip, those bright blue eyes roamed over my figure, drinking me in. "What you tryna do, Kimberly Jamisha Payne?"

My lips once again stretched into a wide smile. Mike and I tied the knot over three years ago after learning of my pregnancy with Jaheem and Kareem. It wasn't huge or over the top ceremony, much to Missy's disappointment. We had a small, intimate backyard wedding with our small group of friends and family there.

Marrying Mike was the best decision I'd ever made. I was head over heels in love with him.

My arms wrapped around his neck, and I kissed him. "I'll give you as many babies as you want, Michael Dontavious Payne." I loved how he loved our boys and me. And as long as he continued to love me with that much passion, he would get everything he wanted out of me.

That was how I knew I'd give him all the kids he wanted.

I was simply in love with what we had, and I was excited to see what the future held for us.

∞ ∞ ∞

I laid against Mike in the lounge chair. My mind and body were in complete bliss as Mike stroked his fingers through my hair. Tilting my head back, I kissed his chin, then along his jawline, causing him to look down at me.

"You better stop." He warned.

My hand grasped the nape of his neck, and I pulled his head down. "What am I doing?" My tongue ran along the bottom of his lip before I sucked on it. "I'm just trying to get us ready for when the kids go to bed." Mike's hand tightened in my hair as his tongue slid into my mouth, causing me to moan. Heat immediately filled the pit of my stomach before it dropped down to my core.

Mike slapped my ass hard before squeezing it. "We don't have to wait until tonight. We got all these babysitters out here." He mumbled against my mouth before deepening the kiss.

My damn body was so turned on, and Mike's tongue intimately stroking mine only caused my pussy to throb more. Once his hand squeezed my throat, I was ready to go.

"Let's go—" I was in the middle of whispering against his mouth when Killian came over, forcing himself on Mike's lap.

"Move, dude." Killian pressed his small hand

against Mike's face and pushed him back. "Gimme kiss, sweetheart." Buddha grabbed my face, and his small lips pressed against mine.

"Man, if you don't get yo' little ass on—" Mike began saying when Buddha turned and mugged him.

"Man, stop blocking—"

"Bitch!" The girls hollered out, cracking the hell up.

"No, the fuck he didn't just tell Mike to stop blocking. Oh, my God! Girl, I know damn well Mike don't be telling him that shit." Ebony asked, cracking up.

My head fell against Mike's chest. I was so embarrassed, even so, I had to laugh. I just wasn't expecting him to say that. "Mike's always saying that to them. I keep telling him to watch what he says because they literally repeat everything. They don't be forgetting shit. These boys too damn much. I blame Mike for how they are. Walking around here calling me sweetheart or shorty. I swear they're his kids. They talk just like his ass." Looking at Killian, I broke out laughing again. "Boy, you need a whooping."

"Nuh-uh." His head shook. "I love you, sweetheart."

"I love you too, baby." I kissed his cheek as Millian, MyKell, Jaheem, and Kareem came over to us. A grunt left my mouth as MyKell climbed on me. "Kells..." I glared at him as he grabbed my shirt and pulled it over my stomach. His head then lay against my belly as small chuckles left his mouth when he felt Kai moving.

My eyes just rolled as I stroked over his small head, caressingly. I loved the hell out of my badass boys.

"Kimmy about to have a whole damn Brady Bunch over here. I just don't see y'all slowing down." Angel chuckled. "Your belly is just big and round. It's so cute." She cooed, reaching over and rubbing my stomach.

Kareem popped her hand, causing my mouth to drop open. "Watch out." He pushed her hand back, then rubbed MyKell's head. "Go to sleep." He told him before kissing his baby brother's head.

Angel stared at me just as surprised before the girls laughed.

"That's not funny. Kareem, you're going to get your ass whooped if you keep on." I threatened. He was definitely on the verge of getting a damn spanking. "Ang, he didn't mean it. He's sorry."

She mugged Remmy while waving her finger. "I'mma get you, watch. You want me to get my ruler?" She told him, and his head started shaking. He knew Angel didn't have no problem with spanking his ass, nor did I.

"I'll whoop his ass if I was you," Mike told her.

"Nuh-uh. Bye!" Getting down, he took off toward the other kids while cracking up. That

caused his brothers to laugh and take off after him
—all except for MyKell. My baby son was tired and
on his way to sleep.

"Ooh, Mike, you need to do something with
your kids, man." I chuckled. They were way beyond
their years, in my opinion.

"Aye!" The sudden loud and demanding yell
from Chris got our attention. "Get yo' ass away from
my daughter!"

My sights settled on Malik, who had sat
down in a lounge chair with Christiana in his
lap. Chrissy's face soon buried into his neck as if
embarrassed from Chris' outburst.

"Man, it ain't even like that. We're just
talking." Malik told him while laughing.

"Tiana, if you don't get yo' ass off that
mothafucka." He snapped at her before his eyes
found us. "Mike, get yo' shorty before I shoot his
ass."

The threat caused Mike and Malik to break out
laughing. Mike's arms went up, and I felt him shrug.
"I ain't got shit to do with that." He told Chris,
chuckling.

"You wanna shoot me?" Malik asked before
saying something to Christiana, who had gotten off
his lap. She now sat in front of him.

"Nigga, ain't that yo' girl right there?" Parker
asked, pointing to Chyna.

Baby girl looked pissed as she mugged Malik

and Christiana.

Malik glanced at her, then shook his head. "Nah, that's my homegirl. Man, yall dramatic as fuck. I'm not trying to do shit with Chrissy. She's my homegirl too." His response caused King to laugh, whereas I groaned, and Christiana hit him. Malik grabbed Chrissy's arms and pulled her closer to him.

"When I beat y'all son's ass, don't be mad," Chris warned us.

"Chyna." He called, beckoning her to him. Although pissed off, she made her way over to them. All the while, Malik continued to talk to Christiana.

After watching the pair, I felt that he liked Chrissy from the way he kept leaning into her, whispering and playing with strands of her hair.

My hand covered my face as I groaned. "Mike, he's not going back out to Bloomingdale no more." I just was not ready for the girl drama with him. I didn't like what I was seeing at all. "Babe, you need to talk with him because this—" I motioned to our son flirting with Chrissy while he had a whole other chick there. "—that shit is not cool."

"Man, leave that boy alone. He ain't tied down to nobody. He's young as fuck so let him have his fun." He stated with a shrug.

I turned to face him. "Fun? What's fun about someone's feelings getting played with, or them being hurt?"

A HEART SO SELFISH 3: FOREVER SELFISH WITH YOU

"Who feelings are getting hurt, Kimmy? Ain't none of them his girlfriend, he just said that." He shrugged, uncaring.

I mugged the shit out of him. "Seriously? So, we're going to pretend like we don't know what none of that—*homegirl*—shit means?" I fussed at him, irritated that he wanted to act like what Malik was doing wasn't an issue.

"Fuck you, I swear to God—" Chyna started yelling. She swung on Malik, then jerked Christiana's head to the side by her hair, hitting her in the face.

"Oh shit." Was echoed as bodies started moving toward them. Everything happened so gotdamn fast that it looked surreal. Where the hell Keema ass came from was beyond me. But she reached them before anybody else.

Keema yanked Chyna back by her hair, slamming the girl on the ground, and went crazy. Although Keema was only eleven, the pair stood 5'3 in height, yet Chyna was thicker than her.

"Bitch, you done lost your fucking mind hitting on my cousin like you're stupid." Keema went off as her fist went stupid as they pounded on Chyna.

King snatched his daughter off Chyna, but Keema still wanted to fight. She fought in King's hold, trying to get free. "Sha'Keema, calm yo' ass the fuck down."

"Daddy! Let me go. That tacky ass bitch gonna hit him. I'll fuck her up!" Keema was going off.

"Nah, bitch, you gonna sneak me for real? See, I've been trying to spare yo' little ass. Now, I'm about to stomp a hole in yo' ass, bitch!" Chyna went off before she tried running up on Keema until Blake quickly grabbed her. "Dude, let me the fuck go!" Chyna practically begged.

"Nah, go on now," Ebony told Chyna, blocking her from Sha'Keema. "Go take a walk and calm yourself down."

"Nah, let me go. Come on, Chyna, I wanna see you stomp a hole in me." Keema's shoe came off, and she threw it at Chyna's head. Blake and Chyna ducked just in time before the shoe could hit either of them.

"Aye, you better calm yo' ass down. That shit almost hit me." Blake snapped on Keema.

"So! Put her ass down then. You shouldn't be touching her anyway!" She went off on him. "Daddy, put me down, please, damn." She was pissed off at King for not letting her fight.

My hand rubbed against my forehead as I glanced at Mike. "So, this is fun?" I asked, motioning to the drama unfolding. My gaze went to my oldest son, seeing him holding Christiana as he and Chris tried calming her down. Chrissy was raging the hell out and fighting the pair hard to get free. Until Chris slung his daughter over his shoulder and walked them into the dirt field.

"Malik!" I called to him. I was beyond pissed off. Once he reached me, I glared at him. "What are you doing?" I motioned between Chyna and Chrissy. Feeling MyKell stir, I shushed and rocked him before he could wake up.

"Momma, that babe clicked out for no reason —"

"No reason, Malik?" I was about to whack the shit out of him when Mike grabbed my arm.

"Baby, I got this." He told me before snatching Malik to him by the back of his neck and dragging him off. Although Mike did that, I could see the grip wasn't tight. Leading me to believe it was only an act to calm me down. It didn't, however.

"Kimmy!" Missy yelled at me. "Bitch, come get yo' gotdamn son." She snapped, holding a fighting Killian.

"She fights my girlfriend." He pointed to Chyna accusingly. "I'll beat her ass." He went off, struggling hard to get free. From the anger on Buddha's face, he was pissed and ready to fight.

"Let him go!" Kareem snapped, running up on Missy with a stick in his hands as if he was about to hit her.

"Boy, give me that—" Angel stopped Remmy before he could hit Missy. She took the stick from him and tossed it.

"Gotdamn bitch!" Kareem snapped while wrapping his arms around Angel's leg, tight.

"Aah! Sonofa—he's fucking biting me, Kimmy! Parker!" Angel hollered at us while she tried pulling Kareem off her leg. He was not letting her go, however. Even when she started hitting on him on his butt. That shit did nothing as he kept his hold on her.

Parker stood off on the side, cracking the hell up with their two sons, Peewee and Ant. Like, they were dead crying laughing.

As I stood there watching the chaos unfold from my eldest son's drama to my youngest baby terrors, I knew our children were going to be pure hell. Far worse than any of the bullshit that we went through.

I was not ready for the hell they were going to bring.

The End...

Swipe or scroll to the next page...

Something Extra

If you all are anything like Kimmy—which I suspect y'all are—I figured y'all nosy butts wanted to know what went down when the guys got Martell and Don...

The scene is on the next page.

Also, I wrote it from Chris' point of view because I felt like he lost the most. He needed this release to finally be able to exhale after years of being suffocated with fear behind Nicki's death.

Okay, that's it. I hope you all enjoy this bonus chapter.

Peach...

Bonus Chapter

Parker

We Can Only Kill Them Once

*A*fter Mike pulled off, Don and Martell glanced at each other before shooting at us. Their bullets did nothing to the bulletproof glass, however. As if realizing their shooting was pointless, the pair took off toward the warehouse.

Chris and I started laughing at their desperate attempt to getaway. Quickly hitting the gas, the tires kicked up dirt as Chris sped down to the pair, swerving the big truck in front of them, causing Don and Martell to halt. They went to turn around but were stopped as Jason blocked them.

"Ain't no running, baby. Y'all might as well stop trying. All of that running and hiding bullshit is over with." I told them as I pushed open my door. Don's gun raised, and he shot, but nothing came out. Smiling at him, I stepped out of the truck. "Baby, don't tell me you're empty?"

Don dropped his gun and laughed. "Might as well get this shit over with but know I'm not begging you bitches." He said, glancing around us before his eyes settled on Chris. He smiled. "I guess you're the one who's going to take me out, huh? I mean, I did take part in killing yo' wife. Shid, it's only fair. So, how we're going to do this shit?" He asked, looking at the gun in Chris' hand.

Chris did the same before he laughed. "Ah, nah, baby, a simple bullet is too good for you. See, I love when bitches beg. That's what I want you to do before I kill you. Baby, I want you begging for death. Mane." Chris called, making Don glance at Mane only to receive a hard whack in the face with a bat. Once Don dropped to the ground, Chris picked him up and tossed him in the truck. He then looked at Martell and grinned. "Y'all don't start the fun without me. Let me get this bitch ready first." After saying that, Chris hopped in the truck and drove down to the units Mike let us use for our playroom.

Martell glanced around at the three of us and started laughing. "Y'all know this some hoe ass shit —"

I headbutted the fuck out of him, causing blood to run from his nose immediately. My fist smacked into his face, making him hit the ground. Once he did, Mane and Jason stomped hard on his face, nearly knocking him out. I squatted beside his head.

Martell spit blood from his mouth. "Fuck you. Y'all niggas some bitches." He spat out.

Laughing, I smacked his ass across the face. "Says the bitch that's been hiding for fucking years. Oh, baby, we're about to be on a lot of hoe shit. You're about to have a long ass fucking night." I laughed. "Before the fun starts, think about all the shit you've done. You had my brother's wife killed viciously, you almost killed me on my wedding day, and to top that off, you had my nigga Ice killed." Laughing, I smiled at him. "I hope you're still stubborn as a bitch. I want yo' ass begging for death too, then again I don't because I wanna torture the fuck out of you. I know you're not going to go out like a pussy and cry for it. Don't let me have that over you, baby." Once again, I smiled at him before I stood up straight.

With a nod to Mane and Jason, the pair began stomping him out.

The bloody steel bat dropped from my hands, hitting the concrete floor hard. It had been well over twenty-four hours since I started beating Don. I've done some of everything to the nigga, from beating him with my fist to pistol whooping him, then pulling out all of his teeth before I grabbed the bat and started playing baseball with his body.

I wanted the nigga to hurt given the way he and his bitch ass brother murdered my wife gruesomely. He needed to feel at least half of what I suffered through the years. Although I knew he needed to die, I didn't want him dead. Death was too easy for him, I felt. In my mind, the nigga needed to live out the rest of his days in pain.

My back hit the wall, and I slid down it, sitting on the floor. All the while, I stared at a bloody unconscious Don. A smile came to my lips at the sight of his swollen and disfigured face.

Yet, as I stared at him, I felt so gotdamn light, like a huge weight had been lifted off of me. For the past seventeen years, the constant pain I've had in my chest eased, making breathing easier.

When I initially learned that Mook had killed my wife, I thought he'd done it solo. My damn soul was never at peace, and I couldn't let her go because I knew Martell had a hand in her murder, and the nigga was still breathing. I never thought Don played a part in it until he said something. So, as he said, it was only right I killed him too.

When Mook died, I felt cheated because, at the time, I didn't know it was him. Now, however, I was able to release every ounce of anger and pain I felt on Don and Martell.

That's why I felt so light, and my chest didn't feel so compressed because I could finally let her go peacefully, knowing I killed the mothafuckas who caused her death.

Light beam into the warehouse as the door opened. Parker walked in, looking around before his eyes landed on me. Coming over, he sat on the floor as well, holding out a blunt.

That's been the first time anyone had come in since I brought Don into the unit. For a long time, we didn't speak as we rotated the blunt. "I did his ass good for the both of us," I told him.

Nicki was like a sister to Parker. He knew her just as long as I did. Plus, since she was with me, that meant she was with all of us. So, he felt her loss just as I had.

"Got us a trophy too." Reaching into my pocket, I pulled out the diamond grill Don once wore. I tossed Parker the top one. "I think I'mma make mine into a charm." Staring at the grill, I smiled hard. Still, Parker didn't say anything as he stroked the grill. Hitting his shoulder with mine, I nodded at his unasked question. "I'm good, P, dead ass. A nigga feels light as fuck, unburdened. I think death is too good for his ass, though, but I know he needs to die."

"A fucking bullet is too good for that mothafucka—both of those bitches," Parker stated, and I nodded in agreement.

Looking at Don, I laughed. "That little bitch got balls. His ass has been screaming like a straight hoe, but not once did he beg me to stop or ask me to kill him." Given Don was a gutta mothafucka, born and bred that way, I didn't expect shit less of him. "Buddy pissed and shitted himself, and still that nigga ain't begged for me to kill him. He must know that shit is pointless." I told him with a slight smile. Exhaling, I chuckled. "I feel good, though." I hit the blunt twice, then stood up, stretching. "We can leave him here for a second. Let's go check on your boy." I motioned toward the doors, making my way to them.

"That nigga, Mike really came through on this shit big time. For a while, I thought his ass was on some bullshit." Parker said, staring at Don's battered body.

I had to agree with him on that. The fact he even reached out to us surprised the fuck out of me. Especially since we knew the nigga didn't care for us. Hell, that mothafucka made the shit known when he called my ass.

"I like the mothafucka to be real with you. That nigga relaxed as fuck, and his patience level is something serious. Mike came through hard." I nodded, agreeing with myself. I glanced around us, taking in the space he let us use to do whatever the fuck we wanted. "Let's finish this up, and we can talk about what we're gonna do with Mike after."

"I think that nigga kill mothafuckas on the low. This is too much fucking storage space for just guns, Lord." Parker said, motioning to the other units that surrounded us.

He had a point. Mike claimed this was a small space, but the shit was enormous as fuck. "Shid, whether he do or don't, it ain't our business. Come on," Grabbing the nape of his neck, I pulled him to the unit where the screaming was coming from. Yet, before I reached the door, I stopped. Seeing the two Ford trucks, a thought came to me. "Sticky." I waved Ice's younger brother over. The nigga was covered in blood. "How you feeling, baby?"

"Better, I won't be completely satisfied until that bitch is dead."

I smiled at that. "I feel you." Taking hold of his shoulder, I pulled him to me. "You gonna take part in that. As a matter of fact, you and P gonna tear that mothafucka apart." The confusion that covered his face made me laugh.

"C, I don't like that look, but I'm intrigued as fuck about what you're thinking," Parker said, staring at me curiously.

"You'll see. Come on." I pushed him to the unit Martell was in. "Damn, that mothafucka beautiful." I grinned, staring at a strung up Martell. They had buddy tied upright to a thick wooden stand. I glanced at Parker, then pointed to the frame.

"That bitch was in here already. I told you, I think that mothafucka kill people on the low." He insisted once again, making me laugh. Parker's

HEART SO SELFISH 3: FOREVER SELFISH WITH YOU

brows furrowed as he took me in. "You seem different. You sure you're really good?"

I nodded, knowing what he meant. Ever since I locked myself in the unit with Don, my damn soul felt at peace. Everything I did to that nigga, I needed to do to let my shorty go. I knew I did her justice. That was why my soul felt at ease.

"Yeah, I'm good. I'll be better in a minute, though." I told him while pointing to Martell. The dude was shirtless, and his body seemed to be leaking from everywhere.

Mane went to crack him with the bat again, but I stopped him.

"Chill, Mane, you don't wanna beat the nigga to death." My hand rubbed over Martell's head before I lifted it up. "Don't drop this mothafucka. You're too good for that, baby." I told him, holding it upright. "You're a smart mothafucka, Lord, I'mma give it to you. Nigga, the way you play Chess with us." I motioned between Parker, Mane, and Jason.

"You outdid yourself for years. Played us like some weak ass pawns. Shid, a tiny part of me respect how you played yo' pieces this whole time. You fucked up when you had my wife killed and tried to kill my brother. My nigga, yo' ass was dead trying to tear my heart out." Grabbing the nape of his neck, I pulled his head to my shoulder. "That's why we're going to tear yo' ass apart. I thought death by fire, but that would be too good for you. I wanna play tug of war with you." Pushing his head back, I stepped away from him. "Don't touch him.

Let that nigga breathe for a minute."

Once we made it outside, Mane and Jason started laughing. "Tug of war? My nigga, what the fuck is that?" Mane questioned.

Jason's laughter stopped once I pointed to the trucks. "Wait..." his brows furrowed as he looked at the black Ford pickup. I nodded at his pause.

"We got all this space. Who gonna hear shit? We might as well play with these mothafuckas. Shit, it's only right given all of the bullshit those bitches did. I wanna see that bitch torn into pieces. P and Sticky can do the shit, unless they wanna watch, like me." That was what I wanted. To watch both of those bitches bodies be torn apart. "What y'all think?" I glanced at them.

"I'll watch that shit. Aside from tv, I've never seen that shit done in person."

"Shid, me either." Mane said, looking at me like I was crazy.

I shrugged at the stare. "A bullet is too easy for Don and Martell. We can only kill these mothafuckas once. I wanna make the most out of it." The shit was only fair in my eyes. Especially given how my wife was killed.

"He has a point." Jason agreed, as did Parker. "Well, I'm watching."

"I'm driving," Sticky stated.

"Shid, me too." Mane said, now sounding excited.

"Nah, let me." Berry chimed in. He and Ice were thick as thieves, so I wasn't surprised by him speaking up.

Mane nodded at him. "You got it."

Going to the truck's bed, I grabbed the thick chains off the back. "Let's tie these bitches up."

∞ ∞ ∞

"Yo, P, Chris, just fucking shoot me!" Martell broke, fear showing in his wide eyes. The nigga looked terrified as he fought hard against Mane and Jason as they held him down while the chains were being locked at his neck, waist, arms, and legs. "Parker, man, come on, Lord. Shoot me." He begged.

Parker walked over to him, kneeling beside his head. "Nah, as my brother said, a bullet is too good for y'all. Take this shit like a man. I mean, you started this shit, baby. We're just ending your game." Parker told him while rubbing over his head. "Remember you and Mook laughed about how you would fuck my wife in front of me before you killed her? That shit has fucked with me for years because I knew yo' ass was sick enough to do it—"

"I wouldn't have killed her. I was just talking shit because I was pissed that you had her. I could never hurt her. Lord, I loved Ang—"

Parker stood up and started stomping Martell in the face. "Don't ever fucking say her name, you pussy ass nigga."

Quickly going up behind Parker. I snatched his big ass away from Martell. "Yo, P, chill out. You gonna kill the mothafucka before we can tear his ass apart, Lord, damn."

Parker pushed me off of him. "I'm good. Sticky, Berry, go. Draw that shit out too." He instructed.

They put the trucks in gear and drove in opposite directions.

"Ahh!" Martell started screaming in pure agony.

My eyes shifted to Don, and the man looked terrified. "Don't worry, baby, you're next."

Don's head dropped, and his swollen eyes closed. Seeing that his mouth was swollen and had no teeth made hearing him harder. Yet as I listened closely, I began making out his words. "Nah, baby, you praying to the wrong mothafucka. God ain't gon' save you. Pray to Lucifer and ask him to welcome yo' ass home."

Don's beat and swollen face rose. I could only guess and say he was trying to mug me, thinking that caused a smile to come to my lips.

"Yea, though I walk through the valley of the shadow of death. I will fear no evil: for thou art with me; thy rod and thy staff comfort me..." Don's words faded, his eyes widened as Martell's body was torn into pieces.

The shit was nasty as fuck and surreal. Yet the scene was entertaining.

Looking at Don, I smiled. "Your turn."

Given all the release we were letting out, the moment felt so gotdamn intimate, so fucking special. It was what we all needed to move on peacefully.

$$\infty \infty \infty$$

"This shit went smoothly as fuck." Mane commented as we sat staring at the blazing furnace. "No lie, I wasn't expecting it to be. I figured it would be more to this." I nodded in agreement.

"Yeah, that nigga set everything up perfectly. I definitely wasn't expecting this shit to be so gotdamn easy." Jason said, making Parker laugh. "We need to pay that mothafucka real decently."

Parker's head shook at that. "Shid, I told that nigga if he could get us Martell on a platter, I'll pay his ass right. That mothafucka told me he didn't want my money. Say, that wasn't the reason he was doing it. With all those gotdamn guns Martell and Don bought, he knew they were coming at us, and Syn would've been dragged into it. He didn't want that to happen. That nigga put himself out there for us, our family. Shit don't get deeper than that for me." Parker stated, zoned out as he stared at the blunt.

Mike didn't know it, but he gave me something I never thought I'd get back. Peace. Without that, my sanity wasn't all the way there. It hadn't been since Nicki's death. Not only that, but fear also consumed me. Fear had a tight hold on me, so much so I couldn't get close to anyone outside of us, the family.

"If he doesn't take the money. We bring him in with us. That man looked out for our family, knowing shit could've turned bad for his ass if Martell or Don would've figured that shit out. Besides, I know Martell's folks are about to be looking at Mike funny for a while. So, it's only right we put ourselves out there for him and his." I glanced at their expressions, trying to read their thoughts on what I said.

Parker started laughing. "Shid, this won't be the first time they've helped us out—although Mike didn't have shit to do with it. Remember that one year at Syn's party, Kimmy's ass was busting that damn Desert Eagle." I chuckled, remembering her and Missy shooting at Mook and Martell. Parker glanced at Mane and Jason, who nodded.

"Letting them into the family could be beneficial on both sides. With the expansion of Fast Line still growing and the drugs we're shipping nationally. Imagine how shit would be if we add running firearms to the business. I'm surprised we haven't gotten into the shit yet. We could expand their shit nationwide if they aren't already. Y'all saw those fucking guns that nigga got for them?"

Mane laughed. "Mike told Chris; we could keep those bitches because they were paid for." Mane stared at the furnace and started laughing again. "I like the nigga, for real. He's blunt and says what the fuck he means. So, I'm for it. We can definitely bring them into the fam."

Jason pointed to Mane. "Everything he said. Plus, it'll make shit easier for us. We can eliminate outside mothafuckas we've been buying guns from. Mike can be our main gun connect, shid, keep that shit in the family. You got to talk to Roc, though." He told Parker, mentioning his cousin and our business partner Morocco who was running Fast Line Shipping and distributing drugs down south.

"He'll know about it later. So, we're all in agreement to bring them in?" Parker asked, looking between all of us.

We nodded.

"So, they're with us from this point forth. Their shit is our shit. They hurt we hurt." He put out there still looking at us to see if we would change our minds. When Parker saw that our minds were made up, he nodded. "A'ight, let's welcome them into the family."

"Cookout?" Mane smiled, rubbing his stomach, making us laugh.

"Of course. That's how we always do it." Parker told him, still laughing.

∞ ∞ ∞

That is how the decision was made to bring Mike, Kimmy, and their badass children into The Family.

Made in the USA
Monee, IL
07 October 2024